PRAISE F(

Truth Be Told (originally published as *Are You Sleeping*)

"[A]n inventive debut . . . The intense plot and character studies are enhanced by the emotional look at the dynamics of a family forever scarred by violence."

—*Publishers Weekly* (starred review)

"A twisty tale that will grip readers as they follow Josie confronting a past she finally cannot escape."

—*Library Journal* (starred review)

"Showing how complicated the truth can be when people have different levels of investment in it. Dark. Moving. Timely."

—Oprah.com

"Josie's dark past becomes fodder for the podcast du jour—if that doesn't hook you, the twist will."

—*Cosmopolitan*

Follow Me

"Soul-cycling, Pilates-perfected, media-savvy readers will devour [*Follow Me*]. Barber's narrative, like social media itself, is as addictive as it is disturbing."

—*Booklist*

"A cautionary tale about the perils of social media . . . [that] keeps you guessing."

—*Kirkus*

"Fast-paced and au courant."

—*Publishers Weekly*

"A commentary on today's obsession with image and technology—and also a great pick for fans of Caroline Kepnes's *You*."

—*Glamour*

"Pretty much perfect escape reading."

—Self.com

Both Things Are True

OTHER TITLES BY KATHLEEN BARBER

Truth Be Told (originally published as *Are You Sleeping*)

Follow Me

Both Things Are True

a novel

KATHLEEN BARBER

This is a work of fiction. Names, characters, organizations, places, events, and incidents are either products of the author's imagination or are used fictitiously. Otherwise, any resemblance to actual persons, living or dead, is purely coincidental.

Published by Lake Union Publishing, Seattle

www.apub.com

EU product safety contact:

Amazon Media EU S. à r.l.
38, avenue John F. Kennedy, L-1855 Luxembourg
amazonpublishing-gpsr@amazon.com

ISBN-13: 9781662525742 (paperback)
ISBN-13: 9781662525735 (digital)

Cover design by Mumtaz Mustafa
Cover image: © Banphote Kamolsanei, © calvindexter / Getty

Printed in the United States of America

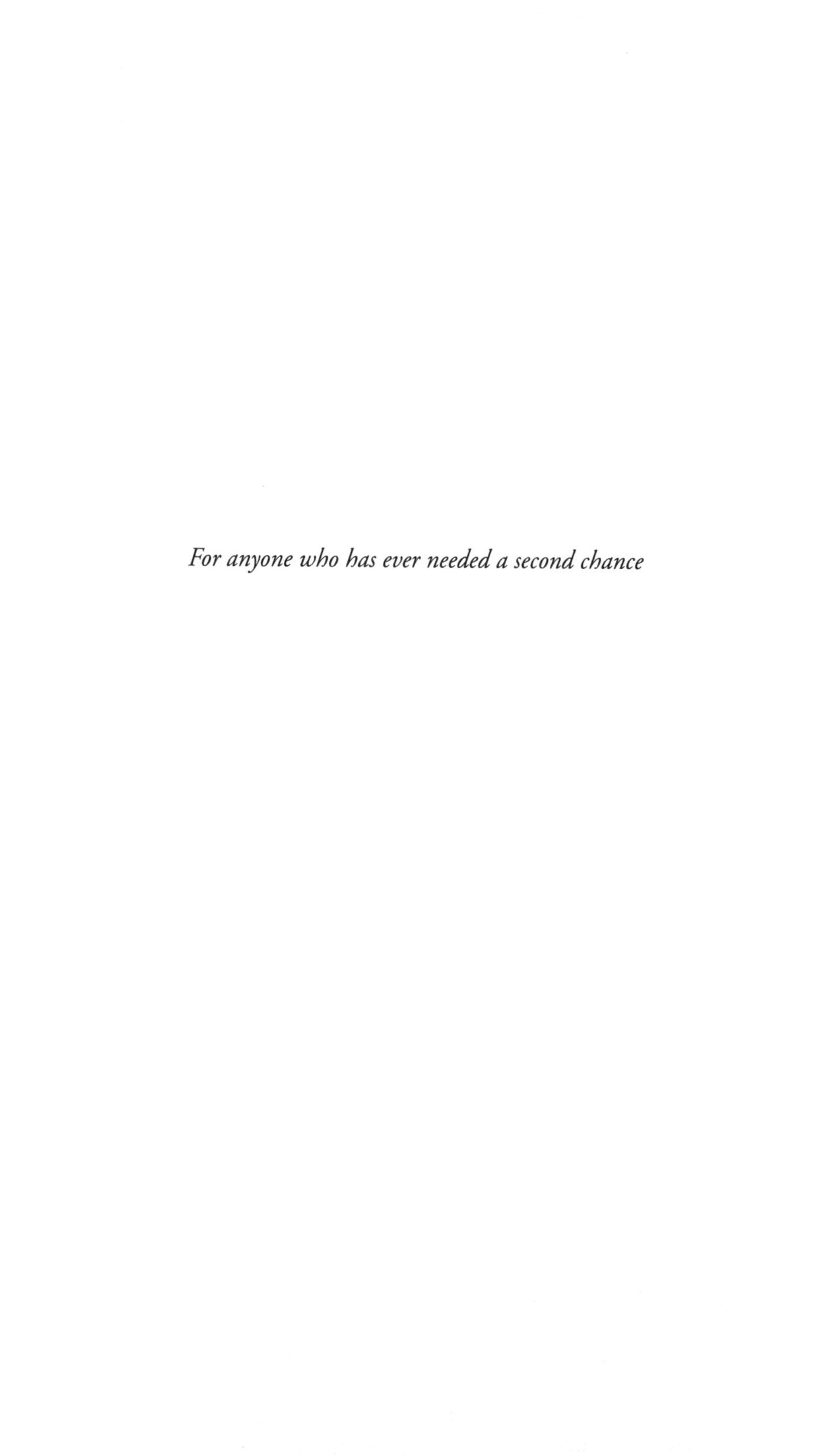

For anyone who has ever needed a second chance

Chapter One

The year before Jack and I got engaged, *New York Magazine* listed him as one of the city's most eligible bachelors. It detailed his storied family, his thriving cryptocurrency exchange, and his diet (which, if you ask me, is just the wrong side of disordered), and included a supremely flattering photo in which Jack, an already gorgeous man, was photoshopped into godlike territory. Legions of women fell in love with him after that profile. All of which is to say, I know that plenty of women—not just women, actually, people of all persuasions—would kill to be in my position. And yet whenever I look down at this diamond-and-ruby ring on my fourth finger, I feel the slightest bit sick.

It's not *all* about Sam. That would be insane. Sam broke up with me five years ago, after all. What kind of person would I be if I was *still* pining over him? I mean, part of my heart still has Sam's name carved into it, but that's true of all first loves, right? *Right?* Don't answer that.

But, truly, I've had doubts about Jack since the beginning, and they go beyond comparing him to Sam. I don't love the cryptocurrency thing, for starters. It feels antithetical to the ahimsa I teach in my yoga classes and my online courses—ahimsa encourages us to live in harmony with all beings, including the world around us. But the greenhouse emissions of Bitcoin mining are alarming, to say the absolute least. And then there's the way Jack's eyes glaze over when I start talking about my career and the superior tone he takes when he lectures me on the supposed benefits of intermittent fasting—and of course there's also the thing with Dolly Parton.

That happened on our third date. The evening had started well: Jack showed up looking, as ever, like a Tom Ford advertisement come to life, all perfect dark-blond coiffure and clean lines, and he took me to this buzzy high-end vegan restaurant that was rumored to have a three-month-long wait list. After our yuzu-bathed mushrooms and our smoked jackfruit, he invited me back to his place for a nightcap.

And, look, I wasn't born yesterday. I knew that Jack wasn't so much interested in another drink as he was in seeing what the pink LoveShackFancy dress I'd rented for the occasion looked like on the floor beside his bed. I almost told him no. The thought of being with anybody other than Sam still made me want to curl up and die, but like I said, it had been years since Sam broke my heart, and last I checked (that very evening as I fastened the halter of said dress), Sam still had me blocked on social media. And so I told Jack that, yes, a nightcap sounded lovely, and I accompanied him back to his minimalist SoHo apartment.

Jack sat me on a sculpted white couch beneath a color-blocked piece of art that he said was an authentic Mondrian (I nodded like I had anything other than the vaguest idea what that meant) and handed me a crystal flute of legit champagne. (I knew because as he handed it to me, he said, "This is the real stuff, you know. Not that sparkling Californian crap.") He toasted the evening and gave me this look, his hazel eyes soft and his sensual lips parted ever so slightly. I knew a kiss was imminent, and I was ninety-eight percent certain I had bits of the red bean mochi we'd shared for dessert stuck in my teeth. I backed away and asked him to point me in the direction of the washroom. He did, and I set my glass down and turned to make my way there.

And that, apparently, was the first time Jack had gotten an unobstructed view of my back. I chose that particular dress largely because the cut showed it off. I consider my back, which is strong and lean from years of daily asana practice, to be one of my better features, and so I was startled to hear Jack cough out a surprised exhalation.

"What?" I asked, looking at him over my shoulder. "Is there something wrong with my dress?"

"No." He laughed softly, covering his mouth with a hand in a poor attempt at hiding a smirk. "Nothing's wrong with the dress."

I craned my neck, trying to see what he found so amusing. "You've never had a 'Kick Me' sign on your back, and it shows," I said crossly. "What are you laughing at?"

"I'm not laughing," he said, unsuccessfully trying to flatten his grin. "I'm just wondering, Vanessa, about that tattoo on your back."

"This one?" I asked, pointing to a circular design across my mid-spine. "It's the phases of the moon."

"I can see that."

"Then you mean this one?" I asked, indicating a black outline on my right shoulder blade. "It's Dolly Parton."

"The likeness is debatable. But I'm less interested in the *what* than the *why*."

I bristled. I didn't like the implication that Jack—a man with whom, by that point, I had only shared three meals and two innocent goodbye kisses—was owed any answers about what I did with my body.

"Hasn't anyone ever told you it's rude to ask about a tattoo's backstory?"

"Come on, Vanessa," he said, flashing me a grin. "I just want to know more about you."

I very much doubted Jack would want to hear the real reason why my body hosted a makeshift shrine to Dolly Parton. I couldn't tell him *the* truth, and so I told him *a* truth instead. "Dolly Parton is a badass. She's, like, the patron saint of hustle. She came from basically nothing and built this amazing career, all on her own terms. She has her own *amusement park*."

Jack looked unimpressed, and I leaned in, determined to spread the gospel of Dolly.

"She's also just an incredible human. That amusement park? She pays her employees' full tuition if they're pursuing higher education, she donated a million dollars to make the COVID vaccine happen, *and* she mails free books to kids under five. Name another celebrity who has done half as much good in the world."

"George Clooney is a noted humanitarian. And he hasn't paid a plastic surgeon to give him boobs like a cartoon character."

If real life were a movie, this was where we'd hear a record scratch. Jackson Dalton remains one of the most physically handsome men I've ever met in real life, but in that moment, he was less attractive to me than a literal toad.

He must have seen the revulsion on my face, because he winced and shook his head. "Shit, Vanessa, that was out of line. I've been spending too much time with Benny."

I scowled, unwilling to let him off the hook just because he'd thrown his obnoxious best friend under the bus. "That comment was gross for so many reasons—not the least of which is that what a woman does with her body is literally no concern of yours."

"Please," Jack said, giving me a hangdog look. "Let's just forget I said that. You're right, Dolly Parton is incredible. She's a goddamn saint." He stepped closer to me and stroked his fingertips over Dolly's face on my shoulder. "If you'll let me, I'll spend the rest of the evening worshipping at her altar."

Maybe I should have knocked those fingers from my body and walked away. But I was tired of longing for someone I couldn't have. I was tired of being alone. And so I promised I would forgive him for that stupid, misogynistic comment.

But I never, ever forgot it.

In fact, it jumps to mind now as Jack erroneously and confidently says, "Beyoncé is overrated."

We're at a housewarming party for Jack's prep-school classmate Gordo, shivering on the private terrace of his sick Hudson Yards condo because Benny wants to smoke a joint. I'm unclear why Benny can't just take a gummy like a normal person, but he has all the maturity of a seventeen-year-old boy, so I assume it's because he thinks smoking makes him look cool. (Spoiler: It does not.) Moments ago, "Texas Hold 'Em" started playing inside, and Benny's girlfriend, Sienna, tugged on his arm because she wanted to go in and dance. Which is how we got to this point: my handsome fiancé casually leaning on the railing of a terrace seven floors up, the Manhattan skyline glittering behind him, while he unleashes his unrequested and astonishingly bad take on the new Beyoncé album.

I flinch, embarrassed. "Jack, Beyoncé is one of the greatest artists of our time."

"Not just *our* time," Sienna says. "*All* time."

"She's right," I agree. "Beyoncé is a living legend. I mean, she's won the most Grammy Awards of any singer *ever*."

Jack shrugs as though this is no big deal. "Sure, okay. She's had a few bangers. But this country album? Nothing but an attention grab."

"She's reclaiming a genre—" I start.

"More like *maiming* a genre," Benny interrupts, then cackles at his own inane joke.

Sienna and I both glare at Benny, but Jack nods in agreement. "For real. Anyway, Vanessa, don't you care that she butchered that one song by your girl Dolly?"

In all the months since our third date, when Jack first commented on my tattoo, he hasn't mentioned it or Dolly Parton herself again. I'd assumed we were filing it next to all the other things on which Jack and I disagree (whether Greta Gerwig was robbed at the Oscars, whether dryer sheets are a waste of money, whether Jack's company should donate more money to environmental causes to offset their emissions), but now I hear the hidden razors in the phrase *your girl Dolly*, and I realize I misunderstood. Jack's no idiot; he knows there's more to the tattoo than I told him. I shift uneasily. Maybe Jack and I should have discussed our exes by now, but we haven't, and here on Gordo's balcony in the middle of a party is neither the place nor the time.

So I pretend I didn't hear the challenge in his voice and lightly say, "In no way did she 'butcher' it, Jack. And you don't just have to take my word for it—Dolly herself introduced Beyoncé's version."

"Hard agree," Sienna says, grabbing my hand. "Come on. Let's leave these philistines here with their skunky pot and go dance."

"Gladly." I loop my arm through Sienna's and stride into the condo with her. I feel Jack's gaze on my back the whole time, and if I know him, he's annoyed that I've walked away from him. Jackson Dalton is accustomed to having the last word.

I use my free hand to gather my long, fuchsia-tipped blond hair over one shoulder, fully exposing my Dolly Parton tattoo in the process. I don't care if Jack hates it. I want him to remember that I'm more than his fiancée, more than a pretty thing on his arm at parties. I'm a wholly separate person who had an entire life before I met him.

On nights like tonight, when I'm standing in a multimillion-dollar Manhattan condo, wearing a silk KHAITE dress and a Cartier LOVE bracelet, drinking a champagne cocktail mixed by a bartender hired for the occasion, my previous life seems like an eternity ago. Sienna drags me across the room to say hi to an up-and-coming actor, and then Jack joins our group, wrapping his arms around my waist and whispering an apology in my ear. I tell him it's okay, but the whole time, I wonder what it means that I would trade this—*all* this, Jack included—for just one more chance with Sam.

Chapter Two

When I was (briefly) a marketing associate, toiling away in a cubicle in Midtown, I used to fantasize about becoming a yoga instructor. I had this dreamy idea that it would mean doing asanas all day in cute leggings and drinking green juice with fellow wellness aficionados. I'm on the other side now, and I can safely say that, yeah, my life has plenty of asanas, leggings, and green juice. But it's not all savasana and inner peace. Teaching yoga involves careful class planning and studying anatomy and promotion and remembering to maintain your insurance and so many other tasks, not to mention all the headaches of running your own small business.

Now, technically, I'm not "just" a yoga teacher. Sienna, who works in branding, insists that I call myself a "wellness coach," and so that's what it says on my website and business cards. Teaching is what I love; it's what gets me up in the morning and propels me through my day. But a person can't eke out a living in New York on teaching yoga alone—not if they want any of that aforementioned green juice, anyway—which is why I do all the other things that fall under the wellness umbrella: creating courses and writing articles and working with sponsors. I know it all sounds kind of crass, but it's what enables me to follow my calling without depending on Jack.

It also keeps me incredibly busy. Today, for example, I started with teaching a 5:00 a.m. class at YogaFarm, followed by back-to-back private sessions at various points in SoHo, then hustled uptown for a podcast interview. I'm teaching again at YogaFarm tonight, plus I need to shoot and edit a new class for my YouTube channel and create some fresh content for my socials, not to mention prep for the retreat I'm leading in the Adirondacks this weekend. I'm overbooked and I know it, but on days like today I feel most alive. Both of my parents still harass me on the regular about my career path (my mother laments the instability of my income, while my father questions the practicality of working in the wellness space, despite having exactly zero legs to stand on because his wife, Cynthia, is about as woo-woo as they come), but I can't imagine things any other way. Yoga put me back together after I fell apart five years ago, and I love sharing its healing benefits with others.

My schedule is so packed today that I nearly decline when Sienna texts an invitation to coffee. I go so far as to type *sorry*, but then I change my mind. I really like Sienna, and it's so rare I get to spend time with her without Benny hanging around. I backspace and instead tell her sure, I'd love to grab some coffee.

Sienna is already at the café when I arrive, wearing a lacy blouse and a killer black leather skirt. Were I to wear that outfit, I'd look like I was cosplaying as a pirate, but on Sienna, it looks devastatingly cool. She's sipping an espresso and frowning at her phone, and I'm reminded that I'm not the only one who's busy.

"Hey," I say, hanging my yoga mat across the back of the chair opposite her.

"Hi, honey," she says, half rising and kissing me on the cheek. I notice that her eyes look a little red—but then again, it's pollen season, and half the city is OD'ing on allergy medication.

"I ordered you an oat-milk latte," she continues.

"Thanks." I kiss her cheek in return and drop into the chair, gratefully pulling the latte to myself. I surpassed my recommended daily allotment of caffeine two hours ago, but espresso hasn't killed anybody yet. I don't *think* it has, at least.

"I'm glad I could steal some of your time," Sienna says. "I know you're crazed. Your retreat is this weekend, right?"

"It is. Three full days without the internet. It's either going to be incredibly restorative or an absolute nightmare."

"Ugh, it sounds amazing." She makes a face at her phone, which is currently buzzing face down on the table. "I mean, to get a break from this thing? Sign me up."

"If you're serious, I'm sure we can squeeze in one more attendee."

"Don't tempt me. If I didn't think my boss would murder me for jetting off in the middle of a major project, I would so be there. An internet-free yoga retreat sounds like the ideal post-breakup getaway."

"Wait." I set down my drink and take in her red-rimmed eyes again. "Did you say *breakup*? Did you and Benny split?"

"Yep. It's over."

My first instinct is to cheer. Benny is an overgrown frat bro who failed into a cushy finance job because of his father's connections, and I never understood what Sienna saw in him. Judging by the tears crowding her eyes, however, I sense cheering might be inappropriate.

Instead, I mold my face into one of surprise and say, "Oh, wow. I didn't see that coming."

"Neither did he." She smiles crookedly and then sighs. "You've never liked him, have you?"

I hesitate. Sienna and I are friends, but the boys are our connection. Jack and Benny were college roommates and still thick as thieves. I'm very aware that anything I say might make its way back to Benny or Jack or both, and I'm also very aware that Jack would consider it a betrayal if I said anything negative about his best friend. Loyalty is important to him.

"I think I saw a different side of him than you did," I say diplomatically. "Do you want to tell me what happened?"

"There wasn't any one thing in particular. I came home from a spin class yesterday morning to find him reading a comic book in bed, and I was just like, what am I doing? Why am I with this person? He has all the ambition of, like, a single-celled organism." She shakes her head slightly, as though dazed. "So I told him it was over."

"Oh, wow." Something stirs in my chest, the notion that breaking up with someone can be as easy as that. "Just like that?"

"Just like that." She blinks, her eyes tearing. "We'd been together for six years. *Six years*, Vanessa. That's a huge chunk of my life, and we were so intertwined. We live in the same apartment. We share the same furniture. Our friends are the same friends." She laughs shakily. "Am I insane? Did I just break up with my entire life?"

"You're not insane," I tell her. "I get it."

And, honestly, I *do*. Splitting with Sam changed the trajectory of my whole existence. Before, I was an extroverted Big Ten sorority girl with plans to join a marketing firm in Chicago postgraduation; after, I was adrift in New York, crashing on my friend Ellie's IKEA futon while I tried to figure out my next step. Even now, when I've rebuilt my life into something beyond my wildest dreams and am engaged to a sought-after man, I keenly miss the more hopeful and less jaded person I used to be, the life I used to have, the man I used to love.

But that's just life, right? Everything is sunshine and puppies until it isn't, and then you move on because what else are you going to do? But no matter how much more sunshine or how many more puppies will be in your future, you're never quite the same again. It's like the teapot my mom inherited from my great-aunt. The summer I was seven, I was doing cartwheels in the living room (in direct defiance of my mother's instruction, she always reminds me) and knocked it off a table and broke it. Mom hot-glued it back together and made sure thereafter to keep it on a higher shelf, where, from a distance, it looks like it always did. Once you get close to it, though, you can see the cracks. There's no ignoring them.

But I don't think Sienna wants to hear me likening her to a broken teapot, and so I tell her, "I know it seems hard now, but it'll be okay. You'll be better off without him."

"I know. Would you believe that Benny thought a pair of handcuffs and a couple of tabs of Molly made for an amazing anniversary gift?" She laughs weakly. "But it feels like a divorce. He gets the apartment and vinyl collection, I get the Peloton and espresso machine, and we're fighting over custody of our friends."

"Getting the Peloton seems like it's working out in your favor. Besides, do you really want custody of Gordo?"

Sienna laughs, the first genuinely amused laugh I've heard out of her this afternoon. "God, no, Benny can keep him and his tacky fake Gucci." Her smile dies. "But Benny's also going to get to keep Jack, and I know that means he gets to keep you as well."

I recoil. "Jack and I aren't conjoined twins, Sienna."

"Of course not, but be honest, Vanessa: How often do you go out with just *your* friends?"

She has a point. My calendar is so crammed with Jack's friends' parties, investor dinners, and other social obligations—not to mention my towering pile of work commitments—that I barely have time to eat, let alone sleep. Occasionally, I find time to go out for meals with women I know from the wellness space, but we end up talking shop and writing off the whole thing on our taxes. I can't remember the last time I went out with friends for *fun*.

"I hear you," I say. "But I'll make time for you. I promise. Listen, I had a really bad breakup once. I remember what it's like and how much I needed other people. I won't abandon you."

My chest tightens the way it always does when I think about losing Sam. I wonder—not for the first or second or even fiftieth time—what it means that I can't put him in my past, that I can't summon the same intensity of emotion for the man I plan to marry.

"Thank you." Sienna smiles warmly and reaches across the table to squeeze my hand. "So you'll still invite me to the wedding?"

"Of course," I say, even as an unbidden thought darts into my mind: *There's not going to be a wedding.*

~

The rest of the afternoon, the conversation with Sienna runs on a loop through my head as I try to get some work done. She broke up with her boyfriend of six years as easily as canceling a dinner reservation. Could it really be that simple? Is that errant thought—*There's not going to be a wedding*—trying to tell me something? Should I follow her lead and break up with Jack?

But that's silly. Right? Of *course* Sienna broke up with Benny. Benny is a man constructed almost entirely of red flags, held together by hair pomade and bad ideas. Jack, on the other hand, is an Ivy League–educated, financially secure entrepreneur who not only knows how to cook but actually enjoys it, and also happens to look like a Disney prince.

But do I love him?

Sure. I mean, yes, of course I do. I must, right?

So what if he doesn't exactly make my heart sing? Who cares if I have never once looked at him and thought *I would die without this man*? Really, who needs that kind of intensity in their life? I needed Sam like I needed oxygen, and look where that got me.

Chapter Three

Two days later, I'm packing for the retreat and still thinking about Sienna. After six years, she shed Benny like an old skin, and now—if Instagram is to be believed—she's living her best life. I'm fascinated by it. Aren't breakups supposed to involve more angst?

Not that I would know. I've broken up with exactly one person my whole life, and I was fifteen years old. Our relationship consisted of holding hands in the school hallway and having his mother drive us to the movies, and it ran its course when he spent the homecoming dance huffing rubber cement in the boys' room instead of doing the "Cha-Cha Slide" with me.

Everyone else I've dated has broken up with me, which sounds pathetic, and maybe it is. I've always been too loyal, too quick to make excuses for bad behavior. I didn't even break up with Jeremy Mullins junior year after he made out with Ingrid Bolton literally an arm's length away from me at the Snowflake Formal, so why would I break up with Jack, who is—on paper, anyway—perfect? Just because of a random, errant thought?

As I fold another pair of butter-soft Beyond Yoga leggings and tell myself that everything is *fine*, I can't help but look around the room and feel a flicker of disquiet. There's nothing wrong with our bedroom, per se. Objectively speaking, it's gorgeous: an exposed brick wall and a twelve-foot ceiling, massive windows overlooking Broadway, a king-size bed covered in a gray duvet that's so soft you'd be forgiven for mistaking it for an actual cloud. A piece of abstract art—this one a Rothko, and yes, Jack told me it was authentic, as well as how much he paid for it—decorating one wall. Not a speck of clutter in sight, unless you count the colorful paperback by my side of the bed. Like I said, it's gorgeous. But it's not *me*.

Up until I moved in with Jack three months ago, I rented a tiny shoebox of an apartment on Avenue B. The studio was so small that in order to shoot my yoga videos there, I had to pile my chair and coffee table onto my bed, but I loved it. I'd painted the walls a cheery pink and covered them in photos, postcards, and other bits of memorabilia. I had a bright blue lamp that I adored, a ceramic cookie jar shaped like a kitten that I'd found at a flea market, and candles on every surface. It was chaotic and colorful and vibrant, and it was so incredibly, perfectly *me*. (The first and only time Jack visited me there, he said he worried it would give him an aneurysm.)

Jack's place is almost laughably the opposite. Other than a handful of high-end pieces of modern art (all hand-selected by his sister, Kathryn, an art dealer), it's almost completely devoid of personality. When I moved in, I tried—subtly, I thought—to spice things up with a few colorful throw pillows here, a collection of wooden elephants I bought in India there, but Jack frowned and told me he didn't like "clutter." Now my tchotchkes live in a box in the back of the hall closet, squeezed between Jack's skis and his scuba gear. I understand Jack's *Architectural Digest*–style vision for his home is classy and upscale—I do. But some days I feel like I'm living in a sterile mental hospital.

Those are the days that I fantasize about how I might live if I left him. Sure, I'd have to give up living in a condo with a doorman and on-site gym (complete with sauna), but I'd have free rein to decorate how I want. I'd paint the walls peppermint pink and grass green and cerulean blue, and I'd pile so many mismatched throw pillows on the couch you wouldn't even be able to see the damn thing. I'd buy that Dolly Parton painting in a bedazzled frame that I've been admiring on Etsy and hang it smack-dab in the center of the wall. I'd keep crystals on my nightstand, only drink out of glassware rescued from thrift shops, and light so many candles the place would look like a cathedral.

But that's nothing more than a daydream. It's fun to think about inconsequential things like decor, but I'm a twenty-seven-year-old woman—an *adult*—and I have more important things to consider. Financial security, for one. Teaching yoga is a dream come true, but it doesn't exactly provide the most stable of incomes. I could lose that revenue stream at any time. Jack, meanwhile, has enough money to never worry a day in his life. His grandfather is Harold Dalton, namesake of Dalton's, the famous department store; his mother's family is awash in oil money; and Jack himself is the founder of Jaxx Coin, one of the most popular cryptocurrency exchanges in the world. The amount of money Jack has access to is totally, completely ludicrous.

But the money, as comfortable as it makes our lives, is not why I'm with Jack. In fact, one of the things that I most admire about Jack is his determination to succeed on his own terms. He built Jaxx Coin from the ground up, soliciting investors and not using his family assets. While Jack is the first to admit his surname gave him an advantage, he's always envisioned himself a scrappy entrepreneur. I see myself the same way, and so we have that in common. And, of course, Jack is charming, with an adventurous, curious side that I love. That's the side of him that flew us to Iceland on a whim because I said I wanted to see the northern lights, and it's also the side of him that knows where to find the best dumplings on the Lower East Side.

We had those dumplings on our first date, in fact. We met a year ago, right after I appeared on the cover of *Yoga Journal* and attracted a wave of attention from people like Jack's sister, Kathryn, who hired me for private sessions. It turned out Kathryn's idea of "private instruction" meant having me bend her body *for* her, and where I normally would have gently guided the student toward independence, Kathryn Dalton is about as approachable as a cactus, and so I decided to just go along with it. I was busy folding Kathryn into sleeping pigeon pose, while she loudly complained, when her apartment door swung open, and there stood Jack.

And Jack—well, the man is good looking enough to stop traffic. As I clocked his golden hair and chiseled jaw, my hands slipped on Kathryn, and she gave an annoyed huff. Quickly, I apologized and renewed my efforts to help her open her hips, but even as I focused on Kathryn, I could feel Jack's eyes on me.

"Jacky!" Kathryn barked. "Can't you see I'm busy?"

I glanced up in time to see him smile slightly and slip out the door. Kathryn didn't mention who "Jacky" was, and I couldn't gather the nerve to ask.

The next night, though, I left an evening class at YogaFarm down on Essex to find the mysterious ocean blue–eyed man on the sidewalk, casually leaning against a pole like he was waiting for someone.

Like he was waiting for *me*, I realized as he straightened and grinned. "Hi."

"Hi," I returned, taking in his neatly combed hair, his light pink button-down with the sleeves rolled to his forearms, and his charcoal-colored pants that looked like they cost more than my rent. "Are you . . . waiting for me?"

"We met briefly at my sister's yesterday but weren't properly introduced." He extended his hand. "I'm Jackson Dalton. It's nice to meet you."

"Vanessa Summers," I said, taking his hand. "But you probably already knew that."

He gave me an abashed smile. "I'm not stalking you, I promise. But Kathryn wouldn't give me your phone number, so I googled you and saw you were teaching here tonight. I thought it would be less creepy than just calling you out of the blue, but now that I'm standing here, I'm wondering if I made the wrong decision."

I laughed. "It's only, like, fifteen percent creepy. But, you know, you could have just messaged me."

"You must get so many messages, though. I wasn't sure you'd even read it—and then how would I convince you to have dinner with me?"

"Consider me convinced," I said, smiling. "Let me give you my card, and we can set up dinner sometime."

"How about now?"

"Now?" I glanced down at my leggings and slouchy sweatshirt, the yoga mat strapped across my back. "I'm not really dressed for it."

"It's nothing fancy. But it *is* the best plate of dumplings you can buy in New York City."

I cocked an eyebrow. "I'll be the judge of that."

"Come on." Jack crooked his elbow, inviting me to take it like an old-timey couple, and I, feeling only slightly silly, obliged. We fell into surprisingly easy conversation about the neighborhood as he led me around the corner to this little hole-in-the-wall dumpling shop that I must have walked past dozens of times, and he bought me a plate of the most succulent cabbage-and-dried-tofu dumplings I've ever had. Jack was right: To this day, I believe those might be the best dumplings in the whole city.

He walked me home afterward, and just outside the scuffed vestibule of my building, he took gentle hold of my chin, tilted my face toward his, and kissed me softly. It was the kind of gentle-yet-assertive kiss that, if I were a different woman, would have lit up all my pleasure centers. As it was, though, my brain flickered and tripped back to my first kiss with Sam. That's how it always happened—the handful of first kisses I'd had since Sam immediately brought to mind the afternoon in Cancún when he and I first met: the smell of sunscreen, the sensation of his sandy thumb grazing my cheek, the softness in his voice as he asked permission to kiss me, and the crush of his salt-stained lips when he finally did. Sometimes I still wake up in the middle of the night, skin flushed and with the faintest taste of tequila in my mouth, and I know I've been reliving that kiss in my dreams. Even now, seven years later, standing in this minimalist palace and folding high-end clothing, like some post-ball Cinderella, I can almost feel Sam's lips on mine, can almost taste their brininess, and that—*that*—is what makes me really think about a happily ever after.

Or it *would* if Sam hadn't blocked me long ago on social media.

I hear the front door open, and there he is: the other reason why that kiss is ancient history. *Jack.* I shake my head to clear it and remind myself that Jack is my fiancé, that he's the one whose lips I should be thinking about. Not Sam's. Never Sam's again.

As I listen to Jack move through the apartment, I toss another pair of socks into my bag and wonder if it means something that I'm not calling out to him. If I loved Jack—*really* loved him, the way it counts—wouldn't I rush across these polished concrete floors to throw my arms around him? Or at least go greet him, ask how his day was? Something—anything—other than wondering what it would be like to redecorate this room with some *color*, or whether I could bounce back from a breakup as easily as Sienna?

Chapter Four

I don't like to brag—okay, I love to brag—but my tech-free retreat was an unmitigated success. The venue was perfect, the half dozen attendees were delightful, and I felt totally and completely in my element.

The only fly in my organic ointment was that the same intrusive thought—*There's not going to be a wedding*—kept swirling through my mind at the most inopportune times. It popped up whenever I tried to meditate or when I led the women in savasana; it circled when I walked in the woods surrounding the property or when I lay on the king-size pillow-topped bed.

My subconscious is clearly trying to tell me something. Maybe I ought to listen.

I'm so caught up in these thoughts that now, as I drag my suitcase into the lobby to check out, it takes me a moment to realize something is amiss. The room is designed to be perfectly serene, a calming cocoon of white, scented with eucalyptus from an essential-oil diffuser in the corner, but the three linen-clad women behind the reception desk are gathered in a tight knot, whispering animatedly. And here's the kicker: They *stop* when they see me. One of them lets out a nervous giggle before turning on her heel and walking briskly out of the lobby, and a second woman follows close behind her, stealing a glance at me as she passes. The remaining receptionist looks stricken, apparently horrified to be left alone with me.

Honestly, that kind of hurts my feelings. I'm no diva. Quite the opposite, in fact. I'm friendly to a fault. I'm often tagged in Instagram photos appended with captions like "Took a class from @vanessa.summers today! She is SO NICE!" Jack attributes it to my Midwestern upbringing and finds it alternately endearing and annoying.

Now the woman behind the desk—Dahlia, as her name tag reads—looks at me like she's concerned I might eat her alive. I offer her one of my most charming smiles, and she actually *flinches*.

I'm beyond confused, but the car I've arranged to drive me home should already be outside, and I don't want to keep the driver waiting.

"Hi," I say, placing my room key on the counter. "I'm checking out."

"Of course, Ms. Summers." Dahlia gives me a shaky smile and slides her eyes away. "How . . . was everything?"

"Perfect, thank you." I try to make eye contact with her, but she keeps her gaze fixed intently on her computer screen. I frown slightly, wondering if there's some sort of problem. Perhaps one of my retreat guests did something she shouldn't have? That seems unlikely. The women who attended were all lovely, not to mention the sort of lululemon-clad, Botoxed thirty- and fortysomethings you'd expect on a retreat in the Adirondacks with a price tag of $2,000 per day—which is to say that I can't really see any of them skipping out on their juice-bar tab or stealing the towels.

"Is Gloria around?" I ask. "I'd love to thank her personally for all her help in pulling off this retreat."

Dahlia freezes, her eyes still on the screen, and then shakes her head jerkily. "Gloria . . . is in a meeting."

My frown deepens. Gloria, the resort event coordinator, has been in nonstop communication with me since I started planning this retreat. In the weeks leading up to it, we emailed multiple times a day, and when I arrived, she greeted me with a bouquet of freshly cut flowers and the sort of hug you'd expect from an old friend. She even stopped me on my way to my room last night to confirm my time of departure and to assure me she'd be waiting for me.

"Are you sure? I think she's expecting me."

"I can leave her a message."

"All right." I place my hands at heart center and offer Dahlia one of my famous Midwestern smiles. "Dahlia, honey, something is clearly going on here. Why don't you just tell me what it is, and then we can figure out how to fix it? Was it one of the guests? Did they—"

"You can't be here!" a loud voice booms.

Dahlia and I both startle, and I turn to see Luc, the resort's concierge—a man who, incidentally, has the arm span of a professional basketball player—standing between me and the grand double doors constructed from roughly hewn wood. He's holding one enormous hand out like a traffic cop to block the path of a young woman doggedly trying to weave around him.

"This is private property," he continues.

"I only need a minute. I—" She stops short when she catches my eye, and her face lights up. "Vanessa!"

I tilt my head, trying to place her. She has a round, baby-like face and brown hair scraped into a tight ponytail, and she's wearing a blue-and-white-striped collared shirt that desperately needs to be introduced to an iron, with a beat-up canvas messenger bag slung across her body. She's certainly not one of my guests. My first thought is that she looks like a friend of Faith's—she appears closer to my sister's age than mine, and Faith has the same unfortunate habit of rushing around in rumpled business casual. But I dismiss the idea almost as soon as it forms. Faith lives in Chicago. Why would one of her friends chase me down in Upstate New York? Why would anyone?

"Again, this is private property," Luc says, placing his body in front of hers. "I cannot let you harass our guests. If you don't leave immediately, I'm going to call security."

"Wait a second, Luc," I say. "It's okay."

He shoots a long-suffering glance at me over his shoulder, clearly telegraphing his displeasure, and then steps slightly to the side, keeping his muscled arms crossed firmly across his broad chest.

"Vanessa, hi," the woman says, stepping forward and extending a hand. "My name is Fern Foxall. I'm an independent journalist."

I blink. I've been a public figure for almost three years now, ever since my first yoga video went viral, and my Google-search results exploded after I started dating Jack last year—I have my own Wikipedia page now and everything—but I'm no celebrity. I'm not the kind of person a reporter drives across town to interview, much less one they would travel *hours* to see. Hesitantly, I shake her hand, then I riffle through my bag for a business card.

"Here," I say, holding a bright pink card out to her. "This is my card. You can reach out later to schedule an interview. I'm flattered you've made the trek to see me here, but now isn't really a good time. I'm in the middle of checking out, and I have a driver waiting for me, so . . ."

I trail off as I realize that everyone in the room is looking at me strangely. I sneak a glimpse in the mirror behind Dahlia's head, wondering if I have smoothie on my face or if I walked out of my room wearing a zit sticker or something, but my reflection looks as expected. Face clean, pink-tipped blond hair in an orderly ponytail, no errant bra straps visible. In the mirror, I see the two receptionists who fled at my approach quietly reentering the lobby through a side door, their eyes wide and expressions eager.

Fern takes the card without looking at it and tucks it in her bag, then produces a handheld recorder. She clicks it on and holds it aloft between us. "Vanessa, would you like to comment on the Jackson Dalton situation?"

I catch my breath. If I somehow manifested harm to Jack with my doubts about our wedding . . .

"What do you mean, 'situation'? Is Jack okay?"

"I mean the situation with Jaxx Coin," Fern says slowly, as though she's speaking to a child.

She might as well be. My fiancé may be the founder of one of the largest cryptocurrency exchanges in the world, but that doesn't mean I understand even the most basic things about it. Once, not long after we first started dating, I asked Jack to explain cryptocurrency to me, but my attention had wandered by the time he said *blockchain*. I told myself I'd read up on it in my spare time, but I never had spare time. I figured I didn't need to understand it; Jack knew more than enough about the subject for both of us.

I look around to see if anyone else is also mystified, but they're all staring at me intently. It's unsettling.

"Do you have a comment?" Fern presses, bringing the recorder closer to me.

As I fight the urge to smack the recorder out of the air, the pieces start sliding into place: The whispering receptionists abruptly going silent when I walked into the lobby. Two of them running away. Dahlia's complete lack of eye contact. Gloria claiming to be in a "meeting." Anxiety roils through my limbs as I realize that whatever this "situation" is, it's something big. Something that's already all over the news.

"Look," I snap at Fern, masking my fear with irritation. "There's no service or Wi-Fi here. I haven't heard from the outside world—Jack included—since I left the city on Thursday night. If you want a comment, first you're going to have to tell me what on earth is going on."

Fern tips her head at me. "That's precisely the question."

I growl in frustration and whirl around to face Dahlia. "That computer you have there. It's hooked up to the internet, right?"

"Um, yeah."

"Perfect. You don't mind, do you?"

Without waiting for a response, I hoist myself up and over the reception counter, ignoring the twinge in my left knee. Dahlia backs away, wide eyed, and I take her place in front of the computer. I reach for the keyboard, ready to google Jack's name, but it turns out I don't have to. The browser is open to cnn.com, where the boldfaced headline reads **CRYPTO CRASH: JAXX COIN VALUE PLUMMETS, FOUNDER JACKSON DALTON SOUGHT IN POTENTIAL FRAUD PROBE.**

I feel like I've walked off the edge of a cliff. *Fraud.* The edges of my vision start to shimmer, and I know it's not just because I've consumed nothing but juice and raw vegetables for the last seventy-two hours. I grip the counter tightly in an effort to keep myself upright.

I curse under my breath.

"Can I quote you on that?" Fern asks, approaching with her recorder.

"No, you may not," I say sharply. "I just need—"

I clamber back over the desk and grab my bag off the floor. With fumbling hands, I extract my cell phone and switch it on. My heart skitters as the service bars dance tantalizingly, then drops as "No Service" replaces them. I kick myself. I chose this location precisely *because* it was so far off the beaten path that, short of building your own tower, there's no way to pull down a signal. I billed it as "an unmissable opportunity to disconnect" and "the perfect site for a digital detox." I assured my guests they'd be reachable via landline in the case of a true emergency, but I'd never once imagined *this* sort of emergency. I eye the landline on the desk, but there's no way I can use it to call Jack. I can't talk to him here, not with that reporter standing there, watching me wolfishly. Not before I know exactly what is going on.

"I have to go," I say to no one in particular and seize my luggage.

"Vanessa—" Fern starts, but Luc, to his great credit, steps in front of her and extends his long arms, holding her back.

I rush out the front door and straight to the black town car parked in the circular drive.

"Ms. Summers?" the driver asks, opening the back seat door for me.

"That's me," I say. I glance toward the resort door, where Fern is now emerging, calling my name. "And I'm sort of in a hurry."

"Understood." The driver shuts the car door behind me and then loads my luggage into the trunk. I can hear Fern still calling my name, and I sink down low in the seat. I clench my phone so tightly that my knuckles turn white, anxious to get to an area with service. I need to talk to Jack. I need to figure out what's going on. This has to be a mistake. It *has* to be. If it's not . . . well, I've reinvented myself once before. I can do it again.

I think.

Chapter Five

One Month Later

"Jack is a coward," my sister decrees through a mouthful of peanut butter toast. She's perched on her faded floral couch, glaring angrily at her television, where CNN is currently displaying a chyron reading CRYPTO CON: WHERE IS JAXX FOUNDER JACKSON DALTON?

"Preaching to the choir, sis," I say from the kitchen area of her apartment as I dump chia seeds into her blender. Faith's blender—like most of the furniture and appliances in her cozy Lakeview apartment—is what she calls a "law student special," by which she means she acquired it for free from her school's listserv. Like all of these "special" items, the blender has seen better days. It has one operational button (plus four that do absolutely nothing) and a suspicious dark red stain on its base. ("Marinara," Faith said when she caught me looking at it. "I think.") I never thought I'd be the sort of person to wax poetic over an appliance, but I'm dangerously close to actually *yearning* for Jack's industrial-strength Vitamix. That beauty could demolish a raw beet in two seconds flat. Faith's blender, in contrast, can barely mash a banana.

"I can't believe you were actually going to marry that bozo."

Pain pricks my heart, sharp and fast, like a needle, as it always does when I think of Jack. Handsome, swaggering, funny Jack, who used to wake me up with off-key serenades of Bruce Springsteen songs and who always saved the best blueberries for me—and also arrogant, power-hungry Jack, who treated my middle-class Midwestern origins like something to be ashamed of and regarded my career as a cute little hobby but didn't mind polishing me up like his personal Barbie doll and trotting me out for the cameras. I might have been contemplating breaking off our engagement, but I was still blindsided by the way things ended.

"I wasn't so sure that I was going to."

Before Faith can respond, I depress the blender's sole button, and the machine chugs grudgingly to life, lazily whirling together coconut milk, spinach, banana, peanut butter, chia seeds, and bee pollen.

Faith scowls. "Don't do that."

"Don't do what?" I ask over the machine's worryingly metallic grinding noise. "Don't make use of your state-of-the-art appliances? What happened to 'make yourself at home, Vanessa'?"

"You *have* made yourself at home. Or are those someone else's sports bras and leggings currently draped all over my bathroom?"

"*Our* bathroom," I correct. "I pay rent, thank you very much."

Faith rolls her eyes good-naturedly. "I should have just found another roommate on the listserv."

"And what? Leave your own flesh and blood on the street?" I put a hand to my chest in mock horror.

"You'll note you're not on the street. But, I don't know, maybe you'll think twice next time before you shack up with a con artist."

"Too soon, sis. And don't act like the timing wasn't perfect—what with you needing a roommate and all."

"A little too perfect," she agrees, casting me a comically suspicious glance. "Am I going to later learn that you paid Corinna to move out?"

"Oh, honey, if I had the money to bribe your old roommate, I'd probably also have the money to get a place of my own with a functional blender. No offense."

"Knock that blender one more time, and that's the last time you use it," she jokes. She takes a bite of her toast and adds, "I know what you're doing, by the way."

"Making a healthful breakfast?" I ask, lifting the blender jar and squinting skeptically at the contents.

"You're changing the subject."

"From Jack? Of course I am. Can you blame me?" I turn my back on my little sister, riffling through her cabinets for a glass.

"I'm your sister," Faith says, her voice softening. "You can tell me things. You don't need to hide behind the noise of a blender or a joke."

My hands shake as I select one of her mismatching glasses. "I'm not hiding—or, I don't mean to be. Look, talking about Jack is hard, okay? I was thisclose to breaking up with him, but that doesn't erase the fact that we still had a life together. I mean, you feel close to somebody when you brush your teeth next to them twice a day, you know?"

I glance over at the television, which currently shows an image of Jack in all his chiseled glory. His ocean blue eyes. His wavy, golden hair. His *cheekbones*. God. Hot tears build behind my eyes, and I pinch the bridge of my nose to hold them back. I've done enough crying over Jackson Dalton to last me several lifetimes.

"Sometimes I feel like it'd be easier to take if I at least understood what happened," I continue, turning away from the television and angrily pouring my smoothie. "I mean, I get that he lost billions of dollars and may have single-handedly brought down the crypto market. But like . . . *how*? Jack isn't some flake. That's what I don't get. How did he not see it coming?"

"I think," Faith says carefully, "that he probably did. Maybe not the extent of it, but he must have known something was about to break. You don't go from running some massive cryptocurrency exchange one day to bankrupting thousands of people the next without having an *inkling* that something is wrong."

"But then, why didn't he *say* anything? I told you how the last time I saw him, he was heading out the door to grab drinks with his dumb friend Benny, right? He gave me a quick kiss and said, 'See you on Sunday, babe.' Just totally normal."

"Like I said, the man's a coward." Faith bites into her toast. "Do you think he'll resurface soon?"

"Jack's the textbook example of an extrovert. There's no way he can stay holed up alone for long."

"Think he'll call you when he reemerges?"

I shake my head. "Literally no clue. But I still have less than zero interest in talking to him if he does. Seriously, I'd rather have a marathon phone call with *Cynthia*."

"But our dear stepmother is *an animal psychic*," Faith says, barely keeping a straight face. "And our father assures us she's *dying* to be a grandmother."

"Hand to God, I would happily sit through another one of Cynthia's monologues about how I really ought to visit Dad more often if it meant that I never had to see or think about Jack again. It's just . . ." I trail off and shake my head. "It feels so weird to have no closure. And usually I think *closure* is such a schmaltzy word, like who really needs it? But to go from thinking that everything is fine to having my life completely upended . . . well, I guess I'd just like to know *why*."

"Greed. Greed is why."

"I don't know. I mean, even without Jaxx Coin, Jack had access to more money than he could reasonably spend in this lifetime. It was kind of gross, actually. So . . . I think there's more to it. Something else happened that led to all this and chased him off to Bermuda or wherever the hell he's hiding out."

"He's not in Bermuda. Bermuda has an extradition treaty with the US."

I grin because of course my sister knows a mundane legal detail like that. "All right, Counselor. Where do *you* think he is?"

She taps her toast against her plate in thought. "Switzerland, maybe? They don't extradite for certain financial crimes."

"God," I say, cringing. "*Crimes.* My former fiancé is a *criminal*."

"I didn't call him a criminal, per se . . ."

"But him fleeing the country doesn't speak to his innocence."

"It does not, no."

I sag against the counter. "Did I tell you we were planning on skiing in Switzerland this winter? I was really looking forward to it."

"Do you even know how to ski?"

"How hard can it be? Gravity basically pulls you down the slope, right?"

Faith stifles a laugh. "I guess it's a good thing his Ponzi scheme melted down before you ended up in traction."

"You're such a jerk," I laugh, throwing a wadded-up paper towel at her. "And what happened to not calling him a criminal?"

"That was me being nice. This is me being honest."

"You really think Jack was running a Ponzi scheme?"

"I don't know a ton about decentralized currency, but from what I've read, it looks like Jack was borrowing money from new Jaxx Coin investors to pay off old investors, and . . . yeah, hon, that's a Ponzi scheme. The biggest one since Madoff, actually."

"But it was, like, fake money."

"Just because you don't understand crypto doesn't mean it's fake."

"Ugh." I sample my smoothie. In a completely unsurprising turn of events, the bananas are still chunky. "Anyway, as uplifting as this chat has been, I really should get moving. I'm meeting Gemma in an hour. Which do you think says 'Please take pity on me' more: my blue romper or my floral sundress?"

"Grown women look ridiculous in rompers, so go with that if it's pity you're after. But, Vanessa, you don't need her to take pity on you. You're really talented. Gemma will be lucky to have you teach at her studio."

"Can you just follow me around today and be my personal cheerleader?"

"I wish, but the law firm is having a kickball tournament today." She rolls her eyes. "It's supposed to make us summer associates think big law is full of camaraderie and fun, but it's not fooling anyone." She shoves the last bite of toast into her mouth and rises from the couch. "Anyway, forget about Jack and whatever number he pulled on your self-confidence. You're Vanessa Summers, the woman who rocketed herself to yoga stardom with just an outdated iPhone and an internet connection. Everything you need to succeed is right in there." Faith taps my forehead with one of her peanut-buttery fingers. "Gemma would have to be out of her mind not to hire you."

I wipe the peanut butter from my forehead and wish that I had half the confidence my sister has in me.

~

By the time I scurry into the Pick Me Up Cafe, I'm ten minutes late. I catch my breath in the doorway and look around the restaurant. I easily spot Gemma, all six feet four of her, seated at a vibrantly painted booth along the side wall. I smooth the wrinkles from my linen romper and curse myself for not managing to arrive on time, just this once. Gemma and I have been friends since we met during yoga-teacher training in Rishikesh three years ago, but I'm about to throw myself at her pedicured feet to beg for a job at the studio she owns, and it would have been nice to start without reminding her how perpetually tardy I am.

"Sorry I'm late!" I call as I approach the booth. "My Chicago geography leaves something to be desired, and I walked three blocks in the wrong direction before I realized it."

"Oh, please, don't even worry about it." Gemma waves away my apology with an elegant hand and rises to greet me. She's wearing a minimalist-chic loose ecru-colored dress, and I realize with horror that Faith was right: I *do* look like a toddler in this outfit. Gemma extends her arms and wraps me in a sandalwood-scented embrace, and I have to extract myself before the warmth of her greeting makes me cry.

"Sit, please," she says. "I ordered you an iced chai."

"That's so thoughtful, thank you." I slide into the booth across from her. "And thanks for making time for me."

"Of course. I was so glad to hear from you. Besides, I still owe you one for saving me from those unruly monkeys."

I laugh, remembering the band of monkeys that lurked around the yoga school's housing. If you left clothing drying outside your window or food on the ledge, the monkeys would snatch it and carry it off—and if you were unlucky like Gemma and had a window that didn't latch, well, you might find the monkeys having a pillow fight in your room.

"Those monkeys were true menaces."

"The worst," Gemma agrees. "You know, I just hired a new teacher who studied there, too. She said those monkeys are still at it. They made off with one of her sports bras."

"I just wish I knew what those monkeys are doing with all those clothes." I force a laugh, but really I'm starting to sweat. Gemma *just* hired someone? Either that means she's actively adding new teachers, or—more likely—she's staffed up and doesn't need me.

"I like to think they're wearing them."

"Like one monkey to one piece of clothing, or are you envisioning several monkeys standing on each other's shoulders to fill out a pair of pants and matching shirt?"

"The latter, definitely," Gemma says, her twists bouncing as she laughs.

"God, I hope so." I take a nervous sip of my tea and decide to just go for it. "Hey, if you're serious about owing me—I have to admit that I invited you here to ask a favor."

"Of course."

I draw back, surprised. "Ouch."

"No, no! I didn't mean *of course* you're asking me for a favor. I meant that my answer is *of course*."

"But you don't even know what I'm going to ask. Maybe I'm here to borrow ten thousand dollars."

"That's not what you're here for," she says confidently. "You want a job."

I nod, humbled. "I'm a good instructor. I'll be on time for class, I promise. I—"

"You don't have to sell yourself to me! I know you're a great instructor. When I took that workshop you led at the *Yoga Journal* conference last year, I was just blown away. You have a really approachable style. My students will love you." She pulls out her phone and taps on it briefly. "Rachel, who teaches my sunrise vinyasa class on Tuesdays and Thursdays, went out on maternity leave last week. I've been subbing for her since then, but I'd be more than happy to have you take over the early class, if that works for you?"

I nod emphatically. "Absolutely."

"I've also been thinking about adding a Friday-afternoon class to the schedule. If you'd like that time slot, we can talk about ideas. And I'm always looking for workshops—"

"Thank you," I interrupt, emotion making my voice hoarse. "Thank you so much, Gemma. You won't regret this."

"I know, honey," she says, leaning across the table to squeeze my hand. "I'm sorry I didn't reach out earlier. How have you been holding up?"

I lift one shoulder in a half shrug. "Fine, I guess? Honestly, yoga's been my savior these last few weeks. If I didn't have my practice, I think I would have just completely lost my mind."

"You're strong, Vanessa. You always have been."

She gives me a sympathetic smile, and I know she's thinking about those nights during teacher training when we, physically exhausted from the long day of asanas but mentally stimulated, would lie on the hard mattress in her room in the dark and talk for hours. Gemma told me about her dead-end job in finance and the long-distance relationship she'd just ended because he wanted her to move to Texas; I told her about the marketing job that had evaporated during the pandemic and, of course, about Sam.

"Thanks for believing in me," I say. "I promise I won't let you down."

But as I reach my hand across the table to take Gemma's, I'm struck by the thought that I can't really promise that. No one can. Sometimes, despite our best intentions, we let people down. Even people we love.

Chapter Six

In the two weeks that I've been teaching classes at House of Om, attendance in my morning classes has steadily increased, and last Friday afternoon, my power *vinyasa* had a wait list. I'm thrilled that my classes seem to be resonating with Gemma's students. The pace of teaching here is different but good. Back in New York, before everything fell apart, I taught a half dozen live classes each week, in addition to the videos I made for YouTube and TikTok, not to mention private classes, workshops, and the occasional retreat. I loved every minute of it, but I was constantly bone tired. I rarely had any time for myself, or to spend with just Jack. Sometimes I wonder if my overstuffed schedule is the reason I didn't notice anything was wrong with Jaxx Coin—or, for that matter, that things weren't quite right with Jack, either. Not that it makes a difference. The past is the past, and no one can change it. I'm trying to focus on the present, on how teaching at Gemma's cozy Uptown studio has reignited an authenticity in my practice I'd lost. It's *fun* in a way that my jam-packed, clout-chasing schedule in New York wasn't.

Like now, as I'm seated cross-legged on Faith's couch, planning out the flow for Tuesday morning's class, I'm *smiling*. Faith, curled up in an armchair with a biography of Sonia Sotomayor, keeps giving me suspicious glances, as though she doesn't trust my happiness. Hey, you and me both, sister. I'm not sure I can remember the last time I felt so *content*. It's been months, certainly, if not years.

I'm debating whether to include *surya namaskar B*—my knee has been giving me problems lately, and I'm a little afraid of chair-posing in front of a crowd—when my phone buzzes on the cushion beside me. I glance down at it and tense when I see the incoming call is from Fern Foxall, the journalist who showed up at the resort and dropped the bomb about Jack. This is the fifth time she's called in as many days—and that's not counting all the texts she's sent. I've been ignoring her messages, just like I've been ignoring the keyboard warriors who keep sliding into my DMs to accuse me of conspiring with Jack, warn me that they're going to "gut that dickbag like a fish" and send me "what's left of his rotten guts," and/or call me a "desgusting crptyo wh0re." (The creative spelling is the only thing I appreciate about those messages.) Sometimes I wonder if Jack feels bad about the terrible situation he left me in, but then I realize that if Jack were capable of feeling guilty, he most likely would not have defrauded people out of gobs of money in the first place.

Anyway, I don't even know how Fern got my personal number; it's not listed on the card I gave her. Her messages have all been about some article she's writing. She keeps insisting that she wants to tell my "side" of the "story" and let people see the "real" me. Both claims set off my bullshit detector. Once upon a time, I considered myself a good judge of people. But then my fiancé made several billion dollars disappear before disappearing himself, and, well, maybe I don't judge people as well as I think.

I resolve to block her number just as the phone finally—thankfully—stops ringing. I pick up the device to do just that, but it vibrates in my hands. My stomach pitches at the sight of Fern's name on the screen once again.

And then I read the message.

Just remember that you had your chance.

"Whatever, drama queen," I murmur, but I'm not fooling myself. Already my mind is spinning as I wonder if I should call her now, if I can head off whatever threat she seems to be making.

"Did you say something?" Faith asks, looking up from her book.

"Just to myself. You won't believe the random—" I cut myself off as my phone buzzes with another incoming message from Fern. This time it's a link. From the phone-generated preview, I can see it's a piece from *The Cut* entitled "The Crypto Con's Girlfriend." Worse, the cover art prominently features my face—a silly promotional shot where I'm winking ostentatiously at the camera. It seemed fun at the time the picture was taken, but now it looks obnoxious, taunting.

"Vanessa?" Faith prompts. "What won't I believe?"

I can't answer my sister. I can't do anything other than slowly raise a finger to click that link, even though every cell in my body screams its objection. But how can I not? I have to know what Fern is saying about me, even though I would vastly prefer to remain ignorant. For years, I devoured every word written about me online. YouTube comments, Instagram Stories, Yelp reviews, and, later, trend pieces. I had a variety of Google Alerts set to ensure I never missed a mention.

But that was before Jack blew up our lives and before people started speculating that we were some sort of more hip, less violent millennial Bonnie and Clyde. Now I've turned off my alerts and taken my accounts private. Briefly, I entertain the idea of just deleting Fern's message and moving on with my day, but I know I can't. As much as I don't want to know what she's written, I *need* to know. I need to prepare myself for what's coming next.

My stomach clenched like a fist, I click open the link and read the full headline: THE CRYPTO CON'S GIRLFRIEND: COCONSPIRATOR OR INNOCENT RUBE?

Somehow, I can tell I'm not going to like either conclusion. Bile rises in my throat as I start to skim.

It's been one month since Jaxx Coin plummeted in value, destroying the world's cryptocurrency market in the process. A lot of people have a lot of questions about what caused this unprecedented crash, but the man with the answers refuses to say anything. Jackson Dalton, Jaxx Coin founder and CEO, is speculated to have left the country to avoid prosecution for wire fraud, and he has remained frustratingly mute. His only communication has been a short video, posted on his sister's Instagram Stories, claiming that he's innocent. The video offered no explanations or excuses—and certainly no promises to answer for what happened.

With Dalton refusing to account for the disaster that was Jaxx Coin, people are starting to ask themselves who *else* might know what happened. Who else might have seen this coming? Who else might have known whether Dalton started Jaxx Coin with the intent of defrauding thousands of innocent people, or whether circumstances led him there? Dalton was vocal about operating Jaxx Coin independent of his wealthy family, and he was famously hands-on, functioning without a board and with little input from anyone else; other high-ranking Jaxx Coin employees were just as blindsided. Dalton's sister, the art dealer Kathryn Dalton, said through her publicist that the single video posted on her Stories is the extent of her knowledge and that she is just as much in the dark as everyone else. She also claims to have lost a "significant" sum of money in the crash, although it remains an open question how Ms. Dalton defines "significant"—a significant sum to the average American, or even a well-off American, is substantially less than anything that would make a difference to the Dalton family.

> Which leaves one person: Jackson Dalton's fiancée, Vanessa Summers. The popular yogi, who rocketed to fame first on YouTube and then on TikTok, was first linked to Dalton last year and, according to sources, moved into Dalton's SoHo loft three months before the value of Jaxx Coin plummeted, dragging the rest of the market with it. Forensic accounting shows that it was during those same three months that Dalton began moving money in suspicious ways, seemingly trying to hide that Jaxx Coin was overvalued and underleveraged. It seems improbable—no, make that *impossible*—that Summers didn't know the business was in trouble. The question, then, is whether she knew enough to be considered an accomplice.

The scream is so guttural, so *raw*, that at first I don't even realize it's coming from me. It isn't until Faith sits beside me and places a cautious hand on my shoulder that I recognize I'm crying.

"Vanessa? What's going on?"

I can't answer her. A dark part of myself insists this is *my* fault, that I *asked* for this. Haven't I been an attention seeker my whole life? Haven't I been chasing fame the way a personal-injury lawyer chases ambulances? I mean, a person doesn't become an influencer of any variety without at least a hint of narcissism. Up until now, I've been blessed with largely good press. Even in the immediate aftermath of Jack's disappearing act, most outlets seemed sympathetic to me, if they mentioned me at all. But every sword has a double edge.

"Vanessa?" Faith asks again, concern threading through her voice.

I thrust my phone at her. "Look."

"Oh God," she murmurs, scanning the article. "Oh, Vanessa."

"She can't *do* this!" I cry. "Can she? You're an almost-lawyer; isn't there a rule against trashing innocent people in print?"

"You're talking about libel," Faith says, her eyes moving quickly as she skims the story. "To be guilty of libel, she has to write something that is demonstrably false. So far, I don't see anything like that."

"Are you kidding? What about this: 'It seems improbable—no, make that *impossible*—that Summers didn't know the business was in trouble.' Or this," I say, leaning over Faith to point out another offensive line. "'Any reasonable person would realize that if something is too good to be true, it usually is.' How is that not *false*?"

"Technically, that's just her opinion."

"Well, her opinion sucks," I splutter, hot tears brimming in my eyes. "Why is she picking on me? I'm a victim, too. Maybe I didn't lose hundreds of thousands of dollars, but my career has suffered. I'll never recover my reputation, not if vultures like Fern Foxall keep dragging my name through the mud. And for *what*? She's acting like Jack and I would sit there and talk about his dumb company over dinner or something, when really that's the *last* thing we would talk about. He had other people to discuss that stuff with. Employees. Friends who were in the business. Why isn't she interrogating *them*?"

"It sounds like she might have interviewed them," Faith says, using a finger to scroll through the article. "But, Vanessa, there *is* one thing she's right about: You were the one who lived with him when things really went off the rails. It's reasonable to wonder whether you might have seen something—"

"Faith," I interrupt. My voice breaks, and I have to try again. "*Faith.* You're my *sister*. Please. I need you on my side."

"I'm *on* your side. Of course I am. I just—"

"You just *what*?"

Faith is silent for a beat too long, then looks away. My body hollows out. If I don't have Faith, I don't have anything. Faith has always been the one constant in my life, ever since she was born when I was three. Our dad was a consultant who specialized in reorganizing hospitals, and we moved around a lot—the better he did his job, the shorter our time in any particular location. I don't think I could have handled all the moves without Faith. Each time we started over somewhere new, it was us Summers girls against the world. When the mean girls in suburban Columbus pelted me with spitballs on the walk home, Faith was the one who let the air out of their bicycle tires. And when an older boy in Springfield kept calling Faith "Dumbo" because her ears stuck out ever so slightly, I was the one who punched him right in his stupid face.

And later, when our parents split up during my junior year of high school, Faith was the only one who understood. She alone knew what it was like to watch our father move once again, this time without us, and she was the only one who understood how awful it felt to witness our mother's clear jealousy over Dad's new freedom. Faith is the one person I can count on no matter what. Whether I need a Band-Aid or a shoulder to cry on, a fresh drink or to borrow a shirt, Faith is always there. There's a reason that I showed up on Faith's doorstep after Jack's disappearance, not my mother's in San Diego or my father's in Tampa, and it wasn't just because I knew Faith needed a new roommate. It was because she is—and always has been—my rock.

But the way she's refusing to look at me feels like a betrayal just as keenly as if she'd literally stabbed me in the back. And, look, I'm not Caesar. I'm not capable of a dignified *et tu*. Instead, I screech like a wounded raccoon and choke out, "You've got to be *kidding* me."

Faith blinks. "Wait, Vanessa, I didn't—"

"I can't," I interrupt, my voice thick with restrained sobs. "I just can't do this right now, Faith. I'm going on a run."

"Now?" Faith glances anxiously out the window. "There's a storm coming."

"It's not here yet." I stalk to the door and step into my sneakers, yanking so hard on the laces I'm surprised they don't snap. "But I won't melt in the rain. Shocker, I know."

"Look, I'm sorry, I just—"

"Please, Faith," I manage. I peel off my oversize T-shirt and toss it across the room, leaving me in my leggings and running bra. I momentarily think about getting a better shirt from my room, but I need to get out of this apartment before I totally fall apart, and, anyway, it's warm outside. "I just need to get out of here."

"Wait," she says, riffling through her purse. She produces her bus pass and holds it out to me. "Take this, okay? I don't want you to get stranded somewhere in the rain."

"I'll be *fine*, Faith," I grind out, but I nonetheless take the bus pass and tuck it into my leggings. Then I rush out the door before the tears can start to fall.

Chapter Seven

I'm no meteorologist, but I realize as soon as I step out onto the sidewalk that Faith is right: It's going to rain, and it's going to rain soon. Dark clouds are gathering in the west, and a cool breeze cuts through the warm air. I reach for my phone to check the weather, but I don't have it. I must have left it in Faith's apartment, and there's no way I'm going back for it now, not after I made such a scene on my way out the door. I'm already embarrassed by my blatant display of self-pity.

Anyway, it's probably for the best. If I had my phone, I'm sure I'd be inundated with texts from "concerned" "friends" who had seen the hit piece, all who would be sending me links to the very social media posts I've turned off my notifications to avoid.

I shake it off like I'm Taylor Swift, and then I begin running down Sheridan Road toward Lincoln Park. Running has never failed me. Ever since I was a kid, barreling down unfamiliar suburban streets in yet another new town, I've used running as a balm for my more difficult emotions. Upset that no one would sit with me at lunch? Run. Overheard my parents fighting once more? Run. Mortified because I tried too hard yet again? Run. I had plenty of reasons to run as a kid, and the habit has stuck with me into adulthood.

For the first block or so, the accusation from the headline—*coconspirator or innocent rube*—repeats through my mind on a loop, interrupted occasionally by a vivid memory of Faith deliberately averting her eyes. By the time I reach the pond, however, my mind is clear—mostly. I remind myself that *mostly clear* is good enough for right now, even as I long for complete, blissful blankness. As a yoga teacher, I often tell students they shouldn't let their quest for a picture-perfect Instagram-ready asana inhibit their practice. *Stop focusing on the outward presentation,* I tell them, *and pay attention to how the movements feel in your body at this moment. Trust yourself.* It's an easy thing to say, but a hard thing to remember.

Even now, with my admonition so clear in my own mind, I'm pushing myself faster, harder, chasing that euphoric feeling I get when my overactive mind finally quiets, when all I can focus on is my own breath, the feeling of pavement beneath my sneakers. Above me, the sky darkens. I've just reached the northernmost edge of the zoo when I feel the first twinge in my knee. I grit my teeth and push forward. My left knee has been bothering me for a few months now, ever since I jokingly popped into a Lord of the Dance pose at a party and felt something tear. Two lessons I learned from the incident: always, *always* warm up and never yoga while drinking.

I've avoided dealing with my knee, telling myself that I'm young and it'll heal on its own. The thing I've been actively denying is that my body can only heal if I give it the time to do so. Instead, I've been pushing myself through classes and practices and runs, and surprise, surprise, it feels perhaps even worse than it did originally. If a student came to me with the same problem, I would tell them to honor their own body and its limits, and I would remind them that ahimsa—the principle of nonviolence—starts with themselves.

I know all that, and I know I should heed my own advice, and yet I can't stop running. If I do, then all the thoughts I'm trying to outpace will come rushing back, and I'll have to confront them: Jack. Fern's accusations—the same accusations I've been seeing online for weeks, the ones that led me to delete all my social apps from my phone. Faith and her heartbreaking lack of trust.

I shove the thoughts out of my mind and push forward, ignoring the now-searing pain in my left knee. As if to underline that I should stop this madness and go home, a sudden clap of thunder sounds, startling me so much that I trip over a crack in the sidewalk.

One second I'm racing across the pavement, and the next I'm lying in a crumpled heap, biting back cries of pain. My palms are scuffed and my pants are dirty, but the biggest casualty is my knee, which feels like someone has sawed it in half with a pair of blunt scissors. It's that moment that the sky chooses to open, pelting me with fat, cold raindrops.

I growl in aggravation and drag myself to a standing position. Almost immediately, my knee folds underneath me. Tears of pain and frustration drip down my face, but I don't even bother to wipe them away. Why should I? No one is here to see. I'm out alone in a rainstorm like some sort of nutcase. I look back in the direction from which I came, and I have to squint because the rain is falling so hard. Faith's building can't be more than a mile and a half away, but with my bum knee and the downpour, it might as well be in Indiana. I'm furious with myself for leaving my phone behind. If only I had that, I could call an Uber.

With a start, I remember the bus pass Faith forced on me, and I would leap with relief if my knee didn't hurt so damn much. I promise myself I will properly thank Faith when I return—I will graciously overlook her earlier betrayal, I will no longer make fun of her blender or her basically useless hair dryer, I might even make her dinner—and I limp ten yards or so to a bus shelter. At this point, I'm not picky about which bus line I take. Anything that gets me out of the rain will be a good start. But once I study the transit map posted in the shelter, I'm glad to see this line will deposit me directly in front of Faith's door. Grateful, I slump against the side of the shelter and wait.

After what feels like an eternity but is, in all actuality, probably only five minutes, a bus pulls to a stop in front of me. The door hinges open, and the driver gives me a sympathetic smile. I can only imagine how I look to him.

I'm soaked from head to toe, loose hairs plastered against my face while my ponytail drips behind me. I know my eyes are red from crying, and my face must be streaked with mascara. My light pink leggings are mud spattered and so wet they're practically see-through, exposing more than a hint of my underwear printed with cartoon pandas. My sports bra is, thankfully, navy blue, but it doesn't provide much coverage, and my gooseskin-prickled arms and torso are on display.

"Hello!" I greet him in a voice that even I can tell sounds slightly manic, and clamber aboard. I dig into my pocket for Faith's bus pass, but my fingers are nearly numb with cold and slick from the rain, and I fumble as I try to free the pass from within my sodden leggings. The stupid card ends up catapulting from my hands into the aisle. I start to crouch to collect it, but my knee screams in protest, refusing to bend. I curse—loudly, causing an elderly woman seated near the front to cluck at me—and clutch my poor knee, sucking in through my teeth to keep from crying out.

"You okay, miss?" the bus driver asks.

"Yeah," I gasp, turning to him while still half-bent over and cradling my knee. "It's just my knee. It—"

"Here."

Faith's bus pass appears in front of me, held by a pair of male-looking fingers.

"Oh, thank you," I gush, forcing myself upright in order to look my fellow passenger in the eyes.

And everything in my body shudders and stops. Because I *know* those eyes. Deep, dark brown, the kind a girl could get lost in if she wasn't careful.

And I don't have a history of being careful.

Those eyes widen, those full lips I remember well—*too* well—drop open in surprise.

"Vanessa?"

I can't breathe. I literally cannot bring air into my lungs.

"Miss?" the bus driver interrupts, his friendly tone all but evaporated. "Are you going to be joining us or not?"

"I . . ." I fumble, backing up. I snatch Faith's bus pass from the man's still-extended fingers.

"Vanessa," he says again, reaching out to catch my hand.

But I'm too fast, even with my essentially useless knee, and I quickly hobble off the bus. Behind me, I hear the bus's doors gear up to close and a familiar voice inside saying, "Wait."

My foolish heart leaps in my chest, even as the rest of me desperately hopes that he does *not* get off that bus. Not now. Not after all this time.

He does not get off the bus, because he is—and has always been—a reasonable, pragmatic person, and reasonable, pragmatic people do not get off buses in the middle of rainstorms to chat with women who ruined their lives, especially when the aforementioned woman currently looks like she's gone feral. I stand, getting pelted with raindrops as I watch the bus drive away, and I realize I can't feel the rain anymore, nor can I feel my injured knee. The only thing I can feel is the aching hole in my heart.

Because that was Sam. *My* Sam. And I just let him slip away again.

Chapter Eight

Faith vaults to her feet when I open the door. "Vanessa! Thank God! Where have you been? I've been so worried! I tried calling your phone, and—"

"I'm fine," I say through chattering teeth. It seemed like ages before another bus came to the stop, and the rain didn't let up in the least. If anything, it got worse. My very bones themselves feel waterlogged.

"You're not fine," she says, surveying me. "You're soaking wet, your pants are muddy, and you're *limping*. What happened out there? Did you fall?"

Any other time, I would tease Faith that as a person who aced the logic-games section of the LSAT (a fact she shares at every opportunity), she should surely be able to deduce that, yes, I fell. But I am wet and tired and in pain and, oh my God, that was *Sam*, and so I am incapable of doing anything other than nodding vaguely.

"You poor thing," Faith says. "Go put on dry clothes, and I'll make you some tea."

"Thanks, but I need a warm bath first." I rub my clammy hands over my goose-pimpled arms and shiver. "That rain is surprisingly cold."

"Good idea. I'll have the tea waiting for you when you're done." Faith tucks her dark blond hair behind her ears and tilts her head at me, her eyes soft. "Hey, listen, Vanessa, if you're upset about that post—"

"I'm just cold," I interrupt, more abruptly than I intended to. Faith's eyes flash briefly with hurt, and I feel a little bad, but honestly, I just can't with this right now. Discussing that so-called journalist's hit job on me is the absolute last thing I want to do while I'm soaked to the bone and still vibrating from my chance encounter with Sam.

"Just let me warm up, Faith, okay?" I say more gently, and my sister nods.

I step into the small bathroom and pull back Faith's shower curtain, patterned with a colorful map of Chicago neighborhoods, then turn on the tap. The interior of the apartment was recently renovated, and the bathroom fixtures are bright white and shiny, but the building itself is old, and the pipes creak and groan within the walls. While I wait for the water to warm up, I shuck off my dripping-wet clothing and pile it in the sink. I plug the tub, dump in some bath salts, and grab the scented candle off the shelf. I look around for the matches before remembering that I left the box in my room the other night. I wrap a towel around myself and pad across the hallway to grab them.

As I reach for the matches on the dresser, my eyes land on my jewelry box. A gift from Jack, the polished mahogany case with its etched-glass lid looks out of place on the set of IKEA drawers. I flash back to last Christmas, perched on a stiff brocade sofa in the Daltons' Park Avenue co-op, unwrapping the box in front of his parents and sister. I was surprised by the gift—the box is beautiful but not at all my style—and I could see Jack's sister, Kathryn, exchanging a look with their parents. I rearranged my face into a delighted smile, and Jack coaxed me to open the lid. Inside, I found a pair of perfect diamond earrings, so flawless that I'm afraid to wear them. Those earrings are still in the box, as is a thin gold chain with ruby satellites that he gave me this past Valentine's Day and the Cartier bracelet. But the diamond-and-ruby stunner he slipped on my finger over dinner at Per Se is gone.

One of the last things I did before I left New York was tuck that beauty into its velvet box, and then slide that box into a manila envelope, which I carried to Kathryn's Chelsea office. There, her black-clad assistant pretended Kathryn wasn't there, despite the fact that I could literally *see* her through a frosted-glass wall. *I'm not the bad guy here!* I wanted to shout, but I restrained myself. I had no interest in causing a scene. For all I knew, that same assistant would film it and post it on TikTok, captioned with something about Jackson Dalton's fiancée's epic meltdown, and I was done letting Jack define me. Instead, I grabbed a pen from the assistant's desk and scrawled "For Jack" on the envelope, and then I walked away, confident I would never see Kathryn Dalton anywhere other than the society pages again.

Now I lift the lid of the jewelry box and reach for the ring that *is* there: a thin brass band, tarnished with age, on which is affixed a misshapen star topped with a chip of cubic zirconia. I slide the ring over my fourth finger, and almost immediately, I can hear Dolly Parton's twangy voice in my head. My chest compresses, and I yank the ring off so quickly I'm lucky I don't dislocate a joint. I return it to the box, grab the matches, and head back to the bathtub.

I slide down into the warm, rose-scented water, relaxing as it starts to thaw my cold body. My knee still throbs, but even it feels better underneath the water. I close my eyes and tip my head back against the cool porcelain, inhaling deeply and ordering my mind to clear.

Of course, this does not work.

All I can see is Sam, a retrospective unrolling backward through my brain: Sam, holding out Faith's bus pass and looking confused; Sam, his dark eyes liquid with hurt, telling me things weren't working; Sam, studiously avoiding my eyes as he mumbles about mistakes; Sam, kissing me underneath a glittering disco ball; Sam, eyes smoldering as he pulls me into his tidy apartment in Ithaca; Sam, holding my hand as we stroll the beach in the dark; Sam, smiling at me for the first time. My heart stutters on this last image, and even though I don't want to think about Sam, I can't stop myself from reliving this one perfect moment in time.

With my eyes closed, I can almost smell the pool at the resort: sunscreen and melted piña coladas and the sharp scent of chlorine. I was twenty years old, and I had been on spring break in Cancún with a gaggle of my sorority sisters for approximately four hours. Immediately upon arrival, we'd decamped to the pool, where we staked out prime real estate at the center of the Corona-guzzling, body-shot-taking, chicken-playing madness. In our string bikinis and navel piercings, we were instantly swarmed by frat boys from New York to Nevada, all offering up tequila shots and cigarettes and their dubiously pleasant company. My friends were eating it up, but before long, I was bored. These boys were nothing more than slightly louder, more aggressive versions of the same dumb guys we knew back at school, and I was over their kind. I was tired of their possessive eyes and their roaming hands; I was tired of hearing the same old lines and being expected to swoon.

As one of these interchangeable guys—this one with a tribal sun tattooed on his pec and an industrial piercing—rambled on about training for a marathon while staring at my chest, I realized I'd been in Cancún for hours but hadn't seen the water. I excused myself from Mr. Marathon—who, I noticed, simply pivoted to his right and started boring my friend Ellie with the same drivel—and wandered to the edge of the resort, where the paved terraces of the pool area gave way to the sandy beach and, just beyond it, the Caribbean Sea.

The beach was empty save for a few people reading in beach chairs, and I skipped past them to the turquoise water. Excitement flickered in my chest. Thus far, my experience with large bodies of water was limited to the Great Lakes. This was something entirely different. I envisioned myself wading up to my waist, trailing my fingers through the gentle waves. I took a couple of steps into the water and paused. It was colder than I had anticipated. Not as cold as Lake Michigan, but cold enough to give me second thoughts. I looked around, wondering whether this was why no one else was in the water. But the glistening surface beckoned me forward, and so I steeled myself and took another step. This one wasn't quite as uncomfortable, and by the next one, I barely noticed the cold. Before I knew it, the water was lapping at my knees.

That was when I felt it: a stinging pain on the back of my right leg.

I yelped in surprise and began hopping around, which in retrospect, was the *worst* thing I could have done because it led me to bring my right foot down on the offending jellyfish. Pain shot up through the sole of my foot, and I screamed bloody murder, momentarily convinced that this vindictive jellyfish planned to repeatedly sting me until I could no longer move and I'd therefore drown in a foot and a half of water.

While that ridiculous thought spun through my head, strong arms seized me from behind and lifted me into the air.

Perhaps I should have been more grateful to be saved from certain death-by-jellyfish, but I'd spent the last four hours being pawed at by drunk, handsy frat bros, and I would rather die than let another one touch me and assume I should thank him for the privilege.

And so I slapped at the strange hands and shouted, "Hey! Put me down!"

"Are you sure?" he asked, his voice a comfortable Midwestern drawl.

"Hands off!" I insisted, squirming.

"Whatever you want," he said and released me.

I put weight on my right foot and immediately screamed in pain, letting loose such a torrent of curse words that I'm surprised all nearby eardrums didn't explode.

"I'm going to pick you up again, okay?" he said, wrapping his arms around me.

"Yes, please," I managed through clenched teeth.

The stranger scooped me up and waded back to shore, depositing me on a lounge chair covered with a striped towel.

"Thanks," I said, gingerly lifting my throbbing right foot and positioning it on the chair, avoiding a splayed-open copy of Kurt Vonnegut's *Slaughterhouse-Five*. I cast an eye over my savior, who was tall and lean, with shaggy, brown hair and eyes shaded by a pair of Wayfarers, and thankfully no ill-conceived tattoos or spray tan in sight.

"Are you okay?" he asked, pushing up his sunglasses to reveal chocolate brown eyes squinting in concern. "Was it a jellyfish?"

I nodded miserably. "I think so. I mean, I've never been stung by a jellyfish before, so I don't know for sure, but *man*." I reached down to touch the tender skin of my foot and immediately wished I hadn't. "God, that hurts. Do you think I need to see a doctor?"

"Yeah, no, I don't think so. There's nothing a doctor can really do." He chuckled. "There's, you know, one thing that you can allegedly do to ease the pain, but no doctor is going to do that for you."

"What one thing?" I asked, nearly blinded by the pain. "This hurts so bad. I'll do anything."

He shifted, looking uncomfortable. "You know."

"I really don't. And I'll— *Oh*." I wrinkled my nose when I realized what he was talking about. "Oh my God. You're not going to . . . pee on it, are you?"

"Not even if you asked me to. My chivalry has its limits." He flashed a crooked smile. "But I will buy you a drink if you think that'd help."

"It would definitely help." I looked warily at the stretch of beach between us and the pool, a distance that had seemed short only minutes before but at the moment seemed interminable. "I don't know if I can walk that far, though."

"I could carry you," he offered.

I glanced back at the bustling pool area, where Ellie was still stuck talking to the guy with the dumb tattoo, and then back again at the Vonnegut reader who had pulled me from the water.

"Why don't I just stay here?" I suggested.

His smile widened. "All right. I'll run to the bar and grab us a couple of beers."

"Make it a couple of tequilas, and you have a deal, kind stranger."

"Tequila it is." He smiled, full lips parting to expose straight white teeth. "And I'm Sam."

"Vanessa."

"Now we're not strangers."

Seven years later, we've become strangers again.

Chapter Nine

When I emerge from the bathtub forty-five minutes later, feeling infinitely more human and more than a little hungry, Faith pounces on me like an overbearing mother hen.

"What kind of tea do you want?" she asks, opening her cabinets and pulling down boxes. "I have lemon ginger and Sleepytime and a decaf chai and Earl Grey and this weird hibiscus tea that—"

"Lemon ginger sounds nice," I interrupt. "Thanks."

"Of course." She selects a tea bag and turns on her electric kettle. "What else do you need? I got a tub of animal crackers at Trader Joe's yesterday—I know you like those. Or—"

"Yeah, thanks. I'm going to grab some ibuprofen, too."

"Let me!" Faith practically shouts, jumping in front of me and pulling open the cabinet.

"Um, thanks." I give my sister a quizzical look. "Is everything okay?"

"*Is* everything okay?" she echoes back. "You stayed out in the rain for, like, forty minutes earlier, and you've barely said two words to me since you got home. Are you still mad about what I said before you left? Because, I swear, I didn't mean—"

"I'm not mad at you, Faith. It's totally reasonable to wonder whether I knew something about . . . about whatever Jack was doing."

"It's not reasonable for *me* to wonder," she says firmly. "I'm your sister, and I will always stand behind you one hundred percent. *More* than one hundred percent. I'm sorry if I made you question that. It's just law school. We're always arguing in class, and that makes me want to be the devil's advocate all the time—but this is not class, and the devil does not need another advocate right now."

"It's fine," I assure her, putting my hand on hers. "Truly. And while we're on the subject of apologies, I shouldn't have shouted at you and stormed out like I did. I've just been so stressed out lately, and seeing that article put me over the top."

"I get it." Faith's kettle beeps, and she pours the boiling water over my tea bag and pushes the mug in my direction. "Listen, I'm here for you, okay? If you want to talk about the article or Jack or anything . . . I'm here."

"I saw Sam."

The words leave my mouth before I think about them, and I can see that Faith is as confused by my non sequitur as I am.

"I don't know what— Oh." She pauses as understanding washes over her features. "*Sam* Sam?"

"The one and only."

"Wow." Faith blinks. "Okay. When?"

"Ninety minutes ago? I'm not sure. I jumped on a bus in Lincoln Park to get out of the rain, and . . . there he was. On the bus."

"Those odds must be incredible."

"I know." I laugh hollowly. "If I was twenty again, I would say it was fate."

"And what do you say at twenty-seven?"

"As it turns out, nothing." I cringe. "I practically flung myself off the bus into the rain just to avoid speaking to him."

"Wait. You saw Sam, and you didn't say *anything* to him?"

"I might have made some word-like sounds, but nothing intelligible." I put my hands over my face, mortified. "It was awful, Faith. A disaster. A car crash with no survivors."

It literally makes my heart feel like it's been shoved down a garbage disposal to realize that, after all this time, after the hundreds—if not thousands—of hours I've devoted to fantasizing about a chance encounter with Sam, *this* was how it happened: me soaking wet, covered with mud, and still carrying around the stink of my felonious ex-fiancé while he stood there, with those puppy-dog eyes and that thick hair, that same heartbreakingly perfect mouth.

I groan with renewed humiliation. "I looked like something the cat dragged in. No, worse. Something the cat *played with* before dragging in. A mangled, decapitated mouse."

Faith quirks an eyebrow at me, letting me know, as only a sister can, that she's unimpressed with my spiraling. "Decapitated, huh?"

"Fine," I relent. "Can we just agree that it was not the reunion I would've preferred? So I just . . . I blanked. I mean, given the circumstances, what was I even supposed to say?"

"I might have started with 'hi.'"

At Faith's bone-dry delivery, I burst out laughing. "Thanks for the hot tip, sis."

"I do what I can," she says, flashing me an impish smile. "So, what's the next step?"

"There is no next step," I say, picking up my tea. "I'm not going to stalk the bus line or anything. It's not like I even know whether that's his usual route or whether he was just trying to get out of the rain like me."

"You can't just do nothing," Faith says, swatting my arm. "Isn't this how a Meg Ryan movie starts? Our heroine finally ditches her terrible fiancé just in time to reconnect with her one true love?"

"One true love?" I repeat. "Who are you, and what have you done with my sister? Aren't you the woman who once made her seven-year-old neighbor cry by telling her that princess movies are antifeminist propaganda and dangerous to her mental health?"

"I stand by that," Faith says, lifting her chin. "Ariel gave up her literal *voice* for that man. Tell me that's not a metaphor. But that's not the same thing at all. You're not some cartoon princess who needs a prince. You're a grown woman fully capable of taking care of herself—"

"Counterpoint," I interrupt, gesturing with scraped palms at my swollen knee.

"Anyway," Faith continues, "you're my sister and my best friend, and I know how much Sam means to you. I just don't want to see you miss a chance."

"I hate to break it to you, but I think I already missed that chance when I flung myself off that bus."

"Not your finest move, I'll agree." She frowns thoughtfully. "How about we look him up on social media? I'm sure we can find some hints about where he lives, and—"

"No."

She blinks at me. "Aren't you curious? This is Sam we're talking about. Sam, who—"

"I know," I interrupt. "And yes, of course I'm curious. But that doesn't matter. Sam blocked me on social media years ago."

"That's no problem. We can use my account or—"

"I can't do it. Sam blocked me for a reason, and I need to respect his boundaries."

"I hear what you're saying, but . . . Vanessa, it's been *years*. And this is *Sam*."

"I know." I pick up my tea and clench my jaw, trying hard not to cry. "And that's why I can't."

It's not that I don't want to. The temptation to peek at his social media and into his life is almost irresistible. I feel desperate in a way that, frankly, scares me, and that's the reason I know that I can't right now. I've never been able to control myself where Sam is concerned, and I'm very aware that one tiny, ostensibly innocent glimpse at his Instagram or Facebook profile or, God, even his LinkedIn page would just be the tipping point. I'd fall headfirst for him again, and that's not an option. Sam has made this clear.

And that's why, even if I was finally ready to throw caution to the wind and tempt my shaky self-control by looking at his social media, I won't. Because Sam *blocked* me. He doesn't *want* me to have that window into his life, and that counts for something. Maybe if I'd paid more attention to what Sam wanted when we were together—*really* tried to understand what was good for him, not just what I wanted—maybe things would have been different. Maybe I wouldn't have lost the only man who ever really saw me, who ever really loved me for me.

Chapter Ten

The good news is that Fern's mud-slinging post caused far less damage than expected. Some of this is sheer luck—within two hours of it dropping, a man formerly famous for his chart-topping songs and currently infamous for being a terrible person posted a shockingly vile rant on TikTok, and it sucked up all the oxygen in the virtual room—and some of it is because Fern misjudged the public's interest in me. They simply don't care that much. People are falling over themselves to read about Jack because he's classically handsome, well pedigreed, and the architect of what's being called "the biggest con of the decade"—a veritable trifecta of clickbait—whereas I'm just a bendy blonde who knows her way around a hashtag. You can't throw a stale bagel in New York without hitting another woman who fits that same description.

The bad news, however, is that it's been four days since I jumped onto that bus in the rainstorm, and I haven't been able to stop thinking about Sam. Like, at *all*. I wake up remembering the way he used to sleep with his face smushed into the pillow, mouth partially open, with his thick, dark eyelashes resting on his cheeks, and I feel like crying before I've even gotten out of bed. I think about him while I'm pouring my coffee—Sam always teased me about the amount of creamer I used. I think about him while I'm riding the bus to House of Om, while I'm leading classes, while I'm staring at the landing page for my YouTube channel and wondering whether I need to make some sort of official statement about Jack. I think about him while I'm showering, while I'm eating, while I'm walking, while I'm reading. At this point, it's easier to list when I'm *not* thinking about Sam, which is . . . never.

I meant it when I told Faith that I wouldn't look him up on social media, but stopping myself from doing so takes literally every ounce of willpower I possess. And, look, I have a robust meditation practice, so I have considerably more willpower than the average twenty-seven-year-old woman. But there, in a nutshell, is the problem: My body wants to orient itself toward Sam like a flower to the sun, and preventing that is physically grueling. I think about sneaking a look; I think about how *easy* it would be to type his name into the Google search bar. But Sam blocked me five years ago, and when I last looked four months ago (in the bathroom at Per Se, Jack's ring sparkling obscenely from its new home on my finger), I was still blocked. Sam isn't impulsive—I can think of exactly one time that he acted hastily, and that did not end well—and I'm certain that blocking me means he does not want me in his life, not even as a voyeur.

"You're being absurd," Faith tells me as we stand shoulder to shoulder in the kitchen, assembling ingredients for our impromptu taco night. "He can't stop you from googling him."

"I know," I say, slicing open an avocado. "But I think it means something that I'm still blocked."

"I guess," Faith says, sounding unconvinced. "But maybe it just means that he no longer uses Facebook."

"I'm also blocked on Instagram and the hellsite formerly known as Twitter."

"Maybe he forgot you were blocked."

"That's actually worse," I say, pulling a face. "I don't like to think I'm *that* forgettable."

"I didn't mean *you're* forgettable." Faith flicks a piece of diced onion at me. "I meant he forgets to manage his social media."

"Maybe," I allow. "Sam never was the extremely online type."

"Yeah." Faith pauses, chewing on her lip in thought. "You know, Vanessa, Sam didn't block *me*, and—"

"I've already told you this. I can't."

"I know, and I hate to be pushy—"

"You *love* being pushy. You *revel* in it."

She shoots another onion cube in my direction. "I *hate* to be pushy, but Sam was the love of your life. You can't just . . . forget about him."

"Trust me, forgetting about Sam is not the problem."

"Then what *is* the problem?" she challenges.

"I ruined his life, Faith. He was at an Ivy League school, and that would have opened doors for him. But he gave all that up for me, and then I . . . I just made it worse."

"That's ridiculous. You didn't *ruin* his life. He—"

"No, I did. Pretending otherwise won't make me feel better. And even if you want to argue, hypothetically, that maybe I didn't, it doesn't even matter. I'd for sure ruin his life *now*. Associating with me—the Crypto Con's girlfriend—would poison his Google results until the end of time."

"You're exaggerating again."

"Hardly. Do you want to read some of the hate mail I'm getting?"

Faith frowns. "No, thank you. And neither should you."

I shrug. "I have a thick skin."

"I don't care if you have a literal exoskeleton. Reading that stuff can't be good for your mental health."

"I'm a *wellness coach*, Faith," I say, jazz-handsing. "I know how to center myself."

"Whatever." She rolls her eyes at me. "I can see I'm not going to win this argument, so how about you go center yourself around making more margaritas?"

Tequila it is, Sam's voice echoes in my head.

Through a lump in my throat, I manage to say, "Tequila it is."

~

"I promise you there's a better way to do that."

Faith sticks her tongue out at me but continues salting the rims of our second round of margaritas by jerking her panda-shaped saltshaker in tiny, precise movements over the edges of our glasses. "You mean like the huge mess you made with our last round?"

"It wasn't that bad," I say, surreptitiously swiping more of the spilled salt off the counter. "And surely more effective than that. I mean, Faith, come on. You have a perfect GPA at a top-ten law school. You are smarter than this."

"*Almost* perfect. Damn Criminal Procedure." She pauses and points a finger at me. "Stop distracting me. This is a delicate operation."

"Fine," I say, lifting my hands comically and backing away. "Just don't blame me when the drinks themselves are salty."

"They'll be *fine*," she insists. "I do it this way all the—" She cuts herself off when her phone buzzes on the counter beside her, and she glances down at the screen. Whatever she sees makes her frown, but she quickly shakes it off and continues. "Like I was saying, I do it this way all the time, and it is *fine*."

"Is everything okay?"

"What? Oh, yeah, everything's okay. It's just Henry—that guy who's my associate mentor at the law firm, you know? The firm has a table at this charity event next Friday night, and he really wants me to come."

"As a date?" I ask, my big-sister alarms going off. "That seems really inappropriate."

"No, no, not as a date," Faith says quickly. "Henry's married, and he's bringing his wife. In fact, he wants *me* to bring a date. Which is just one of the many reasons why I don't want to go."

"Charity events can be boring," I sympathize. "Jack dragged me to a ton of them. But there's usually decent food."

"I'm not worried about being bored." She sets the saltshaker down with a flourish. "Ta-da! Tell me this isn't perfection."

Tentatively, I sip my drink, expecting the margarita to have suffered from Faith's unusual rim-salting practice, but as usual, my sister proves that she knows what she's doing.

"Excellent," I say. "My compliments to the bartender. Now, if you're not worried about being bored, what *are* you worried about?"

Faith sighs. "I know if I go, Henry will spend the entire evening trying to sell me on joining the firm after graduation next spring."

"Isn't that a good thing? Don't you enjoy working there?"

"Yeah, I do. The people are great, and I'm working on really interesting projects. I'm not just shuffling papers or doing make-work like some of my friends are at other firms. And the money is nice, obviously."

"Obviously." I sip my drink. "So why are you hesitating?"

"I'm not sure I want my life's work to be helping massive corporations avoid liability." She licks the rim of her glass thoughtfully. "So Marisa, this girl I know from school, is summering with an environmental action organization. She's doing legal research for this bill they're lobbying for about microplastic reduction. That's something that has a real impact, you know? Meanwhile, I'm parsing language in contracts."

"Interesting. How did your friend get the position with that organization?"

"She just cold-emailed them!" Faith exclaims, her hazel eyes shining with admiration. "Can you believe it?"

"No," I say honestly. "So, what? You're going to see if they need another assistant?"

"No, that's Marisa's thing. It just opened up my eyes, you know? Law school can be such an assembly line, just churning out big-law associates, and it really gave me this myopic view. I didn't even *consider* that organizations like the one Marisa is working for would need lawyers, but of course they do."

"So what are you going to say to this Henry guy?"

"It's not like they've given me an official offer yet. Anyway, once they do, I'll probably accept. Starting my career at one of the top firms in the city would set me up to do whatever I wanted later on. Plus, I don't know when—or even *if*—I'd get interest from some other organization. And then there's the money to think of.

Organizations like the one Marisa works for don't have anywhere near as deep pockets as a large law firm, and as you know, I'm going to graduate with a hefty amount of debt. I need the money."

"Don't trade your life for money," I say firmly. "I mean, look at Jack. He went after the cash and now apparently has to live the rest of his life in hiding."

"Or skiing in the Swiss Alps," Faith corrects. "But don't worry, I'm not about to launch a Ponzi scheme."

"Of course not. Ponzi schemes are so last season." I pause. "But seriously, Faith, you should think about what will make you the happiest. Not just superficially, yay-I-have-disposable-income happy, and not just this-looks-good-on-paper happy, but really, truly, feel-it-in-your-bones happy. Because all that other stuff is temporary. Ask me how I know."

"Hey." Faith reaches over and squeezes my hand. "You're going to be happy again, I promise. I know things are tough right now, but you've got me, and apparently whatever passes for your sense of humor—"

"Hey!"

"—and you'll get through it. *We'll* get through it." Her face lights up as though she's been struck with inspiration. "Hey, why don't you come to the charity event as my date?"

"How does that help you avoid Henry?"

"I'm trying to avoid the conversation, not the man. I see him every day at the office already, and there's a nonzero chance that I'll end up working at the firm with him long term, so I don't want to burn any bridges. Going to the event ensures I maintain that relationship, and bringing you along gives me a built-in buffer in case he starts the full-court press. Win-win!"

"Are you sure you want me to come? I mean, I'm not exactly the most liked person right now."

"You'll be in a roomful of lawyers. Trust me, there will be plenty of people far less likable than you in attendance."

I laugh. "If it's that important to you, consider me there."

"Perfect." Faith taps quickly on her phone. "It's done. No backing out now! One week from tomorrow, we'll be celebrating the Windy City Legal Aid Society at the Cultural Center. Dress code is semiformal."

"Well," I say, smiling around the rim of my drink, "I always do appreciate an excuse to get dressed up."

Faith grins. "This is going to be fun."

I hope she's right. I could use some fun in my life right now.

Chapter Eleven

It has been five days since I twisted my knee running in the rain, and despite my best and most serious attempts at manifestation and smoothie after smoothie laced with an eye-wateringly expensive collagen powder, it still hurts. If I had to quantify my healing process (which is the sort of thing Jack would have asked me to do), I'd have to say it feels only two percent better than it did when I first smashed into the pavement, which is . . . not great. Faith keeps harassing me to see a doctor, but my insurance is garbage—and what would a doctor tell me, anyway? Put some ice on it? Rest? I'm doing all that already.

Well, mostly. I've started planning a series to add to my YouTube channel, and I'm still teaching three yoga classes a week at House of Om, but there's no way I'm giving those up. I promised Gemma I wouldn't let her down, and that means not flaking out on her within the first month. I'm getting through it by crafting classes that are knee friendly (absolutely no *utkatasana*, thank you very much), spending less time demonstrating poses and more time walking around and making adjustments, and popping ibuprofen early and often. It's not ideal, but it's working.

Still, I'm practically gritting my teeth with pain as I finish up my Friday-afternoon class. As the students lie flat on their mats in a restful savasana, I check the time on my phone, mentally calculating how long it will take to put away the props, take the bus home, and draw a warm bath. *Fifty minutes,* I assure myself. *At most. That's how long before I can get some relief.*

Forty-five minutes, I tell myself as they're rolling up their mats. *Now forty-four minutes until I'm sinking into the water, and—*

"Thank you so much, Vanessa!" a chipper voice says, interrupting my thoughts.

I blink and bring my focus to the woman standing in front of me, her mat under her arm.

"I just wanted to say how much I love your classes," she continues. "You're always so *present*."

"I appreciate that," I tell her, feeling like a fraud. "Thank you for sharing your practice with me."

Forty-three minutes, I think.

~

Seven minutes, I tell myself as I hobble off the 36 bus. Seven minutes until I'm standing beside Faith's bathtub, shaking rejuvenating bath salts into the warm water. I'm so close I can almost feel the warmth on my skin, but the Walgreens across the street grabs my attention. I've been slathering my knee in Tiger Balm, and I'm almost out. If I don't get some today, I'll have to get some tomorrow, and I have big plans to spend the morning in bed with some Netflix.

I promise myself I'll pop in and out, and readjust my countdown to ten minutes.

Once inside, however, I decide to treat myself to frozen pizza and ice cream. Faith's law firm has a reception tonight, and she's told me she'll be late. I know I should make myself something healthy for dinner—something with greens and beans and actual nutrients—but just the idea of standing over the stove while my knee throbs in pain brings literal tears to my eyes, and so pizza it is. Technically, I don't need the ice cream, either, but I *want* the ice cream, and self-care is an important component of overall wellness.

I carry my bounty to the self-checkout. I scan and bag the Tiger Balm, then attempt to scan the bottom of the pizza box. The barcode is inconveniently placed near the center of the box, in such an absurd location that I cannot get it to scan no matter what I do. I hold it right side up, I hold it upside down, I hold it at a forty-five-degree angle. Nothing works. Frustrated, I smack the pizza box against the sensor and curse. It's not my best moment, but dammit, I just want to buy my pizza and get out of here. I have a bath waiting for me.

"Yeah, no, I don't think that's going to work."

At the familiar voice, I freeze. *No.* Surely it isn't him. Surely he isn't speaking to *me*. That's just my exhaustion talking.

"Yeah, no, I hear you . . . Okay, let's talk later. Yeah, bye."

I exhale a rattling breath. He wasn't speaking to me. He was just talking on his phone. But that's a small comfort because the voice undeniably belongs to Sam. That voice is tattooed onto my eardrums, his verbal tic of "yeah, no" as familiar to me as my own heartbeat.

My heart tugs, begging me to turn around and face him. My hips start to swivel to do just that before I wrest back control. I cannot turn around right now. Sam *cannot* see me. I am not looking my best: I didn't sleep well last night and have the undereye bags to prove it; I spilled some iced coffee on my tank top as I rushed to the studio this afternoon; and my hairband snapped when I readjusted my ponytail after class, leaving me with ponytail-dented hair and no way to conceal it. Add this to my appearance the last time I ran into Sam—muddy, soaked, and flustered—and there's no question that Sam will be glad he dodged this train wreck five years ago.

With shaking hands, I force my attention back to the infuriating pizza box. I need to scan this thing and get out of here *now*.

"Do you need some help there?"

He's not talking to you. He's back on the phone again. He's definitely not stepping up beside you this very moment, and what the actual HELL, pizza box, why won't you just SCAN?

"Here, if you want me to try—" he's saying as his hands—Jesus Christ, those *hands*, I remember those hands—enter my peripheral vision.

"I can do it!" I say—or rather, inexplicably shout—jerking the pizza box away from him.

"Of course," he says, stepping back with his hands up. "I—"

His eyes connect with mine, and he freezes, hands still aloft like I've just informed him this is a stickup.

"Holy shit," he says.

I don't know whether he means that in a good way or a bad way. My nerves are singing, my entire body vibrating, and I feel dangerously close to vomiting, but I know I have to say something. *I might have started with 'hi,'* Faith's voice echoes in my head.

That's it, I think. *Just say hi.*

I open my mouth to greet him, and instead what comes out is: "Holy shit yourself."

Now I *really* feel like vomiting. I have never wished for a catastrophe—a sudden sinkhole to open beneath me, the self-checkout to burst into flames and give my exit cover—as much as right at this moment. Sam holds my eyes, looking like he also is too stunned to speak, and if things keep going this way, we might be stuck here, staring awkwardly at each other for the rest of the evening, if not our natural lives.

"Are you planning on just standing there, or . . . ?" the woman in line behind Sam demands, tapping her foot impatiently.

"Sorry," I say to her, my voice coming out as a whisper.

"Here," Sam says, holding out his hands. "Can I try?"

"Be my guest," I say, relinquishing the box to him. "As long as you don't judge."

"Me, judge frozen pizza? I would never." His voice is light, but I detect an undercurrent, something that sets all my nerves buzzing. I find myself wondering what he might say if we didn't have an audience of grumpy shoppers waiting in line behind us.

Sam passes the pizza box under the scanner, and, to my utter amazement, it registers on his first try. He sets it aside and reaches for the ice cream in my basket.

"Now, this," he says, holding it up. "This, I might judge. Because what kind of sicko chooses plain vanilla when Phish Food exists?"

"It's vanilla *bean*," I tell him. "And my sister has this jar of super-indulgent fudge sauce that I plan on using."

"That sounds good." There's a playful lilt to his voice, and I almost invite him over for ice cream. *Almost.* Then I remember that it's been five years since we had a proper conversation, and the last thing he said to me was that trying to love me was like trying to stay atop a mechanical bull. *I always end up bruised,* he said. *Want to have a sundae?* is not the logical next conversational step.

"Well," I say, tearing my gaze away from his face, "I should finish up here. There's a line, so." I take the ice cream out of his hands and run it over the scanner. I can feel his eyes on me as I bag it and pay for my goods, and I know color is rising in my cheeks. I need to get out of here before I totally embarrass myself any more than I already have.

"All right," I say, snatching up my bag. "Thanks for the help. I—"

"Wait," he says, placing a hand on my arm as I turn to leave. My skin warms where he touches me, and I'm suddenly irrationally desperate to have that hand on other parts of my body. "I only have one thing. Let me walk you out?"

I nod. As if I could say no.

He barely takes his eyes off me as he scans and pays for a bottle of Claritin. It feels strangely intimate, seeing him buy allergy medication, and also so familiar it hurts.

We walk out of Walgreens together, side by side but conspicuously far apart, and I have a vision of us walking silently down the street together. The idea makes me sad. Once, we had so much to say we constantly tripped over each other's words.

"Which way are you going?" Sam asks.

I point down Surf Street. "This way."

"Me, too." He steals a glance at me as we cross the street. "So that *was* you I saw on the bus the other day, wasn't it?"

I cringe. "If I say no, will you believe me?"

"Nah. I'd know you anywhere, even covered in mud and soaking wet." He runs a hand through his hair, which is just as thick and shaggy as it was the day I met him. "But you were gone so fast I thought I might have imagined you."

"Yeah, well, I was having a bad day."

"Seemed it." Sam sucks on his teeth, and I tense, waiting for him to ask me about Jack. How could I explain him to Sam? The Sam I knew was nothing if not forthright. He would never lie or steal. Sam is a good man—a better one than Jack, a better one than I deserved.

But Sam doesn't ask about Jack, not directly. Instead, he says, "What are you doing in Chicago? Last I heard, you lived in New York."

"I'm staying with my sister for a while. Trying something new."

"Faith, right?"

I blink, genuinely surprised. "I can't believe you remember my sister's name."

"Of course I do," he says softly. "She's important to you, and you were important to me."

Were. Were *important.* The verb tense is as sharp as a knife.

Sam clears his throat. "Does Faith live in this neighborhood?"

"Yeah. She's right up here on Sheridan."

"Oh, nice. I live on Sheridan, too." He smiles at me, and I can't discern whether he *actually* thinks it's nice that Faith lives on the same street. Does he really want to risk running into me at Walgreens all the time? Or is he noting the area where I live so he can avoid it?

"I guess that's why you were on my bus," I say, struggling to keep my voice upbeat even though I feel like I'm choking.

"To be technical, I think *you* were on *my* bus. And you didn't even stay on it." He squints at me. "You dove off into the rain to avoid me."

"Some people enjoy a nice walk in the rain."

"You're not one of them." His voice lowers as he adds, "You forget that I know you, Vanessa Summers."

Something unfurls in my chest, something warm like hope. Like maybe there's another chance for us. Maybe Faith has been right this whole time. Maybe—

I cut myself off as I realize we've reached the corner of Surf and Sheridan and are standing directly in front of Faith's building. I incline my head toward the door. "Well, this is my stop, so."

"You're kidding," he says, his voice unreadable.

"Um, no?"

"Your sister lives here," he says, pointing to the door. *"Here."*

I look at the gray stone face of the 1920s building again, wondering if it's the site of a famous murder or perhaps a known drug den. "Yes? She's in 412."

"Unbelievable." His lips curve into a smile. "I live in 512."

The warm thing in my chest stretches, extending tendrils through my limbs. *Sam lives in the same building.* He breathes the same air, rides the same questionable elevator, showers with water that's traveled through the same rattling pipes.

"That synchronicity is incredible."

"Yeah." Sam stares at me like he's trying to puzzle something out, and from the softness in his eyes, the slight parting of his lips, I get the sense that if I wanted to kiss Sam, I could. And oh God, do I want to kiss him. I want to kiss him and roll back time—before graduation, before Vegas, before the start of senior year, before everything unraveled. I want to go right back to that first tequila-flavored kiss, when all possibilities stretched before us.

But I hesitate, and then the moment passes. He shakes his head as if to clear it and holds open the door for me. "After you, neighbor."

"Thank you, neighbor," I respond. I sneak another look at his full lips and add, "I'm sure I'll be seeing you around."

"Yeah, or we could get coffee sometime. Catch up."

My heart leaps. Catching up over coffee isn't exactly a date, but it's not *not* a date. Before I can tell Sam that *yes*, we should absolutely get coffee sometime, a tall, stunningly beautiful woman charges over to us.

"Christ, Sam," she says through wine-colored lips, throwing glossy, dark hair over the shoulder of her creamy sheath dress. She ignores me completely as she asks, "Where have you been?"

Sam shrinks underneath her sharp gaze. "Walgreens," he says, holding up the Claritin. "I needed—"

She makes a disgusted noise and rolls her eyes. "Come on," she says, reaching for his arm. "We're already late."

"Just a second. Van—" I hear him start to say my name, but I'm already halfway to the elevators, tears burning behind my eyes.

I tell myself I have no right to cry, but I can't help it. A chunk of my heart has belonged to Sam Cosgrove since the moment he lifted me out of that jellyfish-infested sea, and even though we haven't spoken in five years, just a minute ago I thought I still had a piece—a small piece, but a piece—of his as well. From the possessive way that woman touched him, though, I can see how little it matters whether I hold a tiny shard of his heart. The lion's share of it clearly belongs to her.

Chapter Twelve

I'm shaking by the time I reach Faith's apartment. *Sam has a girlfriend.* That much is obvious. And that girlfriend is devastatingly beautiful and appears to have her life together. I mean, I don't think I've ever seen *her* face shared by a reporter from the paper of record with the caption "What is she hiding?" I could be wrong, though. I haven't been on social media much lately.

"Hey," Faith says, looking up from where she's seated at her desk chair, fastening a pair of dressy sandals. "I broke a heel and had to come back and grab another pair before the reception. Do you—" She cuts herself off, frowning, when she sees my face. "What happened? Is your knee okay?"

"Yes. I mean, no. It . . ." I swallow thickly. "I ran into Sam."

"Okay," she says slowly. "From the looks of things, that did not go well."

"It went fine. Sam is . . . God, Faith, he's so *Sam*. Solid and familiar and . . . and get this: He lives in this building. Literally in the apartment above."

Her eyebrows practically leap off her face. "You're kidding. How have I never seen him?"

"Maybe you keep different hours. I don't know. I just . . . Man, Faith, if jumping onto his bus was a coincidence, this is something else entirely. This is *synchronicity*."

"It's wild," she agrees. "And you, what? Ran into him in the elevator?"

"Not exactly." I drop my bag on the floor and cross the room to the couch, gritting my teeth as my knee throbs. "I stopped in Walgreens on the way home to grab some Tiger Balm and frozen pizza, and there he was. In line behind me. And—"

"Sorry," Faith interrupts, eyeing my bag. "But did you say there's frozen pizza in there?"

"Yeah, and I couldn't get it to scan and—"

"I am very invested in this bit of serendipity, I promise, but I'm also worried about your food-safety habits. Frozen pizza needs to stay frozen for a reason, and that reason is E. coli." She scoops up the bag and peers into it. "Vanessa! There's ice cream in here, too. Were you just going to let this melt on the floor?"

"Literally the least of my concerns right now, Faith. Did you hear the part where I saw *Sam*? And he lives in *this building*?"

"I did," she says, her voice softening as she puts my groceries in the freezer and brings the Tiger Balm over to me. "I can't even imagine what you're feeling right now."

"Confused. Because on the one hand, fate, right? I mean, I didn't get a Dolly Parton tattoo because I'm a country-music superfan. I got it because there's a part of me that's always sort of believed that love finds a way. That maybe the universe would give me another shot at Sam. And so for Sam to be standing in front of me and telling me that he, in fact, lives in the apartment right above us? If that's not the biggest, flashiest neon sign in the entire history of signs, I don't know what is. I mean, Faith, he actually asked me to get coffee—"

"He did?" she squeals. "You said yes, right?"

"I said *nothing* because out of nowhere, this glamorous woman swooped over and grabbed his arm and took him away."

Faith frowns. "What do you mean, 'took him away'?"

"You know, she rushed him off stage left for a date or something. I mean, she's obviously his girlfriend. She has to be. The way she put her hands on him, the way she was annoyed with him . . . they're definitely in a relationship." I flop onto my back and use a throw pillow to cover my face. "God, do you think she *lives* with him? Am I going to have to see Sam holding hands with this Priyanka Chopra look-alike in the lobby every day?"

"I can't hear you," Faith says, gently removing the pillow from my face. "But are you sure they're together?"

"If you saw the way she touched him, you'd understand." I draw a breath and try to center myself. "And, look, it's not that I never thought Sam would move on. It's been years. I've lost some of my faith in Dolly Parton and the endurance of love. I mean, look at me. *I* moved on."

The words are hard to choke out. They're technically true: I dated Jack, I lived with him, I agreed to marry him. To any neutral observer, it would seem that I've moved on. But I haven't—not really. Not in any way that matters.

I don't have to say any of this, though, for Faith to understand. In a kind voice, she corrects, "You mean you *tried* to move on."

I bite my lip and nod. "I really did try."

"I know. And maybe you could have moved on," she says, "if you weren't still in love with Sam."

"I'm not still in love with Sam."

"Vanessa, honey, consider the evidence: You're lying flat on your back, crying, because you saw Sam with a woman who may or may not be his girlfriend."

"I'm not crying. And I'm flat on my back because I have a bad knee."

"Vanessa."

"Fine," I say, dragging the pillow back over my face. "I'm still in love with Sam. What am I supposed to do about it?"

After Faith and her nonbroken sandals left for her reception, I tried to distract myself from spiraling over Sam with work tasks. I have emails from sponsors I need to return, leads on private clients I need to chase, hateful comments on my socials I need to delete. But after an initial burst of energy—that lasted maybe all of five minutes—I'm doing nothing more productive than staring at my sad frozen pizza, remembering Sam's familiar hands on the box, and wondering where he and his glamorous girlfriend are at this very moment. Surely doing something more entertaining than *this*.

"Snap out of it, Summers," I say aloud.

I used to be an interesting person, I swear. But having the rug yanked out from underneath me, proving that I didn't really know my fiancé at all, and having my entire career upended by those who found me guilty by association really wrecked my self-confidence.

But forget that. *I'm* not the one who brought down a financial market. *I'm* not the criminal. I'm an innocent party caught in the crossfire, and I'm done feeling like I need to hide.

Decisively, I push away the pizza and call the one friend I'm sure will answer. Ellie Park is a professional party girl, and I don't mean that in a pejorative sense. She and her twin brother, Richie, own an event-planning business, and together they've planned some of the most decadent parties in the Chicago social scene. Ellie has been my close friend since we pledged the same sorority freshman year in college; if anyone can perk me up, it's her.

"She lives!" Ellie exclaims into my ear. "Vanessa, babe, I've been so worried about you. Your social media has gone dark, and I've been calling and calling. I was in New York last week and wanted to see you, but I couldn't figure out how to reach you."

"I'm sorry I didn't call you back. I've been . . . well, you can probably guess how I've been."

"Jackson, that rat bastard."

"Yeah. Anyway, I'd love to see you."

"I'll be in New York again in two weeks. We can—"

"Actually, I'm not in New York anymore."

"Where are you? Please tell me it's somewhere good. I'm dying for a vacation."

"Can't help you out there, hon. I'm in Chicago."

"Chicago!" Ellie whoops down the line. "Even better! Why didn't you tell me?"

"To be honest, El, I've been in a bit of a funk, and I didn't want to see anyone. Don't take it personally."

"I'll try not to, unless you don't come out tonight. Richie's having a gathering at his place. Nothing fancy. I'm texting you the address right now."

My phone buzzes in my ear, and I pull it away briefly to confirm that it's an address. "Got it. I'm in."

"Excellent. I'm heading out in the next thirty minutes. I'll see you there!"

"I can't wait," I tell her honestly.

An hour later, Ellie, who has dyed her jet-black hair cotton-candy pink since the last time I saw her, pulls me by the hand through the door of Richie's West Loop loft. When she described it as a "gathering" that was "nothing fancy," I envisioned a few people sitting around, drinking beer and chatting. I should have known better. This is Ellie and Richie, after all, the duo whose joint twenty-fifth birthday party involved a performance by Billy Corgan. These two don't do anything halfway. At the moment, Richie's darkened loft is lit by a black light, and a DJ is mixing dance music in the corner.

"You didn't tell me this was a full-on party!" I gesture down at my sundress and sneakers—the only shoes I can wear without wanting to kill myself. "I'm not dressed for this."

"It's not a party!" Ellie protests, tugging me along to the makeshift bar set up on Richie's countertop. "Our friend Mikayla just got some new turntables and wanted to test them out, and lately Richie's obsessed with this silly black light he found on eBay. I keep telling him it's outdated—and not in a cool way—but does he listen to his sister? He does not."

"A person ignores Ellie Park at their own peril."

"Exactly," she says emphatically and shoves a hastily mixed vodka soda into my hands. "Here. Now, how the hell are you?"

"Honestly? I'm not all that sure." I gulp at the drink and wince as it burns its way down my throat. "Wow, El. This takes the idea of a *stiff drink* to a whole other level."

"I thought you might need it." She bats her eyes innocently at me. "Come on. Let's go party."

"I thought it wasn't a party."

She laughs and drags me to the center of the action.

Chapter Thirteen

Dancing on my bad knee is not easy—and probably not advisable—but I don't care. It feels so good to be among a crowd of people, to blend in and let loose again. I finish the drink Ellie made me, and then I have another, and by the time I'm on my third, I can barely feel my knee. I've lost track of Ellie, and I'm dancing with Richie, who shares his sister's slight frame but not her pink hair.

"It's good to see you again, Vanessa," he says just before someone pulls him away, and then I'm spinning on the floor by myself. I take another spin, and my knee twinges, and I stumble into a guy standing near me, spilling what's left of my drink on him.

"Sorry!" I apologize. "I lost my footing for a second, and—"

"No worries," he says, waving me off. "I never wear anything I don't mind staining to a party at Richie's."

"Smart man."

"Come on, want me to get you another drink?"

The beat feels like it's thumping inside my veins, and I want to keep dancing, but my knee throbs, reminding me that I really should take a break. I nod in resigned assent. "All right."

"You look familiar," he says, glancing at me as we make our way across the room.

I tense, ready for him to make some comment about me being Jackson Dalton's girlfriend. "I have kind of a familiar face."

"I know." He snaps his fingers, and I start looking for an escape plan. "Poli Sci 101, first semester, sophomore year."

I'm so surprised I laugh. "With that terrible TA who called everyone 'Mr.' and 'Miss'?"

"That's the one." He shakes his head, pleased with himself for solving the puzzle. "I knew I recognized you. I'm Scott, by the way."

"Oh, sure! You were a Delt, right? And you went to Barn Dance with Whitney?"

He nods. "Yeah. The grad dance, too."

I shudder, uncomfortable memories sliding through my mind: Sam skulking in a corner, a shoe flying through the air, someone else's strong arm around my shoulders.

"Have you seen what Whitney's up to these days?" Scott continues, oblivious, as we reach the countertop cluttered with bottles. "What're you drinking?"

"Vodka soda, thanks. And yeah, she just got elected as a state representative, right?"

He lifts a bottle of Grey Goose and nods. "Yeah. Wild, huh? Never thought the girl I smoked up on the roof of my frat house would be a congressperson."

"I mean, to be fair, you got a lot of girls stoned up there, so the odds were good."

He laughs. "You're right. But it can make you feel a bit inadequate, know what I mean? When people we graduated with are up to such cool things. I mean, look at Sam Cosgrove. Hey, you used to date him, didn't you?"

The room abruptly feels too small, and I struggle to inhale.

"Yeah," I manage. "So, what do *you* do?"

And those are the magic words, it turns out. Men love to talk about themselves, and Scott is no exception. He's off to the races, expounding on commercial real estate and mortgage rates. I zone out, nodding occasionally so he thinks I'm still listening, and I hope there won't be a quiz at the end.

Luckily, Ellie saves me. She throws herself against the bar between us and exclaims, "Let's do some shots! Tequila all right?"

Tequila it is.

"I'm in," Scott says.

Ellie glances at me. "Vanessa?"

"Um." I swallow. "Yeah, okay, I guess."

~

One tequila shot becomes two, and the night slides into a blur of dancing and laughing, and then, under Ellie's guidance—or more accurately, her *bullying*—I'm redownloading Instagram on my phone.

"You can't let that asshole Jackson ruin your life!" she screams in my ear over the music. "Take back your narrative!"

"I'm doing it!" I declare, posting a selfie of Ellie and me. "I'm taking back my narrative!"

After being off social media for over a month, I'm like an addict going on a binge. I can't stop shoving my phone in people's faces, forcing them to take selfies with me. I add them to my Instagram Stories, one after another, a parade of increasingly out-of-focus images.

"Hey," Scott says as I smash my face against his for another selfie. "I'm glad you came tonight."

"Me, too!" I squeal, hitting the virtual shutter to memorialize the moment.

He puts a hand on the small of my back and turns his head toward mine, and that's when I realize he's not glad I came because I'm finally getting my groove back. He thinks we're going to hook up.

In another timeline, I might consider it. Scott is cute. He has a gym-toned body and friendly eyes and very kissable-looking lips. Real estate obsession aside, I've enjoyed chatting with him.

But in this timeline, the only man I want to kiss is Sam.

Just thinking Sam's name makes my heart trip. I know I've had enough to drink that if I stay here for just another minute, I'll fall apart in tears, and I know once that happens, there will be no consoling me. So I plant a chaste kiss on Scott's cheek and tell him I'll see him around, and then slip out the door. I text Ellie goodbye from the back seat of an Uber.

The apartment is dark when I return, and I can hear Faith's white-noise machine whirring gently from her room. I creep through the apartment like a cat burglar, hoping to avoid waking her. As quietly as possible, I remove my makeup and brush my teeth, then fall into bed in my clothes. I'm exhausted but too wired to sleep, so I open Instagram. I click through my Stories, and it feels like an out-of-body experience to see myself apparently having such a good time when I now feel so empty.

Seeing Sam has reopened a chasm in my heart, the same one that first cracked open five years ago when he left me. My eyes cloud with tears, and the phone slips out of my hand. As I struggle to catch it, my finger accidentally taps the icon to show who has viewed a Story. I move to close the list, but a username catches my eye.

@samcosgrove

All my nerves fire at once, and I rocket to a seated position.

With a trembling finger, I click on his username. His Instagram page opens, and I catch my breath. I can see it. I'm no longer blocked.

My eager eyes skip to the first picture in his grid, and immediately I wish they hadn't. His beautiful girlfriend, the one I saw in the lobby, dressed casually in an off-the-shoulder T-shirt, bright white against her brown skin, with a slouchy beanie set atop her lustrous, dark hair, smiles mysteriously at me. I don't bother reading the caption. The image alone is enough to make me want to vomit.

Wait, I think. *No, I actually* am *going to vomit.*

I fling the phone down and rush to the bathroom, where all the alcohol I consumed at Richie's comes right back up. In the middle of my retching, I hear a quiet knock on the bathroom door.

"Hey," Faith calls softly. "Are you okay?"

I wipe my mouth and pull open the door a crack.

"I want to be," I confess through tears. "But I don't think I am."

"Oh, sweetie." Faith pushes the door all the way open and pulls me into her arms. "I'm here."

Chapter Fourteen

I cannot rest, not even with the ibuprofen and Gatorade Faith poured into me. *Sam saw my Instagram Stories.* That knowledge bounces around my brain, begging for attention. After all these years, Sam unblocked me, searched out my username, and viewed my Stories. That has to mean something.

Doesn't it?

Maybe he was just curious after running into me at Walgreens. *Wow, Vanessa sure is a hot mess these days; I wonder what the rest of her train-wreck life is like.* I cringe envisioning it, trying to see my posts through his perspective. Would he see my Stories from Richie's party as evidence that I'm still a fun person, or would he find the real-time documentation of my descent into intoxication juvenile? Maybe he thought, *Man, I dodged a bullet there.*

But I can't shake the memory of how he looked at me in the lobby that afternoon. His dark eyes soft, welcoming. *Something* passed between us in that moment, some sort of feeling—evidence that even though we haven't seen each other in five years, the connection between us isn't totally dead.

And then his girlfriend showed up.

Or maybe Faith was right, and she isn't his girlfriend. Maybe the coffee he'd suggested was—if not a *date*, then an opening.

Or maybe she *is* his girlfriend and the coffee offer was exactly what he said it was: a chance to catch up.

But whether or not it's a date or a platonic caffeination, it was decidedly an invitation—and I am going to accept. I close out of Sam's Instagram—I don't think my fragile heart can handle any more glamour shots of his maybe girlfriend—and switch to Messages. There, I key in Sam's name. I could never bring myself to delete his contact information. No matter how long ago or how poorly things ended, the idea of not being able to reach him made me feel sick. Of course, I have no idea if he's changed his number. For all I know, this number now belongs to some random teenager.

Still, I have to try.

Coffee would be great, if the invitation is still open.

I send the message before I can change my mind, and then I stare at my phone as though he might actually respond at four in the morning. Of course, he does not. Somewhere—maybe right above me, maybe beside his girlfriend—Sam is sleeping and oblivious to my message.

~

Somehow I must have fallen asleep, because the next thing I know, light is filtering into my bedroom, and the scent of coffee fills the apartment. I roll over to check the time on my phone, but I'm distracted by the text notification.

Are you referring to actual coffee or one of those ungodly milk-and-fake-sugar concoctions?

Oh no. I'd thought texting Sam in the middle of the night had been part of a weird alcohol-induced dream. But no, it had really happened. I want to die.

But his response—it's playful. Even though he might be happily entwined with that beautiful woman—God, did I even check his hand for a ring? What if he's *married* to her?—he's open to seeing me. My heart flutters.

I bite my lip and tap out, The latter, obviously. Does that change your response?

No because I still believe I can convert you away from the dark side.

You're aware that your side is the literal dark side, right?, I type, laughing. I add, There was a 50-50 chance I got some rando instead of you at this number.

How do you know you didn't?

I guess I won't know until you show up for coffee.

How's 10 am?

So soon! My hangover vanishes in an instant, and I feel like leaping from the bed and dancing. I start to type Yes! but I'm worried about coming across as too eager. Instead, I write, Works for me. Name the place.

Sam sends me a link to a coffee shop a few blocks away, and I smile and tap it into my phone as a new message appears.

See you then. 🙂

Warmth blossoms in my chest as though Sam himself had just smiled at me instead of a silly emoji, and I'm still sitting there, grinning like an idiot at my phone, when Faith knocks on the doorjamb.

"Hey, you. I thought I heard you stirring in here. How're you feeling?"

"Human, thanks to you."

"What are sisters for?" She crosses to the bed and hands me a mug of coffee. "Looked like a wild night."

"Not that wild. Just irresponsible."

"Well, you're still smiling. You must have had fun."

"Yeah, Richie totally outdid himself. There was a lot of dancing and—"

"Drinking, it seems."

I laugh, grimacing as my brain throbs. "Yeah, there was definitely some of that. More than I should have. But . . . I don't know, Faith. It was the first time in a long time that I really felt like *myself*, if that makes sense. Jack kept our social calendar full, and I was otherwise always working. I didn't have time to see my own friends or take care of my own needs. I didn't have any time to just *be*."

"Well, it looks like it did you good. I can't remember the last time I saw you smile like that."

"Actually," I say, glancing down at my phone, where Sam's message is still visible. "It's Sam."

"Sam?"

"I might have drunk-texted him." I cover my face with my hand. "Not my finest moment, I know. But it has a happy ending: We're getting coffee. This morning."

"This morning?" Faith repeats. "*This* morning? What are you doing still in bed?"

"Relax, we're not meeting until ten."

"I hate to break it to you, sis, but you're going to need at least until then to wash that greasy hair and steam the scent of booze out of your pores."

"It's not that bad," I protest, pretending to throw a pillow at her.

"I might be exaggerating for effect," she says, grinning. "It's called *rhetorical hyperbole*. It's not actionable."

"It's unnecessary. I'm going to shower."

"Do more than shower, huh?" Faith says, her tone softening. "This is your second chance with the love of your life."

"He's not the love of my life," I lie.

"Yes, he is," Faith singsongs as she leaves the room.

My chest twitches because I know Faith's right. Sam Cosgrove is the love of my life.

But am I still the love of his?

~

After Faith leaves, I don't head immediately for the shower. Instead, I sit in bed and google him. I have to at this point, don't I? In two short hours, we'll be catching up over coffee. I need to know what I'm walking into. My heart can't take any more surprises like seeing his possible girlfriend. Besides, googling him doesn't feel verboten anymore. The rules have changed. He unblocked me; he viewed my Stories. He's opened the door.

The top hit is a piece published Friday in *The New York Times*, something entitled Meet the Team Disrupting Big Energy, and it features a picture of Sam and the beautiful woman from the lobby. Rekha Agarwal, according to the caption. Hope flutters in my chest. Do they . . . work together? Does that mean they're *not* a couple? Eagerly, I begin to read:

> Sam Cosgrove and Rekha Agarwal, cofounders of Solosol, want to save the planet.

At that, I almost set the phone down. The irony of Sam being an environmentalist while Jack went all in on something that is, at the very least, environmentally problematic doesn't escape me. It's like the universe has cast Jack as the villain and Sam as the white hat. I almost laugh.

I turn back to the article and start again:

> Sam Cosgrove and Rekha Agarwal, cofounders of Solosol, want to save the planet. To do that, Cosgrove says, we must look to the stars. One star, specifically: our sun.

> Solar panels aren't new. But the panel Solosol plans to launch next month, the Solosol Uno, is something different—and potentially groundbreaking. The Uno, designed by Agarwal, a Stanford-educated engineer, is a solar panel smaller than the palm of your hand that is claimed to generate 1,500 watts per hour even in partial shade. If true, that would make the Uno the most efficient solar panel on the market by a long shot. Some experts doubt the veracity of Solosol's claims, but Cosgrove and Agarwal haven't flinched.

I skim the rest of the article quickly, looking for one thing and one thing only: any evidence that Sam and Rekha are a couple. It's not mentioned in the article, and when I open a different browser window and start googling, it doesn't come up anywhere. I relax—but only slightly. I saw the way she touched him in the lobby.

I turn back to the *NYT* article in wonder. It's not that I'm starstruck. After all, I was engaged to Jackson Dalton, and he's been profiled by just about every major media outlet from *The New York Times* to *Rolling Stone*. But that's Jack, a man born into privilege and who has entitlement baked into his DNA. This is *Sam*, the guy I used to sleep beside in an extra-long twin-size bottom bunk. His ascent wasn't predestined. He worked for it, and if I know Sam like I think I do, it was something he worked *hard* for.

My heart hitches. Maybe Faith is right. Maybe I *didn't* ruin his life. I mean, look where he ended up: in the pages of the Gray Lady, about to launch a revolutionary product.

But I can't stop myself from wondering what other amazing things Sam might have already accomplished if I hadn't gotten in his way.

Chapter Fifteen

The Sam I remember always smelled faintly of coffee. He used to joke that he drank so much of the stuff he'd give a vampire the jitters. He was indiscriminate about the type of brew as long as it was caffeinated, and so I'm not quite sure how I feel that he's chosen a local café with pour-overs on the menu rather than a garden-variety Starbucks. Maybe it means his tastes have evolved, or maybe it means I don't actually know him anymore.

I arrive fifteen minutes early, which is significant because I never arrive anywhere early, not ever. Promptness is something I've struggled with my whole life—not because I'm selfish, as my father insists, but because I'm terrible with time management and usually overscheduled. Over the years, I've gotten better by necessity—arriving late to your own yoga class is a bad look—but it's still rare for me to show up more than ten seconds in advance.

I use the extra minutes to buy Sam and I each a coffee and choose a table near the window. Each table is topped with a stack of well-worn books, and I paw through our selection, looking for something meaningful. I'm about to restack them with *Pride and Prejudice*—a romantic classic—on top when I spot *Slaughterhouse-Five* on another table. In an instant, I can feel the Cancún sun on my skin and hear Sam saying, *So there's this guy, Billy Pilgrim . . .* I grab it and place it atop our pile just as Sam walks through the door.

Butterflies the size of bats swarm my stomach, and for the briefest of moments, I think I'm going to vomit. That's all it takes for Sam's voice to echo through my mind again, his words sliding into each other as he says, *I love you so much I want to barf.* The line was absurd when he said it five years ago, and what happened next was even more so, but I'll never forget the tender way he looked at me, the way I could see forever in his eyes.

Now I blink my own eyes to hold the tears at bay. Sam has already seen my messy side twice in recent days, and I want—*need*—to remind him that there's more to me than that. I draw a purposeful inhalation through my nose and let it out slowly through my nose. Breathe in the calm, exhale the anxiety.

Then I arrange my features into a smile and wave at him, calling out, "Sam! Over here!"

He turns his gaze to me, and his dark eyes land on mine. His expression falters—just for half a second, but long enough for me to think he's realized this is a mistake. No amount of exhaling anxiety could make me feel better; I want to disappear in a puff of smoke. But then, just as quickly, his expression morphs into a smile, and he waves back.

As he makes his way to me, I let my eyes run over his body, cataloging the similarities and differences from college: Shaggy, dark hair, unchanged. Muscles that indicate he knows his way around a gym, a new addition. There used to be a softness to his body, a youthfulness. He looks stronger now, more solid. A ripple of desire courses through me.

"Hey, Ness," he says when he reaches me, and the sound of my nickname coming out of his mouth makes my heart explode.

I keep smiling like I'll die if I stop, and rise from my chair. "Hey, you."

Awkwardness follows as Sam and I stand two feet apart, unsure how to greet each other. What's an appropriate greeting for a former lover? Can you fist-bump hello to someone who's seen you naked?

"Hey," Sam says again. Then he lifts one arm and takes a step toward me before stopping, arm still uplifted. "Sorry, is this weird? Can I hug you?"

I nod, not fully trusting myself to speak, and step into his arms. Talk about a mindwreck. Sam's body is warm and smells like it ever did, like coffee and cinnamon and a spritz of aquatic cologne, but the way his arms fit around my body isn't the same. He holds me at a physical distance, hugging me the way you'd hug a cousin, and not even a cousin to whom you're particularly close. Once upon a time, our touch was so electric it could set the air on fire. From the very first day we spent together, huddled on his lounge chair, sipping tequilas while he told me the plot of *Slaughterhouse-Five*, I could practically see sparks whenever we grazed each other's sun-warmed skin. Sam's touch was a form of magic.

Now he's giving me a chaste side hug. I sense he's about to pull away, and I don't want to be the last to let go, so I quickly wriggle from his arms and gesture to the pair of coffees on our table.

"I got you a coffee. You still drink it black?"

"As any self-respecting person does," he says, smiling. "Is yours still eighty percent milk?"

"It's more like twenty percent," I say. "And I use oat milk now."

His expression flickers. "Ah. Got it."

"I tried drinking it black," I blather, anxious to get the smile back on his face. "You know, trimming calories and all that. But, wow, no, thank you. I felt like my stomach was churning acid all day. And how many cups a day did you drink while we were in school? Two or three? Your stomach must be lined with steel."

He chuckles, running a hand through his thick hair. "Remind me not to tell you how much coffee I drink now."

"I shudder to think." I take a seat and summon the courage to ask about his life, afraid of what he might tell me. "But I suppose you need quite a bit if you're launching a buzzy solar panel."

He quirks his mouth into a lopsided grin. "You know what I'm doing, huh?"

"If you're asking whether I googled you, I won't dignify that with an answer."

"That means you did." His grin widens. "Find out anything good?"

"I read you went to business school. Congratulations."

"Thanks." He tilts his head at me. "You know I googled you, too."

I wince. "I wish you hadn't done that."

"Your yoga platform is impressive. Did you work with a business manager?"

I shake my head. "No. Just me and my enormous ego."

"Vanessa," he says, his voice lowering an octave. "There's nothing wrong with your ego."

"Trust me, I know. It's very healthy."

His eyes smolder as he says, "There's nothing wrong with any part of you."

Sam shifts his legs under the table so they press against mine. Heat pools in my lower belly, and I'm desperate to know whether this is intentional. Is Sam hitting on me? Is he *available* to hit on me? Is he actually dating his so-called business partner, Rekha?

Dammit, I'm spiraling again. I order myself to take another centering breath, but the next thing I know, I ask, "Does Rekha know you're a divorcé?"

Sam blinks and moves his legs away. "I'm not sure that's the technical term for it."

"That's a no."

He looks at me as though I have a bomb strapped to my chest, and carefully says, "It hasn't come up."

"And you don't think she deserves to know?"

"*Deserves* to know? No, not really." He cocks his head at me. "Do you tell everyone you meet that you were once married for seventy-two hours?"

"Not everyone. It's not—" I cut myself off.

"Something you're proud of?" he finishes, his expression unreadable.

"That's not what I was going to say," I insist, color rising in my cheeks. "I just meant that it's not something I share with everyone. But, to my earlier point, I *did* tell my ex."

"Your earlier . . . ?" He trails off, shaking his head. "And by *ex*, you mean your ex who's currently a fugitive from justice?"

"Nice."

"I wasn't going to bring him up, but you—" He shakes his head again and holds up his hands. "You know what? I'm very confused about what's happening right now."

I stare into my coffee and say, "All I want to know is whether you told your girlfriend you're having coffee with your ex-wife."

"What?" He furrows his brow. "What are you even . . . ? Oh. You think Rekha's my girlfriend?"

"Isn't she?"

He guffaws as though it's a ridiculous notion. "Yeah, no. She is definitely not."

I bristle. "I saw the way she touched you. In the lobby—"

"Rekha is my business partner, not my girlfriend."

"Really?" I press. "That's all?"

"Really." Sam adjusts slightly in his chair until his knees touch mine again with the barest, most featherlight pressure. "Is it bad that I kind of like your jealousy?"

"You got a kink, huh, Cosgrove?" I slide my legs forward a fraction of an inch, just enough to return the pressure on his knee, and I'm rewarded with a flash in his dark eyes, one of his thick eyebrows tugging upward.

"That's not what I'd call it."

For a heady moment, neither of us says anything. We just sit there, eyes locked, knees touching, a whiff of jealousy vibrating in the air between us. My muscles twitch, desperate to reach across the charmingly scuffed table, grab a fistful of his T-shirt, and haul that dead-sexy man toward me. But it's been years since I touched him in a meaningful way, and so that would be insane behavior.

Still, though, I can practically hear the tension crackling between us. One of us just has to make the first move.

"So," he says, his voice gravelly. I lean forward, skin thrumming with anticipation. "Tell me about you."

It's so pedestrian, so *impersonal*, that I almost burst into tears. Instead, I move my knee away from his and, in the lightest voice I can muster, ask, "What do you want to know?"

"Everything." He shifts forward until our knees are touching again, and that has to mean something, right? "Tell me how Vanessa Summers became a yogalebrity."

Despite myself, I laugh. "Oh God, please don't ever use that word again. I'm one hundred percent not a celebrity of any variety. I'm just a yoga instructor with a nice platform. Actually, wait." I reach into my bag and pull out one of my business cards and slide it across the table. "My friend Sienna wants me to say I'm not just a yoga instructor. I'm a *wellness coach*."

"Wellness coach, huh?" he says, picking up the pink card and studying it. "What does that mean?"

I tell him about the courses I run and podcasts I do, the private coaching and the articles, all of it. Never once does Sam look anything other than riveted, and I feel a part of my self-esteem start to regenerate.

"That's pretty cool," he finally says. "How did you get into the wellness space?"

"Well," I say, chewing on my lip, "I'm looking at the reason."

He stiffens and starts to pull away. "Vanessa—"

"Hey," I say softly, capturing his hand before he takes it off the table. I'm desperate to twine my fingers through his, but I worry that's too much, too fast, and content myself with holding it loosely. "I'm not, like, assigning blame. I'm not here to rehash the past. It's just . . . well, it was formative, I guess. After . . . after everything, I just didn't think I could move to Chicago like I had planned. I needed distance, physical distance. Ellie had a job in New York, you know, so I went with her, and I found a position at a boutique marketing firm. But . . .

it wasn't enough. I needed something else. I needed a little eat, pray, love, but you know me: I don't really like pasta, and I definitely wasn't in the headspace for the love. I couldn't afford to fly to India—not at that point, anyway—so I downloaded some yoga videos, and . . . it was the first thing that made sense to me in a long time. Asanas quell my need to *move*, and the meditative aspect was really a game changer. Then the pandemic hit, and the marketing firm I was working at closed, so I just . . . leaned into it. Started filming myself practicing, went to India to get certified, and the rest is history."

"I—" he starts, then cuts himself off and shakes his head. "I won't rehash the past, either. All I'll say is that I'm proud of you. I've been wanting to tell you that for a while. I saw your face on the cover of *Yoga Journal*—"

"I didn't know you read *Yoga Journal*," I cut in teasingly.

"It was on display in the checkout line at Whole Foods. And I wanted to reach out, but I . . . I just didn't think I should."

"I wish you would have."

Sam holds my gaze searchingly. "Yeah," he finally says. "Yeah, no, I should have."

He inclines his body toward me, his eyes still holding mine, just long enough that I have to wonder if he's about to kiss me, before his phone buzzes on the table between us and we jerk apart as though awoken from a dream. He drags a hand over his face and picks up his phone, but in the instant before he does, I see Rekha's name on the screen. I know Sam said she's only a business partner, but I can't help the flare of jealousy that runs through me.

"Shit," Sam mutters. He looks up at me, his expression torn. "I'm sorry to have to cut this short, but I have to handle something for work."

The phone buzzes again in his hand, and he scowls down at it, muttering another curse as his thumbs tap a reply.

"I'll call you, okay?" he says, his eyes still on his phone as he rises.

"Yeah, okay," I manage, trying to hide my crushing disappointment.

He ruffles my hair in a way that feels both overly familiar and infantilizing, a far cry from the heat I'd felt building between us just moments ago. "See you around, Vanessa."

"Yeah," I say, forcing lightness into my voice. "See you."

Sam doesn't look back as he walks out the door, his face bent over his screen.

Strictly speaking, Sam is correct that he is not a divorcé. Our days-long marriage, officiated by a Dolly Parton impersonator in a Las Vegas chapel decorated with a disco ball, ended in annulment. I'm told this means that, legally, it never happened.

But all the legalese in the world can't change the fact that Sam and I joined hands and promised to love each other always and forever, for better or for worse. I might have been wearing a neon green minidress from Forever 21, and he might have had a spot of spilled tequila on his T-shirt, and our officiant might have serenaded us with a pitch-perfect but wholly inappropriate performance of "I Will Always Love You," but we were *in love*. I was twenty-two years old and could barely conceive of what my life might be like even a year in the future, but I *meant it* when I said "till death do us part." I thought he did, too.

Obviously, I was wrong.

Chapter Sixteen

I open the door to find Faith cross-legged on the couch with an enormous mug of coffee and *The New York Times* crossword open on her tablet. She looks up at me eagerly. "So? How was coffee?"

"Caffeinating."

"Vanessa! Give me something! How was *Sam*?"

His warm smile flits across my mind's eye, and I feel a blush rising in my cheeks. "Funny. Engaging. So adorable I want to die. All the usual."

"Look at you! So it was a date?"

"I don't think so," I say, crossing the room to sit beside her. "I mean, there was definitely something magnetic happening, but he didn't, you know, say anything overt."

"So he didn't mention a girlfriend?"

"No. In fact, he assured me the beautiful woman from the lobby is just his business partner, Rekha."

Faith catches her breath. "Oh, *that's* who you saw. I've seen her picture online. She *is* gorgeous."

"Right? And he *says* she's just his business partner, but I don't know, Faith, you should have seen the way she looked at him yesterday. It was *possessive*, not platonic. Worse, she called while we were having coffee, and he practically vaulted away from me. I mean, I don't blame him. She's stunning. I would date her, and I don't even date women."

Faith smirks. "Looks aren't everything."

"Okay, and she's also brilliant." I shake my head. "Plus, she has the distinct advantage of not having already married *and* lost Sam."

"Vanessa, that was years ago. You were just kids."

"We were *twenty-two*. Adults. That's how old Mom was when she and Dad got married."

"Yes, and look how well that worked out."

"Okay, bad example, but other people do it. They get married young and stay married for sixty, seventy years."

"True. But those people aren't usually married by Elvis impersonators."

I flick her on the shoulder. "It was a Dolly Parton impersonator!"

She flicks me back. "Shouldn't the Dolly impersonators be in Nashville? Maybe you should have held out for Elvis."

"Dolly has global appeal. I mean, come on, she sends free books out to kids. How can you *not* like her?"

"In no way am I shading Dolly Parton," Faith says, holding up her hands. "I'm simply suggesting that perhaps tying the knot on a whim isn't a recipe for lasting marital bliss."

"We were in love," I say quietly. "But yeah, I get it. If *you* got married in a dimly lit Las Vegas chapel that smelled like stale beer, I'd for sure tell you to undo it faster than you can say 'mazel tov.' I just . . . I didn't expect Sam to be so quick to sign those annulment papers his dad had drawn up, or for him to just totally shut me out afterward." I draw an uneasy breath. "Maybe I should have, though. I mean, if I'm totally honest, I knew it was the beginning of the end when Sam transferred from Cornell."

"What are you talking about? I thought you said it was romantic that he switched schools to be with you."

I swallow hard. "I said that back then, but I was stupid and selfish. I should have realized giving up an Ivy League education would derail his future and that he'd resent me for it."

"He said that to you?" Faith asks, looking outraged on my behalf. "Why didn't you ever tell me?"

"Well, he didn't say it in so many words, but he didn't have to. I knew what it meant when he pulled away." Those last few weeks of senior year were brutal, and just remembering how distant Sam was brings tears to my eyes. "And I never told you because it hurt—*hurts* still—too much to talk about. I mean, Faith, imagine finding the love of your life and then losing him because you're incapable of looking further than your own navel."

"You're being too hard on yourself," she says. "It's not like you forced him to apply to Illinois. You didn't hold a gun to his head and make him submit the transfer papers."

"No, but I had him wrapped around my finger, and I knew it." I can see Faith opening her mouth to protest, so I add, "And to make things worse, when I felt him pulling away, when I knew he realized he'd made a huge mistake, I got him drunk and married him."

"Little-known fact, but it takes two not only to tango but to sign a marriage license."

"Joke all you want, but Sam tied his own life to the train tracks for me, and I just stood there and watched."

"You read that *New York Times* article, right? He seems to have turned out more than fine." Faith shrugs. "Anyway, didn't you just come back from coffee with the man, blushing like a ripe tomato? What's with all the doom and gloom?"

I can almost feel Sam's knee against mine, the warmth radiating from his body into my aching joint, and my heart twists. Because here's the thing I don't want to admit: Even if Sam and Rekha aren't together, even if Sam has moved past what happened in college, everything that I did and everything I said—I can't let anything happen between us. Not while I'm still fielding phone calls from reporters like Fern Foxall, not while my inboxes still overflow with random internet trolls accusing me of colluding with Jack. Everyone seems to believe that I knew about what happened at Jaxx Coin, and my name is virtually synonymous with *fraud*. The absolute last thing that Sam, a man about to launch a new company, needs is to be associated with the toxic likes of me.

~

That afternoon, I'm lying on my bed, trying to catch a quick nap to make up for last night's lack of sleep, but my mind can't stop fixating on what went wrong with Sam. I was so quick to call his self-sacrifice *romance*, so eager to believe that our love was written in the stars.

In some ways, it makes sense. I was the kind of child who held elaborate Barbie weddings, who watched everything in the Meg Ryan canon, who started pilfering my mother's bodice rippers at twelve. I loved *romance* and all its trappings, but I struggled to find the real thing. I was a serial dater in high school, quickly disillusioned as I realized that most high school boys' idea of romance was plying me with shoplifted wine coolers and trying to feel me up in the back row of the movie theater. It was mostly the same story with college boys, except they passed me cups of Everclear punch and tried to stick their hands up my shirt at frat parties. It was, in a word, *disappointing*.

Then I met Sam, and suddenly it clicked why nothing had worked for me before. I wasn't *supposed* to be with those boys. I was *supposed* to be with Sam. In retrospect, him scooping me up and carrying me out of the water was the perfect metaphor for him carrying me over the threshold of an entirely new way of looking at life. I loved him from the minute those chocolate eyes hit mine. I knew we were supposed to be, knew it deep within the marrow of my bones. It didn't matter that I went to school in Central Illinois and that he went to Cornell in New York. It was hard, but we did it. We texted so frequently I nearly sprained my thumb, and we talked on the phone almost every night. (And some nights when my roommate was staying with her boyfriend, we did more than just *talk* on the phone.) We saw each other when we could, and over the summers, we both returned to our suburban Chicago homes. Our parents didn't live close enough for us to see each other every day—my mom lived up in Mundelein back then, and his parents were down in Aurora, a distance of just over an hour without traffic—but we lived close enough that Sam drove up to see me a couple of times a week. We spent the summer catching every delicious moment alone together that we could.

Each time we had to part, it was harder. After our second summer together, I was nearly inconsolable when I had to return to school in mid-August for Work Week, the week preceding sorority rush. In theory, I should have been excited. The past spring, I'd been elected Vice President of Recruitment, and it was my time to shine. I'd spent hundreds of hours selecting themes, decorations, and songs, not to mention committing to memory all the recruitment rules. It was time to watch all my hard work come to fruition.

But the only thing I could think about was Sam. When I arranged the members on the interior stairs and instructed them where the handclaps went in the goodbye song ("for pep—*clap*—and vitality—*clap*"), I was remembering an afternoon when Sam and I went into the city and hung out at the Ohio Street Beach. I could feel his hands spreading sunscreen over my shoulders even as I shouted at a sophomore that if she couldn't clap on the beat, maybe she should just *pretend* to clap. When I twisted a garland of silk flowers around the banister, I was remembering buying soft serve at the Dairy Queen and debating what topping was better—I insisted classic hot fudge, but Sam was a sucker for the sweetness of butterscotch. Making decor for an event, I carelessly hot-glued my thumb to a silk petal because I was lost in remembering the sugary vanilla taste of his tongue.

Somehow, though, I made it through Work Week. Everything was in place, and recruitment—and school—would start the following day. At four in the afternoon, the sorority house buzzed with energy. Some girls were getting ready to head over to fraternity houses to pregame for last-day-of-summer parties, and others were getting dressed for the bars, which had been open since noon. The atmosphere was celebratory, but I couldn't bring myself to join. After a summer spent with Sam, nothing would compare.

Instead, I took myself on a punishing run. After six sweaty miles, my mind was finally clear—a state that lasted only until I returned and discovered a line for the shower. I took a seat on my bed to wait, and the memories I'd tried to outrun came rushing back.

I miss you, I texted him. I wish you were here.

Your wish is my command, he wrote back almost immediately.

Tears pricked my eyes as I smiled. When do you think you'll be able to come visit?

Soon? he responded.

God, I hope so. I miss you so much. I miss your lips and your hands and

"Vanessa?"

I looked up, blushing, as a sophomore knocked on the frame of my open door.

"Someone's downstairs for you."

"Thanks." I slid off my bed and headed for the stairs. Odds were good it was the Kappa recruitment chair, who'd spent the past week interrogating me about mundane aspects of our recruitment, with a query about the number of plastic cups we'd purchased or what kind of tape we'd used to affix our streamers. I was so certain it would be her that my brain short-circuited when I saw who was waiting in the rose-colored entry.

Sam.

I stared at him, dumbfounded. He wasn't supposed to be there. Especially not *then*, not with me wearing a T-shirt from a past fraternity party ("Win or Lose, We Still Booze," it read) and with dried rivulets of sweat on my forehead. Not when I smelled the way that I was sure I did.

He grinned crookedly at me and held out his arm, extending a small bouquet of wildflowers. "Hey."

"Hey, yourself." I took the flowers and threw my arms around him, relishing the solid feel of his body. "Sorry if I smell, but . . . God, Sam,

I can't believe you're here. I thought you were supposed to be at school by now."

"I am at school," he said against my shoulder.

I pulled away, blinking and wondering if I was suffering from some sort of delayed-onset heatstroke. "What do you mean?"

"I am at school," he repeated, and that was when I noticed his T-shirt: gray with an orange Block I on it.

I shook my head. "I don't understand. You're saying . . . you *transferred* here? For *me*?"

Sam's shiny white smile flickered—just for an instant, but long enough to plant a seed of uncertainty in my heart. Before I could say anything, though, he tugged his smile back into place and said, "Things changed for me."

If I'm honest, I knew something was wrong at that moment. I knew I should ask him why his smile had dimmed, however briefly—but I also knew that I wouldn't.

Instead, I shrieked with delight and threw myself at him. I wound my arms around his neck and pressed my body against his, no longer concerned about my damp exercise clothing. I caught his stubbled chin in my hand and brought his face to mine, and his mouth opened to receive me. Someone opened the door behind him and whistled, and we pulled apart, cheeks flushed.

"Come on." I tugged Sam's hand and led him upstairs, keeping one eye open for our house mother. Although she usually looked the other way, we weren't technically supposed to have boys upstairs. We made it to my room without seeing anyone, house mother or otherwise, and I pulled him inside and shut the door. As a senior on the executive council, I had my own room—a luxury in the sorority house.

"Vanessa—" he started, but I didn't want to talk about whatever hesitation had crossed his face. And so I placed my hands on his chest and pushed him flat against the closed door.

"Shut up, Sam," I said softly, my mouth against his. "I've missed you."

"It's only been a week," he said, smiling.

"Seven days too long," I said, working on his belt.

He made a noise low in his throat and snaked one hand up through my hair, using it to guide my mouth to his. I kissed him deeply, like I had something to prove, and in retrospect, I thought I did. I thought I had to show him how wonderful it would be to have me around all the time.

"Ness," he breathed, catching my hand as I pushed it down the front of his pants. "Wait. We should—"

I don't know what he was going to say, but I knew I didn't want to hear it. And so I pressed my mouth against his, swallowing his protests, and pushed my hand farther. Once it wrapped around him, he drew a shuddering breath, and I knew I had won.

At least for the moment.

Chapter Seventeen

I'll call you, okay?

I turn Sam's words over in my mind. I'd heard it as a promise, but what if it was only a throwaway line, just something to exit the conversation? The Sam I once knew wouldn't say something he didn't mean, but it's been more than twenty-four hours, and he hasn't called.

Spinning out over Sam is the opposite of productive, and so I take a couple of deep breaths and try to refocus myself. Unfortunately, my mind whirls from one anxiety (Sam) to another (the state of my finances). Because of the capricious nature of teaching yoga, I'd made sure to have a cushion of savings that could hold me over through lean times. But now, more than a month after Jack blew up our lives and my career became collateral damage, that cushion has worn thin. Working at House of Om helps, but I can't get by on only three classes per week. The real money came from my online courses and my sponsorships, and I need to figure out a way to revamp my image and reignite those revenue streams.

It's no easy task, and I've just stepped away from my computer to go on a stress-run when Faith arrives home from work.

"Guess who just called," she announces. "Hint: She badgered me about my postgraduation plans and asked how much a first-year associate makes."

"Hmm." I feign thoughtfulness, tapping my chin. "Gosh, I just don't know. Surely not our mother."

"Ding, ding, ding. Tell the lady what she's won." Faith drops into her desk chair and pulls off her sensible heels, wiggling her toes. "When she wasn't interrogating me about my future earning potential, she was asking about you. She says she's left you messages. *Hundreds*, according to her. She asked whether you'd changed your number."

"I don't think it's been hundreds," I say guiltily. "But she's right. I owe her a call. It's just . . . well, you know. The last time I talked to her, she wouldn't quit suggesting I extort Jack's family for money—not in so many words, of course. Our mother is a *lady*."

"And don't you forget it." Faith gives me a wry grin, then does a double take and frowns. "Hey, what are you doing?"

I pause in the middle of tying a shoe. "Going for a run?"

She stares at me like I've grown a second head. "Are you joking? With your knee?"

"It feels better."

"You're still limping."

"It's fine." Faith gives me a hard look, and I add, "Okay, it's still kind of bothering me, but it no longer makes me want to black out with pain if I dare to so much as look at it, so I'm calling that progress."

"Let me get this straight: Because the pain is no longer debilitating, your plan is to . . . get yourself back to square one as quickly as possible? Ruin your knee forever?"

"That's a bit extreme. And I'll be careful, I promise. But I need to *move*. I can't be so sedentary."

"Vanessa, no one would ever describe you as sedentary."

"You don't understand, Faith. Fern Foxall has been emailing me again, and if I sit still, I'll send her a response that we both will regret." I snap my laces. "I have to *move*."

She looks at me for a moment, seemingly considering continuing the argument. Finally, she sighs. "For the record, you're an exercise addict. But if you truly *must* work out, there's a rowing machine in the building's gym. You should try that instead of running."

Finding the gym in the building's labyrinthine basement takes me longer than I'd like to admit, and I end up in the laundry room twice and the boiler room once. Finally, I find a metal door labeled Gym. Through the narrow window, I can see that it is a "gym" only in the most technical sense of the word. The small room has a low drop-tiled ceiling and a couple of cheap-looking full-length mirrors tacked up on the walls. From where I stand, I can see two treadmills, one elliptical trainer, and the aforementioned rowing machine. Mounted to the wall in front of the treadmills is a small television, currently tuned to CNN.

Fabulous. I was dying to spend my workout listening to talking heads debate whether Jack is a con artist or just an idiot, and whether some congressperson's demand that he testify about what happened with Jaxx Coin will lead to anything. I know it won't. Jack is far too proud to admit he's done something wrong, even—perhaps especially—unintentionally.

Mainstream media has recently shown some images of Jack and me at various parties and events as "evidence" of him "living large" on investor capital. It's ridiculous, considering Jack has more money than most people can even imagine—but then again, Jack seemingly *did* relieve a lot of people of a lot of money, and a picture is worth a thousand words. In this instance, they're just the wrong words.

One of these images I hate in particular. Taken one month before everything fell apart, it shows Jack and me leaving his friend's birthday celebration at a club. Jack, impeccable in a collared navy shirt, has an arm slung around my shoulders, holding me close. I'm smiling—beaming—at the camera. My blond hair is tousled to perfection, my lips are shiny and match the fuchsia streaks in my hair, and the sequins of my dress—also fuchsia—are glittering. It is objectively one of the best photos ever taken of us.

But if you study the photo—*really* study it—you might see that my smile doesn't extend to my eyes, which look ever so slightly bloodshot. You might notice that Jack's arm over my shoulders is tense, the fingers on his hand curled into a tight fist. You might notice that we're smiling at the camera but not at each other. That photo was taken at almost two in the morning, six hours before I had to lead a workshop. I'd been telling Jack that I wanted to leave since eleven, but he kept insisting that I stay, kept saying that it would "look bad" if I left his friend's party without him. Against my better judgment, I stuck around. It was a beginner-level workshop, I told myself, one I'd taught dozens of times before. I could teach it in my sleep. But when someone innocently asked me whether I also worked in tech and Jack laughed—*laughed*—and said, "Oh, Vanessa doesn't work," something inside me snapped. I'd long suspected that Jack didn't take my teaching seriously, but it was one thing to think your workaholic fiancé doesn't fully get your profession and another to hear him dismiss it so flatly.

"Actually," I said, my voice tight with emotion, "I'm an internationally renowned yoga instructor, and I'm teaching a class in the morning, so I need to excuse myself."

I whirled on my heel and stalked off. The next thing I knew, he was at my side, telling me I was making a big deal out of nothing and that I was a buzzkill. He performatively looped his arm around my shoulders, reminded me to smile, and paraded me outside past the waiting photographers.

I wonder if, wherever he is, Jack has seen this image as many times as I have recently, and I wonder if he remembers how miserable we were that night. I wonder what he thinks of that moment becoming one of the images that defines us, defines *him*.

I shake my head and peer through the gym door at the television. CNN is currently running a story about storms in the Southeast, and Jack is nowhere to be seen, not even his name on the ticker running across the bottom of the screen. I promise myself I'll leave the second that changes, and I push open the door.

"Hey, neighbor."

I spin to the side, and there he is: Sam, seated on a previously unseen weight bench, doing bicep curls. He's wearing a plain gray T-shirt with the sleeves cut off, allowing me an unobstructed view of his arms, which are, for the record, very good arms to have.

I realize I'm staring—*gaping*, really—and force my mouth to make words. "Right back at you."

"Sorry about yesterday morning," he says, setting down his dumbbell. "Work is kind of insane right now, and there was a fire that needed putting out. I was going to text you afterward, but it turned out there was no afterward."

"Fire still raging?"

He grimaces. "Unfortunately. I couldn't even justify breaking at six this morning for my usual workout."

"Ugh, I get it."

Immediately, I cringe. What the hell am I even *talking* about? How, exactly, do I *get* a work emergency, much less one that would require dealing with at six in the morning? Gemma never demands that I rush to the studio to solve a yoga emergency, and for the hot second I worked as a marketing associate, I was so far down the food chain that no one was calling *me* for emergencies.

"I mean, I can imagine," I correct. "Do you . . . want to talk about it?"

"Yeah, no, I won't subject you to it." He pauses, eyes meeting mine while his teeth catch his bottom lip. Warmth rushes through me as I wish that I were the one biting that soft, full lip. "But maybe sometime we can—"

"Next up on CNN," a loud voice cuts through the room, "Jaxx Coin founder, Jackson Dalton, still hasn't answered for his crimes, and a close friend of his has new information."

I rear back from Sam and snap my head toward the television. A picture of Jack and Benny fills the screen, a snapshot that I remember taking. Suddenly, I can smell Jack's expensive cedar-scented cologne, the aroma of Benny's musty pot, and my chest tightens. I scramble away from Sam and avert my eyes, turning toward the door.

"I have to go."

"Wait—" Sam says, reaching for me.

"I'm sorry, no." I evade his grasp, my heart banging so hard it feels like it will crack my rib cage. "I . . . I just remembered something I have to do."

I let the door fall shut behind me and race for the stairs as quickly as my legs will carry me. I manage to hold back the tears until I'm in the stairwell. I can't believe I was so close to him. I can't believe I *let* myself get so close to him. I have to remember my promise: I won't derail Sam's life again. I will do everything in my power to protect him from me and the chaos I inevitably bring.

Chapter Eighteen

See you in 15.

I scowl down at Faith's message. My sister knows very well that timeliness is not my strong suit. If she really wanted me to arrive at her charity dinner on time, she should have stuck around to make sure I stayed on track. But she'd taken her dress and makeup bag to work with her, claiming she wouldn't have time to come home after and would instead meet me at the event. Really, this is all her fault.

I should be outside, waiting for an Uber, if not in an Uber already, but instead, I'm in my underwear, leaning over the bathroom sink and using tweezers to apply false eyelashes. When the last lash is finally in place, I take a step back and admire my work. I may be later than a sloth on a Monday morning, but I know how to give good face.

I reach into the closet for the dress I rented for the occasion. Somber navy with a modest square neckline, and with a flirty ruffle across its short skirt, it seemed perfect: boring enough for a roomful of lawyers, but with a hint of flair. According to the comments on the rental site, the dress runs small, so I chose both my usual size and the next size up. I step into the one in my usual size, and at first, everything seems fine. I feel fabric pulling as I shimmy it up over my hips, but I suspect I just have the fabric twisted in an awkward position. Maybe the ruffle has folded in on itself. I get the bodice in place, but something still feels off. I reach around to my back and, with a wish and a prayer, manage to get the thing zipped. It still feels odd, but I tell myself it's probably just that I've been living in leggings for weeks now. Of course a dress feels weird.

But then I see myself in the mirror. Technically, I'm wearing the dress, but there's no world in which this dress fits. The fabric tugs across my hips and chest, and it's short enough to scandalize even me, and I'm the one who filmed a yoga series wearing a sports bra and a pair of shorts so small they were practically underwear.

I snap a quick selfie of myself in the dress, pulling a ridiculous face, and send it to Faith with the caption, wardrobe malfunction. Faith doesn't even "haha" the photo; she just responds, Why aren't you on your way?

I sigh. She's right. I should get going.

But first I need to get out of this dress. I pretzel my arms around behind my body—thanking myself for every time I've led my students in a behind-the-back stretch in class—and catch the tag of the zipper. I start to tug it downward, but after an inch, it stops. I adjust my grip and try again, but it won't move. I turn around in front of the mirror and crane my neck to see what I already know: The zipper has caught a hunk of fabric.

Amazing. Just what I needed. I grit my teeth and try again. It won't move.

I tell myself to pretend I'm Faith and think rationally, but of course that doesn't work because Faith would never get herself in this predicament in the first place. I close my eyes and run through a couple of pranayama breaths—a struggle, considering the dress is practically knitting my ribs together—to bring my anxiety under control, and then I mull over my options. Option one: I can attend the fundraiser in an ill-fitting, partially unzipped dress. Nope. Not a chance.

Option two: I can skip the fundraiser. Again, not a damn chance. Faith is counting on me, and I can't let her down.

Option three: I can walk down to the lobby and beg some random person to help unzip me. I sigh with resignation. That is, unfortunately, the best option. I can only hope that glamorous Rekha doesn't traverse the lobby to witness my humiliation, or God forbid, Sam—

Wait.

Option four: I can ask Sam for help.

My body tingles at the idea. I haven't seen Sam since running into him—and then practically away from him—in the gym the other day. I swore I'd avoid him for his own good, but this is an emergency.

Before I can second-guess myself, I pull out my phone and fire off a text message: Are you home?

He responds immediately: What, can't you hear the blink-182 through the ceiling?

I snicker. Sam, for all his otherwise maturity, is a hopeless fan of vintage blink-182. I used to joke that I knew he was home if I stepped onto his apartment hall and heard Tom DeLonge's whining voice.

Luckily, no. I need some help. Have a minute?

Three dots appear and then vanish, and as I try to parse that meaning, there's a knock on the door. I open it and there he stands: Sam, wearing a Cubs T-shirt and faded jeans, stubble dotting his chin. My pulse flutters. Casual, rumpled Sam has always been my favorite Sam.

His dark eyes run over my impeccable makeup and curled hair to the dress currently doing a boa constrictor impersonation around my midsection. I strike a goofily seductive pose against the doorframe.

"What do you think?"

He frowns. "Do you want my honest opinion?"

I burst out laughing. "It's terrible, I know. And I'm running late to meet Faith. Come on, help me get it off."

"What?"

"Mind out of the gutter, Cosgrove. This isn't a come-on; it's a plea for help." I turn around to show him the mess at the back. "I'm stuck.

The zipper is snagged, I think, and I can't get my arms around enough to free it, so . . ." I gesture helplessly. "Can I borrow your hands?"

"Yeah, no, absolutely."

Sam steps inside the apartment and closes the door behind him. My stomach flutters, and I'm keenly aware that we're alone.

"Let's see what we have here," he murmurs, and I feel his warm hands manipulating the fabric and zipper. I hope like hell he can't see the gooseflesh his touch has elicited.

"You really did a number on this," he says, tugging at the zipper.

"So what you're saying is that I'll have to go to Faith's fancy charity dinner like this? Think anyone will buy it if I tell them it's haute couture? Straight from the runway?"

He chuckles and shakes his head. "I doubt it. But don't worry, I'll get you out of here." He's quiet for a moment, fiddling with the zipper, and then says, "Do you remember Halloween junior year? When you got stuck in that terrible vinyl dress?"

I laugh. "Jesus, yes. You would have thought I learned my lesson."

"To be fair, *this* dress doesn't look like it was purchased for less than twenty dollars at a Spirit Halloween."

"Hey, that dress might have basically been a glorified trash bag, but I was a very sexy Elvira."

"You were always very sexy," he says softly, and my heart stutters as I wonder if he meant that or if he was just absently bantering. I wish I could see his face to know what he's thinking.

At that moment, the zipper releases and yawns open, exposing my whole back. Sam audibly catches his breath, and my bare skin tingles as I realize this is the most undressed I've been with him in years.

"There," Sam says, his voice unusually thick.

He lifts his hands from my back but doesn't step away, remaining rooted to the floor just behind me. If I tipped my hips just an inch, I could touch him. I bite my lip and rock slightly backward, bringing my body to within a hair's breadth of his.

"Thank you," I say quietly. "I appreciate the use of your hands."

He makes a small noise, something that sounds vaguely tortured, and rests those hands on my hips. A delicious warmth radiates from his touch. His fingers splay out, covering my lower abdomen, pressing me ever so slightly against him.

"Sam," I murmur and start to turn toward him, but he stops me, catching me with a hand on my bare back.

"Wait," he says softly, tracing one of his fingers up the length of my spine and over to my right shoulder blade. His finger pads run over the tattoo there, and he asks, "What's this?"

"That," I say hoarsely, "is Dolly Parton. Our Lady of Country Music and Literacy."

"I see that." He drops his hand back to the small of my back, allowing me to complete my turn. I'm pressed against him now, my hands resting lightly on his strong chest.

He licks his lips and asks, "But why is Dolly Parton on your back?"

Sam's voice sounds soft, hopeful, with not a trace of the judgmental tone Jack used when he asked this very same question. But Sam, I know, doesn't need to ask.

"You know exactly why she's there," I say, lightly chiding.

His breath hitches, and his hands tighten on my body. I press myself against him, closing out whatever tiny amount of space remains between us. Sam's hand travels from the small of my back to my hip, grounding me in place, while the other dances gently along my spine, setting off miniature explosions with each portion of bare skin he touches. He sweeps my hair away from my neck and carefully runs a finger along my jaw, studying my face. I feel like I can't breathe.

"Can I kiss you?" he asks, his voice strained. "Or will that ruin your makeup?"

Forget the makeup, I think. *It'll ruin* me.

What I say is, "I have more lipstick."

Sam's lips curl up in a half smile, then they part, and his eyelids lower as he brings his face toward mine. *He's going to kiss me, he's going to kiss me, he's going to—*

And that is the moment my phone loudly blares George Michael's "Faith."

I practically fling myself away from Sam. "That's my sister. I have to go."

"You have to go," he repeats like he doesn't understand the words. "Now?"

I nod regretfully. "Now. Actually, fifteen minutes ago."

He nods and rubs a hand over his face as though trying to reset himself. "Yeah, no, of course. Are you . . . okay with the dress?"

"Yeah. Thanks."

"Anytime." He holds my eyes like he's waiting to say something else, but then my phone rings again, and he nods. "See you around, neighbor."

Sam slips out the door, taking a piece of my heart with him.

Chapter Nineteen

By the time I arrive at the Cultural Center, I'm fifteen minutes late, but that still feels like an achievement, considering I had to not only wrangle myself out of that dress but also restrain myself from dragging Sam back into the apartment. I still feel overstimulated and buzzy, remembering his hands on my body, his face so close to mine, and I can't stop thinking about what might have happened if Faith hadn't called. It might have been blissful or ruinous or both. I'm not even sure anymore.

Instead, I am standing here in this ornate lobby while Faith charges toward me, a cross expression on her face.

"Where have you been?" she demands.

"I'm sorry. There was a problem with the dress, and—" I cut myself off as I get my first proper glimpse of her. "*Faith.* You look incredible!"

She blushes and looks down at herself. "Yeah?"

"Yeah," I confirm. My sister has traded her usual uniform of bland business casual for a trim little black dress with a sweetheart neckline. She's twisted her dark blond hair into a soft updo, and she's wearing a subtle smoky eye and lip gloss.

"Thanks." She does a quick pirouette for me. "I got the dress for fifty percent off at Nordstrom Rack, and my friend Marisa helped me with the hair and makeup."

"She did a fantastic job." I give her a teasing smirk. "You look almost as good as me."

Faith flicks me on the arm and laughs. "Remind me why I invited you."

"Because I'm the life of any party?" I thread my arm through hers. "Have you seen Henry yet?"

She shakes her head. "No. I've just been waiting out here for you."

"Sorry," I say again. I pat her arm and lead her toward the entrance. "I'm here now, so let's do it. Remember, you don't owe Henry an answer tonight. If you feel like he's pressuring you, or you need help in another way, just say . . . I don't know, what should our code word be?"

"Code word?"

"The code word can't be *code word*. That's too obvious." I snicker as she groans. "How about you ask me to get you a coffee if you need help?"

Faith nods. "Okay. If I get stuck, I'll ask for a coffee. But don't actually bring me one. I can't have caffeine this late in the day."

"Have you thought more about what you want?" I ask as we enter the event space. "I know you don't want to talk to Henry about it tonight, but do you think you'd take an offer if they made you one?"

"I'm more confused than ever," she admits. "Yesterday, I felt confident that I wouldn't, but today I'm thinking that I should take it. It'd be hard to pass up that kind of money. I suppose I could always donate to causes I care about."

"But would that make you happy?"

"I don't know." She shrugs. "Isn't that the great gamble of life? You do what you *think* might make you happy, but you don't really know how things will work out. And—" She cuts herself off, straightening her spine and tightening her grip on my arm. "Shh. Here comes Henry."

Henry turns out to be around my age, wearing an expensive-looking suit and an even more expensive-looking smile. At his side is a woman with her own blindingly white smile and glittering diamond earrings, whom he introduces as his wife, Stacey. Stacey is also an attorney, as are seemingly ninety-eight percent of the people here. I *knew* a legal aid charity event would involve a lot of lawyers, but the sheer number of JDs in the room is pretty staggering. I don't have to run a poll to know that I'm the only yoga teacher in attendance.

The conversations run from depositions to discovery to mergers to closings, and are so boring they make me want to stab my eyes out. Faith nods along, occasionally interjecting something that sounds like Latin to me, while I put on my best active-listening face. I sat through more than a few investor dinners of Jack's; I have it pretty well perfected by now. Of course, back then, my mind wasn't writing fan fiction about what might have happened with Sam if Faith hadn't called and interrupted.

"How're you doing?" Faith whispers as I take a seat at the round table beside her.

"I only understand about a quarter of what you people are talking about, but this cabernet is excellent, so it's a wash."

"I owe you one," Faith says, squeezing my hand.

"Nah, it's fine. Like you said, any excuse to dress up." I nod my head to indicate that Henry is about to sit down beside her. "Incoming. Let me know if you need to, you know, *order a coffee*."

Faith glances over at Henry and then nods back at me. "Okay. Thanks for coming, Vanessa."

"Anything for you." I sip my wine and turn to the man seated on my other side.

"Let me guess," I say. "You're a lawyer, too."

"Guilty as charged. You?"

"No way. I'm a yoga instructor."

"Huh," he says, furrowing his brow. "Is the legal aid society a special interest of yours?"

"I'm here as a guest." I gesture toward Faith. "My sister, Faith, is a law student."

"Oh, *Faith*," he says, breaking into a smile. "You should have said so earlier. We all love Faith at the office."

"You're looking at the president of her fan club."

"Wait a second," he says, tapping a finger against his chin. "If Faith Summers is your sister, that makes you . . . Vanessa."

I hold up my hands in mock surrender. "Caught."

He leans forward, his expression changing. "Do you know where Jackson Dalton is?"

"No," I say, forcing a smile even though the mention of Jack makes my stomach tighten into a knot. "I was just as blindsided as everyone else."

"Really? Because I heard his best friend said—"

I wave to the waiter to refill my wineglass. I can already tell it's going to be a long night. Oh, the things I do for my sister.

~

After two hours of slowly served courses and long-winded speeches, we're finally released. It's none too soon, either. I know that I'm tiptoeing the line between tipsy and overserved, and I should get myself home, drink a big glass of water, and head straight to bed. No passing Go, no collecting $200.

"Thanks again," Faith says, squeezing my hand. "I hope it wasn't too terrible."

"Only a *little* terrible." I laugh. "Are you ready? Should I call us an Uber?"

"Actually, I'm going to meet up with some of my friends." She peers at me. "Are you going to be okay going home alone?"

"Of course." I wave off her concern. "You look amazing. You should show yourself off to your friends."

"Are you sure?"

"Absolutely. Here, I'm calling an Uber right now. I'll text you when I'm home."

"Okay." Faith kisses me on the cheek. "Thanks again, sis. Be safe."

"Always."

~

By the time the Uber drops me off, it's almost eleven o'clock. I text Faith as I climb into the elevator and absently press a button.

Made it home. Have fun.

Thanks, sleep well xx

The elevator dings, announcing its arrival at its destination, and the doors slide open. I step off, concentrating on my phone as I add a little heart to Faith's message. Only after the elevator doors have shut do I look up and see a door marked 502 in front of me. I'm on the wrong floor. I jab the down button, but I can see from the lighted panel above the doors that the elevator is slowly making its way to the ground floor. I'll get home faster if I just take the stairs.

Theoretically, that is. Because the stairs are only quicker if you can actually *find* them, and, for the life of me, I cannot. Instead, I look up and find myself standing in front of a door numbered 512. I can hear music inside, something with a quick tempo, and I smile to myself.

Before I can think about what I'm doing, I rap on the door.

Sam opens it, and his eyes widen.

"Van—" he starts, but I don't let him finish.

I throw my arms around his neck and lean into him, covering his mouth with mine. He stiffens, and there's a horrible moment where I think he's changed his mind in the last few hours, that he's going to push me away, but then he responds, and responds with enthusiasm. He wraps his arms around my waist and pulls me closer to him, tongue slipping over mine. I'm delighted and disorientated all at once. Kissing Sam feels like coming home, but maybe a bit like coming home to find someone has rearranged your furniture. It's familiar and unfamiliar at the same time. I remember Sam always tasting of cinnamon Altoids and coffee, his soft lips always finding the perfect rhythm. Now he tastes faintly of beer, and we're slightly out of sync. To make up for it, I lean forward and press my body against his, twining my hands through his thick, dark hair and kissing him more deeply. He makes a surprised noise and pulls away slightly to bite my bottom lip.

"Jeez, Ness," he says thickly. "I—"

"Sam?"

We break apart at the sound of a sharp voice, and I blearily look behind him to see Rekha. She's barefoot in jeans and a Kellogg School of Management T-shirt that's too big on her and clearly belongs to Sam. She holds a beer bottle in her hands, and she looks displeased. Business partner, my foot.

"Sorry," I say, backing away. "I didn't mean to interrupt."

"Wait, Vanessa—" Sam says.

But it's too late. I know that now. And so I just turn and flee, as fast as my heels and bum knee will let me.

Chapter Twenty

I sense something is wrong the moment I wake up. Once I see it's almost nine o'clock, I am *certain* something is wrong. It's too quiet. Faith is an inveterate early riser, even when she's been out until one or two in the morning. I should hear the rustling of her turning pages of a book or the soft murmur of talking heads on CNN; I should smell coffee and bread burning in her law-student-special toaster.

Maybe she stayed out really late, I tell myself. After all, she was just heading out to meet her friends when I left the event. I got home around eleven, which means that Faith—

I can't follow the train of thought. All I can think about is how humiliated I feel after throwing myself at Sam in front of Rekha. Rekha, who was wearing his shirt and drinking his beer at almost midnight. Clearly, she's more than just a business partner, and I was deluded to ever think otherwise.

But he kissed me back, my memory insists. *Didn't he?*

I cannot remember. I had far too much wine last night, and the difference between what *actually* happened and what I *wish* happened feels permeable.

I drag my focus back to Faith. I slide out of bed and pad across the floor, not wanting to wake her if she's asleep—but also knowing that she is not. If she was asleep, I would hear her white-noise machine. Still, I hold my breath as I push open her bedroom door, which stands ajar. She's not there.

So what? I tell myself. Faith is a grown woman. If she wants to stay out all night, that's her prerogative.

But it's unlike her to stay out all night without telling me. I check my messages, but the only one I have is from Sienna, sending me a link to a story I've already tormented myself by reading and in which Benny speculates that Jack defrauded his investors to keep *me* in the life to which I'd "become accustomed." I could kill that moron. I don't have time to dwell on that, though, because there's no message from Faith. Nothing since I texted her when I got home last night.

I dial her number, but it goes straight to voicemail. My chest tightening, I leave Faith a message and then stare at the phone, willing her to call me back. I realize I don't know who she's with or how to reach any of her friends, and I feel terribly negligent. If something happened to my little sister, I will die.

At that moment, I hear a knock on the door. Relief washes over me. *Of course.* Faith must have lost her purse—including her phone and her keys.

Certain it's my sister, I dash to the door and pull it open.

It's not Faith.

Instead, standing there and looking almost offensively good in a soft navy T-shirt and well-worn jeans is Sam.

"You're not Faith," I say stupidly.

He shakes his head slightly, averting his eyes in a way that seems like he doesn't want to look at me but like he can't quite help it, either. I glance down at myself and realize I've answered the door wearing a thin white crop top through which you can see my nipples, with a pair of striped boy-short underwear and nothing else, unless you count the chandelier earrings I neglected to remove and the loose eyelashes that are certainly trailing down my cheeks like spider legs. My cheeks warm.

"I . . . wasn't expecting visitors."

He looks like he's suppressing a smile. "Clearly. Do you, uh, have a minute to talk?"

I bob my head. "Yes. But first—"

I dart to the bedroom and wrap myself in the floral robe Faith says makes me look like I'm auditioning for a *Golden Girls* reboot. I glance in the mirror to find that, yes, I look exactly as bad as I expected. I hear Sam clear his throat in the other room, and I know I don't have time to clean myself up as much as I'd like. Instead, I use a tissue to wipe away the errant eyelashes, run a moistened finger under my eyes to remove (most of) the smudged mascara, and tousle my hair. I remove the earrings and reassess myself. More presentable. Slightly, anyway.

I return to the living room, heart hammering in my chest. I see only two ways this conversation goes: Either he's here to properly kiss me back or to ask me to please never throw myself at him again. Each seems equally likely. Once, I would have known what Sam was thinking just by his expression. The arch of a single dark eyebrow could tell me everything I needed to know about his mood. Now his face gives nothing away. Nothing I can read, at least, and that breaks my heart.

I take a deep breath. "Hi."

His mouth slants in a crooked smile. "Hey."

"Sorry about . . ." I wave my hand to indicate the state in which I answered the door. "That."

"It was my fault; I should have texted."

"No," I say quickly. "I mean, I'm glad you're here. I mean, it would have been nice to shower, but . . ." I force a laugh to stop my rambling. "Sorry, I haven't had any coffee yet."

"I should have brought some. I could have guessed you might need it." He smiles shyly at me. "You . . . well, you tasted a bit drunk last night."

All my cells freeze. *Tasted.* It sounds so intimate.

"Yeah," I say, my voice suddenly hoarse. "About that . . ."

I trail off, unsure what I'm trying to say. There's so much that I *can* say about that kiss: I'd been dreaming of it for years; pyrotechnics detonated in my veins when he kissed me back; it was only an amuse-bouche for the ravenous need lurking inside me, like tossing a peanut to that man-eating plant from *Little Shop of Horrors*. I want him so much I can't breathe, but I'm also very aware that I'm still caught up in the web of Jack's bad behavior—Sienna's text only underscored that—and I care about Sam too damn much to bring him into this. In other words, the kiss, world-rocking as it was, was a mistake.

"Yeah." Sam shifts his weight and peers at me, his gaze still largely unreadable. "About that."

Then his eyes cut away, and I understand. Sam knows it was a mistake. Of course he does; he's no idiot.

But I can't let him say it. I *can't.* Sam is the only person other than my sister who has ever truly loved me for the whole person I am rather than the show I put on, and I will die if he says I was a mistake. And so I interrupt him to say, "My fault. I had too much to drink at Faith's event and was feeling nostalgic. I shouldn't have accosted you like that."

He looks at me oddly, and I can't figure out if he's insulted or just thrown because I've said what he was going to say.

"So that's what that was," he finally says. "Nostalgia."

I swallow hard and nod. "Nostalgia, a healthy dose of alcohol, and muscle memory."

"Vanessa—" he starts, and then shakes his head. "Okay. Well, I guess that's that. I just . . . I guess I'll get out of your hair, then."

A lump forms in my throat. "Sam—"

"See you around, neighbor," he says, but his voice lacks its usual playfulness. I want to reach out to him, to tell him to stay, but he's already out the door. He doesn't look at me again before he pulls it shut, notably with more force than necessary.

~

Fifteen minutes later, Faith slinks through the door, wearing an unfamiliar pair of sweatpants.

"Where have you been?" I demand. "I called you."

"Sorry." She flinches like the light is hurting her. "Drunk Me forgot to charge my phone last night, and it died."

"I was worried about you. I woke up and you weren't here."

"I know, I know. It just got so late, and . . . and so I stayed over at my friend's place." She covers her face with her hand. "I think it goes without saying, but I drank too much."

"That much is obvious." I eye the sweatpants, trying to determine whether they're boy sweatpants. "Do I know this *friend*?"

"Just a friend, Vanessa," she says, blushing. "Hey, is that coffee I smell?"

"Yeah, sit down. I'll grab you a cup." I fill a mug for Faith, add her preferred splash of cream, and then carry it to her. "Here you go."

"Thank you." She closes her eyes and deeply inhales the aroma. "Aah, I needed this."

"Same," I say, curling up beside her on the couch with my own cup.

"Thanks again for coming last night. I know it wasn't your ideal evening, but please tell me you had an okay time."

"I was happy to do it," I say honestly. I spent most of the night bored out of my skull or fielding questions about Jack, but I would do it again in a heartbeat if Faith asked me to. "Did it help having me there?"

She nods. "Henry only brought up an offer once, and obliquely at that. I think he would've done a lot more of that if you weren't there. So thanks. I owe you one."

"I owe you more than one, so let's just say I'm chipping away at my tab."

Faith takes another sip of her coffee and squints at me through a smudged smoky eye. "Is everything okay? You look a little off."

"I might have kissed Sam last night."

"What?" Faith's red eyes go round, and she sits straight up. "When?"

I cover my face with my hands. "Last night, after I got home. I think I was about seventy-eight percent alcohol at that point and ten percent bad decisions, and . . . I knocked on his door and kissed him."

"Oh my God." Faith claps a hand on her chest. "And then . . . ?"

"And then his *business partner* appeared out of the shadows like some sort of monster, and I ran away."

Faith wrinkles her nose. "Wait, what?"

I sigh. "Not a literal monster. She looked gorgeous, of course. But she was in his apartment, Faith. At like, eleven thirty. And I'm pretty sure she was wearing his shirt."

Faith flinches. "Oh."

"My thoughts precisely." I shudder at the memory. "It doesn't matter, though. Just before you got back, Sam came down here to 'talk,' and it's obvious he wishes I hadn't dropped by."

"He said that?"

"He didn't have to. It was written all over his face."

Faith sips her coffee thoughtfully. "Vanessa, can I tell you something about contract law?"

"Please don't."

This, of course, does not stop my sister. "When you're writing an agreement, you have to make sure that everything is explicit. If you leave something out of the contract because you think it's implied, it's considered parol evidence, and, well, you're out of luck."

"And that's relevant because . . . ? I'm not taking the bar exam."

"Because you can't just assume you know what the other party is thinking. You need to clarify, make sure everybody's on the same page. You need to talk it out." She pauses. "At the risk of really overstepping here, Vanessa, you and Sam have *always* needed to talk it out."

I stick my tongue out at her. "All right, Counselor. Duly noted."

Faith pulls a face at me in response. "Anyway, though, I think the more important question right now isn't what he *said* but what he *did*. Inquiring minds want to know: Did Sam kiss you back?"

I can't hide my smile as I unequivocally say, "Yes. He did."

Chapter Twenty-One

Faith might be right that Sam and I should talk it out, but it's a moot point, considering two days have passed and I haven't seen so much as his shadow. I've loitered in the lobby so often the doorman clearly thinks I'm dealing drugs, and I've tried "coincidentally" bumping into him in the gym, but I overslept my alarm, and he was gone by the time I arrived at six thirty. I must have just missed him—the weight-lifting bench was still warm, and I caught a whiff of his distinctive scent. It was enough to drive me half-insane—*almost* insane enough to text him, but not quite. If he'd wanted to hear from me, he would have said "see you later" or "I'll call you." *See you around, neighbor* was shutting a door, not opening it.

I try to redirect my attention from Sam to a course I'd started planning months ago. My original idea was to combine asanas and lessons on the *yamas* into a multiclass program on trusting your intuition, but it feels disingenuous now. Literally no one should take my advice on this—after all, I'm the woman who didn't know her fiancé was perpetrating massive fraud *and* who didn't even realize she wasn't truly in love with said fiancé.

I welcome the distraction when my phone buzzes. I know it's not Sam—I *know* it's not—but there's still a small hopeful part of me that thinks it might be. I grab the phone and check the caller ID. The bad news is that I'm right: It's not Sam. The worse news is that, in my clumsy eagerness, I've accidentally answered the call.

I curse inwardly and lift the phone to my ear, forcing out a pleasant greeting. "Hi, Dad."

"Vanessa," he says in his telephone voice, which is approximately twice as loud as his normal voice. "There you are. Cynthia says you haven't returned any of her messages."

"I've been meaning to call her back," I lie. My father's wife is friendly, sweet, and also nuttier than a fruitcake—and it's nearly impossible to exit a conversation with her. Just as you think she's wrapping up one topic, she segues into something else without so much as a breath.

"I've just been busy," I continue.

"She'd appreciate the occasional text message. It's not like you're working."

I know from experience there's no upside to arguing about my employment status with my father, so I bite my tongue and say, "Got it, Dad. Sorry."

"Things good up there?"

The question is perfunctory. He doesn't want the real answer, but it's not because he doesn't care. It's just that he's a fifty-something-year-old white man who has no emotional literacy. He can't talk about feelings; he can only have surface-level conversations about the weather and local sports teams. If I told my father the truth—that I'm scared my career is over, I don't know where I'm going with my life, and that I may very well have fallen in love with Sam Cosgrove again—there's a nonzero chance that he would spontaneously combust.

I don't want that on my conscience, so I just say, "Yeah, things are good."

"Good, good. Glad to hear it. Listen, the reason I'm calling is that Hal—you know Hal, right? Lives down the hall? Anyway, his kid works at a marketing firm. In Chicago. A good one, too, he says. The kid was down here for a visit last week, and I told him I had a daughter looking for marketing work in Chicago. He said to call him. I have his phone number. You got a pen?"

"Dad," I groan. "I don't need a job."

"Never kid a kidder, Vanessa. Go get a pen, all right?"

Defeated, I flop onto my back on the couch. "Okay, Dad. I have a pen."

He recites a number while I track the progress of a spider on the ceiling.

"You want to read it back to me?"

"No, Dad, I've got it."

"You sure?" he presses.

"I'm sure."

"You'll call him?"

"Yeah, Dad."

"And you'll tell him you're Bob Summers's daughter? Remind him that I bought him and his wife that round at the tiki bar."

"Of course, Dad."

"Good. Let me go grab Cynthia; I know she wants to say hi."

"Actually, Dad, I have to go. But give Cynthia my best, okay?"

"Don't forget to text her."

"I won't."

"And let me know how that call goes."

"Sure thing, Dad."

I disconnect the call and pull a pillow over my face, screaming into it. I know my father means well, but it's just like him to think he can fix my life with some tenuous connection forged at a tiki bar, of all places. (That has Cynthia's influence all over it; the dad I grew up with would never have set foot in anything more exotic than an Applebee's.) It makes me insane that he never recognizes all the hard work I've put into my career, all I've accomplished. I mean, I've been on the cover of *Yoga Journal*. I've taught celebrities. In some circles, I'm considered something of a celebrity myself. (*Yogalebrity*, I hear Sam say, and my heart hiccups.)

But maybe that's all behind me now. I love teaching, but making myself the product isn't as appealing as it once was. My inbox and DMs are crowded with hate mail from people who think I'm hiding Jack, people who think I ruined Jack, and people who think having had anything to do with Jack is a capital offense, not to mention your run-of-the-mill cranks who consider it their solemn duty to verbally assault any woman who dares post on the internet. I've been losing sleep worrying about how I'll resurrect my career. Maybe my dad is onto something. Maybe I should get that phone number for real and sign myself back up for the corporate life.

Maybe I should just give up.

My thoughts of surrender last less than an hour before Gemma asks me to sub a class, which I gladly agree to. Setting foot in the studio instantly reminds me that teaching nourishes my soul. Giving it all up isn't an option; I just need to figure out how to do more teaching and less of the draining social media aspect. I'm turning the idea over in my mind as I return home to find Faith on the phone, grimacing as she says, "Mm-hmm. Yeah. Mm-hmm."

Faith spots me, and relief washes over her face. Into the phone, she says, "Here she is." She doesn't wait for the person on the other end to respond before she shoves the phone in my face, mouthing, "Mom."

I shake my head and wave a hand to hold her off. I'm not emotionally prepared for my mother, especially since I left class to find two missed calls from her, and she'll no doubt point out that I have yet to call her back.

"Sorry," Faith whispers, pushing the phone into my hand.

Reluctantly, I accept it. It's been weeks since I've spoken to either of my parents, so why *shouldn't* both of them call on the same day? The universe is hilarious.

"Hi, Mom," I say as cheerily as possible.

"So, you can answer the phone if it's your father but not your mother."

"I was teaching a class, Mom. I was going to call you after I'd had a chance to shower."

"At least your sister can spare a moment for the woman who gave her life," she continues as though she hasn't heard me.

My instinct is to snap at her that if she'd just *listen*, I was going to *call* her, but I know that'll get me nowhere, and so instead I try a joke. "That's why they pay Faith the big bucks."

She sniffs. "Your father said he found you a new job."

I curse myself for choosing the wrong joke, but now the coincidence of her calling just hours after my father makes sense.

"You talked to Dad?"

"He wanted to let me know he'd quote-unquote 'gotten through' to you. You know he still blames me for you flaking on that job in Chicago."

I sigh deeply and collapse onto the couch. "Mom—"

"I heard that sigh, Vanessa Anne. Do not patronize me."

I pull a face at Faith, sticking my tongue out the side of my mouth and rolling my eyes in a mimed show of death. She gives me a sympathetic look and holds up a bottle of wine. I nod, and she pours me a glass.

"I'm not patronizing you, Mom," I say. "But that was so long ago. Besides—and I say this with love—my career path has nothing to do with either you *or* Dad."

"Then why did he say he just got you a new job? Hmm?"

I gratefully accept the glass of wine Faith hands me and take a sip before saying, "I don't know why he said that. It's not what happened. He just gave me some marketing guy's phone number, that's all. I'm not even going to call him. I've spent a lot of time and effort cultivating my current career, and I'm not just going to walk away from it."

"You mean like your fiancé walked away from you?"

I nearly spit out my wine. "God, Mom."

"I still think that man owes you some money. You might not have been married yet, but you were living together. You were *relying* on him. You should ask Faith if there's a law about that."

"Mom, I'm not taking money from Jack. He's wanted for *fraud*."

"Yes, and that's impacted your own earning ability. He owes you, Vanessa."

"He owes a lot of people, Mom." I hear her inhale like she's about to launch into something, so I quickly say, "But I'll talk to Faith about it, all right?"

"All right. And, Vanessa—"

Her words are cut off by Faith's phone buzzing loudly in my ear, and I jump at the opportunity to sign off.

"Oh, hey, Mom, Faith's getting a call, so I'm going to have to let you go."

"All right," she says, sounding doubtful. "You know I only want what's best for you."

"I know, Mom. Talk soon." I disconnect the call and hand the phone to Faith. "God, she's relentless."

"Like a honey badger." Faith shakes her head. "Between you and me, I didn't even mean to answer. I was expecting a call from someone else and picked up without thinking."

"That's basically how I ended up talking to Dad this morning," I say. "Hey, speaking of, your phone really was buzzing."

"Oh, I just assumed you made that up to get off the call." She taps a thumb to bring her screen to life, and a slow smile spreads across her face. She fires off a text and then looks up at me. "Thanks."

"Sure. So, hey, I think we both deserve a post–Hurricane Mom treat. You want to go out for dinner? There's that new taco place on Halsted."

"I actually have plans." She flashes me a guilty smile. "Rain check?"

"Yeah, sure," I say, struggling not to let my disappointment show. "I mean, I can't believe you'd rather go to some boring law firm thing than feast on delicious tacos with your delightful sister, but there's no accounting for taste."

"It's not a law firm thing." Faith's phone buzzes in her hand, and she glances down at it, a smile tugging at the corners of her mouth. "I'm having dinner with Marisa."

"Your classmate with the do-gooder job? So you're just going to, like, pump her for hiring information?"

Faith's cheeks go splotchy. "I'm not going to *pump* her for anything."

I take a look at my sister's face and recalibrate. "Sorry. I think I'm just off, what with Dad *and* Mom both calling on the same day. I didn't mean to belittle your friendships."

"That's not—" Faith cuts herself off and shakes her head. "Marisa's not my friend."

"Um, okay? Then why—"

"Marisa is more than a friend." Faith takes a deep breath. "You know the other night? When I didn't come home after the fundraiser? I spent the night with her. Like, *spent the night* with her."

"Faith!" I smack my furiously blushing sister on the arm. "You liar! You told me it was just a friend."

"I know!" she says, smacking me back. "I wasn't ready to talk about it. It was the first time something had happened between us, and I wasn't sure what it meant or if it would happen again. I mean, there you were, telling me about how you were certain Sam thought your kiss was a mistake, and it just really got in my head. What if Marisa thought kissing *me* was a mistake? What if she just wanted to stay friends?"

"But you're getting dinner with her tonight, so . . . it's not a mistake?"

Faith's grin spreads and she shakes her head. "No. Not a mistake."

"I can't believe you didn't tell me. What else are you hiding from me?"

"Other than the good chocolate? Nothing." She covers her face with her hands. "I really like her, Vanessa. Like, a lot."

“That’s incredible, Faith. I’m so happy for you,” I say.

And I mean it. Almost entirely. I’m only, like, twelve percent jealous that my baby sister is starting a relationship that makes her glow like a firefly, whereas I’m staring down the reanimated corpse of one that threatens to consume me whole.

Chapter Twenty-Two

Two nights later, Faith once again is spending the night at Marisa's place, and I feel more than a tiny bit jealous—and not just of her love life. I'm envious of my sister's *life*, of how full it is. I'm aware of the irony: Just months ago, I was so overbooked that I would have gladly traded my theoretical firstborn for a single night off to binge reality television in my sweats, and now, when I actually have the time and am starting my third episode of *Real Housewives of Beverly Hills*, I'm acutely jealous of my sister's crammed schedule. I know it doesn't make sense, but, hey, I never claimed to be a rational creature.

I mute a commercial, and that's when I hear it.

A noise. A *scratching* noise.

I freeze, listening intently. Just as I'm about to relax, thinking I imagined the whole thing, it happens again. Scratching and *rustling*.

I've been an apartment dweller long enough to know what that means: rodents. I quietly pull myself off the couch and tiptoe toward Faith's kitchen area, where I think I heard the noise. It's dark, and I think about turning on the flashlight on my phone—but I'm scared of what I might find. Instead, I squint at the shadows on the counter. I think I can account for them all: coffee machine, blender, bananas—and then something moves.

I scream.

I'm immediately embarrassed. What am I, some sort of cartoon character, afraid of a little mouse?

But I saw that shadow, and that was no little mouse. That was a *rat*.

In the apartment with me. Oh God, no. No, no, *no*. This horrible story I read about a rat nibbling on a woman's face while she slept pops into my brain, and I know I can't spend the night alone here with that creature—not if I want to get any sleep.

I grab my phone to call Faith, but I stop myself. What do I think my sister is going to do? Leave the apartment of this Marisa, who makes her smile like she won the lottery, so that she can stay up with me all night and make sure a rat doesn't bite me? It's not like Faith would chase the rat out herself, and it's too late at night to buy any traps.

Then an idea hits me: This is an old building. The kitchen rat is most certainly not the first rat it's seen. Maybe the maintenance team has a process for this. Maybe a trap or, I don't know, a *spray* or something. Maybe they'll at least have an idea.

I slide my feet into a pair of flip-flops and scamper down to the lobby. It's largely empty except for a girl in a sequined tube top sleeping in one of the chairs. The attendant behind the desk is staring at her with obvious displeasure.

"Excuse me," I say, and the attendant drags his eyes away from the sleeping sequin. I give him my most charming smile and say, "Hi. Let's say there's a rat in my apartment. What should I do?"

With all the speed of molasses in January, he lifts a pen and poises it above a notepad. "I'll let maintenance know you have a mouse. What's the unit number?"

"We're in 412. But for the sake of clarity, this isn't a mouse. It's a *rat*."

"Right."

"It's really big."

"Got it."

"Okay." I nod. "So . . . you're going to go get maintenance?"

"I'll let someone know when I see them." He checks the time on a large wall clock. "Maintenance is about to go off shift for the night, so it might not be until morning."

Panic surges through my body. *"Morning?"*

He nods and turns his attention back to the sleeping woman, who is now snoring. "Yep."

"But what am I supposed to do until then?"

He glances back at me, confused. "Whatever you would normally do. It's just a mouse." I open my mouth to correct him, but he gets there first. "Sorry, rat. It's just a rat. Anyway, by the time you get back to your unit, it'll probably have moved on through the walls."

I shudder. "What a lovely thought."

"Good night," he says, and firmly turns his attention away from me.

I sigh, realizing I'm not going to get any more help from him. I head to the elevator and stop when I see the front door swinging open and a tall, rangy form walking through. My heart flutters. *Sam.*

Our eyes connect, and his step falters. Instinctively, I look behind him for Rekha, but she's not there. I exhale a sigh of relief, but then I remember that I'm wearing an oversize T-shirt that says "No Sleep Till Brooklyn," gray sweatpants I've cut off into short shorts, and no bra. It's not the *worst* he's seen me look, but it's not great, either.

"Vanessa," he says, and just hearing him say my name makes me want to melt into a puddle on the floor. He has a way of saying it that makes me feel like we're alone, that we're not in the lobby with the world's least helpful desk attendant just a yard away or the drunk girl snoring in the chair.

I want to dissolve, but I hold myself together and say, "Fancy meeting you here."

His mouth twists up into a half smile, and he looks like he's about to say something, but then he shrugs it off. He nods toward the elevator. "Are you on your way up or out?"

I gesture down to my ratty flip-flops, my threadbare T-shirt. "Out. Obviously. Why would you even have to ask?"

"Ah, yes, how silly of me."

I laugh and then say, "No, I'm heading up. Reluctantly."

He arches an eyebrow. "Oh?"

"Yes." I shoot daggers with my eyes at the attendant, but he's busy doing something on his phone and doesn't notice. "There's a rat in the apartment."

He cringes. "Ugh."

"My thoughts exactly. I came down here hoping for some help, but I was told maintenance is going off the clock and won't be able to come until morning. *Morning*," I repeat, shuddering. "My face could be a rat's breakfast by then."

"I don't think the situation is *that* dire," he says, laughing. "Has Faith seen any rodents in the apartment before?"

"She never mentioned it. And she's out tonight; I don't want to bother her with this."

He looks at me, working his jaw. "Faith isn't there?"

I shake my head. "Just me and Ratatouille."

Sam crinkles his forehead. "Who?"

"Ratatouille? That cartoon rat? From the movie of the same name?"

Sam shakes his head as though what I've said makes no sense whatsoever. "I don't think that was the rat's name. Anyway, I would have gone with Mickey."

"Mickey is a *mouse*," I say, faux aghast. "And a beloved icon. That is *blasphemy*."

He laughs. "You're strange. Come on, though, I'll walk you up to your apartment. And if you want, I'll come inside and check for . . . *Ratatouille*."

There's a flutter of anticipation in my lower belly, and I press a hand against my abdomen as though that will do anything to suppress it. Silently, I sternly remind myself that Sam is coming up solely to check for that horrid rat, and still all my nerve endings sing.

Aloud, I say, "I would appreciate that, thanks."

Chapter Twenty-Three

I open the apartment door and cringe at the state of my living quarters. The nest of blankets and pillows I made on the couch, the open can of LaCroix on the coffee table next to an open bag of popcorn, the pile of fashion magazines spilling onto the floor. The mess I made in the kitchen making tofu scramble for dinner, which I told myself I'd clean up later. The Real Housewives bickering silently on the television.

I'm almost afraid to see Sam's expression, but it's, at most, a minor cringe, not the large-scale revulsion I feared. Then again, I remind myself, once upon a time, Sam slept at my place more than he slept at his own. He's familiar with my housekeeping, or lack thereof.

He glances around and then points to the remnants of dinner. "We should put that away. Otherwise, the rat might eat it."

"Better that than my face."

He gives me an odd look. "What's this fixation with rats eating your face?"

"I read a story about it once. A rat took a bite out of this woman's face while she was sleeping. She had to have plastic surgery, but she never looked the same."

"That sounds like an urban legend."

"Urban legends always start somewhere."

He cocks an eyebrow at me. "You think the guy with a hook for a hand was real?"

"At some point? Yes."

"Vanessa," he says, and he sounds like he's laughing, but not *at* me. Like he's just amused by my existence. It makes me feel warm and melty on the inside.

"A girl in my hometown actually died from mixing Pop Rocks and soda."

"Vanessa."

"It's true!"

He laughs softly and shakes his head, looking at me fondly. "I've missed you."

All my nerves fire at once, but I manage to say, "You missed my earnest belief in urban legends?"

"Yeah. And the way you bounce on your toes when you're animated about something. And the way you talk with your hands." He laughs. "Someday, you're going to put someone's eye out while gesticulating."

"How do you know that hasn't happened already?"

He flashes a smile, then steps closer to me, his gaze softening. "And I've missed the way you smell like vanilla and lemons." He brings a hand to the side of my face. "And the way your skin feels like velvet."

"You think I'm fuzzy?"

"I think you're *soft*," he corrects through a light chuckle. He lowers his mouth to mine, pausing a fraction of an inch away from contact. "I've missed the taste of you."

"Have you forgotten that I mauled you four nights ago?"

"That doesn't count," he says. "It was *nostalgia*."

The reminder of kissing him—and why I *shouldn't*—hits me right in the heart. "Sam—"

His mouth slants into a slight smile. "I knew it."

And then he kisses me, and all reason leaves the vicinity. His mouth . . . God, I've missed this mouth, its soft pressure, the dance of his tongue sliding against mine, the way he catches my bottom lip and sucks gently. This kiss is nothing like the desperate, drunken mess of a kiss from the other night; it's the slow, heat-building kiss I've dreamed about for the last five years. It takes me back to when I first met him, when we spent six days hunkered down in his room at the resort while our friends partied, just tasting each other, touching each other like we were trying to memorize every square millimeter of skin.

Sam slides a hand up underneath my loose T-shirt, the familiar pads of his large hands climbing my ribs one by one. He cups my breast and pinches the nipple, and I gasp and arch against him.

"Vanessa," he hisses against my mouth.

"Shut up," I murmur, wrapping my arms around him and pulling him closer, determined to eliminate any space between us. Sam responds with a strangled groan and joins the cause, pulling our bodies ever closer, locking our hips together. I drag my tongue down the side of his neck, savoring the slightly salty taste of his skin.

"Fuck," he mutters, his eyes rolling back. "God, Vanessa, you—"

He swallows his own words, devouring my mouth once more. His hands slide roughly down my sides, grabbing me and lifting me up onto the counter. He puts a hand on each knee to push them apart and steps between them, pressing his body against mine as he kisses me deeply once more. I'm half-crazed by this point, grabbing him by the hair and holding him to me, lifting my hips in a desperate attempt to feel his strong body against my throbbing core.

The noise that comes out of my mouth is decidedly undignified. "Sam, please—"

He pauses, leaning back to look at me. His eyes are dilated, his cheeks flushed. A devilish smirk stretches across his face, and his fingers walk up the inside of my thigh.

"Oh God," I murmur, but just before his fingers reach their destination, there's a sharp knock on the door.

"Maintenance!"

Our eyes meet and widen, our bodies still inclining together. Sam's finger draws delicate, maddening circles on my tender flesh.

“What should we do?” he asks, his voice low and strained.

I tuck my fingers into Sam’s waistband. “I can tell him to come in the morning.”

“But your face,” he manages, crooking a smile.

“Maintenance!” comes the call again, followed by a sharp rap on the door.

“I’ll—” I start, but Sam has already stepped away from me. He gives me a regretful look and opens the door.

The maintenance man—who has the name “Hank” embroidered on his front pocket—looks from Sam to me. “I hear there’s a mouse.”

“It’s a rat,” Sam clarifies.

“Yep,” I eke out.

“Let’s see,” Hank says gruffly, maneuvering past Sam into the apartment.

I glance at Sam, but he’s already stepping outside.

“Wait,” I say, rushing out to catch him. I twine my fingers through his. “Don’t go.”

He looks at me for a moment like he’s wrestling with something. “Don’t you have an early morning?”

I blink, touched. “You know my schedule?”

“Miss?” Hank barks. I glance over my shoulder and see him frowning at the kitchen mess.

“Just a minute.” I turn back to Sam. “Please. Don’t make me beg.”

There’s a pause in which I’m certain he’s going to leave, going to tell me that this was a mistake just like the last kiss, but then one side of his mouth tugs up into a smile, and he squeezes my hand. “Yeah, no, wouldn’t dream of it.”

Fifteen minutes later, our friend Hank has located and patched up a hole behind the oven that he suspects was the access point for Ratatouille.

"There you go," he says, grunting as he shoves my oven back into place. He wipes his hands on his pants and says, "Either just sealed that rat out or sealed him in."

I stifle a shriek. "You're kidding, right?"

Hank slides his eyes from me to Sam and lifts his shoulders in a "women, am I right?" expression.

"No, seriously—you're *kidding*, right?" I try again, more desperately this time.

"Let me know if you're still having a problem in the morning. I'm knocking off for the night." He gives us a curt nod and lets himself out.

"Did you hear that?" I demand, turning to Sam as soon as the door closes. "He either sealed the rat out *or sealed it in.*"

This is when I notice that Sam is shaking from withheld laughter, literally vibrating from it.

"Oh, you think this is funny, huh?" I ask, cracking a smile myself.

Sam's guffaws burst free. Clutching his side, he says, "Yes. You should see your face."

"Well, get a good look at it now, because it's going to be an all-you-can-eat rat buffet tonight."

He howls with delight. "You're ridiculous."

"I'll look even more ridiculous without a nose."

Sam snorts and covers his mouth. "Hey, if you're that concerned, I know a place upstairs."

My pulse jumps at the implication, but I can't tell if he's serious. I put my hands on my hips and say, "This isn't funny."

Sam stops laughing. "I'm inviting you to spend the night, Vanessa."

I bite my lip. "I know."

He takes a step closer to me and trails his fingers along my cheek, igniting sparks beneath my skin. "I think we have some unfinished business."

The flesh of my inner thighs burns where his fingers had just been, craving his touch once more. But now that we've had a moment to breathe, to *think*, I'm hesitant. All the reasons we shouldn't kiss still exist.

"We do," I say slowly. "But is this a terrible idea?"

"It might be," he admits, then lifts a dark brow. "But would it be our worst idea?"

"Only if you're also inviting a Dolly impersonator." Quickly, I add, "Please say you're not."

Sam shakes his head slowly, sliding his hand from my face down my side and letting it settle in the curve of my hip. "The only one I want is you."

"Yes," I say quickly, willing myself not to overthink it. "Let's do this."

His smile deepens and warms, then he steps toward me, cupping my face in his hands and tilting it toward his like he's going to kiss me. Suddenly, he stops.

"Do you want to, I don't know, brush your teeth or anything?"

I pull back so quickly I nearly fall. "Excuse me?"

"Oh shit," he says, cheeks going red. "That came out wrong. I didn't mean your breath smells. I only meant, you know, for oral hygiene. Before bed. Cavities are bad and all that."

I laugh at his discomfort. "All right. Let me do a little slumber-party prep, and I'll meet you upstairs in a few."

He leans over and presses a featherlight kiss against my lips. "Don't keep me waiting."

~

No more than seven minutes later, I'm standing outside Sam's apartment door wearing my cutest pair of pajamas, this robin's egg blue camisole-and-matching-short set printed with tiny hearts and trimmed in delicate lace. I threw on my *Golden Girls* robe so that I wouldn't give an unintentional show to anyone in the elevator, and a pair of slide sandals for obvious reasons. I've thoroughly brushed my teeth, but I've left my makeup on. Sam's the sort of man who'd tell me that I looked prettiest without anything on my face, but I'm about to spend the night in his bed for the first time in five years, and I'm not doing it with my pores and blemishes on full display.

I pause outside his door to take a couple of centering breaths and untie my robe. He must have been watching from the peephole, because he pulls it open before I've even knocked. My heart flutters to know he's just as excited as I am. The gaze he gives me is absolutely *wolfish*.

"What?" I tease, cocking a hip. "You've never seen pajamas before?"

"I've never seen *those* pajamas before," he says softly. "They're . . ." He trails off and clears his throat. "Very nice."

I give him a little shimmy just as Sam's next-door neighbors open their door and step noisily into the hall. They freeze as we make awkward eye contact, then they quickly turn and hurry to the elevator.

"Get in here," Sam murmurs, wrapping an arm around my waist and pulling me inside.

I laugh and push the door closed behind us. "Did you see the looks on their faces?"

"That's the couple who likes to watch foreign-language dramas at top volume in the middle of the night, so I'm not worried," he says. "They can handle a little noise."

"Sam Cosgrove," I say, twining my arms around his neck. "I didn't know you'd invited me over to watch loud movies."

Sam unleashes a soft growl and kisses me, a slow, deep kiss that makes my toes curl.

"Come on," he says throatily. "Let me show you the bedroom."

I follow Sam through his apartment, which has the same layout as Faith's and mine downstairs, although Sam uses the small second bedroom as an office. I glance at the room as I walk past, and he smiles slightly. "Welcome to Solosol HQ."

"You and Rekha work out of your extra bedroom?"

He nods. "We're saving all the money we can, and we didn't want to pay for an office. We make do here and only rent space when we need a meeting room. It cuts down on our overhead."

"Hmm," I say, although I hate that now I'm thinking about Rekha.

"Here we go," he says, opening the door to his bedroom. The lights are off, but even in the dark, I can see that his bedspread is forest green, the same color as the comforters in both his childhood and college bedrooms, and something inside me cracks. All these years have passed, and he's still Sam, still so undeniably *Sam*. Maybe there's hope for us yet.

"No obvious rat activity," I say. "This passes inspection."

He laughs low in his throat. "Vanessa, do not mention rats again tonight, I beg of you."

"What should I talk about instead?" I ask, turning to him and sliding my robe off my shoulders.

"Fuck," he whispers, his eyes running over me. "Your body."

"Yours isn't so bad, either, Cosgrove," I say, tucking my hand into the front of his jeans.

He makes a soft animal noise and slides his hands underneath the camisole and up my back, those large, warm hands covering my skin. He lowers his head to the soft, tender place at the base of my throat, kissing me gently there and then trailing small kisses up to my mouth.

"I missed you," he murmurs when his mouth reaches mine. "God, I've fucking missed you."

As much as I love hearing this, there's a crack in my heart because I know—*know*—that no matter how much we've missed each other, no matter how much we might want each other in this moment, it is a very, very bad idea for us to be together. My name is inextricably linked to Jack's, and Jack's name is practically synonymous with *fraud*. My reputation has been tainted by association, and I couldn't stand for any part of that tarnish to transfer to Solosol or Sam. And that's before I even start considering our history: what he gave up for me, how I mishandled his love, how he broke my heart. My fear that he'll do it again.

And so, even though it's physically painful for me, I pull away and whisper, "Sam?"

"Hm?" he murmurs, his mouth finding my throat again.

"What are we doing?"

He slides one hand around my front to thumb my nipple, and I hiss.

"This," he says, doing it again, "I believe, is what the kids call *second base.*"

"Believe it or not, I'm actually familiar with that terminology," I say, my hips moving toward his even though I tell them to stop. "But I need to know what we're doing here. What this *means.*"

His hands still, but he doesn't pull away. "Shit."

My heart plummets. "This means shit. Got it."

"No," he says, clutching me. "No, that's not what I meant. I meant, shit, like an expletive, as in 'Shit, I really don't want to think about this right now, but you're right, we need to.'"

"Yeah," I whisper.

"I want you," he says, lowering his mouth to kiss me gently on the lips. "I want you so much, Vanessa. But . . ."

And there it is. The *but*. There's always a goddamn *but*. It's not like I'm not used to it by now. Every man I've ever dated—other than Sam and Jack, and those relationships imploded in their own ways—eventually told me some version of the same thing: *You're a lot of fun, Vanessa, but I'm looking for something else. Something different. Something more. Something* better. I steel myself, knowing it's inevitable that Sam will say something similar, especially since my name is currently being dragged through the mud.

"I have so much on my plate right now," he continues.

He sounds genuinely remorseful, but still I know how to read between the lines: I'm too much, just like I've always been too much, and Sam isn't willing to let a chaos agent like me back into his life.

"I know," I manage while my heart crumbles to dust. "I know, the timing is bad. Solosol is about to launch, and this thing with Jack just will not die."

Sam flinches. "That's . . . Yeah." He looks at me beseechingly. "I don't want to fuck things up again, Vanessa. I don't want to start something only to break it."

I bite the inside of my cheek to keep from crying. "I get it."

"Come here," he says gruffly, pulling me into a rough hug. "I know I'm going to regret this, but you mean too much to me to ruin it."

"You can't ruin—" I start, but he cuts me off with a soft kiss.

"Listen," he says hoarsely as he breaks away. "I want you to know, just for the record, I very much want to spend all night touching and sucking every single part of you."

The parts of me that would most prefer that touching and sucking light up like a pinball machine, and I catch my breath. "You can."

"I shouldn't." His eyes trail down to my mouth, then he yanks them upright to meet my gaze. "*We* shouldn't. But I don't want to let you go. Can I . . . can I just hold you tonight?"

I force myself to take a calm, centering breath and say, "Holding would be good for us."

Chapter Twenty-Four

"There was a *what*?"

"Yeah, that horrified expression you're making right now? That was my reaction exactly."

Faith shudders. "I feel so gross knowing that a rat has been in here with us."

"That's city living for you," I tell her. "You should have seen this place where I used to live in the East Village. I had cockroaches the size of your hand."

"Strangely enough, knowing that a cockroach can grow so freakishly large does not make me feel any better."

I laugh. "All I'm saying is that there are worse pests to have."

"I don't think that's the kind of benchmark I want to use."

"Fair point."

Faith squints at me. "Why are you smiling like that? Am I misunderstanding and these are helpful rodents, like the mice from *Cinderella* or something?"

"Or *Ratatouille*?" I ask, my grin widening.

"Okay, now you're just freaking me out with that smile. What's going on?"

"There . . . might have been a silver lining to the rat incident," I admit, my cheeks warming as I remember Sam's soft touch. "I ran into

Sam in the lobby. And he astutely pointed out that his apartment had no rats, so."

Faith's eyes widen. "So you spent the night? With Sam? Vanessa! Way to bury the lede on that story."

"Honestly, it was mostly just sleeping," I say. "We kissed some, and there was some cuddling, but that was it."

"You're smart to take things slow this time around," Faith says.

My heart twists as I nod, remembering Sam's words: *I don't want to start something only to break it.* Is that what we're doing? Taking things slow? Maybe there's a chance for us yet.

~

"I think," Faith announces, coming into the living room with an overnight bag slung over her shoulder, "that I might spend the night at Marisa's again. Just to confirm we don't have any more rodent squatters."

"Wow, two nights in a row. Things must be getting serious."

Faith blushes hotly and shakes her head. "No, this isn't . . . this isn't *that.* We're just having fun."

"There's no shame in falling in love, Faith."

"I know that." She pauses, chewing on her lip. "I just . . . I don't know, sometimes I think love is for other people."

"Oh, Faith." I touch her shoulder, and she shrugs me off. "You deserve love just as much as everyone else."

"No, I know. That's not what I meant." She studies her short, chewed-on nails and says, "Say I fall in love with Marisa. Then what?"

"Then . . . love, marriage, and a baby carriage? I don't understand the question."

"Marisa is way out of my league. She's . . . she's *gorgeous,* Vanessa. And so smart and so kind and so funny, and . . . How can I fall in love with her? How can I know that this isn't going to end with her ripping my still-beating heart out of my chest and eating it for breakfast?"

"Well, for starters, I guess, no matter how gorgeous she is, you shouldn't date a cannibal."

Faith laughs. "You're terrible."

"But seriously, there's no guarantee it won't end in heartbreak. Anytime you make yourself vulnerable to another person, you run the risk that they'll hurt you." I bite my lip, thinking about Sam telling me that he wants me *but*. No matter what he followed it with, that *but* hurt.

"Well, that sucks."

"I would say 'with great risk comes great reward,' but Jack always used to say that, and we know how that worked out for him, so instead I'll just say this: It's hard to let people in. I know that. God, do I know that. But the times in my life that I've managed to get out of my own way and really open up to someone? That's when I've been the happiest."

Faith looks at me thoughtfully, and I think she might be on the verge of opening up, of telling me more about Marisa, but then she rolls her eyes and snorts. "God, sis, you're cheesy."

"As fondue." I grin. "You know you love me for it."

"Yeah, yeah." She hikes her bag up on her shoulder. "Unfortunately for you, I don't love you enough to spend the night with a potential rat."

"Faith and Marisa, sitting in a tree," I sing. "K-I-S-S-I-N-G."

"Stop, please. I beg of you."

I stick my tongue out at her. "Have fun. I'll see you tomorrow, unless a rat chews off my face overnight."

"Jesus, thanks for that horrible imagery." She pauses on her way to the door. "Hey, Vanessa? You don't need an external reason to talk to Sam. You don't have to wait for a rat, you know?"

I shrug noncommittally. "Yeah, I know."

Faith waggles her eyebrows. "Although it *does* give you a good excuse to climb into his bed."

Cheeks burning, I throw a pillow at her. "Get out of here."

I hear Faith's laughter echoing down the hallway as she walks away, and I wonder if she's right. Maybe Sam and I are at a place where we can show up at each other's door.

Later, I'm neck deep in prep for a workshop and trying my hardest not to spiral because I haven't heard from Sam all day when someone raps "Shave and a Haircut" on the door. *Sam* is my first thought because—well, let's be real, he's been my first thought about *everything* for the past week. Phone rings? *Sam.* Bus goes by? *Sam.* Breeze blows my hair off my neck? *Sam.* It's similar to how my brain operated when we dated in college. Every minute of every day, no matter what I was doing, there was always a small voice in the back of my mind saying, *Yes, and Sam? What about Sam?*

I push myself off the couch, wincing as my knee twinges, heart leaping in my chest, and open the door to find—as hoped—Sam.

"It's you," I say, and in that instant, I can *feel* his fingers on the inside of my thigh, the push of his hot breath on my cheek. I squirm and try to bring myself back to the present. "Hi."

"Hey." He grins at me, but it's not the easy grin I'm used to, nor is it the sexy grin he gave me last night. Rather, I recognize it as the exhausted grin of a man who has had a very long day. He was sleeping like a baby when I slipped out of his bed this morning, and now he looks like he's been through the wringer.

"Sam, are you okay?"

He bobs his head. "Yeah. Fine. Just a little tired. We were— You know what? I'm not here to talk about work. I'm here to see if you want to go out."

"Out?" I echo. "You mean now?"

"Now. I have some steam that needs blowing off, and I'd like you to come with me." He flashes me another strained grin, and I hear his phone buzzing somewhere on his person.

"Um, Sam, I think your phone is ringing."

He shakes his head. "Not important."

I hesitate. Sam has never been one to ignore phone calls or texts, especially lately. "Sam, are you sure you're okay?"

"It's been a long day." He tilts another grin at me. "Now, come on. Don't make me beg."

~

Sam stops on the sidewalk in front of a squat, dark-colored brick building with a rounded entrance shaped like a whiskey barrel. I glance up at the sign above the door, which spells out Friar Tuck in rickety letters. I glance at him to confirm this apparent dive is our destination, and he smiles. The tension around his eyes is gone, and he looks almost eager.

"Come on," he says, pulling open the door. "Ladies first."

I step inside, blinking as my eyes adjust to the darkness. There's a long rectangular bar in the center of the room, crowded on all sides with patrons. Tables occupy about seventy-five percent of the rest of the floor space, and the other twenty-five percent hosts a small stage, where a man in a Chicago Bears T-shirt is singing an enthusiastic but off-key rendition of "Friends in Low Places."

I clap my hands, delighted. "Oh my God, Sam. You brought me to karaoke night."

He grins. "I thought you'd like that."

"I *love* it."

I do. I unapologetically and unironically love karaoke. It's not because I'm so good at it—to the contrary, I couldn't carry a tune if it had handles. Rather, I love the way karaoke can connect a room, and more specifically, I love the way karaoke enables *me* to connect a room. There's nothing like the thrill of getting a barful of jaded drinkers to belt out Journey's "Don't Stop Believin'" with you, or seeing women climb up on their chairs to join you in the chorus of "I Will Survive."

Sam got to see that magic for himself the first time I visited him at Cornell. It was October, six months after we'd first met on spring break. We hadn't seen each other since school started, and we missed each other something fierce, so we saved every scrap of money we could get our hands on until we had enough to buy me a ticket to Ithaca. I was both thrilled and terrified to visit him on his own turf. What if Sam finally realized I was no match for his college friends? They were Ivy Leaguers, kids with the whole world in their hands, whereas I was just a peppy Midwestern sorority girl with no declared major or plan for her future. The night I arrived, Sam took me to a party. Parties were my usual milieu, but I felt stiff, unable to relax. Sam's friends were warm and approachable—of course they were, they were friends with *Sam*—but they grew visibly tired of trying to involve me in discussions about world politics. As I withdrew from the conversation, I could practically see Sam falling further and further from my reach.

And then the host brought out the karaoke machine. My palms started itching when I saw the microphone, but I told myself to hold back. The last thing Sam needed was for me to make a fool of myself in front of his highbrow friends. So I waited while the host started things off with "Norwegian Wood," which is an objectively good song but hardly a banger. I waited as he held the microphone out hopefully, offering the chance to sing to a few friends who all declined it. And I waited while the host then followed up with "Yellow Submarine." And, look, I like the Beatles as much as anyone else, but it was clear that this poor guy was going to make his way through their whole catalog before anyone else took a turn.

"I'll go," I heard myself say.

Sam turned to me, surprised but encouraging. I think he perhaps hoped that I was secretly the next Adele, but, alas, my singing voice is identical to my talking voice, only louder. The thing is, though, that you don't have to be Adele or Beyoncé or even Ke$ha to get a group of partygoers into "Mr. Brightside." All you have to do is shout that you're coming out of your cage, and nine times out of ten, the crowd does the rest. What I lack in talent I make up for in enthusiasm, and as I bounded around, yanking the microphone cord as far as it would go, people stopped their conversations and started singing along. By the time the song ended, a good contingent of the party was howling the chorus along with me.

"Encore!" someone shouted, and everyone cheered. Sam caught my eye and grinned at me.

Two songs later, after someone else finally took the microphone, Sam pulled me into an upstairs bathroom. He had his hands up my skirt before he'd even locked the door—and that's when I learned that although Sam Cosgrove himself is an introvert, my extroversion is a turn-on for him.

Now I feel warmth settling in my belly. Sam didn't just bring me out—he brought me to karaoke night, which is itself an act of foreplay. I reach for his hand and weave my fingers through his. He rubs his thumb softly over the skin of my hand. I lick my lips and glance at him. His dark eyes no longer look tired; they look hungry. Anticipation prickles through my body.

"Come on," he says, tugging me over to a table tucked away in a dark corner. "Let's get a drink."

Chapter Twenty-Five

Fifteen minutes later, I've performed Joan Jett's "I Love Rock 'n' Roll," put my name in for the Britney Spears classic ". . . Baby One More Time," and signed Sam up for a performance slot without his knowledge. Oblivious, he's flipping through the laminated pages of the track listings, making suggestions for me.

"What about 'Dancing Queen'?"

I laugh. "I can't tell if you're being sweetly naive or completely sadistic. There's no way I can hit those notes."

He raises an eyebrow at me. "You say that like you can hit any notes."

"Sam!" I thwack him playfully on the arm. "How about you? What are *you* going to sing?"

"Not a damn thing. You know me. I don't sing karaoke."

"You *didn't* sing karaoke. And a while ago you also *weren't* on the verge of launching a solar panel that will completely disrupt the energy industry. Things change."

His expression darkens for a microsecond—just long enough for me to wonder if I saw anything at all—and then he shakes his head. "Not that much."

"Sam," I say hesitantly. "Are you sure everything is okay?"

"Yeah, fine. Just . . . had a bit of a disagreement with Rekha today. Work stuff."

"Is that why your phone has constantly been ringing? Do you need to fix something?"

He tilts his beer bottle to his mouth. "I don't want to talk about it."

"Okay. But if you change your mind— Hey, what the hell is *that*?" I point at the stage area, where the guy in the Bears shirt has just finished a slurred performance of "I Love This Bar" and is now being handed an inflatable sheep.

Sam chuckles. "Ah. Must be that guy's birthday."

"How do you—" I start to ask, but before I can finish the question, the crowd breaks into "Happy Birthday." Sam winks at me and starts singing along, so I join, too. The guy in the Bears shirt grins blearily at the singing crowd, and once we've finished, he grabs the inflatable sheep by its hindquarters and tilts it up to his face.

I gape at Sam. "Did he just take a *shot* out of that sheep's *butt*?"

"This place has a charm all its own," Sam says, his mouth turning up at the corners. "You should see it on Hat Night."

"After what I just saw happen to that poor sheep, I'm not sure I even want to ask, but: What is Hat Night?"

"Precisely what it sounds like."

"Everyone comes wearing a hat?"

"Everyone chooses a hat from a box near the door."

"Communal hats?" I ask, horrified. "Does Lice Night follow Hat Night?"

Sam shrugs. "I haven't gotten lice yet."

"Sam Cosgrove. You are a reasonable person. I refuse to believe that you have participated in this Hat Night. You must be pulling my leg."

"I'm not, I swear." Sam laughs and lifts his phone off the table, thumbing through photos. He finds the one he's looking for and passes me his phone so I can see a picture of him in this very bar, wearing a saggy jester's hat.

"You look ridiculous!" I exclaim, laughing. I'm about to hand the phone back when I notice a thin arm thrown around Sam's shoulders. The vodka turns unpleasantly in my stomach. *Rekha.* Some masochistic impulse drives me to slide to the next photo, and sure enough, it's a shot of Sam and Rekha together. Her arm is slung possessively around him, and their faces are pressed close together, both of them smiling widely at the camera. She wears a fluffy, bright purple Cossack hat, and to my extreme displeasure, I note that she somehow manages to make even that faux-fur monstrosity look glamorous.

I avoid Sam's eyes as I hand him back the phone. "Purple is Rekha's color."

"Vanessa." Sam wets his lips like he's preparing to say more, but nothing comes out.

"What?" I ask, more harshly than I intended.

"It's just . . ." He trails off and takes a swig of his beer. "Look, I might be off base here, but I'm getting the sense that you're jealous of Rekha, and you really don't need to be."

I gesture to Sam's phone, still on the table between us. "You can tell me all you want that Rekha is just a business partner, but I've seen the way she looks at you. I've seen the way she *touches* you. There's either something going on, or she *wants* something to be going on."

"No way," Sam says, shaking his head. "Nothing is going on, I promise. But . . . okay, in the interest of full transparency, there was. Once."

Bile rises in my throat. The very idea of Sam with someone else—especially someone as beautiful, smart, and, judging by her appearance on Hat Night, *fun* as Rekha—makes me want to scream. I tell myself that I'm not allowed to be jealous. After all, it's not like I didn't date anyone else in the past five years. I even planned to marry someone else. But I can't stop myself from feeling betrayed.

I swallow and say, "I know you don't owe me an explanation, but . . . *when* was there something going on? Are we talking months ago or weeks?"

"Months. Year and a half, actually." Sam twirls his beer bottle in his hands, as if trying to decide how much to tell me. "We met at a green energy convention. We were both late to this talk on advancements in solar energy, and we stood in the back together. We got to talking, and she told me about what she was working on. She'd just finished the prototype of what would become the Uno panel. She built it in her parents' *garage*," he adds admiringly. "She had this amazing creation, and she didn't know what to do with it. She knew she didn't want to sell it to some existing company, but she didn't know how to launch her own. I'd graduated from business school a year earlier and was working as a consultant, but I was really interested in getting involved in the green space. She had the tech skills, and I had the business savvy. It felt like a match made in heaven."

"A business match," I say, allowing myself to believe I've misunderstood and that's all Sam has been talking about this whole time.

"Yeah, and . . ." Sam trails off and shrugs. "I should have known better than to mix business and pleasure."

I make a gagging sound.

Sam cringes, his cheeks reddening. "Shit, that didn't come out the way I wanted it to." He twirls his beer bottle again, keeping his eyes fixed on the amber glass as he adds, "But that's not why we broke up."

"I know I asked, but I'm not sure that I want to hear—"

"We broke up because she's not you."

I pause, unsure that I've heard him correctly. "Sam—"

He lifts his eyes to mine. "No one is you. And—"

"SAM, YOU'RE UP."

We both startle when the bartender calls his name. He narrows his eyes at me.

"You didn't."

"SAM COSGROVE, SINGING BLINK-182'S 'ALL THE SMALL THINGS.'"

I burst out laughing. "You know you know the lyrics."

"You know you do, too." He stands up and grabs my hand. "Come on. I'm not doing this alone."

~

"I *told* you things change," I giggle, holding on to his arm as we descend the stage for the third time.

"If you told me three hours ago that I'd end this shitty day singing 'Don't Stop Believin'' in front of a raucous crowd, I'd have sent you to have your head examined."

"And yet here we are." I sink into my seat and pick up the remnants of my vodka soda. "Do you want to tell me why it was such a shitty day?"

"It's just work stuff." He drains the rest of his beer. "You don't want to hear about it."

"I do," I assure him. "It's clearly bothering you. And who knows, you might feel better if you talk about it."

He laughs shortly. "You sound like my shrink."

"Your shrink?" I repeat.

"Rekha says everyone should be in therapy," he says with a shrug. "That might be because her mom is a therapist, I don't know, but it's been good for me."

"Jack used to say everyone should be in therapy, too," I muse. "I don't really trust his advice, though."

Sam flinches. "Yeah, no, I wouldn't. Maybe only on this one thing."

"I don't want to talk about Jack. I do, however, want to hear what's bothering you."

"Well, all right. Just remember you asked for it when you get bored." Sam sighs. "The way Rekha and I set up Solosol, we split everything fifty-fifty and have an equal voice. In theory, it's great. We share responsibility, and we've historically been good about deferring to each other's expertise—meaning that I let Rekha take the lead on tech stuff, and she steps back on business decisions." He pauses and cracks his knuckles. "Rekha is smart, you know, but she has really shitty business instincts."

"Let me guess: She made a business decision without you."

"She fired our marketing firm without consulting me."

"She *what*? Did she say why?"

"Apparently, the main contact said something sexist to her. And, look, for the record, I am strongly opposed to that. But she shouldn't have fired anyone, much less the entire team, without having a conversation with me first. Our launch date is rapidly approaching, and now we have no marketing at all."

"Well, between you and me, they weren't doing that great of a job anyway. The messaging is all over the place. It's hard to tell who your product is for—or even exactly what it is."

He grimaces. "You get what you pay for. We've got a pretty lean budget. So now we have to scramble to replace the team—not an easy feat, considering everyone else was out of our price range—*and* Rekha is pissed at me because she says I don't support her."

"That sounds really frustrating." I touch his hand. "You should talk to her after you've both calmed down, and, I don't know, maybe you can reengage the firm, but without the sexist guy?"

"Yeah, maybe." He scowls down at his phone. "She's been calling all night, and I haven't answered, so I think she'll be mad about that tomorrow, too." He picks up his empty beer bottle and swings it. "Hey, do you want another drink?"

I pause. I don't really want another drink, but I also don't want the night to end. I don't want to leave this weird little bar, with its sticky floors and off-key singers, and walk back to our shared apartment building, where we'll retreat to our own corners. Sam will probably call Rekha to patch things up, and I'll sit alone in the dark and pine over what might have been. Or maybe Sam will invite me back to his place for another sleepover. Even if I don't get to kiss him again, just sleeping next to him will be more than enough for me.

"Ness?" he prompts, his voice low. He shifts, and one of his denim-clad legs brushes against my bare skin. Instinctively, I press lightly against him. He catches his bottom lip in his teeth, and one of his hands falls under the table, coming to rest on my thigh. His fingertips trace small circles on my skin before curling around the hem of my short skirt. Electricity zings through me, and I am suddenly very aware that Sam and I are sitting in a dark, secluded corner of the bar.

"Yeah?" I respond, so preoccupied with the location of his hand that I can barely get the word out.

"How about that drink?" he asks, his hand sliding around to my inner thigh.

"I don't know." I lick my lips. "I might be ready to call it a night."

His hand stills. "Oh?"

"Yeah." I press my thigh against his. "But the thing is, I'm worried the rat might still be there."

"Oh." Sam's dark eyes twinkle. "I might be able to help you out there."

I open my mouth, but before I can say anything, I notice an older woman with fluffy, blond hair and a pink Western-style shirt taking the stage. She grips the microphone, and the speaker emits a few familiar, twangy notes.

My heart stops. Sam stiffens, his eyes finding mine.

Neither of us breathes as she sings the opening line of "I Will Always Love You." Every nerve in my body fires, and my chest clenches in a sudden iron grip. There is no way I can sit here and listen to another impostor Dolly Parton sing that song, not while Sam's hand is on my thigh, not while his body is so tantalizingly close that I can smell the pepperiness of his aftershave and the fresh scent of his laundry detergent. I cannot physically do it.

"Vanessa," Sam says softly, urgently.

I seize his hand and pull him to his feet. "Let's get out of here."

Together, we step out into the cool night, leaving that song and all its baggage behind us.

Chapter Twenty-Six

Hands entwined, we walk the few blocks back to the apartment building in a charged silence. I steal a sidelong glance at Sam, trying to gauge his thoughts. Did that song ignite something in him the way it did in me? I can't hear those lyrics without remembering that night in Las Vegas, both of us sweaty from dancing, buzzed on cocktails and the thrill of doing something momentous.

The Las Vegas trip was our last hurrah of our college careers. Classes had finished, and as our group clambered aboard the plane, we couldn't stop talking about how *epic* it was going to be. Ellie and Richie had convinced their folks to cash in hotel points for a couple of suites, and they'd used their burgeoning party-planning skills to craft a packed itinerary. I was both looking forward to and dreading the trip. Things with Sam had gotten increasingly strained in the past few weeks, and I had the uncomfortable sensation this trip would bring things to a head.

For a time, our relationship had felt like a fairy tale. The meet-cute on the Mexican beach, the marathon phone conversations, the feeling that we were *fated*. His grand romantic gesture of transferring schools to be with me. Seeing him every single day. But things were different once he was on campus. *He* was different. Sam had always been more introverted than me, but he pulled so far inward he was practically inside out. He had a seemingly unending supply of excuses for why he couldn't join me at parties or the bars: studying, exhausted, *laundry*. And the nights when he *did* agree to come out, he acted like some sort of pod person, staring off into space and nodding along at conversations without following them. Something was up, and I knew I should ask him about it, but I was afraid. Every relationship I'd had before Sam started with laughter and fun and ended with someone telling me I was too much. I would die—just literally die—if that pattern repeated itself with Sam. I loved him too much to hear him say he was bored of me or that he'd made a mistake transferring from Cornell.

And so I resolved not to give him the opportunity to say it. Instead, I planned to drag him to Vegas and surround him with our friends. I let myself believe it would be a magic bullet for us, that it would change things.

And it sure changed things. Just not in the way I hoped.

By that point, our relationship was so tense that I almost expected Sam to cancel on the trip, but he boarded the plane—at least, his body did. He might have been physically there with us, playing the slot machines and downing questionable shots at flashy bars, but he seemed a million miles away. I was afraid he was slipping through my fingers, and it was making me crazy. I should have told him how I felt, but once again, I worried that giving voice to my fears would make them real.

And so I decided the best course of action was to drown both my concerns and his inhibitions.

It worked, sort of. I plied him with tequila shots, and for the most part, we had fun. Our conversations revolved around logistics—where we'd meet our friends, what we'd have for dinner, where we'd drink that evening—and what dirty things we'd do to each other that night, but that was better than silence. I knew it wasn't a sustainable model for long-term relationship success, but it was getting us through a rough patch, and that was all that mattered.

And then came the last night.

Our group had gone in together on bottle service at a club for our final blowout, and Sam and I both had more to drink than was advisable. At one point, all our friends were out on the dance floor, and Sam and I sat alone at the table. He looked at me, and I saw something in his eyes, something that looked almost like sadness. I could feel it coming, could feel him preparing to say something devastating, and I leaned over to kiss him to shut him up. He didn't respond at first, and then he clutched me, holding me so tight I could barely breathe. He kissed me like he was drowning, and maybe I should have stopped him then, but I couldn't. I was drowning, too.

When he pulled away, his eyes were glazed and his voice unsteady. "You know, Vanessa, there was . . . there was this one time in middle school when I had the stomach flu. It was bad, I got really dehydrated and—"

"Sam? Do I want to hear this?"

"Yeah, no, maybe not," he said, laughing a little. "But I want to tell you. So, I had to go to the hospital and get an IV and everything. But before that, everything was shimmery, and dreamlike, and not quite real. I still felt like barfing, but I . . . everything felt like this weird alternate dimension I'd stumbled into." He licked his lips and squeezed my hands. "And it's kind of the way I feel when I'm with you."

I stared at him, unsure whether I was drunk or he was. "I . . . make you feel like you're dehydrated?"

He laughed deep in his throat. "I love you so much I want to barf. God, I'm sorry. I know that's probably not the most romantic thing you've ever heard. I was—"

"Sounded pretty romantic to my ears," I teased. "Only second to a proposal on bended knee."

Sam froze, his eyes holding mine for a beat too long. I knew what was coming next. I knew it, and I did nothing to stop him. If anything, I egged him on.

"Sam?"

Abruptly, he stepped away from the table and dropped onto one knee.

Heart jackhammering against my ribs, I pulled him to his feet. "Come on, you don't know what's on that floor."

"Let's do it," he said, his voice urgent. "Let's get married."

I squeezed his hand so hard I'm surprised I didn't break it, and said, "Yes."

~

Now I sneak another glance at him and wonder if he remembers that night the same way I do. Or is he instead focusing on the sadness of the song, an omen of how things would end? We should never have allowed that Dolly to sing that song; we should have insisted on a different song, any other song. Maybe Faith was right. Maybe we should have held out for Elvis.

"After you, neighbor," Sam says, holding open the lobby door, and my stomach flops. Is this how things are ending? We're back to being "neighbors"?

We don't look at each other as we wait for the elevator, and the silence is agonizing. I want to say something, but I'm afraid of upsetting what feels like a very delicate balance. It feels like Sam and I are standing on the knife's edge, just as close to falling into bed as we are to sleeping alone. The thought of the latter makes me want to die.

Once the elevator doors close, Sam, still looking straight ahead, takes my hand and hisses, "God, Vanessa."

His throaty voice feels like fingertips all over my body, and the ache intensifies, threatening to overwhelm me.

"Yeah," I manage.

Somehow we make it from the elevator to Sam's apartment, and no sooner are we inside than Sam hurriedly shuts the door and pushes my body against it. His mouth descends on mine, rough and hungry. After the minutes of silence, I'm surprised and make a startled little gasp.

"Sorry," he pants, pulling back. "I . . . Is this okay?"

"Yes," I say, pulling him closer. "God, yes. But, Sam, I thought . . . I thought you didn't want to do this?"

"I have *always* wanted to do this." He kisses me again, and I can feel the truth behind his words. Against my lips, he says, "I thought maybe we shouldn't, but I was wrong. I can't . . ." He trails off and strokes the side of my cheek. "I can't stand not touching you."

I pitch forward on my toes, dragging my tongue down his throat. The noise that comes out of him is somewhere between a moan and a growl, I press my body against his, a feeling that's at once familiar and deliciously new.

"You," he says roughly, pressing me more firmly against the closed door. He kisses me deeply, a kiss that steals all my breath, and then pulls back slightly, pinning me against the door with his hips while he looks at me through dark eyes hazy with desire.

"You can't imagine all the things I want to do to you," he murmurs before closing his mouth over mine again.

"I don't know," I respond between kisses. "I have a pretty active imagination."

He laughs, a low, rumbling sound that reverberates through my body, and brings his mouth to the tender skin at the base of my throat. He kisses me there gently while his hands slide up underneath my shirt, then he slips it off and casts it aside. He smiles at my purple bra and thumbs my nipple through the lace. I gasp and squirm, bucking my hips against him.

"Oh my God," I murmur. "You're driving me crazy."

"Me?" he chuckles, pulling down the lace to take my nipple into his mouth. "You make me feel insane. Just totally, completely, out-of-my-head insane whenever I'm around you."

"You know what they say," I manage through moans. "All the best people are."

"You are one of the best people." His mouth moves back to mine, and he unzips my skirt, letting it fall to the ground. He runs a hungry hand down my front, cupping me in his palm, making me cry out. "One of the very, very best."

I pull back slightly, even as his fingers are still stroking me. "Don't put me on a pedestal, Sam."

"Vanessa," he starts, but then shakes his head and buries his face in my neck. "I've got somewhere else I'd like to put you."

Sam hikes my legs around his waist and carries me to his bedroom, where he deposits me on his perfectly made bed. He looks down at me in my undergarments, and a wolfish smile curves across his face.

"God, Vanessa," he says, looking at me appreciatively. "And I thought you looked good in those pajamas."

"It feels unfair that you're not undressed, too," I say, propping myself up on an elbow and reaching for him.

"Fair point." He yanks his shirt off over his head to give me a better view of his taut abs.

"Oh, wow," I murmur, reaching out to touch them. "These are new."

He laughs self-deprecatingly. "Yeah, no, I'm in better shape than I was in college."

"You were perfect," I tell him seriously. "You've always been perfect."

I curl up to kiss him, and he lowers his body over mine, locking our hips together, eliminating any space between us. The warmth of his bare skin, the sensation of it against my own, steals my breath and makes me greedy. I want more, more, more. My core aches to have him close to me, to have him inside me. My hips undulate shamelessly, and my hands reach for the button on his jeans. When I reach my hand inside to grasp the smooth hardness of him, he gasps.

"Fuck," he murmurs.

"Let's," I say, before running my tongue down his throat.

He makes a strangled sound and gently eases me back. "Are you sure? This is—"

"I need you," I say, hearing the ragged desperation in my own voice. "Please, Sam. Don't make me beg."

"Wasn't even a thought," he says breathlessly. "Just give me a second—"

He rolls away and pulls open the drawer on his bedside table. As he sticks his hand inside, his cell phone begins to buzz from a spot on the comforter, where it's fallen out of his pants pocket. My entire body feels like a too-tight guitar string, ready to snap, and I know the only way

I'll get any relief is for Sam to come back *now*, but I can't stop staring at the phone. He doesn't seem to hear it, and even though I want nothing more than for whoever it is on the other end—Rekha, probably—to go away, I feel obligated to say, "Um, Sam, your phone."

"Ignore it." He triumphantly pulls a condom from the drawer and turns his attention back to me, kissing me hungrily. His hand works its way down between my legs, and his fingers push aside the lace, stroking gently and eliciting desperate, needy moans from me. He slides a finger inside, and then his phone starts buzzing again.

"Sam," I manage through panting breaths. "For the love of God, turn that thing off."

He murmurs his assent against my shoulder and keeps one hand working on me while the other reaches for his phone. He turns distractedly to it to shut it off, but then his whole body tenses.

"Shit," he says, abruptly pulling away from me and sitting upright. As if on cue, the phone starts buzzing again in his hand. He stands up, already turning away from me as he says, "I have to take this."

"Who—" I start, but he's already stepping out of the room. My stomach sinks. I know it's Rekha. Who else could it be? She's been calling all night.

In the other room, Sam answers the phone with a low, froggy, "Hello?"

I can't hear what the caller—Rekha—says, but then he clears his throat and says, "No. Nothing. I was just sleeping."

The ease of his lie surprises me, but what really stings is that *nothing*.

Nothing.

To hear him choose that word—well, it opens up old insecurities I'd thought I banished long ago. Before Sam, all my relationships had been mostly physical. Sam was different; he saw me as something more than a party girl who liked to have fun. But now, after everything—after him transferring schools, me dragging him down that aisle, the way things ended—how could I think he'd want me? He's on the cusp of success, and what could I bring to the relationship? My failing career? My toxic association to the Crypto Con? The only thing I'm good for—the only thing I've ever been good for—is a good time.

Alone in my underwear, I feel cheap and exposed. I scramble from Sam's bed and hurry through his apartment, desperate to make it outside before the tears start to fall. I refuse to let him know how much he's hurt me.

I can hear Sam in his kitchen, having a hushed conversation that I can't quite make out, as I move through the living room and collect my clothing from the floor. My eyes burn as I step into my skirt, and the dam threatens to break before I've managed to get the shirt over my head. Desperate to get out of there, I slip into the hallway, my shirt in one hand and my shoes in the other. Across the hall, a young woman opens her apartment door and starts to take a step outside, but takes one look at me and turns around, shutting the door firmly behind her.

I pull the shirt over my head and retreat to Faith's apartment. It's a relief to remember she's spending the night at Marisa's. I'm too humiliated to tell her what happened. Instead, I go to my room and lie down on the bed.

Moments later, there's a knock on our apartment door.

"Vanessa?" Sam calls.

I don't respond.

"Vanessa, is everything okay?"

I bite my lip while hot tears spill down my cheeks. I hold my breath, hoping that he'll say something to make it better, but of course there's nothing he can say. *Nothing.* After I hear his footsteps retreating, I stare at the dark ceiling until, utterly emotionally exhausted, I surrender to sleep.

Chapter Twenty-Seven

Nothing.

The word penetrates through my unconscious, ruining my dreams, and it rattles around my skull while I drag myself out of bed and into the shower. When I emerge, I'm cleaner but no less haunted by Sam's words. *Nothing.* It gets to the heart of what I always feared: that deep down, Sam saw me as less than.

Once, when I visited him at Cornell, I overheard two of his female friends talking about me.

Well, she's not what I expected, one of them said.

I know, right? the other responded. *I pictured someone . . . more sophisticated. She has nothing to offer him.*

The first girl made a noise of assent and agreed, *Nothing.*

Look, I spent my childhood being the new girl. Overhearing people talking about me was nothing new, and it wasn't particularly novel to hear girls being catty. Long ago, I taught myself not to let that kind of stuff bother me.

But Sam has always been my tender spot, my Achilles' heel, and so their assessment pierced me. It haunted me when I couldn't sleep, niggled the back of my mind when Sam seemed distant. *She has nothing to offer him.*

I know I'm not the same girl I was back then. In the five years since I parted ways with Sam, I've made something of a name for myself—but now, even setting aside the fact that Jack sent me back to square one, it's painfully obvious that I'm not enough. How could I be? Sam's launching a company that will do some real good in this world, and I got famous by being a conventionally attractive girl who could stand on her head. I think of all the horrible things people have called me over the years: fame whore, airhead, gold digger. Worse names I don't even want to remember. I wonder if Sam followed my career, if he saw those comments on my socials, if some part of him agrees with them.

I'm startled out of my spiraling by a knock on the door. Hope swells in my chest. *Sam.* It has to be Sam, returning to apologize for what happened last night. We'd both been drinking; things didn't end the way either of us wanted. We can try again.

But it's not Sam.

To my complete and utter surprise, it's Kathryn.

Smooth, sleek Kathryn Dalton, looking wildly out of place in this hallway, with its flaking paint and carpet in dire need of a shampoo. She is, as ever, draped head to toe in black: black cashmere T-shirt and black wide-legged slacks with the murderously sharp toes of her black heels peeking out from beneath the hem. Her platinum hair is slicked back in a perfect ballerina bun, and her earlobes sport enormous princess-cut diamonds.

She lifts one corner of her crimson lips into the laziest approximation of a smile I've ever seen. "It's been a while, Vanessa."

"Kathryn," I say, surprised. "What are you doing here? When I gave you this address, I thought you'd forward the occasional piece of mail, not drop by for a random visit."

Her mouth tightens, and in a voice just shy of mocking, she says, "You've been summoned."

Flashes of representatives on CNN demanding that Jack come home and account for the Jaxx Coin disaster fly through my mind, and I gape at Kathryn. "You mean by *Congress*?"

"Not *subpoenaed*," she says, sneering like she always did when I said something to reveal my allegedly inferior intellect. "*Summoned.* By dear Jacky."

"Jack?"

She frowns. "Yes, Jack. Are you having a stroke or something? Try to keep up."

"I'm surprised, that's all. No, actually, I'm *shocked.* 'Dear Jacky' blew up my life and then disappeared without so much as a 'nice knowing you,' let alone an 'I'm sorry.' I've spent the last month and a half trying to pick up the pieces, and now he *summons* me? I mean, come on, Kathryn, even *you* can see that's messed up, right?"

"You weren't the only one stuck cleaning up his mess." She raises a hand to smooth a stray hair back into submission, and I catch a glimpse of the diamond-and-ruby engagement ring Jack gave me on Kathryn's right hand. I have to smile. Seems like Kathryn figured out how to compensate herself for any "cleaning up" Jack asked of her.

"At least you've spoken to him," I counter. "I haven't heard a single word."

"I don't know anything about that, and I don't care. I'm not here as a mediator. My only role is to ensure you get from here to there with as much discretion as possible."

"And where is 'there'?"

"I can't tell you."

"That's absurd, Kathryn. How do you propose to take me somewhere without me knowing where we're going?"

"We'll be flying by private jet, and frankly, Vanessa, if I recall, your geography isn't that good."

I glare at her. "And what if I don't want to see him?"

"You really don't want to see him?" Kathryn asks, arching a thin brow. "You don't want to hear him out? Or maybe punch him in the face?"

"I'm not going to *punch* your brother. Jeez, Kathryn."

"Suit yourself." She checks the time on her delicate gold watch. "But we're on a schedule here, so I'm going to need you to stop all your performative indignation and put on something other than that hideous towel."

Instinctively, I pull the pink-and-green-striped bath towel more tightly around my body. "I don't know, Kathryn. I have things to do. I can't just jet off to who knows where because Jack snaps his fingers."

"What things?" she asks, looking around as though my obligations might be piled on the floor. "What 'things' are more important than getting an explanation from the man you were going to marry?"

"I have a life here. I'm teaching a six o'clock yoga class on Thursday morning, and—"

"You'll be back in this grim building before you know it. Now, go put on a shirt, or I'll be forced to roll you up in this sorry excuse for an area rug and drag you out of here, and no one wants that." Kathryn steeples her fingers in front of her mouth and sighs. "Look, Vanessa, I know that Jack hurt you. I know you're furious with him, and I think you should be. But you don't know everything. This is your opportunity to ask Jack to explain himself. Don't you want some answers?"

I chew on my lip indecisively. I'm beyond annoyed at Jack dispatching Kathryn to collect me without so much as a single text, but Kathryn's right: I *do* want answers. God, do I want answers. I'm desperate to close the book on Jack and move on with my life, but I can't when I'm stuck perpetually wondering whether this was all some sort of master plan he'd had. When Jack kissed me goodbye before that tech-free retreat, did he know it would be our last? Or was it simply a coincidence that Jaxx Coin crumbled while I was unreachable for days?

"Stop doing that," Kathryn says, staring at my mouth in disgust. "It's revolting."

Jack used to say the exact same thing—albeit in a different, gentler tone—when he caught me chewing on my lip. Despite myself, I smile.

"I want answers," I tell her. "Of course I want answers. But why can't Jack just call me? Or does whatever weird cave he's hiding out in not get cell service?"

"'Weird cave'?" Kathryn sniffs. "Please, Vanessa, do you know my brother at all?"

She's right, but that doesn't answer my question. But maybe it doesn't matter whether or not Jack *can* call me; all I need to know is that he *isn't* calling me. And I *do* want answers. I *need* them. I need to know how, once again, a man I thought I was building a life with could just drop me like a bag of dirty laundry.

"If I go with you, can you promise to have me back in time for my class on Thursday morning?"

She dips her chin in a half nod that may or may not be assent. It shouldn't be enough to assure me, but at that moment, with my self-esteem swirling the drain, it is.

"Fine," I say. "I'll come. Just let me throw together a bag."

"You don't need a bag. Just clothing on your body and your passport."

"My passport?"

From the look she gives me, you'd think I just asserted the world was flat. "Of course. You don't think Jacky's still in the United States, do you?"

"No, of course not," I mumble.

"One more thing," she calls after me as I walk toward my room. "No electronics. No phone, no tablet, no smartwatch. They'll check, and anything you try to slip past them will just be left on the tarmac."

"No electronics," I repeat. "Got it."

A sense of unease washes over me as I shut my door. This is a very bad idea. Boarding a private jet with the untrustworthy sister of my allegedly criminal ex-fiancé and heading out of the country to God knows where without any means of communication? I couldn't have scripted a more terrible plan if I'd tried.

And yet I find myself retrieving my passport from its place in my drawer, selecting a pair of leather leggings that Jack always liked. As I dress, I catch sight of the short floral skirt I wore to Friar Tuck last night on the floor, and a parade of tactile memories assault me: Sam's fingers wrapping around the hem, Sam working the zipper, Sam sliding the fluttery piece of viscose down my hips. I pause, midmovement. *What the hell am I doing? Why am I leaving the jurisdiction to talk to Jack, when the man I* really *want to talk to is just upstairs?*

Just as I'm on the verge of opening the door and telling Kathryn that I've changed my mind, I hear Sam's voice in my head: *Nothing.*

My heart pricks painfully. I might have never stopped loving Sam, but he definitely doesn't love me. Not that it matters. I shouldn't be with him anyway. Last night was a mistake.

"Ticktock, Vanessa," Kathryn calls.

I pinch the bridge of my nose to stave off the gathering tears. I'm done crying over men. I'll see Jack to find out one thing and one thing only: Is he the criminal mastermind the media has made him out to be? In other words, how bad of a judge of character am I? Then, once I'm home, I'll put my exes behind me. *Both* of them.

"Here I am," I say, returning to the living room, passport in hand. "I just need to leave a note for my sister."

"No," Kathryn says. "I thought I was clear that this trip is *discreet*."

"But if Faith comes home from work and I'm not here, she'll be worried."

Kathryn sighs, then pulls a small notepad from her oversize Chloé bag. She scrawls a short note and then leaves it on the counter. "There. Let's go."

I squint at the note. "'Don't worry'? Seriously, Kathryn? That's the best you can do?"

"That's all I'm *willing* to do," she corrects. "Now, come on, Vanessa. Jacky is waiting."

Hours later, I shift in the jet's leather seat and peer out the window. We've landed on a small runway somewhere exceedingly green, with conifer-covered mountains rising on either side. It's gorgeous, arguably the most stunning scenery I've ever seen. I catch a glimpse of a red flag flying above a building. I smile to myself. Faith was right, of course. Jack is in Switzerland.

I turn back to Kathryn, who is staring down at her phone, somehow managing to look supremely bored even while in the middle of an international kidnapping.

"You know, I've always wanted to go to Switzerland."

She frowns. "How did you—" She catches sight of the flag outside the window and sighs. "Ah. Well. You can't tell anyone, you know. Jacky trusts you." As her gaze travels back to her phone, I hear her murmur, "I don't know why."

Honestly, I don't know why Jack trusts me, either. How does he know that I won't fly home and go straight to the Department of Justice? Or *The New York Times*? Maybe I should. Maybe revealing Jack's whereabouts would convince them that I had nothing to do with whatever crime he perpetrated. Maybe that would clear my name.

Or, I think, biting my lip as I look out at the impossibly green countryside. *Or . . .*

Or maybe I stay here. Not *here* here, of course, not with Jack. But somewhere interesting. What's waiting for me in Chicago anyway? Teaching yoga to students who whisper about me behind my back? Chasing an ex-boyfriend who thinks I'm *nothing*? I would miss Faith, of course, but Faith is my sister. She'll forgive me.

It's not like I haven't reinvented myself before. I don't know exactly what my next chapter should be, but I know what I *don't* want, and that's hanging around, waiting for either of my ex-boyfriends to validate me. I suddenly consider something I never have before: I'm letting them define me. At what point should I start defining *myself* by what I want rather than what the men want of me?

Just when I think things can't get any more preposterous, right after I've settled into the back seat of a waiting car, Kathryn pulls a black silk scarf from her handbag and hands it to me.

"Tie this around your eyes," she commands.

"You're kidding."

The dead-eyed look she gives me makes it clear the concept of "kidding" is entirely foreign to her, and maybe it is. I struggle to remember ever seeing Kathryn genuinely laugh unless it was at someone else's expense. I sigh and lift the smooth fabric to my eyes, tying it around my head. The weave is dense, and the darkness is immediate and disorienting. A flicker of fear runs through me.

"Happy now?" I ask.

"Thrilled," she says in a voice that is anything but.

Chapter Twenty-Eight

I sit, blindfolded and feeling extremely vulnerable, in the back seat of a car that smells like cigarette smoke for what feels like over an hour. I, however, am the first to admit that I have no concept of time, so for all I know, it might have been no more than fifteen minutes.

"This is it," Kathryn says suddenly, and the car comes to a stop.

I reach up to remove the blindfold, but Kathryn's cool hand on my arm stops me.

"Not so fast. Jack wants you to keep that on until you're inside."

"This is starting to feel a little kinky."

Kathryn exhales a pointed sigh, making it clear she would rather be doing literally anything besides chaperoning her brother's annoying ex around a foreign country. I hear a car door open, and the sound of Kathryn's heels hitting the pavement. I wonder if I'm supposed to follow her—but *where?*—and fumble to unlatch my seat belt. Just as I'm feeling around for the door handle, my door swings open.

"Come on," Kathryn says, taking my hand and helping me out of the car. "Let's get this over with. We're going to walk about ten feet, then take three stairs, then walk another ten feet, and then we'll come to an elevator. Got it?"

"Yeah." I wave my free hand around in front of the blindfold. "Is this entirely necessary?"

"You know Jacky," Kathryn says, tugging me along. "Once he gets an idea, there's no talking him out of it. He's convinced it's imperative you don't know his location."

"Mission accomplished. I could be on Mars for all I know at this point."

"I'm not taking the blindfold off, Vanessa."

I stumble over the stairs and curse under my breath. "If he's so paranoid about his location, why am I even here?"

"I have no idea." Kathryn sighs and guides me slightly to the left. "It's nothing personal, Vanessa. You can be a lot of fun. But you're not exactly the type of woman any of us expected Jack to marry."

Kathryn's casual cruelty is nothing new, but it still stings. *Nothing,* I hear Sam say. I bite the inside of my cheek to stop the tears from coming and try to keep my voice light as I say, "Good thing Jack isn't marrying me, then."

Kathryn makes a strange noise in the back of her throat, and without seeing her expression, I can't tell whether it's stifled laughter or a muffled cough. I tense, readying myself for a barb, and then she says, "Here's the elevator."

I allow her to guide me inside, and we rise for what might be two or twenty floors before a chime sounds. I hear the doors slide open, and Kathryn grasps my hand and walks me forward. Only once I've heard the elevator door shut behind me does Kathryn finally loosen the scarf's knot. She pulls the fabric away with a flourish, and I blink in the sudden light. There's just *so much* light. We're standing in a foyer with a polished marble floor, high stark white walls, and an enormous skylight above. Straight ahead is an open doorway, through which I can see another blindingly white room. Despite the situation, I catch myself smiling. Of course Jack's secret hideaway is a minimalist paradise.

"He's in there," Kathryn says, pointing one manicured finger straight ahead. "Now, if you'll excuse me."

"Wait," I start. "How will I—"

But Kathryn disappears through a door to my right and shuts the door firmly behind her. I take a deep breath and pivot to face the open doorway before me. *Jack is in there.* My palms itch at the very thought. I've spent the last several weeks imagining what I will do to Jackson Dalton if I'm ever unlucky enough to see him again: smash his precious phone with a hammer, take a pair of scissors to the soles of his obnoxiously expensive sneakers, replace his fifty-dollar-a-bottle shampoo with Nair so all his hair falls out. I dreamed up the most creative ways I could wreak vengeance and the most cutting things I could say. But nothing prepared me for what I actually do when I first see him again.

I cry.

I walk into that stupidly white, starkly luxe room and see Jack seated there on a pale couch, all designer denim and button-down shirt, with the sleeves rolled just so, all wavy, golden hair and unfairly chiseled cheekbones, all *Jack*, and my eyes start to leak.

"Oh, Vanessa," he says, his voice soft as he rises. "Oh, babe."

He opens his arms to receive me, but Jack has, as ever, fundamentally misunderstood me. He thinks I'm crying because I've missed him, when, in fact, I'm crying because I am so, *so* furious that my emotions are short-circuiting. I want to *murder* him for what he's done, but I'm also a yogi who believes in the principle of nonviolence—hell, I have the word *ahimsa* indelibly inked on my body—and so I don't know what to do with myself.

Jack steps toward me, arms spread wide, and without thinking, I shove him in the chest, hard. There are exceptions even to ahimsa, I guess.

Jack stumbles back, his eyes widening so much that I can see white all around the ocean blue of his irises. "What the hell, Vanessa?"

"That's my line." I wipe the tears angrily from my eyes and glare at him. "So what the *hell*, Jack? You have some explaining to do."

Jack sinks onto the couch, putting his face in his hands. Another time, such a pose would have ignited some sympathy, or maybe even a bit of triumph at finally getting Jack on the ropes, but at that moment, all I can do is stare at the crown of Jack's head and think, *Sam has better hair.* The thought is absurd, given the circumstances, but that's how my brain has been lately: absurdly obsessed with Sam. Sam, Sam, *Sam*. Sam appears in my mind, with his thick, brown hair and impossibly dark eyes and full, kissable lips, and a liquid warmth pools in my abdomen—but then I hear his voice say *Nothing*, and my blood turns to ice in my veins.

"You treated me like I was *nothing*, Jack," I spit, the hateful word bitter in my mouth. "You didn't tell me one single thing about what was going on, and then you *vanished*."

"That's not because you're nothing," he says, looking at me with anguish. "God, V, is that what you thought? That wasn't it at all. I did that to *protect* you. Everything went sideways so fast, and I knew I was already fucked, but there was no reason you had to be, too."

I blink, surprised.

"It's not like I intended for any of this to happen," he continues. "You know that, right?"

"I don't know what to think," I admit. "I don't want to believe you're a criminal, but, Jack, I know how smart you are. I just can't believe that you didn't see it coming."

"Oh, I saw it coming, all right," he says, chuckling humorlessly. "I just didn't want to believe it. Toxic optimism, I guess."

"But why didn't you *tell* me?" I ask, voice cracking with emotion.

"There wasn't anything you could do." He shrugs. "It turns out there wasn't even anything *I* could do. But I kept hoping I could turn it around. I thought that with enough confidence—"

"You can't make money out of confidence, Jack."

"Sure you can. Haven't you ever been to Las Vegas?"

I wince.

"The problem, though," Jack continues, unaware, "is that it's much easier to lose money with a lack of confidence. And that's what happened. Some idiot planted a rumor that we didn't have enough capital to cover all our holdings, and that spooked just enough people to cause a problem. Before long, there was a bank run." Jack shakes his head. "All over some dumb rumor started almost certainly by someone at a competing exchange."

"That's awful. I had no idea." I tilt my head in thought. "But can you properly call it a rumor if it's true? I mean, you *didn't* have enough capital, did you?"

He shakes his head like he's disappointed in me. "You don't get it, V. All of this financial shit, even your boring old blue-chip securities, is a gamble. That's the entire point, the whole reason people invest. With great risk comes great reward, right? But it turns out that Jaxx Coin holders didn't have the stones needed for gambling. A few cowards ran to withdraw their money, and the rest were like lemmings jumping into the fucking sea." He sighs. "I tried to calm them down, but they wouldn't listen to me. They wanted out. And we just couldn't produce the cash fast enough. Not because we didn't have the finances, but because they weren't liquid enough."

"I don't know, Jack, that kind of sounds like a fancy way of saying that you didn't have the money."

"Listen, Jaxx Coin wasn't any different than any other cryptocurrency out there—or any traditional security, for that matter. I guarantee you that no one else is sitting on piles of cash."

"If that's true, why is the Department of Justice looking for you? Why are they talking about *wire fraud*? And why are you *here* and not at home, answering their questions? If it's all just some misunderstanding, why did you run?"

"Because it's not just some people asking questions. It's a *mob*. A lot of people lost a lot of money, and they're looking for a fall guy. And don't think I don't know that I'm the perfect person for that role. White, male, conventionally attractive, and from family money. Too much education, too many connections, too much fucking privilege. They would love nothing more than to pin this on me."

"But they'd have to *prove*—"

"You have more confidence in the American justice system than I do, babe. Being innocent and being *found* innocent by a jury of your peers are two totally different things. And I can't go to prison. You know me. I'm not built for that."

"But isn't this a prison, too?" I ask, gesturing around the white room. "A *nice* prison, but still a prison?"

"I may not be able to go to brunch at Balthazar, but there's fine dining here. I can go to the gym. I can go *outside*."

"Okay, fine. So you've chosen luxurious exile for yourself. I still don't understand why this is the first I'm hearing any of this, and I don't understand why you sent your sister to kidnap me rather than, I don't know, placing a telephone call like a normal person."

"Calling it a 'kidnapping' is a bit of an exaggeration, don't you think?"

"She threatened to roll me in a rug, and then she *blindfolded* me."

"Well." He shifts. "I can't have you knowing my exact location if you decide not to stay."

I blink at him. *Stay?*

"Anyway," he continues, "I sent Kitty because I need to talk to you, and you were ignoring me."

"What? I was doing no such thing. Trust me, Jack, as mad as I've been at you, I *wanted* to hear from you. I wanted to hear your side of things. Do you know what they're saying out there? That you planned this. That you're a criminal. God, even Benny is going around telling everyone that you stole money for *me*."

Jack snorts. "That loser."

"Exactly what I've been telling you." I shake my head and return us to the point. "Everyone out there has a story, Jack, but I wanted to hear *yours*. Instead, I've spent almost the last two months slowly going insane, wondering if you were some sort of sociopath and I missed all the warning flags."

"I sent emails. Many emails."

"False."

"I *did*," he says stubbornly. He pauses and rubs his chin. "Although . . . I *did* use a burner address. Check your spam filter."

"I would if your henchman hadn't made me leave all electronics behind in Chicago."

He chuckles. "I won't tell Kitty you called her that."

"Do you know how boring an international flight is without your phone to entertain you?"

"She didn't bring a book or magazine for you?"

"She did not."

He frowns. "Sorry about that. But I couldn't let you bring your phone. Someone could use it to determine your location, and I must maintain my secrecy."

"'I must maintain my secrecy'?" I repeat, rolling my eyes. "God, I can't believe I almost married a supervillain."

Jack affects a hurt expression. "I'm not a *villain*, Vanessa. Although I do appreciate that you think I'm super."

"You really do know how to hear only what you want to hear, don't you?"

He laughs softly and takes my hands, his eyes trained on my ring finger. "I didn't realize our engagement was past tense."

"Jack," I say gently. "Of course it is. You burned our life down and fled the country."

"I didn't want any of that to happen," he insists, squeezing my hands. "Listen, V. I miss you. I miss our life. I know you're mad at me, but hear me out: I have things sorted now. I have access to money again. I'm ready to start living my life, and I want you here with me."

I pull my hands out of his grasp and draw back. "Jack, no."

"Think about it, V. Think about the life we could have here."

"In *exile*, you mean?"

"That's temporary," he says, waving a hand. "My lawyers tell me the statute of limitations for federal wire fraud is five years. Think of it as an extended vacation."

"I don't think so."

"Vanessa—"

"Jack, please," I say, sitting down beside him. "Listen to me. I'm not going to stay here with you, but it's not because I don't want to spend the next five years in Switzerland. I mean, I don't. But I can't stay here, because I'm not in love with you. I knew it before everything happened, but I hadn't figured out how to tell you."

"What?" Jack shakes his head like he doesn't understand. "Is there someone else?"

Sam's face fills my mind, and I swallow hard. "I wasn't seeing anyone else, I promise. I'd just started to have serious doubts that we were meant to be together, that ours was really the life I was meant to live."

He gives me a strange look. "None of us are *meant* to do anything, Vanessa."

I know Jack is right. Nothing is predestined; our lives are the results of the choices we make, the millions of tiny choices we make every day. Sitting here right now, for example, is a choice.

"Let me rephrase," I say softly. "It wasn't the life I *wanted* to live."

Jack twists his handsome face in confusion. "But it *is*. You said you wanted to spend the rest of your life with me."

My chest tightens because he's right, at least to a certain degree. Months ago, when Jack sat across from me, looking sharp in an impeccably tailored navy jacket that brought out the blue in his eyes, and presented me that undeniably gorgeous ruby-and-diamond ring over a dessert plate that looked like fine art, I said yes without any hesitation. Jack wasn't the man I'd once envisioned growing old with, but he was charming and intelligent and curious about the world. I enjoyed spending time with him, even if I didn't love him like a building on fire.

Even if I didn't love him the way I love Sam.

"I know," I say. "And at the time, I meant it. But things changed. *I* changed."

"Vanessa—"

"I will always think fondly of you, Jack. Truly. But I can't stay here with you. I have to go home."

"To Chicago? But Chicago isn't your home. *I* am," he says, catching my hand. "Come on, Vanessa, please. Please stay."

"I can't. I'm sorry, Jack."

I try to pull away, but his hand is tight around mine. For the first time, a flicker of fear runs through me. Despite all the evidence to the contrary, I assumed I could trust Jack . . . but what if I was wrong? What if Jack intends to hold me here against my will? No one knows where I am. I'd become a *Dateline* special, vanished without a trace.

I curse myself for letting Kathryn Dalton, a woman who has *never* liked me and who I'm certain could sell my kidneys on the black market and lose absolutely no sleep over it, spirit me away to a hiding place on another continent. Isn't that the first rule of self-defense? Never let them take you to a second location? I should have realized something was up when she wouldn't let me bring my phone. Now I can't call for help; I can't even google the address of the closest US embassy. I'm furious with myself and my stupid, inconvenient insecurity. If I hadn't been such a mess of self-pity after what happened with Sam, I might have had the confidence to tell Kathryn where to shove it. Jack could call me on the phone or not at all.

"Please let go," I say, trying to steady my wavering voice. "You're scaring me."

He blinks in surprise and drops my hand. "Shit, I didn't mean—" He cuts himself off and shakes his head. "God, Vanessa. I know I fucked up. Trust me, I know. But I've lost so much already. Tell me I'm not losing you, too."

"Jack, believe it or not, this isn't about Jaxx Coin. It's not about you. It's about who I am and who I want to be. Honestly, it's about who I've always been."

He holds my eyes as though searching for hidden meaning in my words, and then he sags. "All right. The thing I've always liked best about you is that you aren't afraid to tell me when I'm being an asshole. I'll have Kathryn get you back to Chicago." His gaze is tender as he runs his fingers lightly down my cheek. “You know where to find me when you change your mind.”

Despite myself, I laugh. “Jack, I have no idea where we are.”

He laughs, too, but there’s a sadness in his eyes as he says, “Yeah, I guess you’re right.”

Chapter Twenty-Nine

There is no private plane on the way home. Kathryn arranges for a car to drive me to the nearest commercial airport, and I fly coach—in a middle seat, no less—back to Chicago. Thankfully, Kathryn took pity on me and handed me a wad of euros before packing me into the car and ordering me to keep my eyes closed, which I used to buy a snack and a paperback novel to entertain me during the flight. I can't focus on the book, though. My thoughts keep swirling from Sam and his dismissive *nothing* to Jack and what he claimed happened with Jaxx Coin, not to mention his delusional hope that I would stay there with him. Perhaps I'm being naive, but I'm inclined to believe him.

In some ways, I feel sorry for him. His fatal flaw isn't criminal greed or even ignorance, but plain old optimism. Jack built that exchange from the ground up, convinced that it was the wave of the future, and poured his blood, sweat, and soul into it, all for it to crumble over a rumor. He lost it all—something that could have been avoided if anyone had just asked the right questions and *listened.*

I shift uncomfortably as I recall something Faith said: *You and Sam have always needed to talk it out.*

After Vegas, when Sam presented me with the annulment papers, I was hurt. I *loved* him, and I thought that his proposal, unconventional as it might have been, meant that he loved me, too. Shoving a stack of legalese in my face felt like the ultimate rejection of that love. It sliced through my bones all the way to my soul, and I couldn't find the words to tell him that. So I didn't. Instead, I pulled into myself. Sam didn't want my love? Fine. I wouldn't give it to him. He didn't put up a fight, just let our relationship die like a forgotten houseplant.

The graduation dance was two weeks to the day after we'd said "I do," and we went together even though our relationship was on life support. The evening—predictably, perhaps—did not go well. Sam refused to even try to enjoy himself. He nursed a beer in the corner and kept checking his phone. He wouldn't dance, he barely spoke, and he was very careful to not actually touch me. Ellie, trying to lighten the mood, made a joke about it, and he stared at her like she'd said she liked to skin cats in her spare time. I was understandably devastated, and self-medicated with vodka sodas until I thought it a reasonable idea to throw a shoe at him. Lucky for him, one of our mutual friends grabbed me around the shoulders and pulled me out of the dance before I threw the other one.

The next day, Sam told me that it was over. *Loving you leaves me bruised,* he said. I wanted to die, but I was too emotionally exhausted to argue. Instead, I got in my car and drove home to my mother's house. I didn't return to campus, not even to walk in the graduation ceremony, and Ellie packed up my room for me. I pulled out of the job that I'd planned to start in Chicago, and I moved with Ellie to New York, where I pretended that Sam Cosgrove didn't still own a chunk of my heart.

The more I think about it, the more I realize that Jack and I have more in common than I thought. When things got tough, we both ran. We're both nothing but cowards.

~

I'm practically asleep on my feet by the time I make it back to Faith's apartment. I shuffle through the door, desperate for a shower, a nap, and a strong coffee, not necessarily in that order, but before I can even remove my shoes, Faith flies out of her bedroom and grabs hold of my arms.

"Where the hell have you been?" she shrieks.

"You wouldn't believe me if I told you."

"That's a nonresponsive answer, Vanessa Summers," she says, shaking me, and I realize that my sister is crying.

"Hey," I say softly, pulling her into a hug. "I'm sorry if you were worried."

"'Worried'?" she repeats, pushing me away. "Why would I be *worried* when there was a note that says 'don't worry' written in someone else's handwriting? Jesus Christ, Vanessa, I almost called Mom! I almost called the *police*!"

I half smile, thinking about how well Jack would have taken *that* development, and Faith smacks me on the shoulder.

"Stop smiling!" she demands. "This isn't funny!"

"I know. I'm sorry. I really didn't want you to worry, and if it was up to me, I would have left a better note, but—"

"What do you mean, if it was up to you? Where have you *been*?"

I hesitate, remembering Kathryn's insistence that I not tell anyone where I was. But I'm not going to lie to Faith for Jack, and so I take a deep breath and tell her, "I went to see Jack."

"You're kidding." She draws back and crosses her arms over her chest. "You left me worried out of my mind so you could go cavort with your criminal ex?"

"No, no. It wasn't like that. It—"

"Then tell me what it was *like*," she cuts in, seething. "Did he offer you another fancy diamond ring? Were you *kidnapped*?"

"No to the former; yes to the latter. In a manner of speaking, anyway."

Faith eyes me distrustfully. "What do you mean?"

"Jack sent his sister to collect me. She made me leave my phone here, flew me internationally on the Dalton family jet, then actually *blindfolded* me—"

Faith gasps. "That sadistic bitch!"

"It was at Jack's request, apparently."

"I'll murder him. Unless you've already done the honors?"

"Trust me, I considered it."

"He still lives?"

"He still lives. In a luxury condo somewhere in Switzerland."

"I knew it." Faith smirks. "Favored retreat of soft financial criminals."

"That's the thing," I say hesitantly. "Jack told me his version of what happened with Jaxx Coin, and . . . I'm not so sure he's a criminal. I believe him, Faith."

She looks at me with concern. "Do you have a concussion? Did Kathryn knock you over the head as well?"

"Just hear me out," I urge. Quickly, I recap what Jack told me about the planted rumor and the resulting bank run, and how he tried to prevent the exchange from collapsing.

When I'm finished, she gives me a skeptical look. "I notice he's painted himself as some sort of tragic hero."

"No, Jack's a coward, and I think he knows it." I pause, picking at a thumbnail. "But I'm starting to wonder if I'm cut from the same cloth."

"You most certainly are *not.* Just look how well you've handled the mess that asshole left behind. I know it's been difficult, but you've pulled yourself together and you're creating a new life."

"I don't know how well I'm actually pulled together, but I'm not talking about now. I'm talking about five years ago. After things fell apart with Sam, I didn't stick around to fix them. I just ran. Eventually out of the country, not unlike a certain crypto bro we know."

"That was years later—and anyway, you went to an ashram to nurse a broken heart. Jack's hiding in Switzerland to avoid criminal charges."

"It was a for-profit yoga school," I correct.

"Whatever. Your situation and Jack's are still hardly comparable."

"Aren't they, though? When you really get down to it? Jack's a coward; I was a coward. Jack made a mess of things, including my life;

I made a mess of things, including Sam's life. I mean, it's no surprise he thinks I'm worthless."

Faith tilts her head. "What are you talking about?"

"I'll spare you the dirty details, but Tuesday night, Sam and I had a few drinks and then . . . well, we were basically naked when Rekha called. He practically fell over himself to answer the phone, and then I heard him say, 'Nothing. I was just sleeping.'" Tears cloud my vision, and I say, "He called me *nothing*, Faith."

"Ouch. What did he have to say for himself?"

"I don't know. I mean, I haven't talked to him."

She stares at me. "He hasn't tried to apologize?"

I shift. "He may have knocked on the door. But—"

"Vanessa," she says sternly. "Have you heard anything you've said over the last ten minutes? You've been bemoaning what a coward you were five years ago to run away from a conversation with Sam, and now here you are again, trying to run away from a conversation with Sam."

I stick my tongue out at her. "I hate it when you're right."

"Life must be very hard for you, then," she says, smirking.

"All right, all right. Stop gloating. I'll go call him."

I don't call him, though. Not immediately, anyway. My phone is dead, so first I have to find my charger (a task that's always harder than it should be), and then I have to plug it in and wait. After it gets enough juice to turn on, I refresh Messages a few times, hoping one such refresh will show a message from Sam. But the only messages are from Faith and Sienna, and there's nothing in the call log.

When I can avoid it no longer, I dial Sam's number. Anxiety flutters in my throat as I wait for him to answer, and I wish I'd spent less time spiraling and more time planning what to say.

About the other night . . .

I heard what you said . . .

The call connects, and my stomach bounces like it's on a trampoline. I start talking before I can second-guess myself. "Hi, this—"

"Hello," his voicemail recording begins, and I sag in disappointment. I hang up and instead open a text thread, but I have no better idea what to say over text than I did over the phone.

Can we talk? I try, but I backspace over it before I send it.

I think we should I start, but I delete that without finishing.

Finally, I type Hey and press send. I clutch the phone so tightly that my knuckles turn white, eager to see the three dots indicating he's typing a response, but nothing arrives. Exhaustion comes crashing down on me like a curtain, and I flop onto my mattress. Almost immediately, I fall asleep, and I sleep for the next twelve hours, holding my phone the whole time.

Chapter Thirty

My mouth feels fuzzy, and my head aches like someone is standing on it. For a brief disorienting second, I think I'm awakening from a raucous night out, but then I remember the strange Swiss interlude. Is it possible to be jet-lagged after such a short trip? I realize I'm still holding my phone, and I look at it, hoping for a message from Sam.

Nothing from him, but there is a message from Gemma.

What happened this morning?

I blink, confused. Then I check the time and date on my phone, and my stomach plummets like it's been dropped down an elevator shaft. It's Thursday afternoon. I missed teaching my morning class.

Nearly sick with anxiety and furious with myself for letting Gemma down, I dial Gemma's number. I leap into a bumbling defense without even waiting for her to say hello.

"Gemma, I am so sorry. So, *so* sorry. I—" I cut myself off, not sure whether I should tell her I've seen Jack. "I wish I had a good explanation, but I . . . I can't really say, and—"

"Stop," she interrupts. "You can't say? We're friends, Vanessa. Have a bit more respect for me, please."

"You're right. I'm sorry. It's just . . . well, the truth is that Jack's sister showed up at my apartment, and she took me to see him. I didn't realize I'd be gone so long, and she made me leave my phone behind. Otherwise, I would have called to tell you."

Gemma makes a noise of disbelief.

"I know how it sounds," I say quickly. "And, look, I wouldn't believe it, either, if I were you. But I swear on my life that's what happened, and I can guarantee you that it will never, ever happen again. I will never, ever miss class again. I will be a model employee. Trust me, Gemma. Haven't I been a good employee?"

"Up until this morning."

"I'll be even *better*. I swear. Just give me another chance. I'll make it up to you. I'll . . . I'll mop the floors. I'll scrub the studio bathroom. I'll wash the windows. I'll—"

"That's enough."

"That's . . . enough?" I repeat hesitantly. "You mean, *Shut up, Vanessa, that's enough out of you*? Or the floors, bathroom, and windows are enough to atone?"

"That's enough begging. I'll give you another chance. And you don't even have to scrub the bathrooms. I have a service for that." She pauses. "But I did just order some new shelving and could use a hand assembling it."

"Absolutely. Of course. Anything. Thank you, Gemma. You won't regret this."

"See that I don't." Gemma sighs. "Look, Vanessa, I don't like being a hard-ass. Especially to you."

"You mean because I saved your clothing from the monkeys?"

She laughs reluctantly. "Exactly. We have a history. And I *like* you, Vanessa. But House of Om is my baby. I have to protect it. A few bad Yelp reviews could wreck everything I've built. Luckily, another teacher was there and jumped in to sub when it was clear you weren't coming. I gave all the students a free pass for a class of their choice to apologize for the confusion and delay. Everyone left happy, but it could have easily gone another way. And I can't risk that."

"I get it," I assure her.

And I do. I understand perfectly: I'm a risk, and that's exactly why Sam can't have anything to do with me.

~

Two hours later, I've dragged myself out of bed, showered, and consumed a salad, and Sam still hasn't called. I keep staring at my phone, at that lonely little *hey*, and wondering if he's even seen it. Maybe he blocked me again. Or maybe he's just ignoring me.

What's that? I imagine Rekha asking as my text came in, lighting up Sam's screen.

Nothing, he probably said, flipping his phone face down.

Nothing. The word makes me feel literally sick. I'm so embarrassed when I remember how stupidly happy I felt waking up with him, how idiotically *hopeful* I felt singing karaoke with him at Friar Tuck. I actually thought we were rekindling our relationship. How could I have been so stupid? I should have known better. Sam is a smart man; there's no way he'd let me destroy his life a second time around.

And yet.

What if Faith is right? Five years ago, I was too cowardly to tell Sam how I felt, and look what happened. We parted ways in every sense of the word: I almost married Jack; Sam partnered with Rekha. Now, once again, I'm too scared to tell him how I feel—and I know the consequences. I could lose him, for good this time—that is, if I haven't lost him already.

Before my bravery abandons me, I leap from the couch and rush out the door. I charge up the stairs and head straight for apartment 512. My fist shoots out and bangs on the door, loud enough that it startles me.

Nerves tingling with anticipation, I wait.

And wait.

No one answers. I knock again, more hesitantly this time.

Again, no one answers. I think I can hear someone moving around inside, but when I lean forward and press my ear to the door, I'm no longer sure that the noises I hear are coming from Sam's apartment.

I knock once more, calling his name this time for good measure. "Sam?"

Only silence greets me. My stomach bottoms out, remembering one time in college when Sam went dark for two days. He didn't answer my calls, didn't return my texts, didn't even respond when I Snapchatted him a picture of me in my underwear. By the time I dropped by unannounced, I was legitimately concerned, but that concern became confusion when he didn't answer the door even though I could *hear* him inside. That confusion became anger when I heard his voice and realized he must be in there with someone else. I pounded on the door and shouted his name, and he quieted, but the door didn't open. The next day, he showed up at the sorority house as though nothing had happened. If I'd had more self-confidence, I would have demanded an explanation, but I was too scared of what he might say, and so I went along with the charade that everything was fine. Still, that afternoon plagued me for years. Why was he hiding from me? Who was he talking to?

Now I feel like collapsing in a pathetic puddle on the hallway floor, but I'm haunted by an image of Rekha dismissively stepping over my crumpled form. Instead, I shuffle back to the stairs and drag myself home.

~

"I love you, Vanessa." Sam's voice is throaty as he kisses his way across my clavicle. "I've always loved you."

"I love you, too," I purr, twining my fingers through his thick hair.

"These last five years have been torture," he murmurs against my breast. He takes my nipple in his mouth and bites gently, making me arch against him. "All I've wanted—"

Sam's words are drowned out by a shrill ringing. I shake my head, telling him I can't hear him, but the ringing gets louder, and then suddenly I realize I'm alone on the bed, early-evening moonlight streaking through my window, my cell phone ringing in my ear.

Still half-asleep, I pick it up and mumble a greeting.

"Hello, Vanessa," a chipper voice greets me. "Did I wake you?"

I pull the phone away to check the caller ID, to confirm what I already know: Fern Foxall is on the other end of the line. I do my best not to groan.

"Hello, Fern."

"I assume you know why I'm calling."

"Fern, it has been a very long day, and I am very tired. Please skip the theatrics and just tell me what you want."

"'A very long day'? Sounds like you're back in Chicago, then. You're not in Switzerland anymore?"

Switzerland. I feel like I've been thrown in an ice bath. Fern knows I was in Switzerland—but *how*? Or is she just guessing, and trying to trick me into confirming Jack's whereabouts? I think he's doing the wrong thing by hiding, but I believe his claim that he's innocent, and his fears of being wrongly convicted in a jury trial aren't totally groundless. I would hate for Jack to end up behind bars just because Fern Foxall *tricked* me.

Carefully, I ask Fern, "What are you talking about?"

"Don't bother denying it. I've seen the photos. How's Jackson?"

"You have photos of me with Jack?"

"That sounds like a confirmation."

"No," I say firmly. "Absolutely not. I don't know what you think you've seen, but—"

"Give it a break, Vanessa. This horse is already out of the barn. Check your messages."

My phone buzzes against my ear, and I pull it away to see a photo of Kathryn and me disembarking the Dalton family jet in Switzerland. On the heels of that, Fern sends me links upon links, all articles with some variation on the same headline: SISTER AND GIRLFRIEND OF FUGITIVE JAXX COIN FOUNDER JACKSON DALTON SPOTTED IN SWITZERLAND.

My heart falls. It's completely and utterly nonsensical, given how Sam and I left things, but my first thought is *Oh God, Sam is going to think Jack and I are getting back together*. Then I remember that Sam thinks I'm *nothing* and that he probably doesn't care if I move to Switzerland. He probably—

Another thought hits me like an anvil. Jack took precautions to make sure no one knew where he was. Is he going to think that *I* had something to do with revealing his location? I hope he—

I cut myself off as I notice something about the photo. I open it and zoom in, my stomach flipping when I realize that it appears as though Kathryn and I are smiling at each other. I'm certain we weren't having a pleasant conversation, but the photograph doesn't catch our words or our tone. It also, unfortunately, doesn't catch the silk scarf in Kathryn's handbag, waiting to be tied around my face.

Of course the whole world will think Kathryn and I are conspiring.

Everyone will think I willingly and happily went to see Jack.

They'll think I've been part of it the whole time. They'll think I am, to quote Fern's earlier headline, a coconspirator in the Jaxx Coin debacle. *Jesus.* This is not good. It is impossible to actually overstate how very not good this is.

I hang up on Fern, press my face into a pillow, and scream.

Chapter Thirty-One

"Are you all right?" Faith asks, looking up from her book as I enter the living room. "I swear I just heard you screaming."

I hand Faith my phone, opened to one of the links Fern sent. "Read this and tell me if I'm all right."

Faith's eyes widen as she skims the article. "Oh no. This says you're an accessory to fraud. Vanessa, this is bad."

"I know. Worse, it's not only Fern making that accusation. The same damn story is running in just about every American media outlet, from *The New York Times* down to niche crypto Substacks. Everyone will see this. There's literally no way to avoid it."

"Oh," Faith says, pulling a face at a notification that just popped up on my screen. "Speaking of 'everyone.' Dad just texted you."

I groan. "See what I mean?"

"Can't talk now, call you later," Faith says aloud as she types a response to our father for me. "Oh, here's another. Sienna wants to know how you're holding up. She says she saw the picture of that—" Faith makes a face and hands me back my phone. "I'm actually not going to read that aloud."

Despite everything, I snicker. Sienna is the queen of colorful insults, and there's never been love lost between her and Kathryn. Quickly, I type her a message saying I'll call her later.

"I wish I'd been here, Vanessa," Faith says. "I wouldn't have let that shady Dalton sister abscond with you."

"No, this isn't your fault. I would have gone with Kathryn no matter what you said. I mean, I know what curiosity did to the cat and everything, but I needed to hear Jack's side of things. Once upon a time, I was going to marry that man. I had to find out if I'd been wrong about him." I frown. "But as relieved as I am to know Jack isn't some criminal mastermind, I could do without my top Google result implying I'm colluding with a wanted fraudster."

"The internet is a cruel mistress," Faith says, shaking her head. "The best thing you can hope for now is that Jack will turn himself in."

"I can tell you right now that's never going to happen. Jack is way too proud to do that."

"So he'd rather—"

"I don't want to talk about it," I interrupt. "I can't control Jack, and thinking about it just fills me with anxiety. I can't stand it. I have to move." I reach for my sneakers. "I'm going for a run."

"You can't," Faith objects. "Your knee—"

"Feels okay," I finish for her. "Besides, Faith, I have to do something. I have all this nervous energy running through my body, and if I don't let it out, I'm going to explode."

"Tearing your knee is not going to make the situation better, Vanessa."

"I'm going to be *fine*," I insist.

"It's dark," she says gently, stepping in front of me. "And you're literally shaking. If you want to go running in the morning, I promise you I won't say a single word. But tonight, please just stay in with me."

My legs twitch, desperate to outrun Fern and her accusations, but I can't ignore the concerned look my sister is giving me. After a moment, I drop my sneakers.

"All right. Tonight, I'll stay in. On one condition."

"Name it."

I push my phone back at her. "You hide that thing from me."

~

True to her word, Faith says nothing when I walk into the living room in exercise clothing just after six this morning. Saying nothing, however, is not the same as *implying* nothing, and Faith's disappointed look is all it takes for me to reconsider my running plans. The truth is that my knee still hurts, and Faith probably has a point that I shouldn't compound the injury just because I'm anxious. I decide to compromise, and head to the basement gym instead. The rowing machine might satisfy my craving for physical activity, and if not, I can try my luck with the elliptical trainer. Strictly speaking, it wouldn't be *great* for my knee, but it would be a hell of a lot better than running on it.

I pull open the metal door marked Gym and immediately freeze. The man on the treadmill has his back to me, but I'd recognize that rangy body anywhere. I know it so well I could pick it out of a lineup with my eyes closed. *Sam.* My cheeks warm as I remember my hands on that body, feeling the strong muscles of his torso, the hardness of his hip bones pressed against mine—

I panic as the treadmill slows to a stop, and I glance behind me, calculating the distance from where I stand to the door and whether I can hightail it out of there before Sam sees me. He hasn't returned any of my messages, and I am very much not in the mood to be rejected once again.

Before I can make a move, however, Sam steps gracefully off the treadmill and turns around, mopping his brow with a white towel. I'm rooted to the spot, hypnotized by his strong arms, shimmering with sweat, and so I just stand there, staring at him like some sort of weirdo as he lowers the towel.

"Vanessa," he says, his voice flat.

"Hi," I manage.

"I thought you were in Switzerland." He spits out the name of the country in a tone usually reserved for the names of war criminals, and I flinch.

I want to tell him that if I'd had my way, Kathryn would never have found me that morning because I would have been in his bed. I want to tell him how the word *nothing* has been ricocheting around my skull for days, and how every time I hear someone say it aloud, I feel like my heart is in a meat grinder. I want to tell him that I love him, that I love him so much it's making me sick.

I love you so much I want to barf.

All I can do, though, is shake my head and say, "No."

He stares at me, his expression one of disbelief, and I'm not sure whether he's astonished I don't have a single thing to say for myself or he's trying to figure out what he ever saw in me. He starts to shake his head, to turn away, and I lurch forward and grab his arm.

"Sam, listen—" He recoils at my touch, and my stomach craters, but I press on, desperate to make him understand what a lie that photo is. "Just hear me out, okay? I know you saw that picture of Kathryn and me, but it doesn't tell the whole story. I didn't want to go with her."

"Are you telling me she had you at knifepoint?" he asks, sarcasm dripping from his words.

"Well, no, but . . ." I take a deep breath and remind myself that the brave thing to do is to tell him the truth, the *complete* truth. "Okay. You're right. I didn't *have* to go with Kathryn. I wanted to."

Sam clenches his jaw so tightly I'm surprised it doesn't crack.

"But," I hurriedly add, "only because I needed to hear what happened from Jack himself. There've been so many rumors swirling around, and I didn't know what to believe."

"He's a con artist," Sam grinds out.

I shake my head. "He's . . . misunderstood."

"Jesus." Sam looks away and rubs a hand over his face. "I knew something was up when you left in the middle of—in the middle of *that*, but I never expected that you were dashing off to reunite with your criminal fiancé. I get that he has more money than God and looks like some sort of action hero, but come on, Vanessa, have some self-respect."

"Wait, no. That's not what happened. I—"

"Don't," he says, holding up a hand. "I can't, Vanessa. Not now. I have way too many balls in the air to get caught up in whatever chaotic shit you have going on."

Sam may as well have reached into my chest and crushed my heart. It hurts so much I can barely breathe, but I manage, "I thought . . . I thought you'd changed your mind."

Something flashes through his eyes, something distinctly like pain, and I know I'm not going to like what he has to say even before he opens his mouth. "I *did*. I *had*. God, Ness, if you knew how much I wanted this to work . . . You're beautiful and captivating and funny and unlike anyone I've ever met. You're fucking incandescent. I want you more than I've ever wanted anything in my life, but you're . . . you're like a sledgehammer. You just shatter me, over and over, and I can't do that right now. I can't be shattered. Too many people are depending on me."

I swallow back my tears. "I don't mean to break everything."

"Shit, Vanessa," he says hoarsely. "I'm not saying this right. I don't mean that . . . Look, I want you, okay? I want you so bad I feel insane."

"You can have me," I say, voice barely audible.

"Vanessa," he says, and I know he means I should have some of that self-respect he mentioned, but that's beyond my capabilities.

"Please," I say, tears streaming down my cheeks. "Please, Sam."

He lays a tender hand on my jaw, and my face instinctively angles toward his. His lips, soft and sweat tinged, close over mine, and for one glorious instant, I think he's agreeing. I think this kiss means, *Yes.* I think it means, *Let's do it.*

But in that same instant, I feel the distance. His lips are on mine, yes, but they're not hungry. We're not building to something. We're saying goodbye.

I feel like I'm falling off a cliff, and I wrap my arms around him, digging my fingertips into his strong back, desperate for purchase. Desperate for him to change his mind.

It doesn't work. He disentangles himself from me and pulls away, and I can see that his dark eyes are bright with tears. In a rough voice, he says, "I'm sorry."

Before I can respond, he turns and strides out the door, taking the last of my hope with him. I want to collapse on the floor and cry, but I tell myself it's better to turn sadness into usable energy, and so I climb onto the treadmill Sam just stepped off. The controls are still slightly damp from his sweaty touch, and I try not to let myself think of that as I turn up the speed.

I run and I run and I run, increasing the speed and the incline until I can barely breathe, until my lungs feel like they're going to explode, until my knee is screaming so loudly I can't even think straight, and then I turn it up again. My feet beat on the band, faster than I've ever run before, and it's still not enough.

Then, with an audible *pop*, my knee finally surrenders, and I come crashing down on the treadmill. The band unceremoniously dumps me onto the concrete floor, and I draw myself into a ball and start to sob. I know I should drag myself to my feet and get upstairs, or at the very least call Faith for help, but I'm incapable of doing so. All I can do is lie here and cry, the blinding pain in my knee no match for the jagged hole in my heart.

Chapter Thirty-Two

When I finally heave myself through Faith's apartment door fifteen minutes later (after ten minutes of lying on the floor in agony and shame, plus five minutes to limp painfully through the labyrinthine basement to the elevator), she—to her great credit—does not say she told me so. Instead, she takes one look at me and lets out a gasp.

"I'm fine," I say, even though I'm grimacing my way through each word.

"Bullshit," Faith says, stepping under my arm to support me on the way to the couch. She eases me down and glances at my knee, the swelling obvious even through my compression leggings. "Do you think we should go to Urgent Care? I can call an Uber."

"I just need ice." I wince. "And painkillers. Lots and lots of painkillers."

Faith fetches me the ibuprofen and a gel ice pack wrapped in a cheerful gingham dish towel, and then she perches on her desk chair and stares at me.

I cast her a sidelong glance. "It's a twisted knee, not a concussion. I don't need constant surveillance."

"I know, but . . ." She tilts her head. "You've been crying. It's not just the knee, is it?"

Sam's face crowds into my memory, disappointment obvious in his deep, dark eyes. *You're like a sledgehammer.* A fresh wave of despair washes over me, and my eyes start leaking anew. I try and fail to conceal a sob. Faith pulls a sympathetic face and comes to sit beside me on the couch, wrapping one of her thin arms around me.

"Oh, sweetie," she says softly. "What happened?"

"Sam was there. In the gym downstairs," I manage. "And he . . . he saw that dumb picture. Of Kathryn and me. I tried to explain, but . . . he wouldn't even listen. He said he had too much going on and that I . . . that I was . . ." I swallow hard, trying to force the words out. "That I was a sledgehammer."

"That dick."

I sniffle. "I mean, it's not like he doesn't have a point."

"No, screw that. I'm sick and tired of hearing about what you supposedly did to him. You know what, Vanessa? Sam Cosgrove is an active participant in his own life. He *chose* to change schools. He *chose* to go with you to that chapel. He *chose* to let you walk away. And now he's *choosing* to be a cowardly, insufferable *dick*."

"Well, I don't know that I would say *that*—"

"You are amazing, Vanessa," Faith interrupts, clutching my hand. "I'm not just saying that because I'm your sister. You are one of a kind, and you are special. And if Sam Cosgrove can't see that, then fuck him to the moon."

Despite myself, I laugh. I squeeze Faith's hand. "I love you, little sis."

Before Faith leaves for work, she sets me up on the couch with a fresh ice pack, snacks, and the controller. She admonishes me to take it easy, but I can't. I have to *do* something. Everything keeps swirling around in my head otherwise. I pull my tablet onto my lap and start work on editing some old images for my socials. Clearly, I can't take any new yoga photos, but—

Suddenly, I bolt upright on the couch. *Yoga.* It's late Friday morning, and I'm scheduled to teach a class in less than six hours. I glance at my knee, which is still the size of a grapefruit. I might be able to make it to the studio, but there's no way I can teach a class. I could call out poses from the front of the room, but I couldn't assist students, and I couldn't make it across the room fast enough if someone needed me. I'm loath to call Gemma and cancel after our last conversation, but I also know how much Gemma would hate it if one of the regulars complained. I have to tell Gemma what's going on and allow her to make the decision. I take a deep breath and dial.

"Hello, Vanessa," Gemma answers, an unsettling note of caution in her voice. Whatever Gemma once thought of me, I know her estimation is nose-diving every minute.

"Hi, Gemma. I'm afraid I'm calling with bad news. I . . . I fell off a treadmill and tore my knee. I can barely walk, and I don't think I'm in any shape to teach this afternoon's class. I can limp my way through it, of course, but I wanted to let you know so you could decide if you want to call a sub."

Gemma is silent for a moment, and I wonder if I've lost her.

"Gemma? Are you still there?"

I hear her exhale. "I'm here. I'm sorry to hear about your knee, Vanessa. But maybe this makes things easier."

I tense. "What do you mean?"

"I've been blocking people from the House of Om socials since yesterday evening. It's like every single troll in the western hemisphere is at-ing me to ask why I've hired a noted fraudster and someone who obviously doesn't live up to yogic principles."

"Oh God, Gemma," I say, my stomach sinking. "I'm so sorry. I never meant—"

"Don't apologize. I knew when we started this that you had . . . shall we say, an air of notoriety about you."

Despite myself, I stifle a laugh. "That's a nice way of putting it."

"I still believe in you, Vanessa. You're a gifted instructor and a good friend. But . . ."

Gemma trails off, and I swallow. "You're firing me."

She hesitates, and I know all I need to know in that two-second pause. My time at House of Om is done.

"I'm not firing you," she finally says. "But you're injured, and the negative attention is upsetting the other instructors and the students. So let's just . . . take a break, all right? Get some rest. Heal. Let the dust settle. And after that . . . we'll talk."

I nod, defeated, and then remember Gemma can't see my head bob. I clear my throat and manage, "All right."

"Please don't take this personally," she says. "If it were only me, I'd just keep blocking them. But I have to protect House of Om and its community."

"I know. I get it. I'm just a sledgehammer."

"A what?"

"Nothing. I'll talk to you later, Gemma."

I hang up the phone and collapse onto the couch, flattened by the reality of the situation. If I can't teach, I can't make rent. If I can't pay my share of the rent, Faith will have to find someone else who can. And that means . . . what? That I'll have to move to California to live with my mom? To Florida to live with my dad and his annoying wife? Or somehow find some other yoga studio that will hire a teacher who can barely walk and is a bit notorious?

My head swims as I realize I have no idea what I'm going to do.

Chapter Thirty-Three

"You need to reapply," Ellie says, holding out a tube of SPF 70.

Ellie, currently wearing an enormous floppy hat and Jackie O–style sunglasses, is serious about sun protection, which is why I'm sure her skin will still be as smooth as glass when she's fifty, and so I'm inclined to take her advice.

I accept it and thank her, for more than just the sunscreen. After Gemma's call sent me in a self-pitying spiral, I phoned Ellie and said fewer than three words before she detected my Eeyore-esque tone and invited me over to the rooftop pool of her River North condo. She brought a chilled thermos filled with rosé and a mini speaker, and we've been lounging on pool chairs and dissecting Taylor Swift lyrics.

"So," she says as I slather on fresh sunscreen, "Richie knows a guy who's starting a new lounge on Hubbard. He's got a soft opening tonight, and Richie can put us on the guest list. Sound fun?"

"It does, but honestly, I don't think I'm up for going out tonight. You should do it, though."

"Is this about your knee? I'm sure Richie can pull some strings to make sure we get a seat. I'll even do you the favor of letting you wear that hideous pair of orthopedic shoes you showed up in."

"Hideous? They're perfectly reasonable cross-trainers."

"If you say so," she says with a sniff. "But they do your legs no favors."

"False. They do my knee all sorts of favors. But it's not about that. I just don't think a big night out is really in the budget right now. Gemma basically fired me today. She told me I *wasn't* fired, but she also told me not to come in, so."

"This'll be on me," Ellie insists. "And who cares about Gemma? I know you think she walks on water, but you're *Vanessa Summers*. You can do whatever you want. You don't need her little studio."

"Gemma has an amazing community," I counter.

"Whatever. You have fifteen million subscribers on YouTube. She's small potatoes."

"Agree to disagree. Besides, my subscriber count isn't quite so impressive these days."

"You're too hard on yourself. You're a goddamn goddess—even when you're wearing terrible shoes."

"You just don't appreciate good arch support." I shake my head at her playfully. "But listen, El, I appreciate *your* support. Really. You're a good friend, and I don't mean to be, like, exhausting or throwing a pity party, but I just don't feel like going out tonight."

Ellie slides her oversize sunglasses down her nose so that I can see her narrowed eyes. "Is this because of Sam?"

"No."

She lowers her glasses even farther so they're practically off her face. "Vanessa."

"It's *not*. I mean, am I upset about what happened? Yeah. But it means *nothing* to him, so."

My voice catches on the word *nothing*, and Ellie groans dramatically. "V, babe, come on. You knew *five years ago* that your relationship had run its course, remember?"

"I mean, that's not entirely true. *He* broke up with *me*, and if you recall, I wasn't exactly happy about it."

She rolls her eyes. "Right. He beat you to the finish line, but you were going to break up with him anyway, remember? You decided to wait until after Las Vegas to avoid ruining the trip, but you were going to cut him loose. Except you morons drank too much in Sin City and turned our early graduation trip into some sort of weird destination wedding."

"What?" I sit up sharply. "Ellie, no. I was never going to break up with Sam."

"Sure you were. You spent literal weeks whining about him and his mopeyness."

"I wasn't *whining*. I was sharing my feelings with a trusted friend!"

She sniffs. "I don't know, V, this seems like revisionist history to me. As I recall, I heard it from both Rachel *and* Zoey."

"But you didn't hear it from *me*." I pause. "Oh my God, did someone tell Sam that I was going to break up with him?"

She lifts a shoulder. "I didn't, but someone might have. I mean, you know Rachel. She couldn't keep a secret if it had a leash."

"Oh no," I murmur as a niggling thought forms in the back of my mind. Our relationship in the months leading up to Vegas hadn't been ideal, but it was the immediately preceding week and the trip itself where things really fell apart. The marriage certificate was nothing but a bandage—and one of those gross, cheap bandages that rip up your skin, at that. So when Sam had broken up with me after the graduation dance, I assumed it had been brewing in his mind for some time. But if my sorority sisters—including Ellie, my closest confidante—were saying that *I* was going to leave *him*, who would have blamed Sam for believing it? What if him breaking up with me was actually him giving me what he thought I wanted?

Spots encroach in my vision, and it suddenly feels very, very important to talk to him about this. I spin my legs to the side of my lounger and reach for the sneakers Ellie hates so much.

"Where are you going?" she asks, surprised.

"Home." I slide my sundress on over my swimsuit and grab my tote. "Thanks for having me over. Sorry to run out on you like this, but there's something I have to take care of."

"Don't do it," she says. "Look, V, I've known you long enough to know that you're going to do whatever you want regardless of what anyone says, but just pause a beat here. Are you really planning to knock on the door of the guy who ditched you, literally in the middle of some heavy petting, so that you can rehash your breakup from five years ago?"

"I just need to set the record straight," I tell her. I think back to what Faith told me. "It's parol evidence."

"I have zero idea what that means. You sound absolutely insane." She shakes her head. "Vanessa, please. I just don't want you to get hurt."

I blow her a goodbye kiss. "Thanks for the concern, but it's a little late for that."

~

I feel electrified, guided by purpose, until I'm actually at Sam's door. Only when I'm staring at the brass numbers 512 do I start to question my judgment. Maybe Ellie is right. All this is in the past; dragging up all those old emotions won't help anything. It won't change what happened: Our relationship broke apart, and I ran away like the coward I am.

And yet I'm here, and my body feels incapable of leaving without at least getting a *glimpse* of Sam. I lift a hand and knock on the door. Almost immediately, I hear footsteps, and then the knob turns.

"Sam—" I start.

But when the door opens Rekha is the one looking at me, her hair glossy and her expression confused. "Can I help you?"

"I need to talk to Sam."

"He's not here."

I squint at her suspiciously. "I just need a minute—"

She sighs. "Vanessa— It *is* Vanessa, right?"

I nod.

"I understand you and Sam used to date and that you seem to believe you two have some star-crossed-lovers thing going on, but it's time to give it a break."

My jaw drops. Her tone is dismissive, mocking, and it makes me wonder what Sam has said to her behind my back. Have I always been more into him than he's into me? Is it that obvious? I want to tell her to mind her own business, but I can't gather the words.

"Sam has enough on his mind right now," she continues. "We're just weeks away from launching a product that will change the world. But in order for that to happen, I need Sam to focus." She pauses to give me a critical look. "Do you understand what that means?"

I lift my chin. "You don't need to treat me like an idiot."

She continues like I haven't said anything. "It means you need to go home, Vanessa. If you love him like you think you do, take a step back and wait for a time when your black hole of need won't obliterate everything we've been working toward."

Anger flares in my chest. How *dare* this woman I've barely met talk about me like she knows me. I want to snap at her that she knows *nothing* about me or my relationship with Sam, but what's the use? She's given no indication she'd listen, and bickering with Sam's business partner won't fix us. If anything, it'll drive us further apart.

Besides, as much as I hate to admit it, I know that she's right. I don't bring anything to the table other than chaos. *She has nothing to offer him.*

Sam is better off without me.

Chapter Thirty-Four

I'm convinced Faith thinks her television only receives CNN and C-SPAN, so when I stomp through the door and find her slumped on the couch in front of some Andy Cohen programming, I'm alarmed.

"Uh, Faith?" I ask, glancing between the melting bowl of ice cream in her hands and Lisa Vanderpump on the screen. "What are you doing?"

"Wallowing." She waves the bowl of ice cream at me. "Obviously."

I limp over to the couch and drop down beside her. "Did something happen?"

She sighs wearily. "You know how some days are just *bad*?"

"Yep." I snatch her spoon and steal a bite of her ice cream. "I'm familiar with the concept of a bad day. I've even suffered through a few of them myself."

She cracks the barest hint of a smile. "Well, I'm having one. I tripped getting off the bus this morning, and all my notes for a brief I'm working on went everywhere. I mixed up cases in a meeting and embarrassed myself, and then I met my old study group for happy hour, but Brian had already gone to another happy hour, so he was drunk and annoying, Katrina kept bragging about this case she's working on, and James was coughing the whole time, and I swear to God, if he gets me sick, I will impale his head on a pencil." Faith scowls down at the ice cream as though it is personally responsible. "And Marisa and I got in a fight because she wanted to tell everyone that we're together."

"And you don't?"

"No. That'll just make it weird when we break up."

I tilt my head. "Sorry, I thought you just said '*when* we break up.'"

"Everyone breaks up," Faith says defensively. "It's inevitable."

"It's . . . actually *not* inevitable."

"And you know this from personal experience?" Faith asks sarcastically. "Or the great model of our loving parents?"

"Okay, so historically, the Summers women have not had great luck in love. But that doesn't mean that you can't be the one to break the mold."

Faith shrugs noncommittally.

"Did you tell Marisa what you're afraid of?"

"I'm not *afraid*. I'm just clear eyed."

"Faith," I say gently. "Honey. You're afraid. It's okay, though. Love can be scary."

"I'm not in love with her. I . . ." Faith trails off as a look of horror crosses her face. "Oh no. Oh *no*. I'm in love with her."

I laugh. "You should tell her."

"Is this you giving me my own advice?" she asks, narrowing her eyes. "Next thing I know, you'll be encouraging me to talk it out."

"Hey, this is fully, one hundred percent a Vanessa Summers original." I bump my shoulder against hers. "Tell the girl you love her."

"But—"

Faith is cut off by her buzzing phone. We both look down at it and see a message from Marisa. Can we talk?

"If you were waiting for a sign, there it is," I tell her, pointing at the phone. "Tell her."

"Ugh." Faith rolls her eyes dramatically and picks up her phone. "Fine."

"Go ahead and say it," I tease. "I'm right."

"A stopped clock is right twice a day." She pokes me with the handle of her spoon. "But I'm only doing this if you are. Go call Sam."

As a general rule, I don't lie to Faith, but I can't bear to confirm her worst suspicions about love and its resilience, and so I nod and say that I will. Instead, I wait until Faith leaves to meet with Marisa before I pop some more pain pills and go to bed early, hoping things will feel different in the morning.

They do not. When I awaken, the hole in my heart feels as fresh as ever, and the pain in my knee is dizzying. My knee, if possible, feels *worse* than it did yesterday. Sam still hasn't called, and the only text message I have is from Sienna telling me that Benny just did a podcast where he again blamed me for the Jaxx Coin disaster. Everything is *fine*.

I want to lie around and feel sorry for myself, but I can't do even that without caffeine, so I start a pot of coffee and then hobble over to the couch, where I slather my knee in Tiger Balm. Even though I know Tiger Balm won't actually heal my knee and works by basically doing jazz hands and distracting me from the pain, sometimes jazz hands are all you need. I sigh as my skin starts to tingle and the searing pain fades to the background.

I'm just leaning back on the couch when someone knocks on the door. *Sam,* my heart insists. *It has to be Sam.* But my heart is often wrong—or at the very least, foolish—and so I ignore it and call, "Who is it?"

"It's me." He clears his throat. "It's Sam. Can I come in?"

My heart does a celebratory cartwheel. Sam might have crushed the hope I've carried all these years and ground it to dust, but I will never *not* feel like walking on air whenever he's nearby. I haul my aching body off the couch and drag it across the room to open the door for him. It's something of a relief to see that Sam looks like he feels about as well as I do, with dark circles under his eyes and stubble on his cheeks. Even so, my body has a Pavlovian response to him, with my heart fluttering and my skin warming.

"Hi."

"Hey." He shifts, not quite meeting my eyes. "Can we talk?"

"Yeah, sure. Come in." I limp back to the couch and try not to groan as I lower myself onto it.

Sam follows me, watching me with concern. "Are you okay?"

Not in the least, I think.

"I'm fine," I say.

"Are you sure?" His gaze travels down my body to my knee, still swollen like a balloon and a fetching shade of eggplant. He blanches. "Jesus, Vanessa. What happened?"

"Nothing," I say, the word bitter in my mouth. "Nothing you need to worry about, anyway. Just a sledgehammer doing normal sledgehammer shit."

He grimaces. "That's what I wanted to talk about, actually."

He sinks onto the opposite end of the couch, and I can't help but notice he's seated himself as far from me as possible. The hole in my heart deepens.

"Listen, I want to apologize for what I said yesterday. I shouldn't have called you . . . *that*. I've just been under a lot of pressure lately, and . . ." He trails off, looking down at his hands. "Well, to be honest, I wanted to hurt you."

"I'm sorry, you *what*? Why?"

"Because you hurt me." He darts his eyes to mine, and they're impossibly dark, a moonless night. "I mean, Jesus, Vanessa. You got out of my bed and immediately flew off to Switzerland to rendezvous with your fugitive ex. You *left* me in the middle of the night for a fucking criminal. That *hurt*."

"*You* were hurt?" I demand, anger flickering in my veins. "*You* were? That's pretty rich, Sam, considering *you* were the one who answered a phone call while your fingers were literally inside me. How was *that* supposed to make me feel? And then you told Rekha that I was *nothing*." My voice shakes as I repeat it for him: *"Nothing."*

"Wait, what? I don't know what—"

He's interrupted by my phone, which begins buzzing noisily across the coffee table.

"Do you need to get that?"

"No. *I'm* not married to my phone," I spit before reconsidering. "Actually, just let me make sure it's not Faith. She's out and—"

"Here." Sam stretches an arm out and hands me the phone.

I glance at the caller ID. *Fern.* With a shudder, I silence the call and flip the phone face down.

"Everything okay?" he asks.

"Nothing I need to address now." I can't help myself and add, "It's not *Rekha*."

Sam makes an aggravated noise. "Look, Vanessa, this is why I said I can't do this right now. Rekha is my business partner, and we're about to launch our—"

"Spare me, okay? Rekha gave me the same spiel yesterday."

Sam's brow wrinkles in confusion. "You talked to Rekha?"

I nod. "I stopped by yesterday afternoon to tell you— Well, it doesn't matter. Just another example of me being what Rekha called a 'black hole of need.'"

"She shouldn't have said that," he says, wincing. "She also didn't tell me you came by. What did you want to tell me?"

"It doesn't matter." It hurts my heart to say this, but it's true. Ellie was right: It's the distant past, and so much has happened since then.

"Hey," he says, his voice soft. "Vanessa, *anything* you have to say matters."

He's holding my gaze when he says this, and I want to believe him. I sigh. "This is ancient history, but yesterday, Ellie mentioned that everyone thought I was going to break up with you in Las Vegas."

Sam blinks and shakes his head, as though this wasn't what he expected me to say.

"I know, I know. It's the long-buried past. I just . . . I didn't know if anybody had told you that, but—"

"They told me." He works his jaw, like he's considering saying something else. "Your friends . . . they all told me."

"God, the *drama* on those girls," I mutter. "Look, I know it doesn't matter anymore, but Ellie told me that, and I just really couldn't stand the idea that you might have thought they were right. It wasn't true, and I just . . . I needed you to know that. I was never planning to break up with you." My voice softens. "I really thought we were forever."

Sam chews on his lip and nods once. "I did, too."

"You did?"

"Vanessa," he says, gently incredulous. "I asked you to fucking marry me."

"But then you undid it."

"I—" he starts, flinching.

"And then *you* broke up with *me*."

"What?"

"You came over the day after the graduation dance and told me you couldn't do it anymore. You told me I left you bruised."

"You threw a shoe at me."

"I didn't really hit you."

"You *did*." He rubs his chest right over his heart. "Right here. And don't think I didn't see the symbolism." He sags. "And I wasn't breaking up with you, Vanessa. Not really. I was just saying we should take a breather. Because of everything that was going on."

I pinch the bridge of my nose to stave off tears. "Vegas ruined us, didn't it?"

"Well," Sam says, looking down at his hands, "it didn't make anything easier, that's for sure. But—"

He cuts himself off as his phone buzzes loudly.

"Let me guess," I say dryly. "Rekha."

"Yeah." He frowns. "She says it's an emergency."

"Of course it is."

"No, she doesn't—"

The phone begins buzzing again, more insistently, and he gives me an apologetic glance and lifts the phone to his ear.

"Hey—" He pauses and listens, his eyes widening and his frown deepening. "Send it to me. I'll call you in a minute."

"What's up?" I ask, aware that something has shifted.

Sam shakes his head, his brow furrowed, eyes trained on his phone. The phone buzzes once more, and all of a sudden, his mouth falls open. "Oh no."

"'Oh no,' what? Is this about your launch?"

"No." Sam runs a hand over his face. "It's about us."

Before I can ask what he means, Sam thrusts the phone at me. All I can see is the headline: SECRET ALLIANCE: THE SHOCKING CONNECTION BETWEEN THE MAN WHO BROUGHT DOWN JAXX COIN AND THE MAN ASKING YOU TO SUPPORT SOLOSOL.

My heart sinks. I know without reading more that *I* am the "shocking connection." With trembling hands, I take the phone from Sam and read the first paragraph:

> Sam Cosgrove and Rekha Agarwal, cofounders of Solosol, the buzzy new solar-energy company, have made a point of claiming transparency. It's how they've been able to raise as much investor money as they have, considering their technology is unproven in the larger market and widely criticized by experts. But it turns out there's one secret Cosgrove has been hiding: He is married to Vanessa Summers, a yoga teacher who has made a name for herself on YouTube—and who happens to be engaged to Jackson Dalton, the CEO of fallen cryptocurrency exchange Jaxx Coin. Cosgrove and Summers's marriage was recorded in Nevada five years ago, and it is unclear whether the pair lives together or how Dalton fits in, but sources

> claim that Cosgrove and Summers have been spotted together in Chicago. As was recently reported, Summers traveled abroad to visit Dalton, where he remains a fugitive from justice.

My stomach is in free fall. This is exactly what I was worried about. Well, not *exactly*. I never thought that some reporter would make the absurd claim that Sam and I are *still* married, but still. I knew I was toxic.

"Oh my God, Sam," I manage. "This is outrageous."

"Is it?" he asks, his expression pained.

"*Yes*. I mean, for starters, this reporter is talking about us as if we're actually married."

"But we were."

"For, like, seventy-two hours."

"Even if it was only seventy-two seconds, we were married, Vanessa."

"It was annulled," I remind him. "Legally, it never happened."

Sam looks at me as though I've pulled out a knife and stabbed him, and fury sweeps through me. Does Sam not remember telling me that we made a mistake? That we needed to "fix" the "problem"? He grabbed that damn knife first and carved my heart out with it.

"Why are you looking at me like that?" I demand, throwing his phone into his lap. "What right do you have to look so hurt? The annulment was *your* idea."

Sam shakes his head. "It was my dad's."

"Fine. It was your *dad's* idea. It doesn't matter who thought it up. The only thing that matters is that *you're* the one who brought it to me. *You're* the one who said it was the right thing to do. *You're* the one who gave up on us."

I let out an anguished sob, and Sam gently, hesitantly touches my shoulder. Softly, he says, "I'm sorry."

I put my hand over his and nod. "Sometimes I imagine what might have happened if we'd stuck it out. I think . . . I think we would have been happy."

He swallows. "I think so, too."

"Sam—"

He shakes his head decisively. "Not now. Please. We have to focus on this."

"Right." I wipe the tears from my eyes. "We have to focus on what's *important.*"

"That's not fair," he says quietly. "People are counting on me—"

I hang my head. "I know. I'm sorry. I just—"

Sam's phone buzzes again. "Shit, Vanessa. That's Rekha. I have to . . . We have to handle this." He rises from the couch and hesitates. "Are you going to be okay?"

"Of course," I lie.

"Vanessa—"

"Go," I tell him. "Please."

He pauses like he might say something else, but then he nods and turns toward the door. After he's gone, I remind myself I knew this was coming. I knew that if I got close to him, I'd ruin things for him all over again. But that doesn't stop it from hurting.

Sobbing, I slather more Tiger Balm on my throbbing knee, and then I add some to the skin over my heart for good measure. It doesn't do a damn thing.

Chapter Thirty-Five

I finally pull myself together and, ignoring all my better instincts, search out the article that Sam showed me so I can read the rest. But when the story is open on my screen, something I hadn't seen before catches my eye.

The byline.

By Fern Foxall

I can barely see my phone through the haze of red, but I manage to call her back.

"Vanessa," she answers, annoyingly serene. "I expected I'd hear from you."

"What is your *damage*?" I demand. "Do you actually get *pleasure* in tormenting me?"

"I tried to give you a heads-up."

"I don't want a heads-up! I want a *retraction*. You're a liar."

"Name one thing I printed that's untrue," she challenges.

"Sam and I are *not* married. Not anymore."

"Is that a fact? Email me a copy of the divorce decree, and I'll issue your retraction."

"I don't have a divorce decree. The marriage was annulled."

"Fine. Email me the annulment decree."

"You don't understand. An annulment means it never happened. So there is nothing to email you."

Fern laughs unkindly. "Are you fucking with me, Vanessa?"

"No. Sam and I got married, yes, but—"

"Vanessa," she interrupts, her voice gentler now. "If the marriage was annulled, there would be a decree. It would have been filed. But I scoured the dockets of every state in the union, and there's no decree. No divorce. No annulment. Just the marriage certificate."

I close my eyes at the mention of the marriage certificate, remembering the Uber ride from the club to the marriage-license bureau, the feeling of euphoria as we held hands in the back of a Prius that smelled like cats. We had won, I thought. We had put whatever was bothering Sam behind us and come out stronger.

I was so, so wrong.

But Fern is, too, and so I tell her, "But that's impossible."

"Like I said, if you have a copy—"

"I don't have a copy! But I'm telling you the truth, I swear. Please, Fern." I draw a shaky breath. "This is going to ruin everything Sam has worked for. Please, I'm begging you. Please retract it."

Fern is silent for a moment, and I feel a flutter of hope, but then she says, "Where's Jackson Dalton?"

The about-face is so abrupt I blink. "What?"

"Jackson Dalton. You saw him. Where is he?"

"You want me to trade my ex-fiancé for my ex-husband?" I ask, aghast.

"Those are your words, not mine. But if I have a different lead to chase . . ."

I hesitate. Jack trusts me not to reveal his location, but then again, those photos have already made the rounds. And Jack, whether or not he did anything wrong with Jaxx Coin, is still hiding from the US government. Sam is the innocent party here. He's the one I should protect.

"Jack is in Switzerland," I say before I can change my mind.

"Everyone knows that. *Where* is he in Switzerland?"

"I'm honestly not sure. We landed at a small airport—"

"Gstaad," Fern says impatiently. "I know. It was on the flight manifest. But I couldn't turn up any record of Dalton actually being in Gstaad. Can you tell me differently?"

"I don't know," I say helplessly. "All I know is that we landed at a small airport in the mountains. His sister and I got into a waiting car, where she blindfolded me, and then we drove for what seemed like a very long time, but like I said, I was blindfolded. For all I know, we were driving in circles. Same story on the return trip—zero concept of where we actually were. The only time I had the blindfold off was when I was inside some condo. It had white walls and a skylight. That's all I know."

Fern sighs. "You're not giving me much to work with here."

"I know. I would tell you more if I could, I swear. Please, please let that be enough. Please don't let this become Sam's problem."

"That's not my concern." She softens her voice so that she sounds almost honest as she says, "I'm sorry, Vanessa."

After I hang up with Fern, I'm tempted to throw my phone across the room. The only thing stopping me is the idea that Fern *might* call to say she's reconsidered, and I don't want to have to drag my hobbled leg around to answer the phone. So the phone is still in my hand when it chimes with an incoming WhatsApp video call from a number I don't recognize. Certain it's spam, I ignore it.

Moments later, the same number messages me: Pick up the ringer, V.

I freeze. There is only one person I know who calls a phone a "ringer." The caller tries to initiate another video call, and this time I hesitate only a second before accepting.

And there, on my screen, looking unfairly well rested, is Jack.

"So you *could* have called me all along," I note.

"I'm taking a risk here, V." He pauses and squints at me. "Have you been crying?"

"What do you want, Jack?"

"I want—" He cuts himself off and sighs. "I really wanted to marry you, you know. And it turns out you were already married the whole time."

"No, I wasn't. I'm *not*. That marriage, it was . . ." I trail off, unable to bring myself to call it a mistake. "We were young, and maybe a little drunk. Anyway, we had it annulled, I swear. That so-called journalist's reporting is shoddy."

"Okay," he says slowly. "Assuming that's the case, why didn't you ever tell me that you had *once* been married?"

"I did," I insist. "I told you that time we went to Paris. Remember? We were crossing the Pont des Arts, and a couple got engaged right in front of us? And I told you I'd been married before?"

Jack guffaws. "Shit, V, I thought you were kidding."

"Yeah, no." My throat constricts around Sam's borrowed phrase, and I swallow hard. "Jack, I cared about you. I might have withheld some parts of myself from you, but I never would have intentionally misled you."

Jack flinches slightly. "Unlike me, you mean?"

"I didn't—"

"It's okay. I deserve it. The thing is, though . . ." He peers at me through the phone, his blue eyes boring into me. "The thing is that I'm lost without you."

My stomach sinks. "Jack—"

"Don't worry, I'm not calling to win you over. I know you said you're not interested right now."

I open my mouth to remind him that I never said *right now*, but he's not done speaking.

"I thought I was getting my life back, but I've realized that I've lost my center without you. You were the only one who ever told it to me like it was."

"You're better off without me," I tell him unhappily. "Trust me. I'm a sledgehammer. I break everything."

"What?" He rears back, surprised. "No way. Look, V, *I'm* the one who made such a huge mess I couldn't even stay in the country."

I laugh a little. "Okay, yeah, that's true."

"But you . . . sure, sometimes you let things get a bit messy, but you always mean well. You always do the right thing."

"I don't know—"

"I could learn a lot from you," he says, rubbing his jaw thoughtfully. "You know what? I should go. Take care of yourself, Vanessa."

He disconnects the call before I can tell him that I certainly do not always do the right thing. If I did, I wouldn't be crying on the couch right now.

~

Thirty minutes later, I'm in the living room attempting to reconfigure my emotions with a guided meditation when I hear a key in the lock, followed by laughter. I pause the meditation just as Faith opens the door, stepping inside with a pretty brunette I assume must be Marisa.

"Hi," I say, and it's only when I hear my squeaky voice that I realize I'm still crying.

"Oh no," Faith says, rushing to my side. "Are you okay?"

"I'm . . . ," I start before a sob chokes me. I swallow and wipe at my wet cheeks. "I'm sorry. It's just . . . been a morning."

"What happened?" Faith asks, pushing my tear-soaked hair off my face. "Does this have something to do with Sam?"

I open my mouth to answer, but I'm cut off by my phone buzzing on the couch beside me. My heart leaps, hoping that it's Sam, but of course it is just my father's wife, Cynthia, texting me for the third time in the last ten minutes, always in all caps as though she's shouting at me from Florida. WHEN ARE WE GOING TO MEET YOUR HUSBAND? YOUR FATHER WILL BE VERY UPSET WHEN HE HEARS.

I shake my head and flip the phone face down on the cushion, then glance at Marisa. "I'm Vanessa, by the way. Faith's sister."

"Of course. I'm Marisa. Faith's . . ." Marisa glances over at Faith.

"Girlfriend," Faith supplies, her cheeks reddening.

Marisa beams, and Faith grins in a way I haven't seen her smile since we were kids—widely, unselfconsciously. Despite everything, I can't help but smile with them.

"It's nice to finally meet you. Sorry it's like"—I wave a hand to indicate my snotty nose and splotchy face—"this."

"Oh please, I'm not scared by a few tears," Marisa says, seamlessly handing me a pack of tissues from her bag.

"Thanks," I say gratefully. To Faith, I say, "She's a keeper."

Faith blushes fire engine red and ignores my comment. "Anyway. Do you want to tell me what's going on? Did you talk to Sam?"

"Yeah, I talked to him. No, I don't want to talk about it. Not right now."

Faith looks at me dubiously.

"Listen," Marisa says. "Faith wanted to change her clothes, and then we're going out to breakfast. Why don't you come with us?"

I hesitate. "I don't know that I'd be a lot of fun right now."

"All the more reason for you to join." Marisa gives me a genuine smile, and I feel something warm in my chest.

"Well," I say, glancing at Faith, "if you're sure."

"We're sure," Faith says, extending a hand to help me off the couch. "Come on, let's go get dressed."

~

"I don't understand," Marisa says, leaning over her omelet. "This reporter is saying that you and this guy are still married?"

"That's what she's saying." I poke my tofu scramble glumly with my fork. "But she's wrong. I'm sure of it. Sam said his dad was really adamant about having it annulled. Sam kept telling me that he couldn't disappoint his dad, not then—whatever the hell *that* meant, like there was a better time to disappoint his father. Sam's dad even roped in *our* dad, who threatened to cut off my tuition if I didn't sign the papers. But of course I was going to sign the papers. What was I going to do, insist on staying married to a man who plainly didn't love me? I'm not a psychopath."

"He *did* love you," Faith cuts in.

I shake my head. "You weren't there. You didn't see how far he pulled away from me. He was practically on another continent."

"He loved her," Faith tells Marisa in a stage whisper. I toss a sugar packet at her, which she bats away easily and continues in her regular voice, "Anyway, joke's on Dad because Vanessa never even *used* that marketing degree he paid for."

"Hey! I used it."

"For, like, all of two seconds."

"Come on, now, that's not fair," Marisa says. Faith draws back in surprise, and Marisa gives her a soft smile and pats her hand. "You're being too hard on your sister. Maybe she didn't use her degree in the traditional sense, but you have to admit she's done an incredible job building her own brand. Obviously, she learned something along the way."

I stick my tongue out at Faith and then thank Marisa.

"I admire you," Marisa says. "Most people just follow the path that's been laid out for them and are too scared to deviate from it. They don't have the courage to forge their own trail. But you did. You crafted a life that's all your own, and that takes vision and perseverance, not to mention fortitude."

"Thank you," I say, touched. "Genuinely, I appreciate that. It hasn't always been easy—most of the time it's not easy, it's a lot of work—but I'm lucky to have made this career that I love. I'm really eager to get it started up again, and I know I'll have to find a new way to teach in person as soon as my knee heals."

"Have you considered opening your own studio?"

"Oh, I couldn't do that."

Marisa tilts her head. "Why not?"

"Because . . . I'm not the sort of person who runs things. I mean, I can manage myself, but other people?" I shake my head. "I'm a chaos agent."

"Don't sell yourself short," Faith says. "Marisa might be onto something. Maybe you *should* think about opening your own studio."

"I don't know." I tap my fork against my plate. "Gemma said House of Om was catching flak because of my relationship with Jack. If I couldn't even keep a couple of classes going, how could I sustain an entire studio?"

"Stop letting people define you by who you used to date," Faith says. "You're a great teacher, Vanessa. Look at what you built up out of nothing. We can do this."

"'We'?" I repeat.

"Of course." Faith reaches across the table and squeezes my hand. "You're not alone, sis."

I return the squeeze. "Thanks. I'll think about it."

For the first time in weeks, I feel a flicker of hope.

Chapter Thirty-Six

The optimism is short lived.

After I part ways with Faith and Marisa, who are meeting some of their friends at a kickball game, I limp back to the apartment only to find Sam outside the door. He's raising his hand as though he's about to knock, and he startles when I say his name.

"Vanessa," he says, turning around. "You're . . . here."

"This is my apartment," I say, gesturing to the door. "Do you want to come in?"

He shifts, suddenly very interested in a dirty spot on the carpet. "So the thing is—"

"That thanks to Fern and her half-assed research, everyone thinks we're still married? Including my stepmother, who seems mortally offended she wasn't invited to the wedding?"

"Fern?" he repeats, looking up at me with confusion.

"The reporter who ran that story. She and I have something of a history, so I called her. She swears she checked the records in every state and couldn't find any official annulment. Which, according to her, means we're still married." I draw a shaky breath. "But she has to be wrong. Right?"

"Right," he says, his voice sounding strangled. "She has to be. I'll call my dad and have him send me the paperwork so you can show it to her. It might take a few days because, well, you know."

Sam grimaces, and I shake my head, not at all sure what he means. Before I can ask, he continues.

"The thing is, though, that damage has already been done. Rekha and I have been fielding calls from investors all morning. They're freaking out."

My chest tightens as I remember Jack telling me that Jaxx Coin was brought down by a rumor.

"You have to get ahead of that," I tell him. "You can't let that snowball. If one of them bails, they'll all start."

"I know. Rekha's working on a statement making it clear that neither of us have ever met Jackson Dalton in any capacity and that he's not involved in our company at all." He pauses and clears his throat. "And . . . well, Vanessa, there's only one link between Solosol and Jaxx Coin."

"Me," I whisper.

He nods, his face crumpled. "Yeah. Rekha is convinced that if we want to truly separate ourselves from your ex, I have to separate myself from . . . *you*."

My vision blurs with tears. "Haven't you already done that?"

"She wants me to make a clean break from you, Ness. She says I need to publicly disavow you . . . or she'll take the company."

"Can she do that?"

"Rekha owns the patent. I'm at her mercy." He searches out my eyes. "I need this company to succeed, Vanessa. I upended everything for it. I fought with my dad about leaving a safe career, and you know—" He cuts himself off, and for a moment I think he's going to cry.

"Sam—" I start, reaching for him.

He shakes me off and continues. "I've poured years of my life and all of my savings into it. I can't afford for it to fail. And . . . and you've seen the press. We have an uphill battle ahead to convince people to give our technology a try. If this is what Rekha thinks we need, well . . . I have to listen to her."

"Of course," I say hollowly.

"Vanessa," he says, his voice breaking, but it's too much. He doesn't get to cry when he's the one breaking my heart.

"Excuse me," I say, my voice cold because the alternative is to dissolve into a puddle on the floor. "I need to get into my apartment, so you'll need to move."

Wordlessly, he moves away. I can feel his eyes on me as I unlock the door and step inside, but I refuse to look at him. If this is the way Sam wants things, this is the way things are going to be.

You always do the right thing. Jack's words echo through my head, and I wish there was truth to those words. I know there isn't. I *want* to do the right thing, but I'm too much of an impulsive hedonist to do it. I've been this way as long as I can remember. Some of my earliest memories are of my parents reprimanding me for not thinking things through: leaping into the deep end of the community pool before I could swim, climbing through my bedroom window onto the porch roof because I wanted a better look at the stars, taking the car for a joyride years before I had my license. *Don't be so impulsive*, they used to say. *Think before you act.*

I never listened.

Especially where Sam was concerned. I *couldn't* think around him, starting the moment he lifted my jellyfish-stung body out of the Caribbean Sea.

But what if things had been different? What if I had really *thought* about things, thought about the long term rather than just my immediate wants? What if Sam and I had taken things more slowly? If we'd spent that first week in Mexico talking rather than just losing ourselves in each other's bodies, or if we'd spent the following months developing and strengthening our bond over the phone rather than devoting most of our time to planning when we could see each other again? Maybe our relationship would have been more secure, and I would have had the confidence to tell him he shouldn't transfer schools for me. If I had done that, maybe he could have gone back to Cornell—or if that was off the table, at least he would have known that I wanted what was best for him. That I wasn't just interested in my own satisfaction.

Or maybe if we had kept our heads about us from the start, he wouldn't have transferred at all. He would have gotten his Ivy League degree and had all the options in front of him, not just the ones that Rekha conditionally handed him.

And of course, if we had our heads on straight, and if we hadn't already stressed our relationship with his transfer, we never would have arrived at the Las Vegas chapel, gift-shop ring in hand. Our marriage would never have been annulled because there wouldn't *be* a marriage, and that particular hole would never have been carved into my heart. I never would have thrown that shoe at Sam, never blown up my own plans, never moved to New York and taken that job with a small marketing firm.

And if I'd never taken that job, I never would have lost my job when the firm went under, and I never would have launched my own yoga business, which means that Kathryn Dalton would never have seen my YouTube videos and hired me for private sessions. If I'd never met Kathryn, I never would have met her brother, who never would have proposed to me with a ring worth the GDP of a small country. And if I never said yes to Jack . . . well, I wouldn't be tangled up in his cryptocurrency scandal. No, instead of being alone, unemployed, and camping out in my younger sister's spare bedroom, I might be living a fulfilling life with the man I love.

I shake my head and order myself to stop. The only thing this exercise will do is hurt me, and I'm hurt enough. I pop some ibuprofen and lower myself onto the bed. As tears start to fall again, I realize that the problem isn't anything I did or anything I failed to do. It's more fundamental than that.

The problem is *me*. The problem is *who I am*. I am irrational and impulsive and driven by my id, and Sam is right to distance himself from me. I'm a sledgehammer, after all. I break everything I touch.

~

"Vanessa?"

I stir at the sound of Faith's voice. It's dark. I must have cried myself to sleep.

"Vanessa?" she says again, and this time I place her voice at the bedroom doorway. "Are you okay?"

"Peachy," I say, my voice cracking. "Can't you tell?"

"You're lying like a corpse in the dark. Seems like the polar opposite of *peachy*." She crosses the room and sits beside me on the bed, looking down at me with concern. "You seemed in good spirits when you left breakfast, considering. Did something happen?"

"I talked to Sam." My throat constricts, and it's hard to get the next words out. "Rekha gave him an ultimatum. He has to choose: me or the company."

"That's ridiculous. Sam is a grown man. He can—"

"He chose the company."

"That bastard." Faith wipes tears from my face. "Oh, honey. I'm sorry."

"The worst part is, I should have seen this coming. Sam and I have been in this exact same place before, and he made the same choice." I bite my lip to stave off a fresh round of tears before I continue. "You remember how Dad threatened to cut off my financial support? He came up with that idea *after* talking to Sam's dad. I would bet the farm that Sam got the same threat. And Sam . . . Sam chose the money."

"Fuck Sam."

"No, but he's *right*. I mess everything up, Faith. His life—"

"Get up," Faith demands. "I'm not going to sit here and watch you wallow anymore over this man who clearly doesn't deserve you."

"No one is forcing you to watch. You're free to leave the room."

"I said, *get up*." Faith grabs my hands and tries to pull me to a seated position, but I resist. Frustrated, Faith stomps her foot. "Come on, Vanessa."

"I can't." I roll over and bury my face in the mattress. "All I do is destroy things, and I'm not fit to be around anyone else."

I hear Faith make an irritated noise, then her footsteps stomping toward the door, and finally, my bedroom door firmly shutting. A fresh wave of sobs wracks my body. Faith, the one person I've always been able to count on, is gone.

I'm all alone.

~

I lose track of time in the dark. It might be five minutes or five hours, but I'm still lying face down on the mattress when I hear my bedroom door open.

I'm about to ask Faith what she wants when I hear a familiar voice say, "You're right. This is bad."

I prop myself up on my elbow and look toward the door. Faith is holding the door open, and beside her is Gemma.

"She's alive," she says, smiling slightly. "How are you doing, Vanessa?"

My instinct is to say *Fine*, but, of course, Gemma has eyes and can plainly see that's not true. Instead, I shrug.

"See what I mean?" Faith says to Gemma.

"Come on, Vanessa," Gemma says gently. "I set up a mat in the other room."

"I appreciate you coming, Gemma, I really do, but I'm not in the mood for yoga right now."

"That's precisely why you should get on the mat. Vanessa, you, of all people, know how restorative yoga can be—not just for your body, but for your soul."

"I can't," I hedge. "Remember my knee? It's swollen like a beach ball."

"I know, honey. And trust me, I don't want to do anything that will hurt it. I thought I'd give you a private session of my famous yin yoga class."

I hesitate. I feel committed to lying in bed, wallowing and not sledgehammering anyone, but a slow, contemplative yin yoga class *does* sound kind of nice.

"Well," I say, sitting up slowly, "I'm not promising anything, but I'll get on the mat."

"That's all I'm asking." Gemma takes a hand and helps me ease off the bed, then guides me to the living room. The overhead lights are off, and the room is lit only by an accent lamp and candles arranged on the coffee table. The couch has been pushed slightly aside to make room for one of my yoga mats, which is spread on the floor beside a pair of large bolster cushions.

I point at them. "You brought those from the studio?"

Gemma nods. "Much to my Uber driver's chagrin."

I picture Gemma loading those awkward cushions into a rideshare and taking valuable time out of her day to coax me out of bed, and something inside me goes gooey. Even after I flaked on class and brought infamy to her studio, she still wants to help me. She still cares about me. Maybe I *don't* break everything I touch.

"Thanks," I say and carefully lower myself onto the mat.

As Gemma guides me through poses and pranayama, I can feel myself returning to my body. Breath by breath, I am becoming more and more like myself. And when Gemma helps me into a reclined heart-opening pose, supported by the bolsters, I swear I feel something crack open inside me. All the pain, all the insecurity, rushes out, and light replaces it.

I am enough.

I open my eyes and smile up at Gemma. "Thank you."

"You're back," she says, returning my smile.

I twist my head to look at Faith, who is hunched on the couch, reading a book in the dim light. "Thanks, Faith. I needed this."

"Anytime, sis. I know you'd do the same for me."

~

After Gemma leaves and Faith heads to Marisa's, I'm tempted to zone out in front of a screen, but I don't want their efforts to reinvigorate me to go to waste. Instead, I'm seated on the bed, my knee propped up on one pillow, a legal pad I stole from Faith perched on another pillow atop my lap. Marisa's suggestion that I open my own studio is looping through my mind, and to that extent, I've written "Own studio?" across the top of the page.

And that's as far as I've gotten.

The idea is tempting but riddled with problems. The first and most obvious is that I cannot—and would never—compete with Gemma. I couldn't repay the kindness she's shown me by opening a rival studio. No, if I wanted my own place, it would have to be in a wholly different area of the city—or maybe even somewhere other than Chicago. Which is not *totally* out of the question, considering Faith is the only thing keeping me here—but I'm not ready to leave yet. Anyway, even setting aside the issue of location, I have no experience running an actual brick-and-mortar business. I've done okay with my virtual business, but I'm not sure I have the capacity to add things like rent and licenses and insurance and who-even-knows what else to the mix. I'd need to hire someone—or someones—to help me, and that just adds another layer of cost and complication. I mean, hello, employee taxes. I get heart palpitations just thinking about it.

No, running a business is for someone made of sterner stuff than me. Look at Sam. He's put everything on the line, and there's a very real chance that it will flop. But he's still pushing forward because he—

Oh.

Something trips in my mind, and I straighten. Rekha issued her ultimatum because she's afraid my toxic reputation will further damage the Solosol brand, and while she might have a point, it's not like the Solosol brand was doing so well on its own. They'd done nothing to counter the articles implying their product wouldn't work, that it was nothing more than Theranos for the green set. All they really did was send press releases to trade journals, but they'd made no effort to define their target audience, they had no consistent branding, and they had no customer engagement. Their website didn't even have a call to action. Even before I came onto the scene, they were in real trouble.

I've been so focused on how I might *hurt* Solosol that I never stopped to think how I can *help* it. Because Sam's wrong. I'm not a sledgehammer. I'm . . . I don't know, a Swiss Army knife or something. I'm bad with tool metaphors, but the point is that I'm capable of doing damage, sure, but I can also provide a valuable assist in the right hands.

And I have an idea how to do just that.

Chapter Thirty-Seven

My idea is this: a Solosol-sponsored pop-up yoga event on the upcoming summer solstice, the longest day of sunlight of the year. The Venn diagram of people interested in yoga, the celestial calendar, and solar power is essentially a circle, so it's an ideal audience for Sam and Rekha's product. In between yoga sessions—cosponsored, hopefully, by House of Om and led by Gemma and my former colleagues—there'll be demonstrations of the Uno, which will make its official launch one week later, and maybe we'll even raffle one off. Ellie and Richie can help me with logistics for the event, and Faith and Marisa with day-of labor. To expand the reach and up the coolness factor, I'll bring in some of my old friends from the influencer sphere.

And therein lies the problem. I used to hang out with a group of other wellness and yoga influencers, but once I started dating Jack, I saw them less and less, and I haven't spoken to any of them after the Jaxx Coin fiasco. At first, they all reached out, but I was too shaken to return their messages, and then, after the good people of the internet started their mudslinging, I *couldn't*. I was too emotionally fragile. Weeks went by, and now here I am, about to ask them to fly to Chicago and volunteer their time as a favor to *me*, the ex-fiancée of the Crypto Con.

I inhale a calming pranayama breath and remind myself that I'm done letting my association with Jackson Dalton define me. I'm stepping out of his shadow and into the sunlight—figuratively and literally. Even if Sam weren't part of the equation, promoting solar energy feels like a necessary corrective after Jack and his destructive Bitcoin mining.

Then I pick up my phone.

~

Hours later, I'm getting excited. This might really work. Gemma is on board, and Ellie is thrilled about the concept. Six of my old influencer friends have agreed to fly in, and two more are tentative yeses—but even better, every single one of them was so genuinely kind to me I feel like bursting. ("Literally no one thought you had anything to do with that mess," one of them assured me. "Some reporter reached out to a bunch of us, and we all told her she was way off base.")

But the pop-up yoga is only part of what I'm planning. After all, I'm a Swiss Army knife: I'm capable of a multipronged approach. I studied marketing, and like Marisa said, even though I only briefly pursued it professionally, I honed my skills through creating and refining my own brand. It doesn't take a professional, though, to realize that Solosol's marketing has been a disaster, especially since Rekha fired the team. They've been going about it all wrong. Dry press releases will do exactly nothing for them. They don't need to go over the technical specs ad nauseum. No, they need *fans*. Instead of just focusing on the product, they need to build a *brand*.

And while I know a few things about brand building, I also count a brand-expert extraordinaire among my closet friends. Sienna agreed with my assessment of Solosol and hopped on a FaceTime to brainstorm with me. I then spent the next several hours in something of a fugue state, scrawling our ideas onto my legal pad. All I have to do now is find a way to get these ideas to Sam. The trouble is, he's made it clear he wants nothing to do with me.

The thought of forcing myself on Sam again makes me feel ill enough that I pause, but I try to remember that this time things are different. This isn't for *my* benefit; it's not about *me*. It's about Sam and, more broadly, the greater good. Sam says this solar panel will shake up the energy industry, and I want to see that happen. I want to help however I can.

But I somehow have to present these ideas to him in person. I can't slide the pages under his door—he wouldn't be able to make heads or tails of them. I could type them up and email them to him, but that would take time—and I have no guarantee he would even open an email from me.

My phone buzzes—another of my influencer friends signing on—and I blink at the time in surprise. It's 6:10 in the morning. I pulled an all-nighter. I haven't done that since junior year in college, and that resulted in me stumbling into a Business Finance final late and falling asleep before I'd finished the last question. Not my finest moment. Now, though, I'm wide awake. Alert. Excited, even. I've been *doing* something, and now I just need to—

An idea strikes me, and I double-check the time. I smile slowly as I realize that I know exactly where Sam is at this moment.

I pause outside the gym door. I look down at the legal pad in my hand and wonder if this is the right move. Sam told me he needed a clean break from me, or he might lose the company he's worked so hard to build. It could be argued that chasing him down at the gym means I don't respect his boundaries.

Briefly, I consider whether I can play this off as a chance encounter—that I just happened to show up for a workout at the same time as him. I'm still wearing the leggings and loose T-shirt I had on yesterday, which could pass for exercise clothing, but I shoved my feet into a pair of flip-flops, which kind of ruins the charade. I consider going back upstairs for some workout-appropriate shoes, but worry that, in doing so, I'll miss Sam—and anyway, there's no real way to explain the legal pad.

Through the door's dingy window, I see him carrying dumbbells to the weight bench. My already frayed nerves shatter. *Sam.* I yank open the door with more force than I intended, and the swing sends me scrambling. At the noise, Sam turns and freezes when our eyes meet. His expression stricken, he glances around the minuscule gym, as though Rekha might pop out from behind a treadmill at any moment and catch us sharing the same air.

"Vanessa," he says stiffly. "I thought I told you. I can't—"

"Be with me, I know. But no one's around, okay? And I'll be quick, I promise." I take a step toward him, holding up my legal pad. "I have some ideas."

He squints at the pad and tilts his head as though he's trying to read it. "Ideas about what?"

"Solosol's image problem."

"Our what?"

"Come on, Sam, it's no secret that you've been having trouble attracting consumer support."

His mouth tightens. "I'm aware of that, Vanessa. But once people see how well it works—"

"*If* they see," I interrupt. "You have to get your product in front of people first—before they can see it work. And to do that, you need to do more than send out press releases. You need to find your audience, and you need to target them. You need to make them believe that they don't just *want* your product—they *need* it. You want them to believe in it so much that they proselytize on your behalf."

"Okay, sure. But that's easy to say and hard to do."

"Think about the product that you're offering. What makes it unique?"

"It's powerful."

"Sure, and?"

"It's small."

"It's *personal.* It empowers the average consumer to harness the power of the sun *on their own.* It's scrappy. It's *American.* A stay-at-home mom in Iowa can order one without breaking the budget, and then she can keep her kids' toys charged without involving Big Energy."

"Yeah," he says slowly.

"So do you think this mom is reading *Tech Daily*? No way. She's scrolling social media when she has a break between doing the laundry and taking her kids to playgroup. And what about a college kid in Nebraska? They're living in a dorm, on a budget—but they, too, can order your product, pop it on the edge of their desk or the frame of their bunk bed, and generate enough electricity to keep their phone powered without having to choose whether to unplug the computer or the minifridge or make some big power-strip maze, *and* they get to feel warm and fuzzy about choosing regenerative energy. Again, are they reading *Business Insider*? No. They're on TikTok."

"Okay," he says, rubbing his chin. "Yeah, okay. So you're saying we should be advertising on social media."

"I'm saying you should *be* on social media. You need a presence there—more than those half-assed accounts you currently have. You need a *personality*. You need a *connection*."

"Personality, huh?" Sam's lips twist up in a wry smirk. "Gosh, if only I knew someone with personality to spare."

"I'm not pitching myself here, Sam. For *anything*." My heart twists, and I have to look away to gather my thoughts. "All I'm doing is presenting you with a path to connect with potential customers—and more specifically, those potential customers who'll tell others about it, who'll make it go viral. You don't need to just sell solar panels, Sam. You need to sell personal solar energy as a way of life. You need to connect with influencers who will make it *cool*."

"Yeah," Sam says thoughtfully. "Yeah, no, I hear what you're saying. But I don't even know how to connect with those people."

"Lucky for you, I do." I flip through the pages until I come to the list of friends who've already signed on and hold it up for him. "This is a list of wellness influencers who've already committed to joining the Solosol Solstice Special."

"The Solosol Sols—" He cuts himself off, shaking his head. "Sorry, the what now?"

"The title is a work in progress. The whole thing is, okay? But if you—and Rekha, of course—are into it, I have the pieces lined up to throw a pop-up yoga event on the summer solstice. It's the longest day of the year, you know, so it's an ideal day to advertise your solar panels. My friend Gemma's yoga studio will cohost, and I have all these influencer friends ready to help promote. If you're able to give one or two Unos away, this thing'll blow up."

"The summer solstice," he mutters. "We should have thought of that."

"You have a lot on your mind."

"Yeah." Sam holds my gaze, and I feel heat begin to pool in my lower abdomen. Sam is so close, so tantalizingly close—all I'd have to do is stretch my arm out, and I could run my fingers down those strong arms of his, coated with a sheen of sweat. One big step is all it would take to bring us nose to nose, and from there, it would just be an inclination of the head, a breath—

I force myself to take a step backward. Sam has made it perfectly clear that nothing like that will ever happen between us again. He chose the company. He chose Rekha.

Tears burn in the back of my eyes, but I blink them back and force a smile. "And the best part is that I don't have to be involved going forward. At all. I can put you and Rekha in contact with the right people, and you guys can take it from there."

"That's not—" Sam starts, but I bulldoze ahead, afraid to let him speak.

Faith's voice echoes in my head—*You and Sam have always needed to talk it out*—but this isn't about Sam and me. This is about Solosol and what's best for the company.

"Here," I say, thrusting my legal pad at him. "I can just give you my notes. I have stuff for the yoga event and also some brainstorming with my friend Sienna, who's like a total whiz at branding."

"You're telling me those are *words* you've written there?" Sam asks, squinting at my legal pad, and then he smiles fondly. "I don't know why I'm surprised that your handwriting remains atrocious."

"I mean, I don't think I'd use the word *atrocious. Free-form*, maybe." I smile myself. "But I understand a square like you might not appreciate it. I'll type this up and email it to you."

"You don't have to—"

"I want to." I pause as my stomach bottoms out. "Unless you're not interested."

"I am. Very interested." He swallows hard and then adds, "Interested in your ideas, that is. I just . . . feel bad asking you to do anything for me. After . . . after everything."

Everything. Such a small word, but such a loaded one.

My smile flickers. "Don't worry about it."

Sam's pitch-dark eyes seek mine, and his mouth opens as though he might speak, but nothing comes out. Instead, his full lower lip remains ajar, looking unfairly kissable, and it takes everything I have to keep my distance. The air between us feels charged with possibility, and in that moment, I know—I *know*—that ultimatum or no ultimatum, if I were to take a step toward Sam, there would be no stopping us. And, God, how I want it. I want it so badly I can taste the coffee-and-cinnamon flavor of his mouth, can actually smell his salty sweat mixed with his familiar musk. I can feel his hands on me, pulling me closer. Need builds inside me until I feel like I might actually explode if I don't touch him, and then I force myself to turn away.

It doesn't matter how much I want him. It doesn't matter if I can tell that he wants me. There are consequences to being with me, and I refuse to ruin one more thing in his life.

"Vanessa," he says, his voice strangled. "I can't do it. I can't *not* see you. I'll tell Rekha that—"

"Stop," I interrupt, not trusting myself to look at him. "Don't say something you'll regret."

"I—"

"I'll email you," I say, pushing through the door before the tears gathering behind my eyes can break free.

Chapter Thirty-Eight

And here is the reason why twenty-seven-year-old women do not pull all-nighters: By the time I return to Faith's apartment, I'm crashing. *Hard.* My eyes feel gritty, and my limbs feel lead lined, and I want nothing more than to crawl into my bed. But I promised Sam these notes, and I want to get them to him soon—before he does something dumb and Rekha makes good on her threat.

Faith has already left for the day, so I make myself a fresh pot of coffee and set up shop at her desk. Progress is initially slow—I'm so tired, and Sam's right, my handwriting is nearly illegible, not to mention the fact that Sienna keeps interrupting my flow with new ideas—but before long, I fall into a rhythm. The chaotic notes are taking shape, becoming something coherent and persuasive and kind of exciting. I'm obviously a biased party, but . . . it's *good.*

When my phone buzzes, I'm startled to realize that I've been sitting at the computer for almost two hours. I roll out a crick in my neck and check the screen.

A text from Sam: Have a minute to talk?

My sleep-deprived nerves dance, and for a moment, I allow myself to believe that he talked to Rekha and everything is fine. Maybe—

It's about the ideas, he continues, and I force myself back to reality.

Yep! I respond and immediately regret the too-cheerful exclamation point.

I'm coming down.

I rush to take stock of my appearance. As expected, I look like someone who's been hit by—and then dragged by—a bus: My eyes are bloodshot and puffy, my skin is dry and uneven, my hair is snarled and in need of a good shampoo. Quickly, I pop in some eye drops and use my rose quartz facial roller in an attempt to deflate my undereye bags. I pat on some facial oil, run a hand through my bedhead-y hair, and then stick a toothbrush in my mouth, just in case.

"Shave and a Haircut" raps on the front door, and I take one final glance at my reflection. I won't be winning any beauty competitions, but, at bare minimum, I no longer look like the living dead. I take a deep breath and march to the door.

Sam, of course, looks unfairly good. He's showered and changed since I saw him last, swapping his gym clothes for those faded jeans I love so much and a black T-shirt that makes his dark eyes look even darker. His hair looks soft and touchable, and his chin is dotted with just the right amount of stubble. He's chewing on his lower lip, which does things to me that I can't even explain, and it takes everything I have not to kiss him in that moment.

"Hey," he says, oblivious to the fact I'm barely holding it together. "Can I come in?"

"Yeah, of course." I hold open the door for him. "You want some coffee?"

"That'd be great, thanks."

He's silent as I head into the kitchen, and my emotions take a tailspin. Jesus Christ, he's thought about it, and now he's taking Rekha's ultimatum so seriously that he's not even *talking* to me in my own damn apartment.

"So," I say, turning to hand him the cup. "Are we just, like, not speaking unless it's strictly necessary anymore?"

"What?" He looks up, his brow furrowed, and I realize he wasn't ignoring me in silence. He was leaning over Faith's desk, looking at the document open on my computer.

Suddenly, I feel self-conscious. Sam's a legitimate businessperson, and I'm basically winging it. It must look so amateurish to him.

"That's not final," I say quickly. "I'm still working on it."

"How long will it take you to finish?"

"Um," I hedge. "I could have it done in another thirty minutes to an hour, I think."

"Good. Because we definitely want to hear more." Sam takes a sip of the coffee and makes a face. "This coffee is . . . surprisingly chewy."

"Tell me about it. Faith has the worst appliances." I shake my head. "Wait. What do you mean 'we'? Did you talk about this with Rekha?"

He nods. "I just gave her the highlights, but she's definitely intrigued."

"You're kidding me. I assumed she'd reject it on principle, just because it came from me."

"Rekha's not petty. She wants Solosol to succeed."

"I know that, but I also know that she hates me."

"She doesn't hate you. She worries about your influence over me."

"But that's—"

"Not entirely unfounded," Sam interrupts, holding my eyes.

A thrill flutters through me, fast as a hummingbird. "Sam—"

"Anyway," he continues, breaking eye contact, "she's in."

"Okay. Wow, that's great. I really think this could be a game changer for you guys." I pause. "I assume she wants me completely offstage? Keeping my filthy paws far away from her pristine solar panels?"

A brief flash of hurt flickers across his expression. "No. Listen, we talked it out. I told her that you're already linked to us whether she likes it or not. I mean, people already think we're married. It's not true, I know, but it's just a detail, and in this absurd post-truth era in which we live, details don't really matter. In the minds of the public, we're bound together, forever."

My heart shivers at the word *forever*, but he continues. "So even if we made some public statement severing our link—which, to be clear, I'm not going to do, fuck her consequences—it wouldn't be enough. It would only make people think that we have something to hide. So we stop hiding our connection, and instead we lean into it. Sunlight is the best disinfectant, you know."

"And you know something about sunlight."

He flashes me a grin that makes me feel like melting. "Just a thing or two."

I smile stupidly back at him for a moment before I remember how much work we have ahead of us. "Then we should get started. I'll finish up this—"

"Vanessa," Sam interrupts, his voice low. "There is one other thing."

I can't quite read his tone, and I'm hoping that he isn't about to say Rekha is issuing some strict demand, like that I communicate exclusively with her.

"Okay," I say slowly. "And that is?"

He steps forward and takes my face in his hands, tilting it up to his so our lips meet. My body thrums with desire, wholly ready to surrender to him, but even as my mouth is opening to his, the word *nothing* slinks through my mind. I shudder involuntarily and pull away.

"Sam, no. I can't."

"Because of the ultimatum?" he asks, looking abashed. "God, I know, I should never have agreed to it, even for a minute. I've been so stressed lately with, you know, everything, and I haven't been thinking clearly." He draws a ragged breath. "If it's any consolation, I was fucking miserable knowing that I'd hurt you."

I swallow around the lump in my throat. "That's gratifying, but . . . God, Sam. We were basically a single breath away from *consummating*, and then you stopped to answer a *phone call*."

He blinks, confused. "What?"

"That night after karaoke. We were—and you answered the phone."

"I had to. It was—"

"Rekha, I know." I can't keep the disgust from trickling into my voice.

"That's not—"

"And you said that you were *sleeping*. You said that I was *nothing*."

His eyes widen. "Whoa. No, no, no. That's not . . . Okay, I did say that I was sleeping. But, Vanessa, it wasn't Rekha on the other end. It was my *mom*. Did you actually want me to tell her the *real* reason I was out of breath?"

My cheeks color at the thought of Sam's mother—a woman who favors cardigans in a variety of pastel shades and who, I'm told, collects china cows—hearing about the state her son was in. She might die of embarrassment. I can understand why Sam would tell her otherwise. And yet . . .

"Your mom? What was she doing on the phone at nearly midnight?"

"Well, my dad is sick again, you know, and—"

"Wait. No. I don't know. What do you mean?"

"The cancer," Sam says, a shadow crossing his face. "It's back."

Chapter Thirty-Nine

The ground tilts under my feet. "Your dad has cancer? And what do you mean, 'it's *back*'?"

Sam frowns. "My dad was diagnosed with prostate cancer six years ago. He eventually kicked it and has been in remission, but a routine scan turned up another spot two months ago."

"I'm sorry, what?" I say, shaking my head in confusion. Each of the words makes sense individually, but I don't understand them all together. Six years ago, Sam and I were together. His dad *couldn't* have been sick. I would have known. Wouldn't I?

"Yeah, it's not great."

"God, no. Sam, I'm so sorry. I had no idea. I . . ." I trail off, shaking my head. "Okay, I can already hear how this is going to sound, and I know you're going to think I'm making this all about me, but: Sam, he was first diagnosed *six years ago*? Are you telling me your dad was battling cancer when we were together and you didn't tell me?"

He shifts guiltily. "I was going to. Once. A couple of times. But then . . . I didn't."

Memories hit me like a fist, over and over: Sam, his expression clouded, asking me to talk that first day he showed up on campus. Sam, his voice hesitant as he called from a visit with his parents, and me, too scared of his feelings to ask what was wrong. Sam, shifting on the bed beside me two nights after those days he'd disappeared on me, his voice strangled as he said, "Ness? Can we talk about something?" Even in the darkness, I could see the pain in his eyes, and my heart stopped. I was certain that was it, the moment he would tell me he'd made a mistake and was headed back to New York. I couldn't let him say it. So I hid my fear behind a seductive smile, tucked my hand into his boxers, and told him I had a better idea. The look he gave me was one of pure relief, and I thought I'd dodged a bullet.

Now, though, standing in my sister's apartment, I see that everything I did to avoid the potential of getting hurt—that night and who knows how many more—only drove us further apart. Sam wasn't going to leave me. He was going to *confide* in me.

"Oh my God, Sam," I murmur. "I shut you down. I am so sorry. I can't believe what a terrible girlfriend I was."

"Stop," he says, putting a hand on my shoulder. "Don't. This isn't your fault. I just . . . Look, according to my therapist, I have a real problem talking about my feelings. And I know I should have been more open with you about what was going on with my dad, but I just . . . I couldn't talk about it. Talking about it made it real, and it was easier to pretend that nothing was wrong while I was with you."

"Oh, Sam."

My heart is a piñata, cracking open and flooding my body with emotion. Knowing that he suffered through his father's cancer diagnosis alone while I was chattering away about parties and vacations and God knows what else makes me feel sick. The fact that, when he tried to open up about it, I silenced him because I was so worried about *myself* makes me want to walk into traffic. It physically hurts not to wrap my arms around him right now, but I hold myself back. Only an emotionally bankrupt asshole would take advantage of this situation.

"God, Sam, I wish you would have told me. Then *or* now. I would have . . . well, I don't know, I would have been less self-centered. How is he doing now?"

"Pretty well, actually. His prognosis is good; his doctors are optimistic. My mom is freaking out, though. She's anxious, but she's trying not to let my dad see how anxious she is, which means that *I'm* the one she calls when she's about to have a panic attack. Sometimes she needs me to talk her down. Even in the middle of the night." He pauses. "That's why I had to take that call and why I didn't want her to think she was interrupting anything."

"I'm sorry. God, I feel like an ass."

"Don't. It's my fault for not telling you. I was just so overwhelmed and I handled it badly. I shoved everything in these separate boxes—my dad, you, schoolwork—in order to deal, but I just made a mess of everything."

"Oh," I say as a thought suddenly occurs to me. "That's why you transferred schools, isn't it? You transferred to Illinois to be closer to your dad."

"Yeah. That, and we couldn't afford private-school tuition anymore. My dad ran his own business, you know, and his insurance wasn't the greatest. All those treatments and medications were expensive. Plus, he couldn't work while he was sick, and my mom's job isn't exactly lucrative. I mean, she's a part-time nursery-school teacher. They were practically burning cash and had no idea what was coming around the bend. I didn't have scholarships or financial aid, and I couldn't justify taking tens of thousands of dollars from my parents to finance my education when that money could mean life-saving treatment for my dad or a roof over my mom's head if—God forbid—things had taken a wrong turn. I wanted to just say fuck the whole thing and drop out of school altogether, but my parents' heads basically exploded when I suggested it. So instead, I transferred to Illinois. The in-state tuition wasn't nothing, but it was way more affordable."

"I wish you would have said something! I feel awful knowing that you carried all that around on your own."

"Yeah, no, I should have." He lifts a shoulder. "But . . . I don't know, Ness. I was really not in a good way, and I loved you too much to drag you down with me."

"I would have gone anywhere with you," I tell him softly.

He nods slightly. "I know. That's why I couldn't."

I close my eyes and let the weight of his words sink in. When I open them, I say, "This is going to sound insane when I say it aloud, but, Sam, all these years, I thought you transferred schools to be with me."

"Ah, well." Sam avoids my eyes. "I might have told you that because I thought it sounded romantic."

"You *jerk*!" I exclaim, not entirely playfully. "I mean, yes, it sounds romantic, but it was also a huge burden on me. I thought you threw away your Ivy League education—I thought you *ruined your future*—for me."

"Oh, Ness," he says gently. "I had no idea you felt that way. I'm so sorry."

"You were so distant," I continue. "I thought you regretted your decision. I thought you regretted *me*, but you were just preoccupied with your dad."

I look to Sam for confirmation, and he nods. "I was a mess that year, Vanessa. I felt like everything was out of my control. The only thing that was keeping me sane was you."

"If only you would have told me what was going on, I could have . . . I don't know. Helped you somehow. Not dragged you into some skeezy Vegas chapel because I thought I was losing you."

Sam blinks. "You didn't drag me anywhere. I proposed to you, remember?"

"You didn't know I'd take you up on it."

"Yeah, I did," he says, voice soft as flannel. "I just didn't know how things were going to end up. I didn't think any further ahead than that night."

"Maybe that was part of the problem. You were just trying to get through the night, and I thought it was a new start. Instead, it just broke everything."

"You mean because we had it annulled?" Sam asks. "That was . . . Ness, my dad was *pissed*. He wanted different for me. Education, a job, *then* marriage—including a nice wedding my mother would get to help plan. I should have known that, but I was so stupid in love with you that I couldn't even think straight. Once I saw how upset he was, though, I couldn't stand being the cause of it. Not with him so sick."

I shake my head in frustration. "Why didn't you just *tell me* that? I would have understood. Instead, you avoided me. I thought you hated me."

"Jesus, no. Of course I didn't. Look, I fucked up, okay?" He runs his hands through his hair. "I couldn't talk about my dad. I *couldn't.* I thought he was going to die, Vanessa, and I just . . . I couldn't handle it. So I was already messed up over that, and I felt like I was letting people down left and right. My dad, my mom—and most of all, you. You were so mad at me, and I thought you didn't want to be with me anymore. And that absolutely crushed me because I loved you, Vanessa. I loved you so fucking much."

"Then why didn't you fight for me?" I demand, tears starting to slip down my cheeks. "If you loved me so much, why didn't you fight to stay with me? Why didn't you tell your dad that you weren't signing the papers?"

"Because I knew he was right. We shouldn't have gotten married when we did."

"But if you loved me—"

"Vanessa," he says softly, taking my hands and holding my eyes. "I loved you with all of my heart. We should not have impulsively married in Las Vegas. Both things are true."

I lower my face so he can't see how hard I'm crying. On some level, I know he's right. Spontaneously tying the knot in front of a Dolly Parton impersonator was not the answer to our problems, and attempting to course-correct didn't mean that he didn't love me. Yet that flies in the face of everything I've told myself for the last five years, and it's hard for me to accept.

"Look at me, Ness," he urges, using a gentle hand to tilt my chin. A tear escapes from the corner of one eye, and Sam uses the pad of his thumb to wipe it away. "Vanessa Summers, I love you."

I freeze, unsure if my ears are playing tricks on me. *Love.* Present tense.

"I love you," he repeats, trailing a finger along my jaw. "I have never stopped loving you. You are the first thing I think of in the morning and the last thing I think of before I fall asleep. God, Ness, I love you so fucking much."

"I love you, too," I tell him, tears now sliding freely down my cheeks. "You have no idea how much I love you. You're the standard against which I measure all other people."

Sam lowers his face to kiss me tenderly, reverently, upon my lips. "I need you in my life. Please say you'll give me another chance."

"Of course I'll give you another chance," I manage through my tears. "If you're sure. I don't want to ruin things for you. Not again."

"You've never ruined anything for me, Vanessa, and you won't ruin this. The only thing you'll ruin is *me* if you tell me we can't make this work."

"We can make this work," I assure him, leaning forward on my toes to kiss him.

He wraps his arms around me and pulls me closer, and I melt into his embrace. His arms are warm, welcoming, *home*. His mouth descends on mine, and the kiss is slow and tender. I can feel the desire pulsing through both of us, practically crackling in the air, but for once, I don't feel in a rush. We have all the time in the world, and that knowledge thrills me.

Sam pulls away, his lips swollen. "I didn't even ask. Is Faith here?"

I shake my head. "Nope."

"Are you expecting her back anytime in the next three hours?"

I arch an eyebrow at him. "Three hours, huh?"

"Better make it four," he says with a smirk. Then he lifts me off the floor and carries me into my bedroom, laying me down gently on the bed. I see his eye catch a poster over my bed, a Degas ballerina scene that I've always liked.

"Is that the same poster you had in college?" he asks.

I nod. "I can't believe you remember what artwork I had in college."

"I remember everything about you," he says, positioning himself over my body. "I might have been a disaster back then, but you were my guiding light, the one bright thing in my life. Every detail about you is burned onto my brain."

"I hope they're good memories," I say, running my fingers through his thick hair.

"The best," he says softly, looking down at me adoringly. "God, that first night with you is etched onto my soul. I couldn't believe someone as stunning as you wanted to be with me. I was almost convinced I was hallucinating."

"You're wrong," I inform him, sliding my hands underneath his shirt and feeling his strong back. "After our first night together, you spent the entire next day insisting that you never did anything like that. You obviously thought I was easy."

"No, wait, that's not how it was!" he laughs into my mouth. "I was worried you thought *I* was easy. In truth, I was just totally, helplessly smitten with you."

"Baby's first communication error."

"It's kind of a miracle we communicated at all," he says wonderingly.

"Well," I say, trailing one of my hands down his taut side and tucking it into the waistband of his jeans. "We might not be superstars at traditional communication, but we've always been very good at communicating in other ways."

My hand slips farther into his pants, and he purrs and presses against me.

"Very good," he manages, then closes his mouth over mine, cutting off further discussion.

Chapter Forty

Two Weeks Later

Sun and Salutations (the much improved name for the Solosol Solstice Social) is, against all odds, a complete success. I'd hoped for Millennium Park, but even Ellie and Richie couldn't make that happen on such short notice. They were, however, able to secure a permit for a smaller, more intimate park not far from Navy Pier. They worked a few connections—including their friends at a coconut-water company, who donated a few cases of a new flavor they were testing—and their friend Mikayla brought her turntables. Gemma and the House of Om staff led a series of yoga classes, and I even taught one. I was terrified that no one would show up, or that people would only show up to heckle me, but it was exactly the kind of class that I loved to teach: sweaty, invigorating, and full of serious students. We set up charging stations powered by Solosol Unos, which my influencer friends used liberally as they shared dozens of images from the event and talked up the product.

The event will cap off with a short presentation from Sam and Rekha and a raffle for one of three Unos. All day, Sam's been worried that no one will stick around, but the crowd has swelled over the course of the day, and now the park is crowded with people wearing free Solosol swag—hats, sunglasses, and T-shirts—and clutching raffle tickets.

"Holy shit," Sam mutters at my side, surveying the crowd. "This is out of this world. The preorders we've gotten just in the last few hours . . . Vanessa, I don't know how to thank you."

My heart swells, and I wrap my arm around his firm midsection. "I wanted to help. I believe in this, Sam. I believe in *you*."

"You're incredible," he says, his eyes softening as he leans forward and kisses me gently.

"Ugh," a voice says behind us.

We break apart and turn to find Rekha, her arms crossed over the goldenrod-colored jumpsuit that Sienna convinced her to wear for the occasion. (She'd assured her it gave "sun" without being too yellow.) Rekha wrinkles her nose and asks, "Must you do that here?"

Even after all the hours and effort I've poured into remaking Solosol's image in a couple of short weeks—not to mention coordinating with Sienna to get Unos into the hands of a few key influencers and celebrities, which dramatically raised its coolness factor—Rekha still treats me no better than a wad of gum stuck to the bottom of her shoe. I'd try not to take it personally if I didn't know that, in fact, it *is* personal.

I give her my most charming smile. "Are you guys ready? It's time."

"Yes," Rekha says with a firm, confident nod.

Sam offers a less-confident shrug. "I may or may not vomit, but other than that? Sure, I'm ready."

"If you vomit onstage, it'll probably go viral," I say faux-thoughtfully. "So maybe lean into that."

"You're a strange woman."

I laugh and twine my fingers through his. "Seriously, you'll be fine. I'll be right there in case you get nervous."

"'Get' nervous?" he jokes, squeezing my hand.

"Sam! Rekha!" Ellie calls, hustling over in her own Solosol T-shirt, knotted above her navel, with her pink hair sticking out of her Solosol baseball hat. "You're on!"

Sam gives me one last grateful look, and then he and Rekha follow Ellie to the small stage. I glance around the crowd, determined to soak in this moment, all these eager faces, and then I see something that makes my heart stop. Brown hair pulled back in a tight ponytail, a button-down shirt in a sea of athletic tanks and sports bras.

Fern Foxall.

~

There's no reason for Fern to be here. No good reason, that is. Acid roils in my stomach as I imagine all the ways she might ruin this day for Sam and Solosol. If that happens, I know Rekha would never forgive me. It's exactly what she's always worried about: my baggage negatively impacting everything they've worked for. I need to get Fern out of here *now*, and I start threading my way through the crowd toward her just as Ellie switches on a microphone and begins to speak.

"Thanks so much for coming, everyone! Let's give a big round of applause for House of Om, which generously sponsored this event. Don't forget that each of your registrations comes with a unique code for fifteen percent off a class package."

Everyone in the crowd applauds. Except Fern, who is neither clapping nor smiling. Her arms are crossed firmly over her chest, and her gaze is trained unblinkingly on Ellie. As I take a step closer, I note she has dark circles under her eyes and a sheen of grease along her hairline. As if she can feel me staring at her, she glances toward me. She blinks once as our eyes meet, and then, pressing her mouth into a determined line, she turns away.

"And now," Ellie says, "it's my great pleasure to introduce Rekha Agarwal and Sam Cosgrove, the cofounders of Solosol and our major sponsor. Let's give it up for Rekha and Sam!"

The crowd breaks into another round of applause, and I glance toward the stage. Sam is grinning, his cheeks adorably flushed. He looks around the audience as though he's searching for someone, and when his eyes land on me, his smile widens. He taps his heart and winks at me, and it's all I can do not to melt into a smitten puddle on the lawn. God, I love that man.

At his side, Rekha lifts her chin and begins speaking. "Thank you all for coming. It's so heartening to see so many here to support green energy. Now, it's our pleasure to give you a sneak peek at our upcoming product: the Solosol Uno, the very first solar panel small enough to fit in your purse but powerful enough to charge your computer."

Someone whoops in the crowd, starting a cascade of cheering. I glance around for the initiator, certain it was one of my influencer friends, but as near as I can tell, it was someone I've never met. Excitement zips through me. It's working. Sun and Salutations is generating the buzz Solosol needs.

As Rekha continues her remarks, I refocus my attention on Fern. The more I watch her, the more obvious it is that she's tense and jumpy and up to no good. I need to get her out of here before she does something annoying. I slip beside her and latch my hand around her arm, pulling her to me as I hiss, "What are you doing here?"

"Watching your boyfriend," she says, shaking me off. "He's impressive. What does Jackson think of him?"

I grit my teeth, unwilling to take the bait. "You can't be here."

"Actually, I can." She holds up her phone to show me her Eventbrite pass. "I'm a registered attendee."

I curse myself for not checking the attendee logs, and try for a new strategy.

"Listen, Fern, you're wasting your time. Other than the foil-hat types on what's left of Twitter, you're literally the only person who still thinks that I'm some sort of coconspirator in Jack's alleged fraud. Give it up. Didn't you see that *New York Times* story where they looked up the Solosol investor lists and verified that none were Jack or me or aliases of either of us?"

"I saw it," she says tightly. "But those reporters are either on the Dalton payroll or didn't look closely enough. I *know* they're wrong, but because they published their half-assed findings and people still apparently care what *The New York Times* says, *my* editor won't print *my* story without more evidence. So I need to find it."

"There's nothing to find," I say, holding up my palms. "What's that old adage? 'Follow the money'? Well, I don't *have* any money. If I had any role in what happened with Jaxx Coin, wouldn't I have at least some of those billions of dollars? Wouldn't I be doing something other than sharing a rat-infested apartment with my sister and wearing leggings bought on clearance from Old Navy?"

She looks uncertain, and for a second, I think I've gotten through to her.

Then I hear Rekha say, "We have a few minutes for questions, if anyone has any."

Immediately, Fern shoots her hand up in the air.

"Put that down," I snap, swatting at her, but it's too late.

"Yes?" Rekha says. "You in the striped shirt. You have a question?"

"I do." Fern flashes me a coldly triumphant look and says, "Mr. Cosgrove, would you care to comment on your relationship with Jackson Dalton's fiancée? As we all know, Jackson Dalton is the fugitive founder of Jaxx Coin and currently suspected of committing massive financial fraud. How can consumers know that Solosol is a legit operation and not a money-laundering front by Jackson Dalton, considering you're romantically involved with his fiancée?"

A murmur picks up around the crowd, and Sam looks dumbfounded. I'm paralyzed, torn between wanting to defend myself and not wanting to cause a larger scene.

"I'm not Jack's fiancée," I hiss at her.

"What an interesting question," Rekha says. She smiles at Fern, and her smile is precise and dangerous. "I find it ludicrous that while I'm standing here discussing technology that will revolutionize the energy industry and has the potential to dramatically reduce our reliance on fossil fuels, someone is idly wondering about the sex life of my partner here. Still, allow me to set the record straight: Neither Sam nor I have ever met Jackson Dalton, and our company has nothing to do with him or Jaxx Coin. Moreover, I'd encourage you to use common sense. If my partner stole Jackson Dalton's fiancée, why would Dalton ever want to have anything to do with our company? Besides, the man ran a cryptocurrency exchange. His mission was to destroy the world; ours is to save it."

Sam clears his throat. "Yeah, obviously, I agree with what Rekha just said. There's no link between our company and Jaxx Coin. Our technology is important and life changing, and that should be the focus today, not my relationship with my girlfriend."

Girlfriend. I flush. Sam just called me his girlfriend in front of a live audience. He catches my eye and offers me a quick smile.

"But since someone just implied that she was somehow involved in whatever went down at Jaxx Coin," he continues, "let me be perfectly clear: Vanessa is one of the most honest people I know. I trust her implicitly. I have no reason to doubt her when she says that she knew nothing about the inner workings of Jaxx Coin, and neither should anyone else."

Rekha nods sharply. "Now, does anyone have any questions that aren't stupid?"

I turn back to Fern, but she's already gone.

Chapter Forty-One

One Week Later

The Solosol launch party is, in a word, *epic*. Even though I know Ellie and Richie well, it was only three weeks ago that I came to them with the ideas for *both* Sun and Salutations *and* a launch party, and I'm stunned at how seamlessly and successfully they pulled off both events. Sam and Rekha had said they didn't have the budget for a launch party, especially after the solstice event, but I convinced them it was well worth rearranging some line items for a party. (I'd said nothing gets people more excited than a party, and Rekha had sniffed but ultimately, begrudgingly, agreed.) I brought on Ellie and Richie, who forwent their usual fee and pulled some strings to create a dazzling event. I trawled through the contact lists of Solosol, Ellie, Sienna, and myself to create a guest list, and then we ran a contest online to get invites to a select group of fans.

True to form, I'm late to the party. I *tried* to get there on time—really, I did—but Faith's apartment blew a fuse while I was getting ready. Apparently, the century-old building isn't wired for two women in the same unit to simultaneously use a blow-dryer and a curling iron. Also contributing to my tardiness was my knee: Most days, it feels almost normal, but dragging it up three flights of stairs in high heels to reach the rooftop wasn't easy and took some time.

I'm actually glad we're late. By the time I arrive with Faith, Marisa, and Sienna, who has flown in for the event, the party is in full swing—and it takes my breath away. I didn't say anything to Sam because he has enough on his plate, but I was worried that between the late invitations and spartan budget, the party would be sparsely attended or otherwise awkward. It's gratifying to see just how wrong I was. The rooftop is crowded—not fire-hazard crowded, but happening-place-to-be crowded—and there's a tangible buzz of excitement in the air.

Across the room, I see Sam talking to a small group of sharply dressed individuals—potential investors, maybe. I don't want to interrupt him, but he stops midsentence when our eyes meet. He holds up a finger and says something to the group and starts making his way across the room to me, his hungry eyes never once leaving my face. Heat builds in my body, and I self-consciously run my hands down the sides of my dress, making sure it's in place.

I rented a dress for the occasion—several dresses, actually, scarred as I am by the disaster with the dress for Faith's charity event—and the one I chose is the color of lemon custard, a shade that catches the fresh highlights in my hair. It is also clingy and practically backless, and is, as Faith said, "a look."

"Wow," Faith breathes at my side. "This is quite a party."

"Well, it's no legal gala," I say as a server appears with a tray of Sunbeams, the signature cocktail created just for this event—a sunny, bubbly concoction featuring passion-fruit puree, sparkling wine, and, of course, tequila.

"Think they need any lawyers?" Marisa asks jokingly.

"Excuse me," Sienna says, clutching my arm. "Who is that man over there?"

I follow her gaze to where Richie is speaking to the DJ, and then look back at her. "That's my friend Richie Park. He and his sister are the event organizers."

"*That's* Richie Park?" she asks, eyes roaming over him. "We exchanged some emails, but I didn't know he looked like . . . that."

I suppress a smile. Richie does look particularly nice this evening, with a well-cut suit and his black hair freshly trimmed. "Do you want me to introduce you?"

"No need." She tosses her hair over her shoulder. "But I am going to go over there and say hi."

Sienna makes her way across the room to Richie just as Sam finally reaches me.

"You made it." Sam's voice is husky as he places a hand on the small of my back, and the touch of his fingertips against my bare skin sets off a chain reaction of fireworks in my body.

"Of course I made it," I say, twining an arm around his waist. "I wouldn't have missed this for the world."

"She's also only thirty minutes late," Faith says. "For Vanessa, that's practically showing up *early*."

"Oh, I remember," Sam says, chuckling.

"Stop it, you two," I say with a laugh.

"Faith, Marisa, nice to see you both," Sam says. "If you don't mind, I need to steal Vanessa for a minute."

"She's all yours," Faith says, holding up her hands.

"Enjoy yourselves," Sam says to them before leading me back toward the group. As we cross the room, he leans in and says softly, "You look incredible. Good enough to eat."

A thrill runs through me. "Are you hungry, Sam?"

"Very." His voice is low and rough, reverberating through my body.

"Me, too."

He stalls at my side. He cuts his eyes toward the crowd and then over his shoulder, and turns back to me and says, "There's a little private coatroom in the hall. The door locks."

All the desire centers in my body fire at once, but I fight them back.

"Sam," I force myself to say levelly, "this is the launch party for your company. You are the man of the hour. I'm not going to let you spend your own party making out in a coat closet."

He clears his throat. "I was planning on doing more than making out."

And even though I very much want to shove him into said closet and get my hands on him, I control myself and promise him, "Later."

"I hope not *much* later." He gives a low whistle, tracing his fingers down my spine. "This back. This dress should be criminal."

"I thought you'd like that." I smile at him. "No zippers to get stuck."

"I don't mind helping you with zippers." He glances at my bare back and smiles softly. "Hey, I have something I want to show you. When we get to the later portion of the evening."

"Yeah?"

"Yeah." He grimaces slightly. "First, we have mingling to do. Lots and lots of mingling."

⁓

As the party enters its last hour, I congratulate myself on avoiding Rekha the entire time. She's there, of course—midway through the event, she gave a short speech about how satisfying it is to see her vision become reality, and I've otherwise seen her socializing all evening. It's hard *not* to see her—Rekha always looks stunning, but this evening she's an absolute vision in a glamorously minimalist black dress, a column of pitch-black silk that flows over her hips and shimmers ever so slightly when she moves. I've kept out of her way as much as possible, even going so far as to excuse myself from Sam's side when he approaches her. I want to believe it's selfless, that I'm trying to ensure Rekha doesn't have to deal with me, whom she so clearly despises, at her own party, but the truth is that I don't want to have to interact with her, either. I'm not sure I'll ever forgive her for giving Sam that ultimatum.

But I congratulated myself too soon, because moments later, I exit a stall in the women's room, and there she is. Rekha stands directly in front of me, touching up her glossy lips in the mirror. She immediately stiffens when she sees my reflection.

I hesitate, considering whether I should simply say nothing. I assume that's what she wants. Rekha has made it clear to me that she believes I am toxic, a veritable hex on her company, and I'm sure she'd be delighted to make it through her launch party without having to speak my name.

But she's *wrong*.

I am not toxic, and she wouldn't even *have* this party if it weren't for me. Besides, whether Rekha likes it or not, Sam and I are together. She can't avoid me forever.

I raise my chin, approach the sink beside her to wash my hands, and say, as casually as I dare, "Hey, Rekha."

"Vanessa," she says simply. She dabs at her lips again, then adds, "That's quite a dress."

I know it's not a compliment, but I don't care.

"Thank you," I say, flashing her a megawatt smile. "You look nice, too."

Rekha frowns slightly, as though trying to parse whether I've just given her an insult.

"I mean it," I say. "You look phenomenal."

She purses her lips and caps her lip gloss before tucking it into her black satin clutch.

"Wait," I say as she starts to turn away. "I just . . . Congratulations. On everything you've accomplished. It's truly incredible."

"I know."

I can't help myself; I laugh. "Your confidence is refreshing."

"I don't understand why I should pretend to be humble," she says, crossing her arms. "And to *you*, of all people. I worked *hard* for this. Why *shouldn't* I be proud?"

"I wasn't being sarcastic. I really admire your confidence."

"You say that as though you're some sort of shrinking violet, but I know you. You love attention."

I give her a half smile. "Craving attention and having self-confidence are two different things, trust me."

Rekha tilts her head, her dark, glossy hair cascading over her shoulder as she studies me. "Look, Vanessa, I will never understand what Sam sees in you. But one of the reasons we make such good business partners is that we see things from different angles. It's also one of the reasons our attempt at dating was such a disaster. He—" She cuts herself off, shaking her head. "Well, if you think I was trying to keep you apart because I wanted him for myself, you're very, very wrong. We couldn't have been more mismatched."

"I don't know, I would have thought that you two were a perfect pair. Smart, ambitious, early risers."

"Sam sings in the shower," Rekha says stiffly. She drops her voice and adds in horror, "*Dolly Parton songs.* If I never hear '9 to 5' again, it will be too soon."

My heart swells in my chest, but I grin and say, "Well, at least you didn't witness his Lady Gaga phase."

Something almost like a smile flickers across Rekha's face. "Small mercies. Anyway, what I've come to realize is that I don't have to understand Sam's attraction to you. It's enough that you make him happy. He's been walking on air these last couple of weeks. I've never seen him like this."

I bite my lip to keep from smiling too much. "I love him."

She rolls her eyes. "How touching. Now listen to me, Vanessa: I value Sam's happiness, but Solosol is my priority. If you do something to jeopardize the company, I will personally take you apart."

"I would never do that," I promise. "You can trust me."

She makes a noncommittal noise, then turns back to her reflection and smooths a hair back, frowning when it immediately pops out of place.

"Do you need a bobby pin?" I dip into my bag and hand her one.

"Thank you," she says, taking it from me and pinning it into her hair. She cracks half a smile at me in the mirror, and I decide to take a chance.

"Hey, Rekha, do you think we could maybe . . . be friends?"

She grimaces slightly. "No. But friendly is doable."

"You're stone cold," I say, grinning in admiration. "Friendly it is."

Chapter Forty-Two

"Come on," one of Sam and Rekha's mutual friends urges as we stand in a tight group outside the bar on Hubbard Street. "Let's keep this party going!"

"Nah," Sam says, tightening his arm around my shoulders. "I appreciate you guys coming out for us, but I'm beat."

There's a rumble of discontent throughout the group, and I rise on my toes to whisper in Sam's ear, "Are you sure? This is your night. Don't you want to celebrate?"

"They're just going to do shots until they can't feel their faces," he whispers back. "I have a different idea of how I'd like to celebrate."

His voice is electric in my ear, and when he accentuates his point by slowly walking his fingertips down my bare spine, my insides dissolve into a pool of want. It takes significant restraint to keep myself from gasping aloud. As discreetly as I can, I slide my hand between his suit jacket and his shirt, reveling in the heat coming off his firm back. Sam makes a noise low in his throat, a soft growl that only I can hear.

"Lame, Cosgrove," another friend says. "You've been hiding out for weeks now. Give us tonight!"

Rekha glances over at us and curls her lip slightly, seemingly in disgust. I brace for her to add to the chorus, but then she shakes her head minutely, as though even she can't believe what she's about to do, and says, "Leave him alone, guys. Sam has been killing himself on this launch for months now. The man deserves a rest."

"And you?" one of them asks. "Are you going to bail on us, too, R?"

"Not a chance," she says. "I'm made of sterner stuff than Sam."

"Thank you," I mouth at her, and she rolls her eyes before giving me a small smile.

Friendly is good enough.

~

Sam and I are all over each other before his door is even fully shut. The desire that's been building since the moment our eyes met across the crowded rooftop has reached a fever pitch, and we're desperate to touch each other. His kiss is bruising; his hands are everywhere at once. He pushes me against the door, hitching up the side of my dress to run one hand along a thigh while the other cups my breast through the delicate fabric. He hikes one leg around his waist, and I flinch.

"Sorry," I mutter. "That's my bad knee."

I pull back long enough to unlatch my high heels and plant both feet on the ground, but when I reach for him again, he starts leading me down the hall.

"Come on," he says between kisses. "Bedroom."

We only make it halfway down the short hallway before we lose control again. This time it's me pushing him against the wall, dragging my tongue down the side of his neck and loosening his belt. He groans and pushes me away slightly, saying, "We're so close—"

Somehow, we make it all the way to Sam's bedroom. I'm ready to explode; every inch of my skin is desperate to be touched. I grab him by his undone belt and pull him to the bed, gently shoving him down and lifting the dress to my waist so I can straddle him. He gasps and fits his hands on my hips, pulling me against him.

"Vanessa," he rasps, somehow making even my name sound dirty. Then suddenly his hands still. "Wait."

"Hmm?" I manage, barely able to think through my haze of lust.

"I have to show you something."

"Right now? Can't it wait?"

"Trust me, if I thought it could—" He cuts himself off, looking almost pained, and carefully removes me from his lap.

"What is it?"

Sam rises, giving me a devilish smirk as he shrugs out of his suit jacket. He tosses it aside and then starts unbuttoning his shirt. Apparently, what he wants to show me is some sort of awkward striptease? An odd time for it, but okay. I laugh and tuck my fingers into my mouth, rewarding him with a wolf whistle.

"Yeah, baby!" I call. "Take it *off*."

Sam's cheeks redden adorably as he laughs. He unbuttons the last button on his shirt and tosses it onto the ground with the jacket, then peels off his undershirt. At the sight of his sculpted midsection, even more heat pools in my belly, and it's all I can do not to grab him and yank him back to me. Independent of my body, my hands reach for him, but he dances away from my fingertips.

"Are you ready for this?" he asks.

"Ready for—" I start, but he turns around before I can get out the entire question.

I gasp.

On Sam's right shoulder blade, under a slip of shiny protective see-through film, is a fresh tattoo of Dolly Parton.

"Oh, Sam." I crawl onto my knees and reach out, lightly touching the skin around the tattoo. "You got Dollied."

"That I did. Our Lady of Country Music and Literacy, on my body for all eternity."

"We have matching tattoos," I say, unable to keep the smile out of my voice. "You know what that means. We're stuck together forever."

"Ness," he says, turning around and taking my face in his hands. "I already knew that."

"You mean that, don't you?" I ask, almost afraid to hope. "This time it's for real."

"It was always for real." He kisses me tenderly on my forehead. "But this time I'm more mature. I'm emotionally equipped to have a serious relationship. And I've spent every day of the last six years thinking about you, and you're crazy if you think I'm going to let you go."

"We both know that I am a bit crazy."

He laughs. "All the best people are."

I start to respond, but Sam silences me with a smoldering kiss, which he follows with another and then another, until I'm ready to black out from happiness.

~

Sometime later, Sam and I are lying awake in the dark. We're both still buzzing from the excitement of the party and the thrill of being together, and neither of us wants to go to sleep first.

"So . . . ," Sam says, tracing a finger along my bare shoulder. "There's something we have to talk about."

"Oh?" I ask, catching his finger and pulling it to my mouth to kiss lightly.

"Yeah. My dad called just before the party."

I tense and drop his hand. "Is everything okay? Is he—"

"He's doing well, health-wise," Sam interrupts. "It's not that."

"Then it's because he saw me on your Instagram," I say. "You hadn't told him that you were back together with me, and he's still convinced I'm some sort of bad influence."

"That's not it, either." Sam strokes my hair. "He *did* see a photo of you, and technically I guess I hadn't told him that we were back together—"

"Sam!" I protest, pulling away. "I thought things were different this time. I thought you were a better communicator."

"I *am*. I promise. I've just been so preoccupied between the launch and, well, *you* that I hadn't talked to my parents for long enough to do anything other than check in about my dad's health and listen to my mom's worries. I wasn't hiding anything from them, I promise. And Dad doesn't think you're a bad influence."

"He did."

"He questioned my judgment. It was never about you." He shakes his head. "Anyway, I'd asked him a couple of weeks ago about what that reporter said. About how the annulment papers were never filed."

"Oh." Something cold settles in my chest. All those wonderful things Sam said, the way he touched me, and . . . he's been thinking about how to prove that our marriage legally never happened. "And your dad found them? I knew Fern had to be wrong. She—"

"She's right."

I shake my head, not sure I've heard him correctly. "What?"

"The lawyer never filed the papers because my dad never paid him."

"*What?* Why not?"

"He'd just started a new round of chemotherapy, and my parents had other things on their minds. Dad was sure he gave Mom the bill to pay, but they couldn't find a record of it. They tried to call the lawyer but found out he died not long after we signed those papers. Heart attack, I guess. They made some calls, and . . . as best anyone can tell, my parents never paid the bill, and after the lawyer died, no one followed up on it. So the annulment was never filed."

"So," I say slowly, almost afraid to voice what I think this means, "you're telling me it's not a mistake and that we really have been married for the last five years."

Sam quirks a smile and nods. "It's kind of funny when you think about it."

"You think this is *funny*?" I demand, whacking him playfully on the chest. "I almost married someone else!"

"You wouldn't have gone through with it."

"How can you be so sure?"

"Well, for one, you wouldn't have been able to get a marriage license." He catches my chin and tilts my face toward him. "But more importantly, I know you would have come to your senses."

"You're right, you know. I was going to break it off with Jack even before everything happened with Jaxx Coin." I lick my lips and add, "I never stopped loving you, Sam. I thought about you all the time."

"It can't be half as much as I thought about you."

I shake my head in disbelief. "I really thought you hated me. I really thought you resented me for ruining your life."

"That's what we get for being such trash communicators."

"But no more," I remind him, taking his face in my hands. "Now we tell each other exactly what we want."

"Exactly," he murmurs, leaning down to kiss me.

"Like right now," I say softly. "I want your hands right about . . . here."

He smiles as he slides his hands down between my legs. "I'm listening."

"Good boy." I draw him in for another kiss.

"Just so you know," he says, coming up briefly for air, "I'm committed to being a better communicator this time around. I'm never going to shove you in a box again. I'm going to be completely open with you, even if it's too much."

"You could never be too much," I tell him honestly. "You're always the right amount of much."

"So are you." His eyes hold mine. "Never change, Vanessa."

My heart swells as I lean forward to kiss him.

Chapter Forty-Three

One Month Later

I survey Faith's crowded living room and feel ready to burst with happiness. Just a couple of months before, when I'd shown up on her doorstep, freshly abandoned by my fiancé, sponsors, clients, and friends, I'd felt completely and utterly alone. Now the room hums with faces I know and love—or if not *love*, exactly, have come to respect: my sister, of course, smiling radiantly at Marisa, the two of them squeezed into one of Faith's slouchy armchairs; Ellie, who is leaning back in Faith's desk chair with her glitter-encrusted ankle boots on Faith's desk; Gemma, fresh off teaching a class, seated on one end of my couch; Rekha, still not my friend but also not *not* my friend, perched on the other; Sienna and Richie, lounging on yoga bolsters on the floor, their hands intertwined; and, of course, Sam, who is sharing Faith's less beat-up chair with me and has one of his strong arms wrapped around my waist. My heart is full, and not just because of the found family in this room, all gathered to celebrate my newest professional venture.

That's right, as of about ten o'clock this morning, I am officially a co-owner of the House of Om. After the success of Sun and Salutations, Gemma came to me with an offer. House of Om was growing beyond her wildest dreams, and she wanted to expand—but she was already stretched thin and needed a partner to make that happen. It took me less than thirty seconds to agree. Soon, we'll open a second studio space, conveniently located just blocks from Faith's and my apartment, and I'll be managing it. We have a lot of work to do to transform the space into the serene House of Om branch we're envisioning, but I'm looking forward to it.

Now Gemma raises a chipped coffee mug that says I ♥ TORTS. (Faith has only two plastic champagne flutes and three mismatched wineglasses. The rest of us drink our sparkling wine out of juice glasses, mason jars, and the aforementioned law-school mug.)

"To Vanessa," Gemma says. "I'm excited to see what's in store for House of Om, and I can't think of anyone I would rather have as a partner for this next chapter."

"Even though she's practically allergic to timeliness," Sienna jokes, raising her glass.

"That's part of her charm," Ellie argues.

"Charming or not, I'm working on my punctuality," I promise. "And while we're toasting, I'd like to raise a glass to you all. These last couple of months have been some of the most challenging of my life, and I'm honestly not sure that I would have made it through them without you. *All* of you. Even those of you who actively wished I would just take my ridiculous antics and go away. Not that I'm naming any names, Rekha."

She offers me a guilty smirk. "To be fair, I only wanted you to go away until we'd gotten the Uno launched."

"And she couldn't even do that," Faith teases.

I pluck a piece of popcorn from the bowl on the coffee table and toss it at my sister's head. "Thanks for the support, sis. Next time we're celebrating you, I'll be sure to roast you."

"Speaking of . . . ," Marisa says, eyes glittering as she leans forward.

"Don't," Faith mutters, blushing.

Marisa squeezes her hand and continues, "Faith accepted an offer with the EPA today."

"You got it?" I squeal. "And you didn't tell me?" I launch another piece of popcorn at her.

"They called while you were in the shower," she says, blushing. "I didn't want to take away from your celebration. But . . . yeah, I'm really excited. I'll start after graduation, and I feel like I can make a real difference there, in a way that I couldn't at a law firm."

"I'm so damn proud of you!" I raise my glass in the air. "To Faith!"

Faith squirms under the attention, her cheeks turning beet red, and says, "Hey, what about Sam and Rekha? Shouldn't we be toasting them, too? I read today that you guys have sold over a million units. In just a month! That's incredible."

"Thanks." Sam blushes endearingly. "Yeah, no, things have really taken off."

"'Taken off' is an understatement," Sienna says. "You're up among the stars."

"Some might say the biggest star of all: the sun," Richie adds, gently ribbing Sienna. "I read the waiting list is a month long."

"It's not *that* long," Sam says. "But, yeah, we weren't prepared for the insane demand. We're working double time and doing everything we can to get those Unos into the hands of the people who want them."

"Meanwhile, all those haters are eating crow," I add.

"Haters?" Rekha repeats. "Who hates solar energy?"

Marisa raises an eyebrow. "Aside from the coal lobby?"

"She means all the so-called 'experts' who were always talking about how unlikely it was that your solar panel would even work," Richie says.

"But I knew it would," Rekha protests.

"You knew it because you created it," I say. "Everyone else just had to take your word for it. And look at it now."

Rekha gives me a rare genuine smile. I suppress a grin.

"Faith is right," I say, lifting my glass high. "Cheers to Sam and Rekha!"

"Mother Earth thanks you," Gemma adds.

"Hear, hear," Ellie says. "Maybe when you guys release the next product, you'll give me more lead time, and we can have an even bigger, better party."

"What could be better than *that* party?" Faith asks, wide eyed.

"Oh, sweetie," Ellie says, extending out an arm to ruffle Faith's hair.

"It'll be a while before we release another product," Sam says. "We have our hands full with this one."

"That's not all you have your hands full with," Sienna says with a smirk.

"And on *that* note," I say, laughing as I rise from my place on Sam's lap, "does anyone need a refill?"

I'm answered by a chorus of yeses, and I make my way to the kitchen to retrieve another bottle of sparkling wine. Faith gaped when I lugged ten bottles into the apartment earlier, but I pointed out that nothing's sadder than a celebratory dinner that runs out of bubbly. I'm unwrapping the foil from the top of a fresh bottle when my phone begins buzzing in my pocket. Expecting it to be the pizza I ordered, I pull it out of my pocket and am about to answer it when the caller ID stops me cold.

Fern.

I silence the ringer. Fern Foxall has never once been the bearer of anything but bad news, and I refuse to let her ruin this evening.

Still . . . I can't help but wonder what she wants. It's been months since Jack cratered the cryptocurrency market; the public's attention has long since moved on from him, and certainly from me. I haven't heard from Fern since Rekha gave her a dressing down at Sun and Salutations. If she's calling me now, that means she thinks she has something newsworthy. It might be better to know about it now rather than be blindsided by it later.

"What is it, Fern?" I demand, answering without a greeting. "Make it fast. I'm hosting a dinner party."

"And you didn't invite me?" She makes a tutting sound. "I thought we were friends."

"Your invitation must have gotten lost in the mail. Now, out with it: What garbage are you going to spread about me this time?"

"It's not about you."

"That's what I've been telling you for months."

"Reasonable minds differ. But this isn't garbage, and it's not about you—although I think it will be of *interest* to you." Fern pauses, then adds, "I know you think I've been unfair to you, Vanessa. It wasn't personal."

"What was that you were saying about reasonable minds?"

"Touché," Fern says. "Listen, I'm offering an olive branch here. A preview of my next story."

"Enough with the theatrics. My guests' glasses are empty, and they're getting restless."

"I have it on good authority that Jackson Dalton's lawyer has cut a deal with the US government."

I blink, surprised. Of all the things I thought Fern might say, this wasn't even on the list.

"A deal?" I repeat. "What does that mean? Jack is turning himself in?"

"He's expected to arrive in Washington, DC, tomorrow morning."

"But that doesn't make any sense. Jack insisted he was innocent. That it was just bad luck, not fraud."

"I understand he's maintaining his innocence, but he's no longer running. There'll probably be a trial. He may testify before Congress. I don't have the specifics."

"I'm shocked," I admit. "I know Jack better than most people, and this . . . Well, *unexpected* is not a strong enough word. Do you know if something happened? Did someone give up his location?"

"You mean, more than you did?" she asks, her voice smirking. "No, as far as I know, nothing like that happened. My source provided me with a private message Dalton sent to a friend, in which he said he'd decided it was time to, quote, 'do the right thing.'"

You always do the right thing, I hear Jack's voice say in my head. *I could learn a lot from you.*

A hand flies instinctively to my heart. "Good for Jack."

"Good for everyone," Fern corrects. "Now we'll all finally get to hear what went down at Jaxx Coin."

Relief bubbles up inside me. Fern's right—everyone will hear the truth, and everyone will finally realize that I had no part in the disaster. The shadow of suspicion that's been hanging over me since Jack fled will finally lift. I'm almost giddy as I think about it.

"I trust you'll report on the *truth* as vigorously as you reported on everything else."

"Of course," she says, sounding mildly offended. "I'm a journalist, Vanessa."

"Vanessa?" I glance up at the sound of my name and see Sam hovering nearby, his brow furrowed in concern. "Everything all right?"

I flash him a reassuring smile, then tell Fern, "I have to go, but thank you for calling."

"Not so fast. You didn't think I was calling solely out of the goodness of my heart, did you?"

My hand tightens on the phone. "That implies you have a heart."

"Now you're just hurting my feelings." She laughs. "No, Vanessa, I'm working on a scoop about Dalton's imminent arrest, and I want to know what you, his one-time fiancée and alleged coconspirator, have to say about it."

"If you promise to never call me an 'alleged coconspirator' again, I'll comment."

"Deal."

I take a deep breath and turn away from Sam. "I wish Jack all the best. He made some mistakes, but he's a good man. I have full confidence he'll do everything in his power to make it right with his investors." I bite my lip and cut another look at Sam. "And, well, everyone deserves a second chance."

Fern sighs. "I was hoping for something with a bit more fire, but I guess that'll have to do."

"Can I tell you about ahimsa, Fern?"

I can practically hear her eyes rolling. "No. Enjoy your party."

There's a note of finality in her words, and as I lower the phone, I think with relief that might be the last I ever hear from Fern Foxall.

"Who was that?" Sam asks. "Did I hear you say 'Fern'?"

"Yeah. It was Fern Foxall," I say, picking up the partially opened wine again.

"Fern who? Wait—not that reporter?"

"That's the one." I remove the foil with a flourish. "She said Jack is turning himself in."

Sam freezes, clearly unsure how to act. "Huh. Are you . . . okay with that?"

"Better than okay," I assure him. "Once Jack explains what really happened, people will see that Jack made an error—okay, a series of errors—but he isn't a criminal. And once people realize *he* didn't set out to run a fraud, they'll know I couldn't have been abetting him."

"No one thinks that."

"Yes, they do. Take a quick scan of the comments on any of my socials. That new video I uploaded to YouTube this morning? The flow class I've been working on? It was up for *five minutes* before some rando posted a novel in the comments about how I'm a criminal and the FBI is going to arrest me any day." I shrug. "I'm pretty good at ignoring nonsense like that, but truthfully, I'm tired of it. I'm ready to have my name cleared. And Jack's testimony will finally do that."

"Well, then, that's great." Sam leans in to kiss me, but as he does so, I notice one of his hands is curled closed.

"Wait," I say, holding him at bay. "What do you have in your hand there?"

Sam bites his lip and gives me a devilish smirk. "Just something I found in your room."

"My room? What is it?" I try to peel open his fingers, laughing when they remain closed tight. "Sam! What is it?"

"Hey," he says throatily, moving my hand away from his. "Here."

Slowly, he unfolds his fingers, revealing a tarnished, misshapen ring in the palm of his hand.

I clap a hand over my mouth in surprise. "Sam Cosgrove, what were you doing looking through my jewelry box?"

"I wanted to know your ring size. And then I found this." He looks at the ring wonderingly. "I can't believe you kept it."

"Of course I kept it," I say softly. "Like I had any other choice."

"Well." He licks his lips and lifts the ring between two fingers. Holding it out to me, he says, "Vanessa Summers, I love you so much I want to barf. I know that's not the most romantic thing you've ever heard—"

"Are you kidding me?" I ask, happy tears leaking from my eyes. "Second only to a proposal on bended knee."

His eyes twinkle, and he steps around the counter, dropping to his knee in front of me. "Would you do me the honor of being—of *staying*—my wife?"

"Yes." I laugh. "God, yes. The honor would be mine. Now, please, Sam, get up. My knee is barely healed, and it's starting to ache in sympathy."

He slides the ring onto my fourth finger, both of us smiling as it fits perfectly. He brings my hand to his mouth and plants a soft kiss on it, then rises, catching me in his arms and bringing me in for a dizzying kiss. Happiness floods my body, and I'm suddenly grateful for every supposedly wrong choice I made that led me to this moment. Over the last few years—and the last few months, in particular—I've spent so much time thinking about all the ways my life would be different if I'd made other decisions, but then I wouldn't have ended up here, locking lips with the man I love on the day I signed a contract to co-lead a yoga studio, surrounded by true friends, and the most joyful I've ever felt.

"Hey!" Faith's voice calls out. "What just happened over there?"

I pull away from Sam to beam and lift my hand to show off my new—*old*—ring.

"Look at that!" Ellie cries, clapping her hands excitedly. "They just got engaged!"

"Aren't they already married?" Marisa asks in a low voice, leaning toward Faith.

Yes, I think as Sam pulls me in for another kiss. Yes, we just got engaged, and yes, we are already married. Both things are true.

Acknowledgments

I am very lucky to be able to do what I love, and very, very lucky to have a whole host of incredible people to help me do it. A million thank-yous to everyone who pitched in to turn this idea of mine into the book you're reading now! I owe the biggest thank-you to Lisa Grubka, my absolutely stellar agent—thank you for encouraging me with this project and for always going to bat for me!

So many thank-yous are due to Melissa Valentine, who took a chance on Vanessa, Sam, and me; Jodi Warshaw, whose thoughtful edits notably improved this book; and Nancy Holmes, who is shepherding this story (and me!) through the publishing process; Carissa Bluestone and the rest of the team at Lake Union, including Angela Elson and others.

Thank you, of course, to my wonderful husband, Marc Hedrich, without whose love and support my writing career would not be possible. Thank you to my fab mother, Mary Barber, for being an early reader and always championing me, and thank you to my darling little monsters for being patient with me while I worked on this book on the playground, at ballet and soccer practice, and while on vacation. Thank you to all the rest of my family (my brother, David, and all the Hedrichs, Hanlons, Pughs, and so on) for their ever-present encouragement and support. A special thank-you to Angelica Castillo, without whose loving care of my children I would literally never have had the time to write this.

Thank you to Kristin Rockaway, Suzanne Park, and Chelsea Resnick—if you ladies hadn't looked like you were having so much damn fun with your projects while we were on our retreat, I might never have written this. I have so much gratitude for so many members of the writing community that I can't possibly list them all here, so I'll just give a special shout-out to a subset of my DC crew (Ed Aymar, Angie Kim, Christina Kovac); Vera Kurian's brunch group; and Jenna London, Sarah Keller, and Tania James, all of whom had to listen to me freak out about this book at various times. Thank you to my boss bitches (Cate Parkin, Ashley Philippi, Johanna Maska) and my AGD besties (Liz Heisler, Molly Hammond, Kristen Dawson) for always cheering me on. And, of course, side hugs to the law school clique—you know I have pictures of some of you taking shots out of a certain inflatable sheep's hindquarters!

And finally, thank you, thank you, thank you to all the readers who have welcomed my books onto their shelves. I sincerely appreciate it, and I hope you enjoyed reading this story half as much as I enjoyed writing it.

About the Author

Photo © 2024 Tim Coburn

Kathleen Barber is the author of *Follow Me* and *Truth Be Told*, which was adapted into a series for Apple TV+ by Reese Witherspoon's Hello Sunshine media company. A graduate of Northwestern University School of Law and a former attorney, she now writes full-time and lives in Washington, DC, with her husband and two children. For more information, visit www.kathleenbarber.com.